THE
SPIDER

Lars Kepler is a No.1 bestselling international sensation, whose Killer Instinct thrillers have sold more than 17 million copies in 40 languages. The first book in the series, *The Hypnotist*, was selected for the 2012 Richard and Judy Book Club. The most recent, *The Spider*, became the most sold novel in Sweden of 2022. Lars Kepler is the pseudonym for writing duo, Alexander and Alexandra Ahndoril. They live with their family in Sweden.

THE SPIDER

Lars Kepler

ZAFFRE

Originally published in Sweden by Albert Bonniers Förlag in 2022
This edition published in the UK in 2023 by

ZAFFRE

An imprint of Bonnier Books UK
4th Floor, Victoria House, Bloomsbury Square, London, WC1B 4DA
Owned by Bonnier Books
Sveavägen 56, Stockholm, Sweden

A CIP catalogue record for this book is
available from the British Library.

Hardback ISBN: 978-1-83877-786-9
Trade paperback ISBN: 978-1-83877-787-6

Also available as an ebook and an audiobook

1 3 5 7 9 10 8 6 4 2

Typeset by IDSUK (Data Connection) Ltd
Printed and bound in Great Britain by Clays Ltd, Elcograf S.p.A.

Zaffre is an imprint of Bonnier Books UK
www.bonnierbooks.co.uk

Lars Kepler would like to give readers advance warning that certain events and details from *Lazarus* and *The Sandman* are revealed in *The Spider*.

Once upon a time, there was a serial killer by the name of Jurek Walter. He was more cruel, and he killed more people, than any other murderer in northern Europe.

The man who eventually brought his killing spree to an end was Detective Superintendent Joona Linna. Joona doesn't believe in innate or metaphysical evil, and would probably suggest that Jurek had simply lost the part of his soul that enables a man to be human.

Only a handful of people knew of Jurek's existence, but the majority would no doubt argue that the world became a better place without him.

Jurek Walter is now dead, but just because something is gone doesn't mean it has disappeared entirely, as though it never existed. When something ceases to exist it leaves behind a dangerous void – a void that will eventually be filled in one way or another.

1

Margot Silverman hears the thudding of the horse's hooves against the bark chips as it gallops along the illuminated trail.

The sky is dark, the August air cool.

The trees race by on either side of her, fading away into the night before reappearing in the glow of the next lamp post.

Margot is head of the National Crime Unit in Stockholm, and she goes riding in Värmdö, to the east of the capital, four times a week. It helps to clear her head and centre herself.

The horse charges along the narrow trail, and the quick pace makes her heart race.

She catches brief glimpses of things in her periphery: fallen trees, the far edge of the field, a damp sweater with a smiley face on it, draped over a barrier.

Margot leans forward and feels the breeze on her face.

The horse's movements are asymmetrical as it gallops, its left hip higher than the right.

Each three-beat gait ends with its right front leg pushing off from the ground, followed by a moment of suspension.

In those few seconds as they fly through the air, she feels a tingle in her thighs.

Catullus is a Swedish warmblood gelding with long legs and a powerful neck, and Margot needed only to shift her outside leg back and push her hip forward to help spur him into a gallop.

Her braid thuds against her back each time his hooves hit the ground.

She sees a deer bolt across a clearing through the swaying ferns.

The lights are broken on the last part of the trail, and Margot can no longer see the ground in front of her. She closes her eyes and puts her faith in Catullus, allowing herself to be carried forward.

When she opens her eyes, she spots the bright stable between the trees and slows to an extended trot.

Margot's chest and back are sweaty, and she can feel the lactic acid burning in her muscles after an hour's interval training.

She walks Catullus in through the gates and dismounts.

It is almost 11 p.m., and Margot's silver Citroën is the only car still parked outside the stable block.

She leads the horse through the darkness towards the building. His bit clinks, hooves beating softly against the dry, trampled grass.

From one of the stalls inside, she hears a couple of loud thuds.

Catullus stops dead, lifting his head and pulling back slightly.

'Hey, what's up?' Margot asks, squinting into the darkness between the tractor and the nettles.

The horse is afraid, exhaling heavily through his nostrils. She strokes his neck and tries to coax him towards the stable, but he refuses to budge.

'What's going on, buddy?'

He shudders and veers sharply to one side, as though he is about to bolt.

'Whoa-oh-ho.'

Margot grips the reins and firmly leads him in a half-circle, through the tall meadow grass and out onto the gravel. The lights outside the stable block give everything nearby three sharp shadows.

Catullus snorts and lowers his head.

Margot squints at the end of the building, and though she can't see anything, she shudders.

Once they are safely inside the bright stable building, she takes off her helmet. The tip of her nose is red, her blonde braid heavy against the back of her quilted jacket. Above the tops of her long boots her jodhpurs are dirty.

The smell of hay and manure hangs heavy in the air.

The other horses are quiet as she leads Catullus to the wash stall, takes off his saddle and hangs it up in the heated tack room.

A couple of stirrups clink against the wooden wall.

Her first job is to rinse Catullus down and give him a blanket, then she needs to take him to his stall, feed him, give him a little extra salt and turn out the lights before heading home.

She reaches into her pocket to make sure she hasn't lost her father's old hip flask. She uses it for hand sanitiser rather than liquor – not because it's especially practical but because it brings her luck and amuses her.

The door onto the yard creaks, and Margot feels a rush of unease. She steps out into the main area and peers towards the front of the building.

She hears Catullus shuffling in the wash stall behind her. The hose is dripping, a dark trickle of water flowing around the sweat scraper towards the drain.

Several of the other horses snort, their hooves striking the ground, while the electrical cabinet on the wall emits a low hum.

'Hello?' says Margot.

She holds her breath, standing perfectly still with her eyes on the door and the dark window for a moment before turning back to Catullus.

She can see the ceiling light mirrored in the curve of his black eye.

Margot hesitates, then takes out her phone and calls Johanna. Her wife doesn't pick up, and she feels a knot of anxiety in the pit of her stomach. For the past two weeks, Margot has had the sense that someone is watching her. She even began to wonder whether Special Investigations or the Security Service has her under surveillance. She isn't a paranoid person, but a number of anonymous calls and a pair of missing earrings have left her wondering whether she or Johanna have themselves a stalker.

Margot tries calling again. The phone rings and rings, but right as the voicemail is about to kick in, she hears a crackling sound.

'Drenched and naked,' Johanna answers.

Margot smiles. 'How do I always manage to call at the right time?'

'Hang on, let me put you on speakerphone.'

Something rustles and the background noise changes. An image of a nude Johanna, standing in the middle of their brightly lit bedroom, fully visible from the apple orchard outside, flashes through Margot's mind.

'Sorry, I'm just drying off,' says Johanna. 'Are you on your way back?'

'Need to give the little man a quick hose down first.'

'Remember to drive carefully.'

Margot can hear Johanna rubbing herself with a towel as they talk. 'Make sure you close the curtains and check the door is locked,' she says.

'It's like we're in *Scream*. You're watching me from the garden right now, aren't you? And by the time I manage to lock the door, you'll already be in the house.'

'This isn't funny.'

'OK, boss.'

'Ugh, I don't want to be the boss anymore; I'm no good at it. I was fine as a detective, even if I was a bit cocky, but now that I'm in charge—'

'Stop,' Johanna interrupts her. 'I'd have you as my boss any day.'

'Oh la la,' Margot laughs, her mood improving.

She hears Johanna lower the blind, the cord clinking against the radiator.

'Put the blue lights on and come home,' Johanna tells her. Her voice sounds faint, distant.

'Were you able to get the girls into bed?'

'Yeah, although Alva asked me whether you like your horse more than you like her.'

'Ouch,' Margot says, laughing.

The minute they hang up, the feeling of unease comes creeping back up on her. She can still hear a faint clinking sound, which continues for a moment or two before stopping. It must be coming from somewhere in the stable building, Margot thinks. It sounds like when the buckets hanging in the aisle knock together.

One of the horses pushes up against the wall, making it creak.

Margot turns towards the door.

It looks like someone tall is trying to hide in the shadows over by the feed room. The rational side of her knows it's just the cabinet where they keep the brooms, but it seems to be standing much further out than usual.

The wind barrels over the metal roof, shaking the windowpanes.

Margot walks down the aisle. She sees the bars of the stalls flickering at the edge of her vision, heavy horseheads gleaming in the light's glow.

She has to make a real effort to stop herself calling Johanna again to ask her to double check the outside door; the kids always have trouble bolting it properly. All she is going to do is see to Catullus, drive home, take a shower, and crawl into her nice, warm bed to go to sleep.

The light flickers and dims.

Margot stops to listen, peering past the wash stall to the changing room.

The stable block is quiet, but then she hears a rapid ticking sound, like something metal rolling across the floor.

She turns around, but the noise stops. She can't tell where it was coming from.

Margot steadies herself against one of the stalls and peers over to the main door.

She hears the ticking again, getting closer and closer now behind her.

Catullus anxiously raises his head, and Margot feels something slam into her back. One of the horses must have kicked her, she thinks as she falls.

The world disappears for a moment, and she hears a roaring sound in her ears.

Margot is lying face down on the floor, her lips and forehead bleeding where they struck the concrete. She feels a strange burning, tugging sensation in her spine, and can smell something sharp in the air.

As it dawns on Margot that someone has just fired a gun at her, her ears start ringing. The horses are frightened, shifting in their stalls, bumping against the walls, stamping their feet and snorting.

She has been shot, she thinks.

'Oh God, oh God . . .'

She needs to get up, drive home and tell her daughters that she loves them more than anything.

She hears footsteps, and feels a sudden jolt of fear.

There is a creaking sound, followed by the same clicking she heard earlier.

Margot's lower body is numb, but she realises that she is being dragged towards the door by her legs.

Her hips scrape against the rough concrete.

Margot tries to cling to a trough of feed, but she is too weak.

A bucket tips over and rolls away.

Her jacket and undershirt ride up.

Her breathing is shallow, and she knows that the bullet must have hit her spine. Wave after wave of pain shoots up through her torso.

It feels like she's been struck with an axe.

As she's pulled across the floor, Margot feels like an animal being dragged away to slaughter, like a bark boat caught in a current, like a zeppelin floating above the fields.

She knows she can't give up, that she has to keep fighting, but now she's so weak she can no longer keep her head up.

Her face has been torn to shreds by the rough floor, and the last thing Margot notices before she loses consciousness is the slick trail of blood on the floor.

2

Lisa is standing with her back to the window, resting the cold glass in her hand on the window ledge. It's the middle of the night, and she and two men are in a single-storey villa in Rimbo, around fifty kilometres north of Stockholm.

One of the men is in his fifties, wearing a suit and a pale blue shirt. His short hair is greying at the temples, and his neck seems stiff. He tosses the empty ice cube tray into the sink, pours some gin into a pitcher and then tops it off with tonic water.

The other man is in his early twenties, broad-shouldered and tall. He has a shaved head and is smoking a cigarette by the extractor fan.

Lisa says something and covers her mouth as she laughs.

The older of the two men leaves the kitchen, and the light in the bathroom comes on a moment later. From outside, his shadow is visible through the thin curtains.

Lisa has just turned twenty-nine, and she is wearing a pleated skirt and a silvery blouse that stretches over her breasts. Her dark hair is glossy. She was born with a cleft lip, and she has a pale scar above her mouth.

The younger man drops his spent cigarette into a beer can, moves over to Lisa and shows her something on his phone. He studies her reaction with a smile, says something and then pushes her hair back from her cheek.

She looks up and meets his eye, standing on tiptoe to give him a peck on the lips. His face turns serious, and he glances back towards the hallway before leaning in and giving her a deep kiss.

Saga Bauer watches through the display on her camera as the younger man reaches beneath Lisa's skirt and cups her between the legs. Saga has been filming the villa from the neighbour's garden for the past hour, perched on top of a wheelbarrow beside the tall fence. The light from the large windows in the kitchen and living room spills out onto the trunks of the pine trees and the cones scattered across the grass.

The older man reappears, pausing in the doorway, and the others break off their kiss and move towards him.

Saga rests her telephoto lens on top of the fence in order to get a sharper image, but the threesome have already made their way into the hall.

Lisa's husband was in the same class as Saga at the police academy, and he ended up joining Norrmalm Police after graduating. He suspects his wife has been cheating on him while he works nights, but he hasn't confronted her yet. Instead he got in touch with the detective agency where Saga now works. She warned him during their very first meeting that he might not actually want to know the truth, but he hired her anyway.

Lisa and the two men are now just outside the dark bedroom. Saga can't see what they are doing, but their shadows are dancing across the skirting board and through the open doorway.

She double checks that the camera is still filming.

One of the men turns on the floor lamp by the bedside table. All three have started stripping, and Lisa is standing with her back to the window. She tugs down her underwear, steps out of them and scratches her right buttock. Her tights have left a groove around her waist, and Saga can see a bruise on one of her calves.

The walls are the colour of honey, and the enormous bed has an ornate brass headboard. The bright lamp glares in the glass of a framed photograph of the boxer George Foreman, but when the younger of the two men sits down on the edge of the bed, he blocks out most of the light.

The older man lies down and takes a condom from the top drawer of the bedside table. Lisa moves over to him, straddles him and waits until he is ready.

She says something, and he grabs a yellow cushion from the floor and pushes it beneath his hips.

Lisa crawls upwards and kisses him on the chest and lips. Just as he is about to enter her, her face disappears into the shadows again.

The younger man is still sitting on the edge of the bed, trying to get himself hard enough to put on a condom.

The floor lamp by the bed starts rocking in time with Lisa's movements, causing the golden tassels to shake.

Saga waits patiently for her face to come back into view. Unless she manages to capture her face on film during the act itself, Lisa can always deny she has been unfaithful. She could show remorse for kissing another man and claim she left the house just as the other woman arrived.

Denial and lying always go hand in hand.

A light comes on in the house behind Saga.

Lisa pauses, puts a hand on the younger man's back and says something to him. He reaches for a bottle of massage oil from the other bedside table.

Lisa is still straddling the older man's hips, but she leans forward as the younger man climbs up onto the bed.

Her thighs shake as he penetrates her from behind. The threesome are perfectly still for a moment, and then the two men slowly start thrusting.

The light still isn't good enough.

Saga hears someone crossing the lawn behind her, and she glances back over her shoulder. The neighbour has spotted her.

'This is private property,' he shouts. 'You can't—'

'Police,' she snaps, turning to look at him. 'Stay back.'

The man has a white moustache and hunter's waistcoat, and he approaches her with a stressed look on his face.

'Can I see your ID?'

'In a minute,' Saga replies, turning back to her camera.

The light spills past the threesome on the bed, casting a shadow onto the dusty window. The younger man's face occasionally comes into view in profile, his nose and his taut mouth. Wet skin glistening in the light, a bent neck and tense thigh muscles.

'I'll call the police,' the neighbour threatens.

One of them knocks the bedside table, causing the lamp to topple over and hit the floor.

Lisa's face is suddenly awash with light, her mouth open and her cheeks flushed. She says something and closes her eyes, pale breasts trembling and hair swinging across her face.

Saga films the scene for another moment or two before hitting stop, replacing the lens cap and climbing down from the wheelbarrow. The neighbour backs away from her with his phone to his ear, and she holds up her expired Security Service ID just as he gets through to an operator.

She strides past him and across the lawn, climbing the fence and following the road down to the jetty where she left her motorcycle by the bins.

Once she has packed her camera away, she calls her boss and gazes out at the smooth rocks and the dark water.

'Henry Kent,' he answers.

'Sorry for calling so late,' she says. 'But you wanted me to report back—'

'That's how we do things,' he cuts her off.

'OK, well, I'm done here, I've got it all on film.'

'Good.'

Saga's blonde hair is tied up in a ponytail, and despite the dark circles beneath her eyes and the deep crease on her brow, she is still strikingly beautiful.

'I was wondering . . . Since it's so late, could I drop off the camera in the morning?'

'You need to bring it in now.'

'It's just that I have to get up early to—'

'What is it you don't get?' he says, raising his voice.

'Nothing, I just . . .'

Saga trails off when she realises he has ended the call. She sighs and shoves her phone into the inside pocket of her jacket, zips it up, pulls on her helmet and climbs onto the bike, rolling out of the parking space and off along the road.

After being out on leave for so long, she hadn't wanted to return to her job with the Security Service. Instead she put in a request with the National Crime Unit. The HR manager got in touch to say that while they didn't currently have any vacancies, they were very much interested in what Saga had to offer and would take it up with management.

It soon transpired that however ready Saga felt to get back to work, she first had to be given the green light from a psychologist at the Crisis and Trauma Centre. While she waits, she has been working for the Kent Detective Agency, mostly investigating affairs and running background checks. Outside of that, she spends almost all her spare time as a support person for two children with Down syndrome.

Saga lives alone, but she is currently sleeping with the anaesthetist who cared for her half-sister at the Karolinska Hospital in Huddinge a little over three years ago.

It's three-thirty in the morning when she pulls up outside the detective agency's offices on Norra Stationsgatan, enters the code and takes the lift to the third floor. She unlocks the door and disarms the alarm.

Out of habit, Saga checks the mail tray just inside the door and finds a small taped-up box with her name on it. She carries it through to her cubicle, puts it down on the desk and takes a seat. After logging in to the system, she takes the memory card from the camera, pushes it into the card reader, transfers the footage and archives it.

Saga is tired and her eyes drift towards the window, to the late night traffic, the roads, bridges and bright entrances to the tunnels.

The whirring of the hard drive drags her back to the present, and she gets up, locks the camera in the safe and returns to her cubicle.

Eyes heavy from lack of sleep, she tears the brown tape from the box and opens the flaps. She holds it under the desk lamp, reaches inside and pulls out what seems to be a crumpled child's drawing.

Saga unwraps the ball of paper to reveal a small bundle of white cotton and lace.

Using a pen, she pushes back the thin fabric and finds a small, grey object inside. A metal figurine, no more than two centimetres tall.

The dull metal shines in the light.

Saga angles the lamp and sees that the figure is a man with a bushy beard and a winter coat.

3

The broken glass crunches beneath Joona Linna's feet as he slowly crosses the hotel room. In the window, the man with the wrinkled face swings back and forth, his neck broken.

The front of his shirt is dark with blood from the deep wound caused by the noose.

Tiny shards of glass litter the window ledge beneath him.

His last whisper echoes through Joona. The words twist around him like snakes.

Joona knows that the man is dead, that his cervical vertebrae are severed, but he still feels like he has to check for a pulse.

He has just reached out to touch his throat when he hears a ringing sound.

* * *

Joona opens his eyes and grabs his phone from the bedside table, answering quietly before the second ring.

'I'm sorry to call so late,' says a man's voice.

Joona gets out of bed. He sees Valeria open her sleepy eyes, and he strokes her cheek before heading to the kitchen.

'What is it?' he asks.

'This is Valid Mohammad from Stockholm South. Margot Silverman's wife Johanna called 112 at twelve-thirty. She said that Margot went riding at the stables near Gustavsberg some time around nine and that she should have been back long before midnight. Johanna couldn't leave the kids home alone, but she was worried Margot might have had an accident, so dispatch sent a unit out there. We've just heard back from the responding officers . . . They didn't find Margot,

14

but it seems like there's a lot of blood on the floor in the stables . . . I don't know, I thought maybe you'd want to know.'

'I'll head over there now,' Joona tells the officer. 'Can you make sure no one touches anything? It's important; tell your colleagues not to move a muscle until I get there. I'll take over, I'll bring my own technician.'

He ends the call and phones his old friend Erixon.

It is now five minutes past two, and the first patrol car arrived at the stables forty-five minutes ago.

Ninety-five minutes have passed since Johanna called 112.

Joona knows there is no point in setting up any road blocks. All they can do now is examine the scene and try to work out what might have happened.

'OK,' Erixon whispers.

'I know your back's been bothering you, but I—'

'Don't worry.'

'I just need our best technician on this,' Joona explains.

'But he didn't pick up, so you called me instead, right?' Erixon says in an attempt to mask his anxiety.

They arrange to meet by the turn off to the stables, and Joona goes back to the bedroom and starts getting dressed. Valeria gets out of bed in her thin nightgown and pulls a cardigan around her shoulders.

'What's going on?' she asks.

Joona puts on the watch his daughter Lumi gave him. She bought it because she thought the face was the same shade of grey as his eyes.

'I just got a call,' he replies as he buttons his trousers. 'I have to go, it's . . .'

He trails off, and she meets his eye.

'Someone you know,' she fills in.

'Yeah, it's Margot. She went riding and hasn't come home,' he says as he pulls on his shirt.

'What did the responding officers have to say?'

'They found her car. And there was blood in the stables.'

'God . . .'

'I know.'

Joona hurries over to the gun cabinet, enters the code and takes out his Colt Combat. He slides it into his holster and fastens the straps as he makes his way back out into the hallway. Valeria follows

15

him, giving him a quick kiss and locking the door behind him as he runs towards the lifts.

As he waits for the garage doors to open, Joona thinks back to the first time he met Margot. She was pregnant, newly promoted to detective superintendent, and she welcomed him into her investigation despite the fact that he was no longer an officer.

He drives up the ramp and out onto the narrow back street, turning left onto Sveavägen and accelerating towards the Klara Tunnel.

There is almost no other traffic on the road at this time of night.

Central Stockholm disappears into the distance behind him. Tower blocks and brightly lit shopping centres race by, as well as industrial buildings, residential areas, and countless bridges over inlets and bays.

As a detective superintendent with the National Crime Unit, Joona Linna has solved more complex murder cases than any other officer in northern Europe.

There are two patrol cars by the turn off to the stables, one on either side of the lane. Their blue lights sweep across the trees and the tarmac, making it look as though they are underwater.

Erixon's van is parked on the other side of the road. The forensic technician lives in Gustavsberg, only a five minute drive away.

Joona pulls over onto the verge and gets out to greet his colleagues, asking them to set up a cordon across the turn off.

The night air is cool, and everything is dark and quiet. Other than the stables, there is nothing out here; nothing but forests and meadows.

Joona sees Erixon's bulky frame moving through the bright head-lights. The forensic technician is standing by the sandy tyre tracks left by vehicles that have cut the corner onto Ingarövägen, pouring liquid plaster into each one.

'Here's hoping this is all just a misunderstanding,' he mutters.

Joona murmurs in agreement.

When he's finished, they get into Erixon's van and drive the short distance to the stables, their headlights carving a tunnel of pale trees and grass through the darkness.

The gravel crunches beneath their tyres.

They pass enclosures with rows of feeders and a trampled paddock before they spot Margot's car parked outside the stable block.

Erixon pulls over and switches off the engine.

There is nothing to say. The two men pull on disposable overalls and make their way over to the car, photographing it and shining a torch through the windows.

The light glares on the glass, illuminating the front seats inside: the steering wheel, an energy drink in the cup holder, sweet wrappers and a thick case file.

They turn and walk over to the building.

In the headlights from the first patrol car, they see a tractor and a clump of nettles against a red wall.

Three jackdaws screech above a cluster of trees.

For the next few minutes, Erixon photographs the scene, spraying fixative onto all the footprints and tyre tracks, numbering everything and scribbling in his incident log.

An officer in uniform is standing perfectly still in the pale light from the open boot of the patrol car, a roll of police tape in one hand.

'Where's your partner?' asks Joona.

'Inside,' he replies, gesturing wearily.

'Don't move,' says Erixon, beginning to secure any evidence around him.

Joona knows it is a truism that the simplest explanation is often the most likely, but it still bears repeating at times – especially when hope informs their thinking.

Right now, he simply cannot bring himself to accept that he will probably have to tell Johanna and the kids that Margot is dead.

He and Erixon slowly approach the stable block. The outside lights are switched off, but the glow from inside seeping out through the gaps around the door is bright enough for them to see that the ground has been swept.

'Can you use UV on that?' asks Joona.

'It's probably about time, isn't it,' Erixon says, sighing.

He trudges over to his van and loads everything he needs onto a trolley, grabs the ultraviolet light and switches it on.

'Jesus . . .'

The gravel in front of the door to the stable pales in the invisible light, but the blood stands out in dark, stringy clusters.

Though the ground has been swept, a large amount of blood is still visible, leading in a straight line from the door. After about two metres, it disappears.

Erixon takes more photographs, then collects samples of the stained gravel from five different spots, tipping it into separate evidence boxes.

'I need to get inside,' says Joona.

Erixon makes his way over to the stable block, scanning for fingerprints on the door handle, the door and the wall inside.

'My mentor always used to put elastic bands around his shoes, but I always preferred step plates instead,' he says, tearing the plastic from a new pack.

He opens the door and, breathing heavily, places the first plate onto the threshold and pulls on a pair of shoe covers.

Joona follows him inside.

The bars on the stalls gleam in the yellow light. The other police officer is standing stock still outside the tack room.

There is a large pool of blood in the middle of the concrete floor, a long drag mark stretching out to the area that has been swept.

From there to the door, they can see parallel streaks of blood left by the broom.

The perpetrator must have worked backwards, sweeping away their footprints behind them.

'Joona Linna,' says the officer. 'I almost didn't believe you were serious, but I thought . . . well, maybe it was best to keep still, just in case.'

'Appreciate it.'

While Erixon sets out the step plates, Joona studies the scene. Other than a black gelding shifting anxiously in the wash area, the horses are all dozing in their stalls.

The perpetrator wasn't trying to cover up the crime, Joona thinks. He just wanted to erase any trace of himself.

Erixon shines a powerful raking light across the floor, but there are no visible footprints in the aisle. He sighs and tries another angle, then gives up.

'No footprints, and the handle's been wiped clean,' he says.

Joona moves forward over the step plates.

Most of the blood has dried, though there is a patch in the middle that is still sticky and coagulated.

There is no sign of any spatter, no real blowback.

Margot was probably shot with a handgun. A pistol with a relatively low muzzle velocity, using a hollow-point bullet that failed to exit her body.

18

Erixon soaks swab after swab in a sodium chloride solution, dabs at the dried blood and then seals them in evidence bags.

Joona's eyes are focused as he moves forward, allowing the lingering shadows of whatever happened to surge through him.

There is a lot of blood. It's impossible to say how long Margot was on the floor, but the blood was still pumping from her body and hadn't yet started to coagulate when she was dragged outside.

He notices that one of the black plastic feed troughs is slightly out of place and that it has left a drag mark on the concrete.

'What are you thinking?' Erixon asks, following Joona's eye.

'Could you spray some Bluestar around the bloodstain?' he asks.

Erixon grabs the bottle and sprays all surfaces where there is no visible sign of any blood.

The chemicals in the spray give blood a temporary luminescence, meaning that even the smallest droplets develop an icy blue glow.

Joona stands perfectly still, trying to make sense of the scene now that all the blood is visible.

He registers the shape of every drop in relation to gravity and the surface on which it landed.

Around thirty-five centimetres from the main pool of blood, he notices a few pale glowing spots.

Joona moves towards them and leans in close.

There is a smear of pink lipstick on the concrete between the blood stains.

Margot's face must have struck the floor when she fell.

Erixon photographs everything, and Joona continues to the other side, bending down to study a row of six glowing droplets to the right of the main pool.

Blood has a higher surface tension than water, meaning that any droplets that fall onto a relatively smooth surface will retain their rounded edges rather than splitting, just like the series of drips on the floor in front of him.

The first five have a slightly pointed shape, thanks to a rightward motion, but the last is perfectly round.

'Check for gunshot residue in these,' says Joona, pointing to the six drops.

'Never heard that one before, but sure.'

'The shooter is right-handed. They pressed the muzzle to Margot's body from behind, fired one shot and followed through on the movement before swinging the gun away, like this, pretty slowly, before eventually stopping.'

'So you think these dripped from the barrel of the gun?'

'Margot fell forward with the bullet still inside her. Her face struck the floor and she split her lip.'

'We don't know whether the blood is Margot's,' Erixon says half-heartedly.

'That's her lipstick.'

'Are you sure?

'I'm sure of the colour.'

'I'm sorry to hear that,' Erixon mumbles.

'Yes, but Margot was still alive, because she tried to grab hold of that feed trough.'

'I'll try some Amido Black.'

'The shooter dragged her out by the feet while she was still alive and bundled her into a car. He then came back inside and swept up his footprints, wiped the handle and door, swept the yard right up to the car, took the broom and left.'

4

The water is as smooth as silk when the group moors their rented motorboat in a bay on the west of the island in the hazy sunshine. They take off their life jackets, grab their things and walk a short distance up the sandy beach before stopping to rest at the edge of the wood.

Samir is short of breath, spluttering into his handkerchief, and Lennart unfolds a camping chair with trembling hands and slumps down into it. Leaning against her walking stick, Emma considers telling the others that she had thought they were still young and fit enough to manage a walk of no more than a hundred metres.

Sonja hitches up her mustard yellow coat, sits down on a rock and opens her rucksack.

'No touching the food before we get there!' Lennart snaps.

'I'm just grabbing my medicine,' she replies, digging out a small prescription bottle.

They have brought a picnic of boiled eggs, potato salad, cold meatballs with a Dijon mustard dressing, tuna sandwiches, hotdogs, pancakes with raspberry jam, a thermos of coffee and a small bottle of cognac.

Emma lights a cigarette and peers back at their footprints in the sand, past the driftwood and other junk that has washed ashore. Further down the beach, it looks as though someone has dragged something heavy all the way up into the woods.

'Sometimes it feels like I'm looking at everything through a piece of glass, Bernie,' she whispers.

Bernie is her late husband, but she has continued to talk to him since he passed away. Some days she even opens the wardrobe and talks to his lightweight summer suit. She tells her friends she is enjoying her newfound freedom, but the truth is that she misses him dearly.

'Maybe it's time for us to give up and let the next generation take over?' says Samir.

'Like hell,' Lennart mutters, getting to his feet.

Emma leads them to the windswept woods, around the crumbling rocks. Her stick gets caught between two roots that have been forced up out of the earth, and as she tries to tug it free it feels as though someone else is pulling on it, dragging her down into the ground.

She feels a sudden urge to call off their excursion, to claim she doesn't feel well, but she walks a little further towards the glade before pausing to let the others rest again.

Lennart unfolds his chair, and Samir claims – with a smile – that he is seeing bright spots.

'I'm coughing up blood,' Sonja mutters.

After losing their partners, the four friends decided to form the Occult Seniors, a group with the motto: We've already got one foot in the grave! They travel to haunted places, hold seances and talk to spiritualists. None of them actually believe in ghosts, but they think it's a fun way to spend time together, and have been genuinely scared on a number of occasions.

'Listen up, everyone,' says Emma, standing in front of the others. 'Something like 100 million people died of cholera in Europe during the nineteenth century.'

'I remember it like it was yesterday,' Lennart says.

'Marx claimed that history repeats itself,' Emma continues, 'first as tragedy and then as farce. The Swedish authorities wanted to stop the spread at the border, so they set up a quarantine station for ships from Russia and Finland on an island called Fejan.'

Somewhere in the distance, a crow caws as the sun disappears behind a cloud. The woods suddenly feel much less welcoming.

'Fejan is around four kilometres east of here,' Emma goes on, using her stick to point. 'The people who died there were buried on uninhabited islands, and it just so happens that one of the biggest cholera cemeteries in the entire archipelago is right here.'

Their eyes turn towards the glade visible between the dwarf pines and sloping trunks.

'And it's haunted?' asks Lennart.

'Like your arse is by all those haemorrhoids,' Sonja mumbles.

'Didn't catch that, I'm afraid,' he says with a laugh, turning his good ear towards her.

Sonja leaves her picnic bag on the ground and makes her way into the glade. The bilberry bushes shake behind her, and Emma watches as she disappears among the trees.

'Seriously, though,' Emma speaks up again. 'I've read all sorts of texts from the folk archives and the Archipelago Foundation. No one living in the archipelago would voluntarily set foot on this island, but . . .'

Something catches her eye, and she trails off. She thought she saw a person between the trunks and brush, right behind Sonja. A short man wearing Bernie's linen suit. It looks too big for him, the shoulders sloping oddly.

'Hey, come and look at this,' Sonja calls from deeper inside the glade.

The others make their way over and find her standing by a large bundle on the ground. One end is narrower than the other, propped up against a birch tree. The bundle is probably around two metres long, made from sheets and plastic, bound with ropes that are looped around the surrounding trees.

'What the hell is that?'

Emma realises this must be what she saw behind Sonja. She wonders whether it could have blown in during a storm. There could be life jackets or fenders inside, wrapped up in a bit of old sail canvas.

'Maybe it's an art project?' Samir suggests with a smirk.

Emma nudges the bundle with her stick. Whatever is inside is as soft as a cow's udder, and much too heavy to have been carried on the wind.

Lennart mutters to himself as he unfolds his pocket knife and moves forward.

'I think we should leave it alone,' says Emma. 'It doesn't feel . . .'

She pauses as Lennart makes a long incision at the thick end of the bundle. From the hole, a greyish slime with brownish-red streaks and jelly-like lumps oozes out onto the ground. An acrid chemical smell hits them, making them back away. As the thick liquid drains away into the grass, they notice there is a half-dissolved foot among the brown sludge.

* * *

There are currently thirty-three police officers working full-time on Margot Silverman's disappearance, plus an additional fifteen experts at the National Forensic Centre.

The investigation is being run out of a large conference room at the National Crime Unit in Stockholm, where four detectives are gathered around the table with coffee, water, laptops, notepads, pens and reading glasses in front of them.

Maintaining a sense of professional objectivity has proved challenging for some, and several arguments have already flared up.

'This is Margot we're talking about, for fuck's sake. Our Margot!' Petter Näslund snapped before leaving the room.

The core group is being led by detective superintendent Manvir Rai. His parents both emigrated to Sweden from Goa, and he likes to cite that as the basis for his complete lack of prejudice towards anyone but the Portuguese.

Manvir is eloquent and sharp, with a constant frown on his face, always dressed in a black suit, white shirt and slim black tie.

Flecks of dust shimmer in the glare of the projector as he briefs the team on the photographs taken at the stables in Värmdö. He wraps up by going through any possible threats, whether linked to cases Margot has worked or directed at the police force more generally.

'We've got a team working to produce an initial report by this evening. They're making a list of everyone who has been released from prison or granted leave recently,' he concludes.

Joona stands up, leaving his jacket draped over the back of his chair as he turns to his colleagues.

His shirt is unbuttoned at the collar, his sleeves rolled up. His face seems tired, almost feverish, but his intense grey eyes are like polished steel.

Though he spends a lot of time behind a desk, his muscles and scars bear testament to the many years he has spent working in the field – as well as his military training in unconventional close combat.

'As you're all aware, the National Forensic Centre has now confirmed that the blood on the floor is Margot's, as is the urine, spinal fluid and marrow,' he begins. 'They're working quickly to compare the foot and fingerprints with the regular visitors to the stables. The technicians found 2,800 separate impressions, but it doesn't feel especially likely that we'll find anything belonging to the perp.'

'He's cautious but not professional,' says Manvir.

'We have a tyre track from a small lorry by the turn off that doesn't match any of the frequent visitors, so it could belong to the vehicle we're looking for.'

'What's the next step?' asks Greta Jackson.

Greta is an expert in profiling, with a doctorate in behavioural science and criminology. She has pale blue eyes and short greying hair, and is wearing a pair of tight trousers and a soft pink velvet jacket.

'We're still waiting on the results from various analyses,' Joona replies. 'And I just learned that the handprint on the feed container that you saw earlier was made by Margot. That means she was alive when she was dragged out. I'm repeating that now because it also means there's a chance we can still save her life . . . I know everyone is prepared to give their all right now, but I want to emphasise just how urgent it is, because we believe she was shot in the spine.'

'Do we know for sure she was shot?' asks Greta.

'I can't see any other way to read the blood evidence,' Joona replies as someone knocks at the door.

Saga Bauer's ex-boyfriend, Randy Young, enters the conference room with his service mobile in his hand. He is wearing jeans and a dark blue knitted sweater, plus a pair of glasses with black frames. His head is shaved, his hair nothing but a dark shadow on his scalp. Randy made the move from Internal Affairs to the National Crime Unit fourteen months ago.

'Joona, you've got a call from Stockholm North. Sounds pretty important,' he says, handing the phone over.

'Linna,' Joona says down the line. He hears a sharp intake of breath.

'Hi. I just wanted to say that we . . . uh, we've been following everything to do with Margot Silverman's disappearance over the incident channel,' says a shaky male voice. 'And I think . . . Obviously we haven't been able to verify it, but . . . Jesus Christ, I . . .'

'Who am I speaking to?' asks Joona.

'Sorry. Rickard Svenbo, Norrtälje. Inspector.'

The man falls silent again, and Joona hears a low whimper. His colleague is clearly in shock, struggling to express himself coherently.

'It's OK, Rickard, I'm listening. Just take your time,' Joona says softly.

'We've found some remains. Human remains, we think. It's completely fucking awful, completely fucking awful.'

'And where are these remains?'

'Where? On the ground . . . on, uh, a small island just off Kapellskär.'

'Could you tell me what makes it so awful?'

'They've been dissolved . . . In acid, it looks like. But we also found a hip flask in the middle of all the gunk, and it's engraved with the name Ernest Silverman.'

5

Joona is sitting opposite Astrid, one of the children with Down syndrome that Saga helps to support, in the hobby room at Enskede School.

Astrid is eleven, with long, dark hair and big, dreamy eyes. She has rounded shoulders, and her little face is almost always cheerful.

She has a white plastic box of nail varnish on the table in front of her, and as she takes out her favourite shades and lines them up in front of Joona, she tells him their names.

'Rouge Noir,' she says, holding one up.

'Nice,' he says.

'Do you want that one?'

'I'm not sure. Pink is nice too,' he says.

She rummages through the box and places another small bottle in front of him.

'Lady Like.'

'Ah, my favourite,' he says.

Joona came straight to Enskede from Kapellskär, leaving Erixon and six other technicians on the island.

The body had been dragged up one end of the beach by the natural harbour at the west of the small island, and as before the perpetrator had swept away any footprints they might have left. Erixon did manage to find a few shoeprints in the woods, but considering how cautious the killer seems to be, Joona doubts any of them are his.

By the time they arrived, there were flies crawling all over the foot and the other pieces of bone scattered in the grass.

Talking on the phone to Nils 'The Needle' Åhlén, professor of Forensic Medicine at the Karolinska Institute, Erixon had said that the remains resembled the stomach contents of some sort of animal, like food at varying stages of digestion.

'The bag has a thick rubber liner, and I'm guessing the perp used caustic soda to dissolve the body,' he explained.

Joona doesn't want to think about it, but he knows there is a chance that Margot was still alive when the chemicals began to take effect.

Astrid's lips are pursed in concentration, her long eyelashes trembling behind her glasses as she paints Joona's nails.

'Oops,' she whispers with a grin as some of the varnish ends up on his skin.

'My nails are too short.'

'Yeah, but it still looks pretty.'

'Really pretty.' He smiles.

Joona watches her calm brushstrokes, and before long the deep crease in his forehead starts to soften. It leaves behind a pale mark that slowly fades as she moves on to his other hand.

Saga called him earlier to say that she needed to meet as soon as possible, but when he arrived she had to help Nick take a shower after football.

Joona thanks Astrid and is busy blowing on his nails when Saga and Nick come into the room.

Saga is wearing a pair of pale blue jeans, basketball trainers and a knitted Icelandic sweater. Her long hair is gathered in a tight plait, and her face is bare.

Joona gets up and shows them his nails.

'Wow.' Nick laughs.

'Very nice,' says Saga.

Joona thanks Astrid again, telling her he has never felt so pretty. They head outside, and Saga makes sure the kids get onto the school bus before she and Joona start walking along the pavement in the sunshine.

'So, how's life as a private detective?' he asks with a wry smile.

'It's actually pretty unbearable.'

'Sorry to hear that.'

'Yeah, but I need a job – I can't claim sick pay anymore.'

'You know I can always lend you some money if—'

'I know,' she interrupts him. 'Thanks, but it's OK, I'm fine . . . I just need to get back onto the force.'

'Of course.'

'I've actually applied for a job with the NCU,' she tells him.

'Not the Security Service?'

'No, I think I'm done with them,' she replies. 'I need something much more concrete. I'm good at murder investigations, that's what I'm best at ... and to be perfectly honest, I want to work with you.'

'That would be fantastic,' he says quietly.

'But I swear, they won't even look at my application before the psychologist gives me the all clear.'

'That's always the way.'

'I really need this,' she says without looking at him.

If she is to have any chance of the psychologist declaring her fit for work, she has to be able to demonstrate that she is stable and self-aware, that she can take care of her finances, and manage a social life and a steady relationship.

'In any case, I asked you here because I only have half an hour before I have to be at a work meeting,' she explains, pausing by her motorcycle. 'My boss treats me like a ... I don't even know what. Anyway, I think ... I feel like I need to talk to you about the find on Kapellskär. I can't tell you who told me about it, but—'

'Randy.'

'I'm not saying a word.' She smirks.

Joona feels an ache in his chest when he sees that the harried intensity is back in her eyes. Saga pulls a plastic folder from her rucksack and holds it out to him. Through the milky plastic, he can see the postcard she received over three years earlier.

I have a blood red Makarov pistol. There are nine white bullets in the magazine. One of them is reserved for Joona Linna. The only person who can save him is you.

    Artur K. Jewel

Joona nods in recognition, turns the postcard over and studies the black and white photograph from 1898. The image is of the old cholera cemetery on Kapellskär, where Margot's remains were found.

'I know, but Jurek is dead,' he says.

'The Beaver isn't.'

'True, but he's in jail in Belarus, on manslaughter charges. We've tried to bring him back to Sweden, but there's no extradition treaty.'

The Beaver was recruited by Jurek, and remained loyal to him until his death. He then disappeared without a trace – until a year ago, when Interpol discovered that he was being held in a secure facility in Belarus.

A gust of wind makes the trees shake, and a few locks of blonde hair blow across Saga's face.

'OK, but . . . I just have the feeling this killer is influenced by Jurek somehow.'

'I really don't know, Saga. The fact that Margot's remains were found in the cholera cemetery is a bit of a coincidence, I'll give you that, but . . . It's just so hard to think that her murder could have anything to do with me. I mean—'

'But it is about you, it is,' she interrupts him, turning the postcard over. 'To me . . . The way I see it, Margot's death is some kind of message, proof that the threat against you is real.'

'This postcard is three years old,' he argues.

'But this is happening now.'

6

Saga parks her motorcycle and makes her way into the dimly lit bar. The TV screens on the walls of Star Bar are showing a German football match, the floor is scratched and dented, and the bottles behind the bar are glowing in the blue LED light.

She finds Simon Bjerke in one of the booths towards the back, dressed in full police uniform. He has a large beer in front of him, and is staring down at a laptop covered in stickers.

His face is furrowed, his moustache badly trimmed and his eyes puffy. When he spots Saga, he closes the lid of the computer and leans back with his arms folded.

'Saga Bauer, top of the class, the hottest—'

'That's what you said last time.'

'The hottest, the smartest, but never interested in dating or playing spin the bottle . . . And now here you are, down in the dirt with the rest of us.'

'Can't control everything,' she sighs, taking a seat opposite him.

'So, you had something to show me?' he says, sipping his beer.

'We've completed our investigation, which means you have the right to see what we've found – now or whenever you like.'

He studies her with cloudy eyes. 'I have the right?'

'You can also choose not to,' she explains.

'So she's been cheating on me?' he asks with a tense smile, a muscle twitching beneath his right eye.

'Do you want me to answer that?'

'Are you really sure? My Lisa? I mean, it's not all a misunder-standing?'

'Do you want to know what we think?'

'What the hell are you smiling for? What's so fucking funny?'

'I'm not smiling, I'm trying to be friendly in a situation that's clearly getting to you.'

'It's not getting to me, I just want to know the truth.'

'The truth about what?'

'Whether my wife's a fucking whore.'

They both sit quietly for a moment, and Simon gulps down another mouthful of beer. Saga notices that his hand is shaking as he lowers the glass.

'You came to us because you suspected your wife had been seeing another man while you—'

'I'll take that as a yes,' he interrupts her.

Saga hands over a dark grey folder with the words Kent Detective Agency printed in silver in the top right-hand corner.

'This details exactly what we found, our observations and conclusions. And here are all the supplementary files and pictures,' she says, passing him a USB stick.

Simon opens his laptop and pushes the stick into the slot. There are greasy fingerprints and splash marks all over the screen, the lights above the bar reflected in the grubby glass.

'Maybe you should read the report first,' Saga suggests.

He double clicks on the video file and hits play.

A floor lamp has fallen over, and is resting against an armchair. The bulb paints two ovals of light across the wall, illuminating his wife as she has sex with two men.

Lisa is straddling one of them, bracing herself against the mattress on either side of his torso. Her face is flushed and her mouth open, and the scar on her upper lip pales with every gasping breath she takes.

The second man is on his knees behind her, holding her backside and thrusting forward with a look of concentration on his face, his back glistening with sweat.

The short clip ends.

'Go fuck yourself,' Simon barks, throwing the rest of his beer over Saga. 'You fucking pig, fucking scum . . .'

There are a handful of other people in the bar, and they all turn towards him. The bartender starts making his way over. Saga's shirt and trousers are both drenched, and she gets up and leaves without another word.

'I hope you fucking die!' Simon shouts after her. 'I hope you get raped and humiliated and die!'

As Saga comes out onto the street, she glances down at her phone and realises she doesn't have time to go home and get changed. The boss sets a tight schedule for his employees, and he is notoriously strict. All of the other detectives are out on various jobs for the rest of the day, and Henry doesn't like the office to be left unmanned when he goes to the gym at two. She also has a report on a case of insider trading that is tearing a family business apart due in by four.

Saga shivers in her damp clothes as she drives back to the agency's offices, takes the lift and unlocks the door.

The lights are on in the empty office, though her colleagues' computer screens are all dark. Through the glass wall, she can hear Henry's rasping voice. He is on his phone as always, blinds closed.

Saga hurries inside, peels off her wet clothes and drapes them over the radiators beneath the two windows. She then sits down at her desk in nothing but her underwear, logs in and realises she got here just in time. She gets to work on her report.

Her old white bra is drenched in beer, the waistband of her blue underwear damp.

She stopped boxing several years ago, but her stomach and shoulder muscles are still visible in the harsh lighting.

Saga shudders when she realises she can no longer hear Henry's voice. He has CCTV cameras throughout the office, even in the bathrooms, though he claims those are only active at night.

She stops typing and finds her mind drifting to the postcard and the discovery of Margot's remains in the cholera cemetery. It bothers her that she has no idea how she might be able to protect Joona. She knows he will never go into hiding, that he will never accept protection of any kind.

Saga can't help but think that his lack of fear might prove dangerous this time, that underestimating the threat may well come back to bite him.

The door to Henry's office opens, and Saga turns her attention back to her report. She hears him drop something into the tray for outgoing mail and then turn in her direction.

Henry Kent is thirty-nine, with short dark hair and a neat beard, a small, straight nose and greenish brown eyes. He likes expensive suits, and he is incredibly sociable.

His father punished him with lit cigarettes when he was a boy, and Henry loves to show off the round burns on his arms and chest, explaining with a smile that although he hates his father, he also learned discipline from him.

He slowly makes his way over to the window behind Saga and peers out at the rush hour traffic and the bridges blocking the view over to Brunnsviken and Haga Park.

'Was the client happy?' he asks, turning to her.

She stops typing and meets his eye.

'I followed protocol, but he insisted on watching the footage. He got angry and threw a beer over me.'

'We'll add the dry cleaning bill to his invoice,' he says, moving closer to her.

'Like I said yesterday, it would have been better if you'd summarised everything for him,' she says.

'This suit is worth more than your entire wardrobe.'

'All I'm saying is that it was an uncomfortable situation.'

'You can dry your underwear on the radiator in my room if you want,' says Henry.

'Very funny.'

'Or maybe you like having wet underwear?'

'Stop,' she warns him, looking him straight in the eye.

'Stop what?'

'You know what I mean.'

'I'm not opposed to all this "me too" business, but a man has to be allowed to make a joke or pay someone a compliment,' he says, gazing back at her.

'I agree.'

'You look good. You've got a decent body.'

'OK, that's enough.'

'You could say thanks,' Henry replies, raising his voice.

'Thanks.'

'I know you need this job.'

'Like I've told you, it's really important to me.'

'If I fire you, you won't even be able to get a job as a security guard.'

'I'm sure.'

Henry looks away. 'I have to go soon. Remember to send me the summary of Johnson versus Johnson before four.'

'I will. I'm working on it now.'

He starts making his way over to the door, but pauses and turns around.

'Do you really think the NCU is going to hire you? Seriously, the National Crime Unit?'

'Have you been reading my private emails?'

'You'll never be a police officer again,' he says as he leaves the room.

7

Joona often helps Valeria in her nursery garden on the weekends. The physical labour helps him get his thoughts in order.

The NCU is working overtime to track down Margot's killer, but it feels as though their investigation has ground to a halt.

They have absolutely nothing to go on.

Margot's murder seems mysterious, almost like it was random.

Their attempts to tie any prints to the perpetrator have so far proved futile, and they are still waiting for the report from the forensic post-mortem and the delayed results of a number of lab tests.

Joona carries eight bags of peat up from the root cellar and puts them down beside the raised beds. He is wearing boots, old jeans and a navy blue sweater, flecked with paint from when he touched up the woodwork last autumn.

He pauses to watch Valeria as she pushes a wheelbarrow of top dressing between the young fruit trees. She has a plaster on one cheek, and her curly hair is full of straw and dry needles. She is wearing work gloves, black jeans, a dirty red quilted jacket, and a pair of rubber boots covered in dry clay.

So beautiful, Joona thinks to himself.

He has wanted to propose to her for a long time, and he thinks she would say yes if he asked. But only because she doesn't know the truth about him.

Joona hasn't told her that he smokes opium on occasion whenever he feels like he is making the world a darker, more dangerous place.

He can't bear the thought of losing her.

After graduating from high school, she fell head over heels for a man who was a few years older than her. He was an addict, and she tried to help him, even had two sons with him, but ultimately ended up becoming hooked on heroin herself. She hit rock bottom after being arrested and sentenced to prison for attempting to smuggle eight kilos of Estonian hash into the country.

Despite all the time that has since passed, despite never relapsing, despite having single-handedly raised both sons after her release and always keeping on top of her work, she has never forgiven herself.

And she would never forgive him.

Joona has no idea why he occasionally needs to sink so deep that he senses his own dissolution. He has tried to convince himself that it's just his way of processing grief, of admitting his own weaknesses in order to be able to keep up the fight, but that isn't true.

The truth is that something happened to him when he put the noose around Jurek Walter's neck. Joona still hears the echo of Jurek's last whisper whenever he wakes in the middle of the night.

Dust billows through the pale sunlight as Joona starts shovelling the peat.

Valeria pauses, pushes her hair back from her face and peers off down the cracked tarmac lane.

A white van is approaching.

Joona leans his shovel against the raised bed and moves over to her.

'That's Erixon,' he says.

'Did you know he was coming?'

'No, but I think I can guess what he's going to say,' he replies.

The van pulls up in the turning circle, and when Erixon opens the door to climb out an empty crisp bag tumbles to the ground.

'Quite some place you've got here,' he tells Valeria, gesturing with one arm. 'It's magical.'

'Thanks,' she says.

She smiles and pulls off one of her gloves to shake his hand.

'My fondness for the plant world isn't mutual, unfortunately . . . You don't have any nice plastic flowers, do you?' he jokes, pulling a sad face.

Valeria laughs. 'No, but I can order some if you like.'

'He'll still manage to make them wilt,' says Joona.

'Probably.' Erixon sighs.

Valeria gives Joona a quick glance to let him knows that she understands the situation.

'I thought I'd head inside and get washed up before making a start on dinner. You're very welcome to join us, Erixon,' she says, turning towards the house.

The men stand quietly for a moment, watching her walk away, and then they start wandering aimlessly between the rows of young trees.

'I didn't want to do this over the phone, but they've confirmed that the DNA is Margot's. The remains in the bag are hers.'

'We already suspected as much,' says Joona, slumping onto a stack of pallets.

Erixon kicks at the gravel and looks down at Joona with watery eyes.

'Honestly, it's one of the worst things I've ever seen . . . There was a rubber liner inside the plastic and fabric, and the killer dissolved the body at the scene, using sodium hydroxide – caustic soda. Impossible to say what the cause of death was.'

'So she could have been alive in the bag?'

'I don't know. Have you seen the pictures?'

Erixon holds out an A5 envelope and then turns away as Joona opens it and pulls out two colour photographs.

In the first, the contents of the bag have been laid out on a high-edged autopsy table. Margot's tissue is nothing but a grey-ish-yellow, half translucent slime with a few bigger lumps dotted here and there.

Beside her spinal column, which has been almost completely stripped bare, he can see a bright red foot without any toes.

In the second photograph, The Needle has rinsed away the chemicals and residue and lined up the more intact pieces of Margot's body.

A skull with a little hair still attached, scraps of neck muscle and windpipe, more bones – a thigh and a grey, blood-smeared piece of pelvis and tailbone.

'As for the stable . . .' Erixon says, clearing his throat. 'You were right, the lab found gunshot residue in the five blood drops on the floor, and this is where it gets interesting . . . They found traces of antimony, as expected, but also potassium, tin and mercury.'

'The bullet had a mercury primer,' says Joona, pushing the pictures back into the envelope.

'I've looked into it. They don't make them anymore. Bullets like that were only produced for a few years, back in the Eastern Bloc, but I'm sure it's possible to find old stores of them if you know where to look.'

'Did you find the bullet among her remains?' Joona asks, pressing two fingers to his left eyelid as the flicker of a migraine rears its head.

'Yeah, I've got it in my lab in the van. I thought you might want to take a look.'

The wind whistles through the young fruit trees as they walk over to the van.

'The strange thing is that the casing is as white as snow,' says Erixon, turning to Joona.

'What kind of metal?'

'It can't be anything other than fine silver. All silver contains a little copper, as you know, even sterling silver, but I think the perp must have heated up the casing until the copper oxidised ... And after that, they used acid to remove the copper oxide, leaving the round with a layer of fine silver, as it's called, on the outside.'

Erixon opens the van doors and climbs inside with a sigh, switching on the lamp above a small desk and loosening the straps around the chair. Ducking down in order to avoid hitting his head, Joona follows him in.

'There are no fingerprints on it,' Erixon continues, opening a drawer. 'Sit yourself down. Just let me know if you need a phase-contrast microscope.'

'Thanks.'

Erixon grabs a pair of porcelain-tipped pincers, lifts the bullet from a small box and sets it down on a microscope slide.

Joona takes a seat by the desk and angles the lamp towards it.

The bullet is badly deformed, its white casing like a tulip in bloom and its lead core flattened like a button.

'Hollow-point,' he says.

'The diameter is 9.27mm, which makes it a quarter of a millimetre bigger than the rounds you use.'

'So it's a Makarov?'

'Yup.'

'With a mercury primer and a fine silver case.'

'It's incredibly strange,' Erixon sighs, turning to Joona. 'Don't you think?'

'Mmm,' Joona replies.

'Do you want to tell me what's going on?'

'All in good time.'

* * *

Once Erixon has gone, Joona carries the spade and wheelbarrow over to the tool shed. The sun has dipped behind the treetops, filling the forest with shadows.

Yet again, he finds himself wondering what the macabre decision to dissolve Margot's body really means.

The nursery garden is bathed in a soft grey dusk, the sacks of peat lined up and the water in the rain barrel twinkling like an eye.

There is now little doubt in his mind that her death is linked to the postcard Saga received. Artur K. Jewel is an anagram of Jurek Walter, and the pistol the author mentions is a Makarov. According to the message, it also contains nine white bullets.

One of those bullets is meant for me, thinks Joona. And if we can believe the sender, Saga is the only person who can save me.

Who could have written the postcard?

Jurek Walter's family is long dead and his right hand man, the Beaver, is in prison in Belarus.

They aren't dealing with a copycat; this killer's modus operandi is completely different to Jurek's. Jurek never resorted to games, anagrams or mysteries, Joona thinks, as he makes his way towards the row of greenhouses.

To avoid the risk of leaving any drawings or written material behind, Jurek created a complex mind palace. From my point of view, thinks Joona, that was almost like a riddle, but to Jurek it was nothing but a visual system of coordinates to keep track of his victims' graves.

He never managed to complete his system, either. There were no graves at the last point, over by Moraberg.

Still, it's clear that whoever sent the postcard has some sort of connection to Jurek, and therefore also to me and Saga, he thinks.

Joona would like to continue his conversation with Saga, and he decides he should speak to the acting head of the NCU about temporarily bringing her on board while they wait for the green light from the psychologist.

A blood red Makarov containing nine white bullets.

9x18mm Makarov rounds fit the Makarov pistol, developed in the Soviet Union shortly after World War II and still used, albeit in a modernised form, across large swathes of the world.

The killer crept up on Margot in the stable and shot her in the spine. They then dragged her outside, hauled her into a vehicle and dissolved her body in sodium hydroxide in the Kapellskär cholera cemetery, some 120 kilometres away.

Joona empties the bag of leaves onto the compost heap and gazes between the trees, over the bilberry bushes and heather, until he can see no further.

A bird flaps anxiously from the branches of the spruce closest to him.

Two pinecones drop to the ground.

Joona turns around and makes his way back over to the tool shed, the tall meadow grass righting itself in his wake. He hangs the bag beside the rakes and looks over to the house. Golden light spills out from the kitchen window, and he can see Valeria's shadow dancing across the curtain inside.

As he winds the hose onto the reel, he notices that the door in the furthest greenhouse is ajar, and he wipes his hands on his trousers.

The gravel path crunches beneath his boots.

He sees his silhouette in the panes of glass, surrounded by the faint glow from the kitchen.

The choppy rattle of a helicopter passes overhead somewhere in the distance, quickly fading to silence.

Joona walks along the row of greenhouses until he reaches the furthest one, which Valeria uses as a storeroom.

He peers inside and sees a grey cat slink around a sack of chicken manure.

He opens the door and steps onto the concrete slabs in the middle walkway.

The sharp scent of tomato plants hangs heavy in the air.

Their leaves are straining upwards on both sides of him, pressed against the glass, forming a passage that ends in darkness.

There is no sign of the cat.

A relay switch clicks, and he hears the low hiss of the watering system.

Joona slowly makes his way down the narrow walkway.

He can see the cluttered storage area up ahead.

Above the glass roof, the evening sky is dark.

A dirty plastic bag has been shoved into a terracotta pot.

Joona keeps going.

The cat hisses and bolts away.

He hears a crack as a twig breaks outside.

A spade with a broken shaft has been left in a wooden crate.

Joona pauses and studies Valeria's old furniture.

Two of the legs on the big mahogany chest of drawers have collapsed, and everything that was stacked on top has fallen to the floor. Valeria's Portuguese sailor's chest is lying on its side, lid open. A blue tile with a compass rose painted on it has cracked, and a few photographs have fallen out.

The door creaks, and Joona wheels around. He grips the shaft of the spade, only letting go when Valeria flicks the switch for the overhead light.

'So this is where you're hiding?' she says, making her way over to him. 'What's happened here?'

'The legs must've collapsed,' he explains.

'I'll deal with it tomorrow. Dinner's ready.'

He picks up the three photographs and hands them to her.

'This was for Dad's fortieth,' says Valeria, showing him a studio portrait of the entire family.

'You should frame it.'

'Or this one,' she says, smiling.

He takes the faded colour photograph from her. Valeria must be around five in it, grinning and holding a football beneath her arm.

'Look at you,' he says.

She is studying the last of the pictures with a frown. In it, three teenage girls with long hair have waded out into the water. They are carrying a large pale blue sculpture of a woman in a flowing dress and a veil of pearls.

'Is that you in the middle?' he asks.

'No, I don't understand . . . This is a ritual, Mãe d'Água. It's really popular where I'm from, but our family never bothered with it. Dad could be quite strict sometimes.'

'Are they your friends, then?'

'No, I . . . honestly, I have no idea. I've never seen this before.'

* * *

Brandon has finished his pizza – a 'Millennium', with kebab meat and extra sauce – and is busy working his way through his fifth beer of the evening at Blå Bar.

He has his phone in his hand, flitting between several dating apps to keep the various conversations going, but none of the people he is talking to are ready to meet.

Brandon often finds himself thinking that he should move back to Uppsala. It's just that he doesn't have the energy to get his life in order, and his job at Kristinagården is fine, thank you very much.

He has made up his mind never to go to the churchyard again, but for some reason he can't shake the image of the raked gravel, the narrow walkways and the benches in the darkness between the lamps.

That was where he met Erik.

His only real relationship. It lasted seven months, until the summer, when Erik left to go interrailing and said he wanted to be free.

Once Brandon gave up any hopes that Erik would come back, going to the churchyard almost became a kind of compulsion.

Not that it does him any good. It doesn't help his self-confidence, doesn't bring him any comfort – it isn't even sexually satisfying. At best, it's intense and exhausting enough for him to be able to drift off to sleep when he gets home.

His old friends still hang around at the football pitch or over in Hallstavik Square, but the last thing he wants is to bump into any of them; that's why he has taken refuge on this side of town.

He knocks back the last of his beer, gets up and tucks the green chair beneath the table, bracing himself against one of the grubby pillars. He then turns and walks across the creaky floor, calling over to the bartender to say thanks.

The summer air smells like it used to when he stayed out late during the school holidays. The sky is dark, and a cartoon clown advertising ice cream thuds against the railing around the seating area with every gust of wind.

Brandon sways. He knows he should head home, but his restlessness takes him up the little road that runs alongside the paper factory.

The place is huge, with enormous industrial buildings, windowless brick facades, great piles of wet woodchip and timber, rumbling lorries.

It's like something out of a fucking sci-fi dystopia, he thinks.

He turns off the pavement, onto the freshly-cut grass between the silver birches and linden trees. The church itself is illuminated, but the car park is bathed in darkness. A new-looking Volvo is parked up against the wall.

Brandon pauses and feels a wave of dizziness as he sees the movements on the other side of the steamy car windows.

He staggers up the slope, over to the winding road and the empty bench he always seeks out.

The darkness beneath the maples is almost absolute.

He stands beside the bench and looks around.

Down on the main road, a car drives by. Once it is gone, all he can hear is the wind in the trees. A soft rustling sound, the thinnest branches stirring, followed by a muffled cry.

It's so quiet he barely notices it, and then it is gone.

Brandon's gaze is drawn down the narrow curve of the road that runs through the cemetery.

He sees a middle-aged man in a brown leather jacket standing behind a bush, a wry smile on his face.

Right then, Brandon feels something drip onto his neck.

A heavy raindrop that burns like boiling water. He reaches up to wipe it away, and another drop hits his fingers.

'Shit, what the . . .'

He steps to one side, out onto the narrow road, and looks up. Hanging from the branch above him is some sort of plastic and fabric cocoon, wrapped up in tape and rope. The big bundle shakes and starts swinging slightly, making the thick branch creak.

8

A large cortège carrying Margot Silverman's remains in a white coffin winds its way through Stockholm. The procession starts at the red brick station in Haninge Centrum where she first began her career as a police officer, and ends at Maria Magdalena Church, where the vicar who conducted her marriage to Johanna will lead the service.

The first six police motorcycles escorting the black hearse emerge from the Söderled Tunnel and turn left.

Hornsgatan has been closed to all other traffic between Slussen and Timmermansgatan.

Margot's cortège swings left just before Mariatorget, driving around the block and up to the church.

The bell rings solemnly as six of her colleagues, all wearing white shirts, black ties and mourning armbands, carry the coffin over the cobblestones. They pass the military colour guard and enter the dark church.

*　*　*

Through the grubby windows looking out onto lines of traffic and a pale sky, a melancholy light filters into the office.

Saga hasn't left her desk or stopped to eat in five hours. She is hunched over her keyboard, headphones on, attempting to transcribe thirteen separate conversations at double speed.

Her fingers dance across the keys, her heart pounding.

She has requested two hours off work to attend Margot's funeral, and the boss has agreed – providing she has the transcripts ready before she leaves.

'I could come back later to finish them off,' she suggested instead.

'Don't bother coming back at all if you leave before you're finished,' he snapped.

Saga speeds up again, trying not to miss a single slip of the tongue or filler phrase.

Her forehead is slick with sweat.

After working a shift last night, she is still wearing a pair of red leather trousers and a T-shirt with Damien Hirst's glittering skull on the chest.

She kicks off her heels as she finishes typing, then saves the transcriptions, sends the encrypted document to her boss, logs out and switches off her computer.

She hurries out into the hallway and pulls on her boots and jacket.

'Done already?' Henry asks from the doorway to his office.

'I just sent you the document.'

'But I need a physical copy in my hand.'

Saga pulls off her boots, returns to her cubicle and powers up the computer. She logs in, opens the document, hits print and collects the sheets from the printer, stapling them together before she knocks on his door.

When he fails to answer, she hurries back to her computer, logs out, turns off the lamp and quickly tidies her desk, then tries again.

'Come in,' Henry says after a moment.

She opens the door and steps inside. Her boss is sitting in his armchair, reading *Connoisseur* magazine.

'Here are the transcripts you—'

'Thanks, you can just leave them on my desk,' he says without looking up.

Saga does as he says, making her way back out into the hallway and pulling her boots back on. She hurries out of the office, doing up her jacket as she runs down the stairs.

When she reaches the street outside, she unlocks her motorcycle with trembling hands, rolls it across the pavement to the road, climbs on and starts the engine.

She drives a little too fast, almost losing control as she turns off onto Klarastrandsleden. There isn't much room between the concrete wall and the slow-moving traffic in the tunnel, but she manages to maintain her speed.

She knows that her job at the detective agency is unsustainable, but there is no way the police psychologist will give her the green light to return to the force if she is fired.

In the middle of Centralbron, a train travelling in the opposite direction thunders by alongside the right-hand lane. The cables overhead spark, and the breeze makes her sway.

Saga's plan is to head back to her apartment and get changed. The church is only five minutes from where she lives, and she doesn't want to show up to the funeral in red leather pants and a T-shirt with a skull on the front.

It's after three by the time she pulls up outside her building, and the ceremony has already started. She leaves her motorcycle right outside the door and decides not to bother checking the CCTV cameras like she usually does before heading inside. She simply runs up the stairs and tramples on the post lying on her hallway mat before kicking off her boots.

Saga unbuttons her trousers as she rushes through to the bedroom, tugging them down and kicking them away. She drops her leather jacket to the floor and struggles into a black dress. As she heads back out into the hallway, she pulls on a black jacket and grabs her running shoes instead of the pumps she put out earlier, then hurries out of the apartment.

She sprints down Bellmansgatan, grabbing the black metal railing in her left hand and swinging around onto the stone steps, pausing as a bus thunders by on Hornsgatan.

Saga runs across the road and up the steps to the churchyard, darting between the graves and over to the church. She holds up her ID to one of the uniformed officers by the entrance, and once he ticks her name off his list she makes her way into the dark vestibule inside.

After she first got home from the rehabilitation centre on Idö, she requested a one-on-one conversation with Severin Balderson, the elderly priest at Maria Magdalena Church. She has often thought about the fact that she simply got up and left in the middle of their meeting, having realised over the course of their conversation that she needed to become a police officer again in order to forgive herself.

When she saw his name on Margot's funeral notice, she decided that she would try to talk to him after the ceremony, that she would apologise for her overly hasty letters, in which she complained to the archbishop about his provocations that God was all-powerful and the protector of all children.

Saga comes into the church just as the police choir starts singing 'Glorious is the Earth'. She takes a seat in the back row, beneath the organ loft, and takes off her jacket.

The white coffin at the front of the church is laden with red roses, and the glow of the candles flickers up the whitewashed arches and vaulted ceiling.

Margot's immediate family said their goodbyes in a smaller ceremony earlier, but Johanna has stayed behind and is now sitting tall beside Joona in the front row.

The church is full of officers in uniform, all wearing mourning bands.

The choir finishes their song, and the candlelight glitters on the men's tie clips as they move away.

A young priest steps forward, making his way down the steps into the nave before pausing. He looks out at the congregation and starts talking about lives taken too soon, deaths that we simply cannot comprehend.

Johanna's shoulders start shaking, and Joona passes her a tissue.

Saga quietly opens the order of service and sees that Severin Balderson is supposed to be conducting the ceremony, just as she had thought.

But this isn't him.

Why has another priest taken over?

She feels herself break out in a sweat, unable to focus on the prayers.

Saga knows she has a manic side, but she can't help but dig out her phone.

The woman sitting beside her notices its pale glow and flashes her a look of disappointment.

Saga attempts to hide her phone beneath her jacket, leaning forward as she searches for Severin Balderson online. She finds his Facebook page and stares down at the image of his bearded face and bushy brows.

The little metal figurine that arrived in the post looks just like him. She needs to examine it more closely, using a magnifying glass.

She must talk to Joona.

* * *

The poignant tune of the final psalm echoes through the nave of the church as Joona leads Johanna down the aisle. He can feel how weak she is, her legs constantly threatening to give way beneath her, and he keeps her upright with an arm around her waist.

The pews are full of mourners dressed in black, heads bowed.

They walk through the dark vestibule and out into the pale summer light. There are house sparrows chirping in the bushes, blackbirds singing in the trees.

A black taxi is waiting for Johanna at the bottom of the hill.

'I still can't believe it,' she says.

'It'll take time,' Joona tells her.

People begin to flood out of the church, streaming past them on both sides.

'I think I might need to see her after all,' she says. 'To really wrap my head around the fact that she's dead. I know you think it's a bad idea, but I'm afraid I'll regret it if I don't see her one last time. What if I never manage to process the fact that she's gone? What if I keep thinking she'll come home and crawl into bed with me every night?'

'We can go back inside. The church will be empty soon, and you can stay there for as long as you like, but I really don't think you should open the coffin.'

'OK,' she whispers, swallowing hard.

'Do you want me to ask the taxi to wait?'

'I don't know, I should probably get home to the girls . . . It's just that I can't bear the thought of Margot being all alone, and . . .'

Johanna bursts into tears again, and Joona wraps his arms around her until she manages to calm down. He walks her over to the taxi, helps her inside and then closes the door and watches the car pull away.

Joona turns back to the church. Some people have begun to leave, but others are chatting in small groups. He sees Saga talking to the priest by the church doors, and he notices something flicker across her face every time one of the other mourners stops to thank him for the ceremony.

Joona takes out his phone and switches it on. Manvir Rai has left him a voicemail.

He moves over to one side, beneath one of the maples, to listen.

'*It's me, Manvir. I know you're at the funeral, but we've found another body. Same method, same killer . . .*'

Joona listens to the entire message, then drops his phone back into his pocket. Saga has spotted him, and is hurrying across the cobblestones. He walks towards her between the graves.

'I need to talk to you,' she says.

'Walk with me, I'm in a bit of a hurry,' Joona tells her, making his way down towards Bellmansgatan.

'What's going on?'

'They've found another body, by Hallstavik church this time.'

'Just now?'

They cut across the gravel and into the alleyway.

'Someone called it in last night, but the responding officers didn't take it seriously until—'

'What the hell?' Saga groans.

'The man who reported it was pretty drunk, apparently. He kept talking about a cocoon from outer space.'

'OK,' she sighs.

They come out onto Bellmansgatan and follow the pavement to the left.

'The Needle is there now.'

'Have they identified the body?'

'No, it's completely dissolved; it must have been hanging there longer this time,' Joona explains as he unlocks his car. 'But The Needle did find a ring from the theological institute in Uppsala, which suggests they were probably a priest.'

'His name is Severin Balderson,' says Saga, meeting Joona's eye.

9

Joona has accompanied Saga back to the detective agency, and is now sitting in the meeting room in front of a large microscope with a digital display. The silvery grey reflection of his wristwatch dances across the wall.

Saga is wearing a pair of latex gloves when she returns from her booth carrying a small box.

'This came in the post on Thursday.'

She carefully folds back the paper and a layer of thin white fabric and produces a small figurine, around the size of a pistol cartridge, setting it down on the microscope slide.

'It must be him,' she says after a quick glance at the display.

Joona studies the figurine's crudely sculpted face: a man with a full beard, thick eyebrows, deep-set eyes and a slender nose.

As grey as a corpse in the morgue.

Saga holds up her phone to show him a picture of Severin Balderson. There is no doubt about it, the little metal figurine does look like him.

'I spoke to the other priest,' says Saga. 'No one has heard from Severin in days. He goes through drinking bouts, apparently, so the other priest wanted to give him a little time.'

'OK, I'll call The Needle and ask him to run a DNA analysis.'

The door to the meeting room opens and Saga's boss Henry Kent comes into the room with a look of disappointment on his face.

'What's going on here, Saga?' he asks.

'I'm helping the police with a—'

'That's great,' he interrupts her. 'But do I need to remind you that you're on the clock here?'

'I still have another hour.'

'OK, but I need your help collecting a few shirts from the dry cleaner.'

'Do you want me to have a word?' Joona asks quietly.

'I've got it,' she replies, turning back to her boss. 'Henry, I need a moment with Joona here, but the minute I'm done I'll go and pick up your shirts. I'll even take off the plastic and hang them on those cedar hangers you like.'

'Have you been snooping through my desk?' Henry asks, his eyes on the little metal figurine.

'Why would I have . . .'

Saga trails off and gets to her feet, pushing her boss up against the wall with one hand.

'What are you doing?!'

'You were talking about the figurine, weren't you? When you asked if I'd been snooping through your desk?' she asks, her voice sharp.

'Take it easy, Saga' Joona warns her.

'That arrived in the post on Thursday,' she continues.

'OK, but—'

'You weren't here on Thursday,' she cuts Henry off.

'Sounds right.'

'So why are you asking if I've been looking through your desk?'

'I thought—'

'Because more of these figurines have arrived for me, haven't they?'

'I have one,' Henry replies. 'It's in the bottom drawer of—'

'And was that parcel addressed to me too? Was it? Have you been taking my private mail? That's fucking illegal!' she shouts.

'This is my agency and my . . .'

Henry pulls away with a frightened look on his face, following Saga as she marches into his office. She flings open his drawers, tossing papers, files and shoe trees to the floor. When she spots a small cardboard box similar to the other one, she lifts it out.

'You're fired. You're so fucking fired.'

'Shut up, Henry,' she snaps. 'I quit, and you'll give me all the references I want – otherwise I'll be back.'

She shoves his computer to the floor to make room for the box, sweeping pens and folders aside and setting it down on the desk.

'Joona!' she shouts.

The boss is trembling, and he takes a step back as Joona comes into the room. Saga grabs a pen and carefully pushes back the cardboard flaps.

Joona moves closer.

Saga slowly folds back the bubble wrap and a crumpled sheet of paper from a book, revealing the small figurine inside.

'Margot,' Joona whispers.

10

After speaking to Joona, Morgan Malmström, the acting head of the National Crime Unit, declared the two murders a so-called 'extraordinary event'.

The primary purpose of declaring an extraordinary event is to prevent the rest of the police force from becoming overwhelmed during particularly resource-intensive operations. Instead, the unit tasked with investigating the incident is temporarily fenced off as a separate entity, with its own organisational structure, support staff, budget, experts, legal team and operative resources.

Morgan Malmström appointed Manvir Rai as strategic commander, and he immediately gave Saga Bauer a probationary position as an investigator.

It is 6.15 on Monday morning when Saga follows Joona into the glass foyer of the Police Authority building, swipes her temporary pass and continues through the revolving doors.

'Welcome to the NCU,' Joona says as they leave the lifts on the eighth floor and start making their way down the corridor.

They pass the empty pantry and one closed door after another. The strip lights glare off the plastic floor, and a poster billows away from the wall in their wake.

Manvir, Greta Jackson and Petter Näslund are deep in intense discussion when Joona opens the door to the large meeting room, but they quickly stop talking when they spot Saga.

Drone shots of the find sites have been pinned up on one wall, as has an image of the stables where Margot Silverman was shot.

Between the coffee mugs and laptops on the table, there are printed close ups of the two metal figurines, plus copies of the preliminary analyses from the lab.

'Thanks for letting me join you,' Saga says, shaking the three detective superintendents' hands. 'I know I'm going to learn so much from working with you, and I hope I can help to find the killer.'

Manvir tells her to sit down at one of the computers, then clears his throat and explains how to log in. Petter offers to help, his voice oddly strained.

'It's probably none of my business,' Greta begins, 'but I would imagine she's sick of being judged on her looks; she wants to be respected for doing her job well.'

'They said the same about me when I first joined,' Joona jokes.

'Of course they did,' Greta says with a laugh, putting on her glasses.

There is a knock at the door, and Verner Zandén, the head of the Security Service, comes into the room before anyone has time to respond. He is almost six foot five, wearing a pair of crumpled trousers and a brown blazer.

'Saga, I was hoping you'd come back to us,' he says in his booming baritone.

'You might have mentioned it,' she says.

'I just thought . . .'

'Thought I would have said no?'

'Sorry to interrupt, I just wanted to check whether any of you know how to do magic. I promised the grandkids I'd make their granny hover.'

'You're going to make Maja hover?' Greta asks with a wry smile.

'Verner, we're trying to work here,' says Saga.

'Right, yes, sorry,' he replies, striding back out of the room.

Down on Polhemsgatan, a car alarm starts blaring. Someone pushes a squeaky trolley along the corridor, and the air conditioning unit hums non-stop.

'OK, shall we get started?' Manvir asks, clearing his throat. 'Joona has told us all about the postcard and the nine white bullets, the Makarov pistol and the threat against, uh, against . . .'

'Him,' Saga fills in.

'This whole thing is fucking nuts,' Petter mutters.

'I know. But at least we have a pattern,' she replies. 'The hunt is on, but so far it's all been on the killer's terms.'

'And that leaves us feeling the pressure,' Manvir says with a nod.

'What do you have to say, Joona?' asks Petter.

'I usually—'

'Don't tell me, you've already solved it?'

'No, but I will. And soon.'

'That's great, just great.'

'Take it easy, Petter,' Greta warns him.

'This is personal for me. I loved Margot,' Petter snaps back, his chin trembling.

'It's personal for all of us,' she replies.

Petter sighs and moves over to the window, taking out a tub of snus and pushing a wad of the tobacco beneath his lip.

'I have a few questions for you, Saga, before we get down to work . . . Is that OK?' asks Greta.

'Of course.'

'Would you like a cup of coffee or anything?'

'No, thanks, I'm fine,' says Saga, leaning forward in her seat.

'OK. My first question,' says Greta, flicking through to a blank page in her notepad, 'is whether you have any idea why the killer reached out to you?'

'No, but I aim to find out.'

'OK, let me rephrase that. Why do you think he sent you the postcard?'

'Because I'm the only person who can save Joona. That's the reason he gives, anyway.'

'Does he want Joona to be saved?'

'I think he wants the burden of responsibility to fall on me.'

Petter moves back over to his chair and slumps down into it.

'But why you, specifically?' Greta presses Saga, not taking her eyes off her for a second.

'I don't know, but I think there must be some sort of connection to Jurek Walter.'

'The anagram on the postcard,' Manvir fills in.

'And what do you think that connection might be?' asks Greta.

'It's probably someone who identifies with Jurek, who admires him for managing to remain active for so long without being caught.'

'But why would he want to kill Joona?'

'Because Joona killed Jurek.'

'And why does he want you to stop him?' Greta asks, leaning forward.

'Maybe because I failed to stop Jurek?'

'You mean he wants to make you responsible for stopping the killings, and then to see you fail?'

'Yes.'

'Interesting.' Manvir nods.

Joona has to make a real effort not to betray his pride in her. Saga managed to give them clear, concise answers without attempting to mask or smooth over her own failings.

'I attended an FBI symposium on serial killers in Texas,' Greta tells the others. 'Most of the participants concluded pretty early on that the idea that a serial killer wants to be caught, that they want to be stopped, is a myth.'

'It's probably not their primary driving force, that's true,' Joona agrees.

'I know. What I'm saying is that it's a misconception based on the fact that serial killers often get cocky after a while. It's not that they *want* to be caught, it's that they don't believe they *can* be.'

'Though many serial killers do communicate. With the police, the media, even though there's no practical reason for them to do so,' Joona points out. 'And the idea that they're getting cocky doesn't quite explain it.'

'No, absolutely not, I agree with you there. I actually made a similar point at the seminar,' Greta nods.

'I don't have the same experience as the rest of you,' says Saga. 'But isn't it linked to the idea that many serial killers were pyromaniacs as children? That the same urge reoccurs once they're older, only . . . in the form of a game, or whatever you want to call it, where they lose control and therefore rid themselves of any responsibility? As though they're trying to say, "I'm going to start a fire now, and it's going to spread and cause damage unless someone puts it out."'

'Yes,' says Greta, fixing her serious eyes on Saga. 'Because that's precisely what I think our killer is saying. "Saga, I've warned you, and you know what will happen if you don't put the fire out. I've got nine white bullets, so from this moment on you bear complete responsibility for anyone who dies."'

'And he can say that because I could've saved both victims if I'd been able to work out what he was saying in time.'

'The figurines were posted to Saga before the murders took place,' Joona elaborates. 'They reveal who the victim will be while there's still time to save them.'

'We've got two guys from surveillance watching the detective agency so that we don't miss any more,' Petter speaks up.

'Thanks,' says Joona.

Manvir gets to his feet, grabbing one of the detailed images of Margot's figurine. He studies it, his forehead creased.

'What do we know about the killer?' he asks, tossing the image back onto the table.

'Only what he wants us to know,' says Joona.

'Are we sure about that?' Greta counters.

Manvir buttons his jacket and moves over to the whiteboard, grabbing a pen from the shelf. Tip squeaking, he starts writing:

Communicative perpetrator: possibly in an attempt to abdicate responsibility.
References: Jurek Walter, Saga and Joona.
Metal figurines: sent to Saga, indicate next victim.
Ammunition: 9x18mm Makarov rounds, fine silver casings, Russian mercury primers.
Murder and discovery sites not the same.
Bodies dissolved in caustic soda, rubber body bags.
Victims: one middle aged woman, head of NCU; one elderly man, priest at Maria Magdalena Church.

Manvir turns back to face the others. He looks like he is about to say something, but he holds his tongue and lowers his hand.

'We're dealing with a serial killer here,' says Joona. 'He has nine bullets in his pistol. It's possible he's killed before, we have no idea, but I'm certain he'll kill again unless we can find him soon.'

'Nine victims,' Saga mutters to herself.

'Why nine?' asks Petter.

'That could prove to be key,' says Joona.

'Should I add that to the board?' asks Manvir.

'Yes.'

Serial killer with nine intended victims.

Manvir turns back to them again, pushing the lid onto the pen and then holding it up to get their attention.

'We have no fingerprints, no DNA, no fibres that don't belong to the packaging . . . But the gunshot residue found in Margot's blood can't have been deliberate,' he says.

'Maybe not,' says Joona. 'But it only confirms what the killer has already shown us.'

'I still think we should take a closer look at the mercury angle,' says Greta.

'Good idea,' says Joona.

'According to the lab, the figurines are made from ordinary tin, as we'd already guessed. Impossible to trace,' says Manvir, turning back to the board.

'And you don't need any special equipment or tools to work with tin; the melting point is so low that an ordinary kitchen will do,' Saga explains as Manvir writes.

Lack of evidence: suggests caution and awareness of forensic methodology.
Material knowledge: casting tin, producing fine silver, using caustic soda.

They pass around the enlarged images of the figurines: Severin's crudely carved face, beard and brows; Margot's prominent nose, the crease on her brow and the plait resting against her shoulder.

'I used to make clay models for animation when I was younger,' says Petter. 'And let me tell you, I was much more careful . . . I mean, our killer hasn't even bothered doing any tidying up; they haven't filed it, haven't got rid of the lumps and bumps.'

'I know, I made tin soldiers myself,' Manvir says with a nod, adding yet another point to the board.

Not a perfectionist.

Greta gets up and pins the two large photographs of the figurines to the wall. She returns to the table and pours herself a glass of water, taking a sip and dabbing at her mouth with a napkin.

'The parcels were posted from two different locations around Stockholm,' says Manvir. 'One was dropped off at the newsagent on Odengatan, and the other came from the post desk at the Co-op supermarket in Midsommarkransen . . . We've got two teams checking CCTV in the area right now, but we decided not to put the locations themselves under surveillance, since he's hardly going to go back to the same place when he has several thousand to choose from.'

'There are no fingerprints on the boxes, the tape or anything else in the parcels,' says Petter. 'We're analysing the torn out page, the bubble wrap, the child's drawing and the old fabric, which . . .'

He trails off as everyone in the room receives an alert over the police network.

Another parcel has arrived for Saga Bauer.

11

A police car races from the Kent Detective Agency offices on Norra Stationsgatan to the station in Kungsholmen, lights flashing and sirens blaring. Two forensic technicians are ready and waiting outside when it pulls up at the kerb. They take the parcel and lower it into a larger box, then hand it over to members of the bomb squad.

The squad's dog eagerly sniffs the package before they quickly scan it for explosives and use an X-ray to inspect the contents.

All they can see inside is a small, rough lump of metal.

The technicians take the box back from the bomb squad, hurry into the foyer, past security, and take the lift to the laboratory where the investigation team is waiting in protective clothing.

The detectives watch impatiently as one of the technicians lifts the parcel addressed to 'Saga Bauer c/o Kent Detective Agency' out of the larger box, places it on the light table and starts taking pictures.

The only visible marks are a number of glove prints, likely from the sorting office.

A technician uses a scalpel to cut away the bottom of the box, pulling out a ball of crumpled paper and unfolding it to reveal a small bundle of white cotton.

'Hurry, hurry,' Greta mutters.

While everyone is watching the woman open the bundle, the two other technicians start searching for traces of the perpetrator on the inside of the empty box and the wrapping.

'Come on,' says Petter. 'We don't know how long we've got to identify the next victim, but it's fucking urgent.'

'Check for prints, there must be something!' Manvir blurts out.

'Microscope! Come on, come on.'

'Careful now,' Petter warns the technician.

With soft, almost tender movements, she unfolds the scrap of fabric around a small tin model, around two centimetres tall. Using a pair of pincers, she sets it down on the slide beneath the microscope.

The five investigators gather around the technician as she adjusts the magnification level and focus. A dull grey glow appears on the screen. The figurine's head is out of shot, but the little metal figure is wearing a short-sleeved shirt with epaulettes and an emblem on its right arm.

'A police officer,' says Joona.

The figurine also has a pistol and a baton on its belt, and is holding a hat in one hand.

The green-eyed technician adjusts the slide so that the model's head comes into focus, then steps aside.

The detectives stare down at the crude face, which has a thick moustache and bags beneath its eyes. The man has a thick neck and small eyes, and there are a couple of strange bumps on his bare head, almost like the beginnings of a pair of horns.

'We've got 35,000 officers to choose from,' Manvir mumbles, leaning forward.

'What the hell do we do now?' Petter asks, sounding stressed.

Saga's face has paled, and she takes a step back. Joona looks up from the microscope and peers over at her.

'OK, listen up, everyone,' says Manvir. 'We need to share photographs of his face force-wide as soon as possible.'

'You recognise him, don't you, Saga?' says Joona.

'I think his name is Simon Bjerke, he works for Norrmalm district,' she replies.

'Simon Bjerke? Who is that?' Manvir asks, taking off his protective mask.

'All I know is that he hired the detective agency where I worked recently,' she says.

'You sound sure,' says Greta, her voice intense.

Saga nods.

'Are you? Are you sure?'

'We were in the same class at the academy.'

'This might give us the head start we need to find him before it's too late,' says Joona.

'OK, let's get going,' says Manvir.

The five hurry out of the lab, pulling off their protective clothing as they go. Petter's overalls get caught on his shoe, trailing behind him until he manages to shake it off. Manvir peels off his gloves and shoves them into his pocket.

As they run down the corridor, Petter manages to get hold of Simon Bjerke's home address, phone number and radio number. While he calls Simon's mobile, Manvir tries to reach him over the radio.

'I'll get in touch with command,' says Greta.

She talks to the duty officer as she walks, and quickly learns that Simon Bjerke is out on patrol.

'Quiet, everyone,' she says, switching her phone to loudspeaker. 'Where is he?'

'I can see,' says the officer, 'that Simon and his partner Haron Shakor just responded to a call out in Årsta, but—'

'What kind of call?' asks Greta, stopping dead in the middle of the corridor.

'We received a report about a group of men harassing the owner of a halal butcher.'

'So they're there right now? Can you put us through to them?' asks Greta.

'I can't, they seem to have their radios switched to direct mode,' the duty officer replies.

'Send units out there,' says Joona.

'Are there any other cars in the area?' asks Greta, setting off down the corridor again.

'Let me check ... Yes, we've got one by the Globe Arena and another on Östbergavägen, by the park.'

'Send them to the scene,' she says.

The five detectives break into a run towards the lifts.

'I'll go,' Joona says as he presses the button.

'What's the plan?' asks Petter.

'Getting there before the killer this time,' says Saga.

'Simon is probably safe so long as he's with his partner,' says Manvir.

'I'll bring him back here,' says Joona, opening the door to the stairwell.

'Do you want me to come?' Saga asks.

'Only Joona is permitted to work operationally,' Manvir quickly interjects.

'What the fuck?'

The sound of Joona's rapid footsteps on the stairs is muted as the steel door swings shut with a dull thud.

'Let's head back upstairs and piece together everything we know about Simon; we need a complete profile,' says Manvir, irritably jabbing at the lift button again.

'What's the deal with Simon Bjerke? Why would anyone want to kill him?' asks Greta. 'Do you know, Saga?'

* * *

Joona overtakes a petrol tanker, passing Liljeholmen on the E20 before getting into the left-hand lane and swinging off onto the 75.

He has just learned that the two patrol cars have reached the scene and are in the process of setting up a cordon.

Joona turns off into the industrial area that has sprung up around the freight terminal, past a rundown Best Western hotel, a Burger King and a large petrol station with a car wash. He can see the blue lights of a police car sweeping across the tarmac and the buildings up ahead.

Wholesalers, rubbish bins and loading docks race by at the sides of his vision.

He pulls up in front of the patrol car, which has been parked across the road.

The officers have taped off a large area.

Joona gets out of the car and hurries over to an officer in uniform, holding up his ID.

'What's going on?' he asks.

'We're not really sure, but our colleagues responded to a thirty-five about an argument or a robbery, and it looks like they went in . . . Last we heard, it had developed into a hostage situation. Command told us to hold off, but since that . . . nothing.'

Mounted beneath the overhanging roof on the yellow brick building is a green and white sign reading HALAL BUTCHER, with a round emblem in green and black. The steel door is closed, and the blinds in the three small windows are down.

The fan unit for the cold room has been mounted on the flat roof, a scrap of tape flapping in the breeze.

On the ground between the car park and the building, there are a number of old refrigeration units and cabinets.

'Have you been in?' asks Joona.

'We've been ordered to wait for backup.'

Simon and Haron's patrol car is parked between a rusty van and a silver Hyundai with the butcher's logo on its door.

'When will they be here?'

'Twenty-five minutes is the last I heard.'

'I need one of you to the rear and one on the roof next door,' says Joona, heading back over to his car.

He opens the boot and takes out his bulletproof vest, quickly pulling it on. Right then, he hears an agitated voice behind him:

'You're not listening to what I—'

'I'll listen once you've come this way,' one of the officers replies sharply.

'But it's my dad who—'

'Be that as it may, you can't be here right now; this area has been cordoned off.'

Joona fastens the Velcro around his torso, turns around and watches the officer attempting to stop a middle aged woman from getting any closer to the butcher's shop.

'This is my dad's business,' she continues. 'The display counter is new, the fan is new, it's his life's work. Let me go, I have a right to be here!'

'No, you don't, this . . .'

Joona moves around a yellow rubbish bin and doesn't hear what the officer says to the woman, but she is still agitated when she replies.

'OK, I'll come with you if you listen to me,' she says. 'My dad is in there, and he's an old man. They're harassing him, you know. You have to do something! There are three of them, they've got guns and . . .'

She trails off at the sound of raised voices from inside the shop.

There is a thud against the wall.

Something crashes to the floor.

Then, silence.

12

The officer lifts the plastic tape and escorts the woman out of the cordoned-off area. They walk along the edge of the building, pausing after twenty or so metres in front of a row of closed aluminium fronts.

He grabs her arm, but she pulls away.

Dust swirls across the parking area in the August sun.

Joona hurries to catch up with them, telling the officer that he will take over and then turning to the woman.

Her eyes are big and bloodshot, her full lips trembling. She is wearing jeans, a white windbreaker and a Burberry scarf.

'My name is Joona Linna. I'm a detective superintendent with the National Crime Unit, and I'm going to do everything I can to help your father.'

'I've been trying to tell—'

'Just hold on. I know you're scared, and I'm going to listen to what you have to say, but first why don't you tell me your name?'

'Nora, but it doesn't matter. They're attacking my dad in there. There are three of them, and he's an old man.'

'I hear what you're saying, Nora. Could you tell me what's happened so far?'

She tucks a few stray locks of dark hair behind her ear. 'Everything was like normal this morning. I was in the shop, helping Dad with the prices,' she says, rubbing her mouth. 'And then the Brothers showed up. We saw their van outside and Dad told me to call the police and leave through the back door, through the office by the cold room.'

'Who are the Brothers?'

'My dad, Aias, he put their shop out of business ten years ago, and now they want payback . . . I know one of them from school, Branco.

He's actually a pretty nice guy, he was on the football team Dad used to coach.'

'Are they career criminals?'

'I don't think so, but they've sent letters, called in the middle of the night, tried to take him to court. We're talking about a lot of money here, lots of meat; Dad can't even keep up anymore.'

Her tears have caused her kajal to run, collecting in the creases beneath her eyes.

'OK, Nora, I need you to keep your distance and listen to these officers. You'll be making our job harder otherwise – you understand that, right?'

She nods and wipes her nose with shaking fingers.

'I'm just so scared they're going to hurt him.'

'I know, but I'm going to go in and talk to them now.'

'You're going in?'

Joona turns away and lifts the blue and white tape, walking past Andersson Fruit & Veg.

By the back entrance, there are three plastic chairs around a table. The beer bottle on top is full of cigarette butts.

He keeps going, stepping over a low fence and gesturing to his colleagues to let them know he is going in. He moves along the edge of the halal butcher and knocks on the door.

'Simon? I need to talk to you,' he says, turning the handle.

'No one's coming in here!' a gruff voice shouts.

'Take it easy, I just need a quick word with Simon,' says Joona, making his way in with his hands above his head.

'What the hell?'

To the right of the door, almost by the counter, is a bearded man with a shotgun.

'You fucking deaf or something?'

'No, but I don't have time for this,' Joona tells him. 'I need to find Simon, they told me he was in here . . .'

Joona immediately reads the situation: the five people in the butcher's shop are on the verge of a bloodbath. The surface tension of their fear is all that is saving them right now.

Behind the display counter, around fifteen metres away, Aias is standing in his white coat, a knife to Branco's throat.

Branco's pistol is lying on the bloody workbench.

The bearded man by the door is holding a Benelli M4 Super 90, pointing it at Aias.

Over by the drink refrigerator, Haron the police officer is down on one knee. He is using his left hand to steady his right forearm, training his Sig Sauer on the bearded man.

At the very back of the shop, by the table of pump thermoses and plastic cups, a thin man with a blonde ponytail is shifting nervously with a Glock 34 pointed at the officer.

'Haron, you and Simon responded to the call. You came out here together,' Joona continues in a soft voice.

'He's out back, I think,' Haron replies, maintaining his aim.

'OK, I need to report that back to command,' Joona says neutrally.

'Don't fucking move,' the blonde man shouts, his voice faltering.

'I'm just taking my phone out,' says Joona.

'I'll shoot your friend. I will, I'll shoot the pig.'

'Chill out, Danne, we've got this,' Branco shouts.

Joona slowly pulls his phone from his pocket and calls Manvir.

The tension in the room is palpable, everyone teetering on the edge of losing control. Over the stench of raw meat and damp concrete, Joona can smell nervous sweat.

'Manvir.'

'You've heard about the situation in Årsta, I take it? Simon Bjerke isn't here, he's likely to the rear of the building.'

'Who the fuck is Simon?' asks the blonde man.

'I'll let the team know,' says Manvir.

'I'll shoot, I'll fucking shoot,' the bearded man whispers, staring at Aias with wild eyes.

He is extremely agitated, the gun in his hands trembling. The collapsible stock is unfolded, the magazine capable of holding five rounds, and Joona has little doubt he would hit the old man from this distance.

'OK, everyone listen to me,' says Joona, dropping his phone back into his pocket. 'We've clearly hit a deadlock here. The three of you are brothers, just think about that for a minute. If any one of you fires your weapon, two of you will die and the other will be sentenced to life in prison.'

'Shut it,' the bearded man barks.

'Just wait. If you shoot Aias, he'll have time to cut Branco's throat and my colleague will shoot you,' Joona explains, keeping his voice calm. 'Danne might have time to fire his Glock and injure my colleague, but I'll be able to disarm and arrest him.'

There are raised voices outside, and Joona hears Nora cry out in despair. Aias is now shaking, and a trickle of blood runs down Branco's throat.

Joona studies the slowly swaying plastic curtain into the cold room and Branco's hands in the hazy reflection on the white tiles.

'Branco is bleeding, for God's sake!' the blonde brother shouts.

'It's fine, I'm fine,' he yells back. 'I swear, it's fine, no one—'

'Enough now, let's do this,' the bearded man wheezes, taking a step forward.

'It's just a scratch, Aias didn't mean any harm,' Joona says, attempting to cool the situation. 'Aias, be careful with that knife. Your daughter is right outside; she says she knows Branco from school?'

'I know that,' the old man replies.

'He was on the football team you used to coach, and—'

'I know, I'm sorry, I'm trying—'

'We don't give a shit if you're sorry,' the bearded brother shouts.

His finger is trembling on the trigger, and a bead of sweat drips from his nose.

'Listen to me. I want to make sure you understand just how much of a deadlock you're in before I make a suggestion,' says Joona. 'None of you can do anything without all these guns going off simultaneously. You can't even look at me; you need to keep aiming. I could easily take my Colt from my holster.'

'Don't do it,' the bearded brother shouts back. 'Are you stupid or something?'

'None of you can aim your weapon at me,' says Joona, slowly taking his pistol from his shoulder holster and loading a round into the chamber.

'This can't be happening,' Danne whispers.

Branco burps in stress and closes his eyes for a moment.

'There's nothing you can do about it,' Joona explains. 'I could walk right up to any of you and take a shot, but—'

'Seriously, is this guy out of his fucking mind?'

'Just listen to me,' Joona continues. 'We don't have much time, and I want to resolve this before the task force kicks the door down.'

'What the hell do you want?' the bearded brother screams.

'I know that Aias put your father out of business, and that he didn't do it nicely. I also know that the—'

'I worked harder,' the old man protests.

'. . . that the three of you came here today planning to take it all back, but that isn't how it works. All that will happen is you'll end up in prison.'

'Great,' says the bearded brother.

He licks his lips, and the barrel of his shotgun thuds against the glass display unit.

'But there's a better solution,' says Joona. 'Haron, would you mind lowering your weapon?'

'But . . .'

'Just do it, it's OK.'

His colleague's eyes are panicked as he lowers his Sig Sauer. The fans on the cooler unit whirr to life, and the bottles in the fridge start to clink softly.

'Now you do the same, Danne.'

'No,' the blonde replies with a stressed smile.

'But you could at least take your finger off the trigger?'

'Fine, I'll do it,' he says.

Joona slowly moves towards the man with the shotgun. A few pieces of gravel from the parking area outside crunch beneath his feet.

'I want you to come to some sort of agreement with Aias,' Joona continues. 'There's a huge demand for halal meat—'

'What the fuck d'you think this is about?' the bearded man barks.

'A much bigger demand than Aias can manage on his own; it's big enough for all of you . . . And I saw that there's an empty unit not far from here, it's actually in a much better location, closer to the hotel.'

'Don't listen to this bullshit.'

Joona holds up his Colt Combat, removes the magazine and drops it into his pocket. He then racks the slide back and lets the round in the chamber clatter to the floor.

The bearded man is shaking with adrenaline, unable to suppress his thirst for revenge. There is a real risk he might fire the shotgun at any moment.

'You could rent it,' Joona continues. 'And that way you'd have a shop . . . You could take the cooler unit and the counters from outside. They can have them for free, right, Aias?'

'Yes, yes, just take them,' the old man nods.

The blonde man lowers his pistol, hand trembling and cheeks flushed. The bearded man mutters to himself, gripping the shotgun so hard that his knuckles have turned white.

'And you could start coordinating your deliveries,' Joona says as he makes his way over to the counter. 'Aias, you can show them your receipts, let them see just how much profit you all stand to make if—'

Mid-sentence, without a single glance to the side, Joona swings his arm out and grabs the barrel of the bearded man's gun just as it goes off with a deafening crack.

The shot hits the light fitting on the ceiling.

Joona wheels around and rams the butt of his Colt into the bearded man's forehead, snatching the shotgun out of his hand and turning it on the blonde.

Glass and chunks of plaster rain down on them.

The bearded man staggers back, hitting his head on the wall and slumping to the floor with his mouth open, blinking mutely.

The light fitting and the metal mesh falls from the ceiling, shattering the display cabinet and studding the meat inside with shards of glass.

The blonde drops his pistol.

Haron kicks it away and pulls out his cuffs.

Aias tosses the knife to one side, turns away and covers his eyes with his hands, sobbing. Branco wraps an arm around his old football coach's shoulders in an attempt to comfort him.

13

The wind blows a paper plate across the parking lot, carrying it off in a cloud of dust past the cracked loading bay towards the next row of buildings.

Aias is sitting on a gurney behind an ambulance, with Nora gripping his hand as he talks to a police officer.

Joona runs across the parking area, stopping when he reaches Simon Bjerke's colleague Haron Shakor, who is busy loading his bulletproof vest into the boot of his car.

'Simon wasn't behind the building, we can't find him anywhere,' says Joona.

'Weird,' Haron replies without looking up.

'And his radio isn't on direct mode, it's switched off.'

'I don't know what to tell you.'

'This is urgent.'

The National Task Force leads the brothers out of the butcher's shop. All three are cuffed, and the bearded man has a bandage around his head.

'The deal still stands,' Aias calls after them. 'I'm a man of my word!'

Branco smiles and holds his eye as he gets into one of the dark National Task Force vans.

'Listen to me, Haron. I know you're trying to protect Simon,' Joona continues. 'But going in alone like you did was really dangerous.'

Haron shakes his head. 'I wanted him out back, but . . .'

He trails off as a message comes in over the radio. He loosens the device from the strap on his jacket and turns up the volume.

'Haron, come in,' says a weary voice.

'Simon?' He moves a few steps away from Joona. 'There's a detective from the NCU here, he wants to—'

'I'm on my way,' the voice interrupts him. 'I just need to take a leak and buy—'

There is a loud bang, followed by the crackle of static, then silence.

'Simon? Simon, come in,' Haron shouts. 'Simon, come in!'

'Tell me where he is,' Joona orders the officer.

Haron turns to him with a blank look on his face.

'It just went dead . . .'

'Haron, if you know where Simon is, now is the time to tell me,' says Joona, unlocking his car.

'What's this—'

'Just tell me,' Joona barks.

'He's been at L.A. Bar all afternoon. It's over there, by the sports field,' he says, pointing over the rooftops.

'Come with me.'

They get into the car, and Joona screeches away.

As they speed over the roundabout above the motorway, he calls regional command to let them know where he's going.

'So he drinks?' Joona asks Haron.

The officer tells him all about Simon's alcoholism, explaining that his colleague has repeatedly promised to get his act together, but that things have only got worse.

'I've been covering for him for years,' he says.

Haron had dropped Simon off at the bar an hour before the call came through about the disturbance at the butcher's. He tried to reach his partner, and when he realised that Simon had switched off his radio, he decided to go in alone.

Joona pulls up outside L.A. Bar with two wheels on the pavement. He leaps out of the car.

The bar is in the corner unit of a creamy-white apartment building with red balconies, and the dusty awnings provide shade to the deserted terrace outside.

Joona runs over and tears the door open.

There are three men quietly watching a football match at separate tables inside, each with a glass of beer in front of them.

The karaoke area is empty, and the bartender is sitting down with a coffee behind the bar, playing on his phone.

Joona strides over to him and holds up his ID.

'Where's the police officer? The uniformed officer?' he asks.

'He paid and left maybe ten minutes ago,' the bartender replies, moving a small bucket of napkins and cutlery to one side.

'Was he alone?'

'Always is.'

'Do you know where he was heading when he left?' Joona asks. In the mirror behind the counter, he sees Haron come into the bar.

'I just saw him turn right, but—'

Joona turns around and hurries back towards the door. Haron holds it open for him and follows him out.

'It sounded like he was outside when he said he needed to take a leak,' says Haron.

Joona starts running down the length of the building, past Thai Spa, down a set of stairs and around the corner to the parking garage.

A crow flaps up from one of the bins.

Joona draws his service weapon and makes his way into the quiet, leafy courtyard behind the building. The roots from the tall birch trees have broken through the tarmac on the footpath, and he can see a playground with a red slide up ahead.

Joona looks all around and starts walking along the back of the building, towards a tall exterior staircase with a rusty handrail.

He hears a crunching, scraping sound on the other side of the stairs and gestures for Haron to follow him in a wide semi-circle.

The swings in the playground creak in the breeze.

Joona moves forward without a sound. His shoulder brushes up against the base of the stairs, and he catches the scent of damp brick and rotting leaves, followed by the unmistakable metallic tang of blood.

He hears the same crunching sound as before, much closer this time.

Joona takes a step forward, aiming his pistol at the dark corner behind the stairs.

The basement window has been lined with silver foil, and two rats scurry away.

The ground by the stairwell is slick with blood, and there is a long drag mark along the wall, stretching around three metres before disappearing completely.

Joona starts running, continuing along the length of the building until he emerges from the courtyard on the other side. His eyes scan the empty street, swinging right and coming to a halt at the crossing.

There are no cars, no people.

They were too late, yet again.

Joona radios command, requesting road blocks and helicopters, then he calls Manvir to give him an update.

When he returns to the courtyard, he finds Haron staring down at the blood. The officer's arms are hanging limply by his sides, and his face looks utterly drained, like someone about to doze off behind the wheel.

Simon Bjerke's body camera is lying on the ground beside the trail of blood, and by the rusty drain cover, a milk-white bullet casing glitters in the light.

* * *

Joona and the other detectives are back in the meeting room at the NCU. Erixon has taken over at the scene, with orders to report even the most insignificant finds immediately.

Hundreds of cars have been searched at the road blocks around Årsta, but so far their efforts have been fruitless, as has the helicopter surveillance of the area. There are no CCTV cameras on the streets around the scene, but a team is currently knocking on doors in the neighbouring buildings in the hopes that someone might have seen something.

IT expert Johan Jönson is wearing what looks like a pair of loose pyjama bottoms and a T-shirt bearing the slogan 'Got the T-Shirt'. He plugs his phone in to charge and opens his laptop.

One of the police technicians takes Simon Bjerke's camera out of a box and holds it up like a priceless item at auction.

'We've already checked it for prints, but please be careful with it,' he says, trying to wiggle his glasses higher onto his nose.

Johan Jönson pulls on a pair of latex gloves, takes the camera from him, shakes it a little and then puts it down beside the laptop.

'Movie time,' he says, clearing his throat for effect.

Simon Bjerke's body camera was on 'stealth mode', which means that the camera was recording even though it looked like it was switched off. The little red LED on the front wasn't blinking like it would have otherwise.

All police body cameras buffer continually to the internal memory, which means that the playback also includes the thirty seconds prior to the moment when the actual recording began. The purpose of this is to ensure that the reason the camera was activated – often a key event in terms of the investigation – is captured on film. For reasons of privacy, however, there is no audio for the first thirty seconds of footage.

'Do you want sound or not?' asks Johan.

'There isn't any,' Manvir replies, sounding almost annoyed.

'Of course there is. It just gets deleted when the material is transferred . . . Actually, not even then, if I'm really honest.'

'Then we want sound.'

'Good, that makes things a bit easier for me,' says Johan, copying the memory card to his laptop.

He returns the camera to the technician's box, takes off his gloves and turns his laptop to the others.

'Are you ready?' he asks, looking up at the detectives.

'Yes,' says Saga.

The film begins abruptly, with wind roaring in the microphone and crunching footsteps on the tarmac. The camera was mounted on Simon Bjerke's torso, and the image rocks in time with his gait as he approaches the steps to the rear of the building.

'Simon?' Haron's stressed voice crackles through the speaker on his radio. 'There's a detective from the NCU here, he wants to—'

'I'm on my way,' he interrupts him.

Simon swings in behind the stairs and pauses in front of the basement window. The lopsided silver foil behind the glass creates a distorted reflection of his listless face. In the blurred greenery of the park behind him, the slide in the playground looks like a red star, and something grey seems to rush towards him over the grass.

'I just need to take a leak and buy—'

A hunched shadow appears behind him, moving at lightning speed, and before Simon has time to finish his sentence a loud crack drowns out all other sounds.

The ground rushes up towards the camera, and there is a thud and the screen goes dark.

The sound of Simon's heavy breathing fills the meeting room.

He cries out in agony as he rolls over onto his side and activates the camera. The sound immediately becomes much sharper. It's obvious he is in terrible pain, whimpering between shallow breaths.

All they can see is the sun-dappled crowns of the birch trees above him.

There's the sound of a slow-moving vehicle that approaches and comes to a halt, and they hear someone running across the tarmac.

The camera shakes and turns back towards the ground.

A whirring, mechanical noise cuts through Simon's muffled cries. There is a flash of light, and the building swings into shot and drifts upwards before settling.

'His camera fell off,' says Joona.

The whirring continues, a metallic rattling sound, and they hear Simon groan.

'It sounds like he's being fed into a fucking meat grinder,' Petter whispers.

'He's being winched into the back of a truck,' says Joona.

Silence fills the room. There are a couple of loud bangs, then the car rolls away. The camera is still lying on the ground, filming across the tarmac.

It doesn't take long for the first rat to appear, immediately followed by two more. A moment later, they hear slow footsteps approaching.

'That's me, I must have just missed them,' says Joona.

'Play it again,' says Saga.

14

Johan Jönson tears the corner from a pack of Pop Rocks and pours the candy into his mouth. The pressurised carbon dioxide in the little sugary crystals is released by his saliva, making them crackle.

'Is it possible to enhance the footage of the shooter?' asks Greta.

'No can do,' he says, leaning back. 'There are no sharp lines; it's just a cloud of dust.'

Manvir gets to his feet, smooths his tie and moves over to the corner of the room, standing with his eyes fixed on the point where the two walls meet.

Staring at his back, Petter opens his mouth to say something, but Greta stops him.

'Just leave him,' she says quietly.

Johan Jönson clicks on an icon depicting what looks like a maze, and his screen turns black.

'I can try a programme called X-terminal, but I don't think it'll make much difference . . .'

As Joona studies the preliminary forensic report from the courtyard in Årsta, Greta compares photographs of the three victims. Petter flicks absent-mindedly through a copy of the Police Union magazine, and Saga hovers behind Johan, staring down at the computer screen with a frown.

'No luck?' she asks.

'Nope, can't get it any better than this,' he replies, looking up at her with bloodshot eyes.

With Manvir still in the corner, the rest of the team gathers around Johan's computer. The sharpest image of the perpetrator that they have is still nothing but a grey haze behind Simon's back. They can make out the killer's shoulders and head, but no distinguishing features, no limbs or items of clothing.

'Shouldn't we be able to work out their height?' asks Greta.

'Tricky,' Johan replies. 'It looks to me like he's hunched over or . . . there's something weird about him, anyway.'

'Look, we might not have much to go on,' says Joona, 'but we've had a first glimpse. We've seen how quick he is, how he takes his victims by surprise.'

'Like a predator,' Greta whispers.

'And we know that he's quiet, that he doesn't say anything to them,' says Saga.

The computer screen goes to sleep, making the room a little darker. The radiator stops whirring, and the only sound comes from the warm casing, which clicks quietly.

'We were close,' says Greta, meeting Joona's eye. 'We would've caught him if luck had been on our side.'

'Who knows,' says Joona.

'If you'd got there five minutes earlier, or if Simon hadn't switched off his radio . . .'

'Seems that way,' Joona replies, nodding to the whiteboard and the images on the walls. 'But we're still playing the killer's game. He came up with the rules, and we're probably still moving at his speed.'

'But I'm thinking . . . If we'd just been a little faster, a little smarter,' Greta continues. 'We know that Margot was shot at the stables and then found in the old cemetery outside Kapellskär. We don't yet know where Severin was shot, but he was found in a cemetery in Hallstavik.'

'Two graveyards, that could be a pattern,' says Saga.

'And Simon was shot outside a bar,' Greta goes on. 'But his body hasn't been recovered yet.'

'He could still be alive,' Petter points out.

'Yes, I know . . . I know he's probably fighting for his life in a rubber bag right now,' says Greta, looking away.

'That's the awful truth,' says Petter.

'I know,' Greta says. 'But I can't bear thinking about it, I just can't. Not if I'm going to be able to focus on my work.'

'I just thought I should say, but—' Petter blurts,

'Yes, you've done it now,' she interrupts him.

'But the real question is what the hell we're supposed to do now,' Petter says, running his palms across the table.

'We need to find him,' Greta says in a low voice.

'Our killer is active across a pretty big area,' says Saga. 'I mean, the stables in Värmdö and the cemetery in Hallstavik must be about seventy kilometres apart . . . If we take that as the diameter of a circle, then we're looking at, what? Almost four thousand square kilometres.'

'And there's no reason to think he'll stay inside that circle,' Greta points out.

'Who cares? We can't just sit here and do nothing,' says Petter, getting up from his chair. 'Right, Manvir?'

'Just leave him,' Greta repeats.

'Let's double the diameter and reach out to the regions affected, tell them to send patrols out to all cemeteries,' says Joona.

'I'll get right on it,' says Petter, moving to leave just as a knock comes at the door.

Randy steps into the room, wearing black jeans and a grey jacket. His sharp brows give his otherwise friendly face a slight hint of sternness.

'I've heard back from all the units in Årsta,' he says, clearing his throat. 'Nothing yet, unfortunately . . . We've tried knocking on doors, road blocks, speed cameras, searches.'

'Tell them to keep going,' says Greta.

Randy briefly attempts to catch Saga's eye, then whispers 'Okay' before leaving the room and pulling the door shut behind him.

Without a word, Manvir turns away from the corner and makes his way over to the whiteboard. He grabs a marker from the shelf and updates their list with the information that the third victim has brought to light:

Serial killer with nine intended victims.
Victim number 1: female, middle age, head of NCU.
Victim number 2: male, elderly, priest at Maria Magdalena Church.
Victim number 3: male, early middle age, alcoholic police officer.
Communicative perpetrator: possibly in an attempt to abdicate responsibility.
References: Jurek Walter, Saga and Joona.

Metal figurines: sent to Saga, indicate next victim.
Shoots victims from behind, at close range.
Ammunition: 9x18mm Makarov bullets, fine silver casings, Russian mercury primers.
Has a vehicle with an electric winch.
Murder and discovery sites not the same.
Bodies dissolved in caustic soda, rubber body bags.
Lack of evidence: suggests caution and awareness of forensic methodology.
Material knowledge: casting tin, producing fine silver, using caustic soda.
Not a perfectionist (lack of finesse on tin figurines)
Moves extremely fast, like a predatory animal.

Manvir pushes the lid onto the marker, takes a few steps back and reads through the list before turning to the others.

'Saga, you mentioned at one point that the killer identifies with Jurek Walter in some way?' he says.

'Yes ... because of the anagram on the postcard. It could be a game or an attempt to provoke us,' she replies.

'But how does he even know about Jurek when all the material from that case is classified?' asks Greta.

'There was a serious leak,' Joona explains.

'If a handful of police officers know something, the whole world knows it too,' Manvir mutters.

'There were a lot of people involved towards the end of the preliminary investigation,' Joona goes on. 'And afterwards, a large group was tasked with following up on any cold leads in an attempt to find the missing bodies.'

'But why Jurek?' asks Greta. 'If we look at this in terms of approach, our perp isn't a copycat.'

'There must be some other connection,' says Saga.

'We've had three murders so far, but what do we actually know about his MO?' asks Manvir, gesturing to the board.

'He studies his victims, probably over a long period of time; he knows where and when to strike,' says Saga, getting up from her chair.

'Well-planned,' says Manvir, adding another point to the board.

'He sneaks up on them from behind, attacks them without warning, and shoots them in the back from close range,' Saga says.

'We've got a third silver casing . . . The measurements are the same as the 9x18mm Makarov,' Manvir adds.

'I think the bullet is meant to paralyse the victims prior to being transported,' says Saga, pointing to the images of the blood found in the stables. 'We don't know why he doesn't kill them immediately, but it's clearly part of the plan.'

'I agree,' says Greta.

'And shortly after abducting them, he dumps their bodies in a new location, possibly a cemetery,' Saga continues with increasing intensity. 'In a bag lined with rubber, filled with sodium hydroxide, wrapped in plastic, sheets and rope.'

'The Needle wasn't able to establish a cause of death for either of the first two victims. We don't know whether it was the bullet wounds or something else,' says Joona. 'We don't even know if the victims were dead when the corrosive process began.'

'God,' mutters Petter.

'He doesn't just want to kill his victims; he wants to obliterate them,' Joona says quietly.

Saga sits back down at the table, and Manvir's face is pale as he pulls the lid from the marker and starts writing again:

Perpetrator is highly organised, studies the victims, knows their habits and routines.

Has a reason to keep victims alive.

Obliterates victims.

Manvir puts the marker back on the shelf and returns to the table. He unbuttons his jacket and hikes up his trouser legs slightly before sitting down.

'The tin figurines are the most tangible clues,' he says. 'They're the killer's way of communicating with us.'

'So how are we supposed to interpret them? Why tin? Why make little sculptures at all?' asks Greta.

'My immediate thought was toy soldiers,' says Manvir. 'When I was a boy, we used to cast and paint them and then re-enact various historical battles.'

'I think you'd struggle to sell that to kids today,' Greta says with a smile.

'Please, let's focus,' Manvir continues without returning the gesture.

'The boxes sent to Saga are the most common kind in Sweden, impossible to trace. The same goes for the tape – they're both things you can buy anywhere,' says Petter, holding up two photographs.

'The tin figurines seem to have been wrapped in whatever the killer had to hand, possibly just random bits of rubbish,' says Greta. 'Old pieces of paper, scraps of fabric.'

'Though forensics didn't manage to find any prints or DNA on anything,' Petter points out.

Joona opens one of the folders and takes out the images of the packaging. He spreads them out on the table and looks at each in turn.

A ripped T-shirt featuring the emblem of the Los Angeles Dodgers, plus half a pub menu.

A piece of bubble wrap with a sticker from the Gustavsberg porcelain factory on it.

A page torn out of an encyclopedia. On one side, there is part of an article about the trogon family of birds and the mineral troilite. On the other, a large photograph of a Trojan horse on an amphora dating back to 670 BC.

A small scrap of fabric with a lace trim and a photocopy of an old hand-drawn map of a city called Al-Majdal on the edge of a lake.

There is a child's drawing in red crayon on the back of that sheet, depicting a family at a dinner table.

Greta studies Joona's focused face and the photographs on the table in front of him.

'What are you thinking, Joona?' she asks.

'Margot's figurine was wrapped in an article about the Trojan horse and a piece of bubble wrap from Gustavsberg. The Gustavsberg factory was in Värmdö,' he replies. 'Simon's was wrapped in a bar menu and a piece of fabric with the emblem of a Los Angeles baseball team on it.'

'The stables and L.A. Bar,' Saga gasps.

'The Predator is telling us where he's going to shoot his next victim,' Joona continues.

'Oh God,' Greta whispers.

'The priest's figurine was wrapped in this fabric,' says Joona, handing the image to Saga.

'Probably from a christening robe. I looked up Al-Majdal, but it doesn't exist anymore,' Saga says, her phone in her hand. 'It used to be known as Migdal, or Magdala in Aramaic, the language Jesus spoke . . .'

'Mary from Magdala,' says Greta.

'Can someone find out whether Maria Magdalena Church is missing a christening robe?' asks Joona.

'I will,' Petter offers.

'So he's giving us advance warning of who he's going to kill and where, and we still haven't managed to stop him,' Manvir says with a sigh, loosening his tie.

'It's almost enough to make you feel like we bear some responsibility,' Petter mumbles.

'Stop it,' Greta snaps.

'Sorry, it's just so fucking frustrating.'

'I know,' she says, sighing. 'I feel the same way, but at least we've worked out the rules of the game now. And when the next figurine arrives – which it will – then we'll be better prepared . . .'

15

Francesca Beckman is one of the psychologists at the Crisis and Trauma Centre, which works closely with the police, and she is responsible for determining whether or not Saga is fit to return to active duty.

Three years ago, Saga's hunt for Jurek Walter finally caught up with her. In the blink of an eye, she became the prey, desperately fighting to save her family.

When her half-sister Pellerina died after being trapped in a coffin, everything came crashing down around her. The Security Service funded two-years' rehabilitation and specialist psychiatric help at a treatment centre on the island of Idö, and by the time she returned to Stockholm she finally felt strong enough to think about doing something other than taking her own life.

The afternoon light filters through the swaying branches outside, into Francesca's office. It feels as though the entire room is spinning, tumbling down some dangerous slope.

Saga is perched on the very edge of her pale blue armchair, and she nods weakly and meets Francesca's brown eyes.

In place of personal photos or children's drawings, the psychologist has a large framed picture of a forest scene on the wall. Saga finds herself gazing at the dappled glade and the small stream snaking between moss-covered rocks.

'You've made real progress, there's no doubt about that; you're on time for all of your sessions here, you've managed to hold down a job, you're a support person for two young children,' Francesca tells her. 'And that's why I told the acting head of the NCU that I was happy to recommend a return to desk duties.'

Francesca has a pretty face, despite the fact that her cheeks are covered in small scars, all the way back to her ears and scalp.

She is in her fifties, and so tall that she has to sit with her legs outstretched to avoid banging her knees against the desk.

'But I'm operational. I've always worked operationally, that's who I am. I thought I'd made that clear,' says Saga.

'I know,' the psychologist replies, taking off her glasses.

'It's really important to me,' Saga continues, bouncing her foot up and down. 'I think it would do me good to get back to work, to feel like I can handle the operational side of things, because I know I can.'

'I hear what you're saying.'

'Plus, they need me right now. That might sound over the top, but—'

'It's too soon, Saga,' Francesca Beckman interrupts her gently. 'That's my assessment. You've made definite progress, but—'

'You don't know anything about me.' Saga snaps, getting up so abruptly that the chair slams into the wall behind her. 'You don't know a thing about police work, what we go through, what it really takes.'

'OK, why don't you tell me?'

'Sorry,' Saga mumbles, sitting down again. 'I'm just so disappointed.'

'I thought you'd be happy because I'm supportive of you working with the police again.'

'I am, but I'm just not made for desk duty, I . . .'

Saga trails off and clasps her hands in an attempt to keep them still.

'So you weren't happy today, at the NCU?'

'It's the best thing that's happened to me in years. It was interesting and I know I was useful, that I contributed . . . I just feel like I could do so much more if you'd let me work operationally with Joona.'

Saga's gaze wanders across to the flickering sunlight on the wall beneath the window.

'Have you spoken to Randy yet?' Francesca asks.

'Yes . . . Well, I've *seen* him, he came in to give a debrief today.'

'How did that feel?'

'OK. I mean, it was fine.'

Francesca puts her glasses back on and flicks through her notepad. 'You told me you ended things with him in order to punish yourself.'

Saga takes a deep breath and turns back to the psychologist.

'I don't feel that way anymore . . . I just couldn't stand myself at first, I've told you that. I didn't think I deserved anyone's love, I didn't think I even had the right to live.'

'But you're in a new relationship now . . . with Stefan?'

'Yes.'

'Do you want to tell me about him?' the psychologist asks after a moment.

'I don't know, it's a bit early. I have no idea if it'll go anywhere, I don't want to force it; we both have our own lives, but we see each other regularly and that's enough for me right now.'

'Do you think you deserve his love?'

*   *   *

Saga leaves her motorcycle in a parking space by the end of a grey building, enters the code at the entrance and takes the stairs to the second floor. She knocks quietly and lets herself in, locking the door behind her, kicking off her boots and hanging up her jacket.

Stefan is on his laptop in the kitchen, and he doesn't look up when she comes in. He is on an online forum, she notices, writing a review for a business called Yemoja Massage. He's given it five stars and is leaving a comment about one of the sex workers.

She waits a few seconds and then heads to the bathroom, where she gets undressed and turns on the shower. As ever when she comes over to see Stefan, she feels a jolt of anxiety in the pit of her stomach.

The anaesthetist lives with his wife and two sons in a villa in Djursholm, but he has access to a small apartment on Blomgatan in Solna, just a few minutes' ride from the hospital where he works.

Saga knows that he is sensitive to even the slightest hint of perfume, so she takes care to rinse every last trace of soap from her body before drying herself off, hanging the towel on the rail and leaving the bathroom, walking to the bedroom.

The blinds are closed, but there is still a soft, murky light in the room, spilling across the plastic flooring and drab furniture. His cleaner must have been round today, because the bed is made and Saga can see a strand of white yarn from the mop beneath the skirting board under the radiator.

By the time Stefan comes into the bedroom almost an hour later, she is so cold she is shivering.

He pulls back the bobbled blanket on the bed. 'Lie down or go home.'

'I don't want to go home,' she replies, doing as he says.

Saga often tries to convince herself that all she wants is a physical relationship, that it's all she can manage right now, that this is how she wants to live.

Stefan pushes her legs apart and climbs on top of her.

He doesn't like it when she gets wet. There have been a couple of occasions when she has, times when he has shown her a modicum of tenderness, but he always just gets up, grabs her clothes and throws them into the stairwell, snapping at her to go home.

It doesn't matter. Saga can't afford to lose him, so she just bites her tongue whenever she starts to feel herself getting carried away.

She stares up at the ceiling light in order to avoid meeting his eye, focusing on a tiny string of dust that keeps swinging in the air.

Stefan's thrusts are quick and aggressive; he swears at her if she doesn't lie perfectly still, calling her vulgar names, whispering that he will let all his friends have a go at her.

After a while, he grips her throat with one hand and squeezes hard.

Saga lets herself go completely limp, the lack of oxygen causing flashes of light to dance across her eyes.

All she can hear is the creaking bed and his wheezing grunts as he finally ejaculates and pulls out.

Saga rolls over onto her side, coughs into her elbow and breathes as quietly as she can.

Stefan is flat out on his back, breathing heavily, his ears and his chest red.

He doesn't know it, but she is connected to him; he was on the team at the hospital the day her life came crashing down around her.

Stefan was her sister's anaesthetist. But he doesn't remember Saga.

When she first recognised his picture on Tinder, she ran to the bathroom and threw up. Sleeping with him is her way of holding on to her grief, because even this is so much more than nothing.

'I'm working with the NCU now,' she says.

'What's the pay like?'

'I don't know, I just want—'

'Smart,' he sighs.

'Shall I call for some food?' she asks, getting up from the bed.

'No time, I want to try to get some sleep before I hit the gym.'

'I thought—'

'You don't *have* to come over here, you know,' he interrupts her. 'It's not that fucking good.'

'Don't get annoyed just because I asked if—'

'I don't want to eat with you; I'm not your boyfriend.'

He gives her 1.5 milligrams of Levonorgestrel to ward off any chance of pregnancy, watching her closely as she swallows the pill.

Whenever Stefan is drunk, he always starts talking about how much he hates women who think they're irresistible, women who have a career. How much he detests women who have caesarean sections and how he hopes they end up with ugly scars.

Saga gets dressed without showering, knowing he likes the idea of her feeling his semen between her legs as she rides her motorcycle. He has told her that the thought of it trickling down her thigh during an important meeting makes him laugh.

The minute she gets out into the stairwell, however, she grabs a tissue from her bag, wipes herself down and throws it into the rubbish bin outside.

The tears don't start to fall until she is back on her bike. Grief wells up inside her, making her throat tighten so much she can barely breathe.

As she drives home, she realises that Jurek is still shaping her life. The fact that she is no longer a police officer, that she can't cope with love: both boil down to him.

She would give anything to turn back time and get another chance to kill him.

It should have been her.

Saga passes the Karolinska Institute and sees the Norra Tornen residential complex looming up ahead, but she turns right, towards the motorway.

What was it about Jurek Walter? How did he infect her so thoroughly?

Once a person has let him into their head, he seems to stay there forever.

She occasionally catches glimpses of that in Joona's eyes.

He isn't free either.

The new killer must feel something similar, she realises out of nowhere. He has lost his way in Jurek's labyrinth, spent too long staring into his eyes.

Saga drives over Västerbron, the burnt yellow glow of the evening sun bouncing off the rough water down below.

The thought sends shivers down her spine. The killer is lost in Jurek's labyrinth.

But almost everyone who ever crossed paths with Jurek is dead, so who could it be?

The lines of sunlight make the trees in Långholmen look like they are ablaze.

Was he a victim? One of the people Jurek tried to recruit? Someone who managed to break free from the long line he cast?

16

She parks her motorcycle a block from her apartment, takes out her phone and, out of habit, opens her home security app. Saga studies the real-time footage from the four cameras in her apartment: one in the hallway by the front door, one in the kitchen, one in the living room and another in her bedroom.

Everything is quiet.

She opens the history tab. The footage is only saved when the cameras detect movement, so the last clip is of Saga herself in the hallway, pulling on her shoes and standing with her hands and forehead pressed to the door.

She watches herself stand there for several minutes.

Saga always feels anxious before she goes to meet Stefan. She knows full well she is punishing herself, but she hadn't realised quite how long she hesitated before leaving; she had thought she just paused to gather herself for a moment before heading out.

The minute she's back inside, she throws her clothes into the washing basket and jumps into the shower, her new theory still racing through her head.

Their killer, the Predator, has been damaged by Jurek somehow.

She dries herself off and pulls on her pink dressing gown.

It is seven-thirty in the evening when she climbs into bed with her laptop and types Jurek Walter's name into the search bar.

Despite the fact that all material about him is classified, the search engine throws up over three thousand hits for his name inside quotation marks. Most of them are blogs and podcasts focusing on true crime and cold cases. Certain phrases reappear almost word for word, claiming that Jurek Walter is an urban legend, a dark shadow in the missing person records.

On one forum, someone has written that a trusted source within the Oslo Police revealed that Jurek Walter desecrated graves and took trophies from his victims. Another user mentions a number of mass graves outside Madrid.

Saga realises she will need to try more specific search terms, investigative phrases or exact locations, but instead she adds her sister's name beside Jurek's and hits enter.

This time, there are only thirteen hits. She skims through the list and shudders when she notices a website called 'The Jurek Walter Files'. The hair on the back of her arms stands on end, and she takes a deep breath and clicks on the link.

A quick glance is enough to tell her that whoever created the page made use of dozens of classified files from both the NCU and the Security Service.

She scrolls down and finds herself staring at the last picture taken of Jurek before he escaped from the secure psychiatric unit at Löwenströmska Hospital. The sight comes as such a shock that she has to close the lid of her laptop for a moment and focus on her breathing.

Saga clicks between low-res images of the Polish passport Jurek used to enter Sweden, the custody forms that were filed following his arrest in Lill-Jans Forest, forensic documents and the beginnings of a biography.

She quickly establishes that almost all the material is authentic, and directly linked to Jurek Walter. There are only a handful of images that might be fabrications, such as a photograph of a bloody chair purported to have been found at Hasselgården home for dementia patients.

The website doesn't seem to serve any other purpose than to get as much material about Jurek Walter as possible out into the public domain. Almost like some sort of fan page, she thinks.

The admin is listed as someone calling himself Karl Speler.

Saga runs a quick search and discovers that it isn't a pseudonym, that Karl Speler moved to Sweden from South Africa and now lives in Älvsjö. He spent a few years working as a tabloid journalist at *Expressen*, and seems to have become paranoid since he was fired from the job.

She has a vague memory of what happened. *Expressen* published a report on Jurek Walter, and the Security Service stormed in and seized the whole print run the minute they found out.

Karl Speler must have been the author of that piece.

Saga turns her attention back to his website, clicking through to the partial biography and reading a short interview with Susanne Hjälm.

Susanne spent years working as a doctor in the secure bunker where Jurek Walter was imprisoned, but she allowed him to get into her head and is now serving a lengthy prison sentence of her own in Hinseberg.

Karl asks her a number of direct questions, but Susanne's answers are all incredibly vague. Despite that, it is clear that meeting Jurek Walter ruined her life. Susanne is now divorced, has lost custody of her two daughters, and receives no visitors in prison.

The interview ends with her hanging up when Karl asks about Joona Linna.

Saga clicks on the contact button and writes a brief email to info@ jurekwalterfiles.com to say that she would like to speak to Karl Speler, signing off with her name and telephone number.

She hits send, and before she even has time to return to the homepage, her phone starts ringing.

'Saga,' she answers.

'This is Karl Speler,' says a man's voice. He sounds short of breath. 'Am I speaking to Saga Bauer?'

'Yes, I just sent you an email.'

'Oh wow. Sorry, I'm just a little starstruck,' he blurts out.

Saga assumes that Karl Speler decided to publish the truth about Jurek Walter because his work was confiscated and his article removed, because he was fired.

She hears his heavy breathing and thinks about how he must have spent a long time tracking down and piecing together the whole story.

A story in which she and Joona play the main roles alongside Jurek.

It must be strange for him to be speaking to someone he has followed, documented and studied from a distance for so long.

'Do you have time to talk?' she asks.

He lets out a short, stressed laugh, holding the phone away from his mouth.

'Do I have time to talk to a fallen angel? Yeah, I think I can probably spare a few minutes from my incredibly full and meaningful life.'

'You seem to know more about Jurek Walter than anyone else outside of the police force,' she says.

'No doubt about it,' he replies, his mouth now much too close to the microphone.

'Even more than the police, in some cases.'

'Very possible.'

'I'd be really grateful if you could help me narrow down a list of people who have met Jurek and lived to tell the tale.'

'Of course.'

'I'm interested in absolutely anyone who might have crossed his path.'

'OK, but . . .'

'You've got my email address,' she says.

'But if I'm going to share my research, I want to meet you first. I want to sit down with you and show you what I've got over a coffee or something.'

'I've got a lot on my plate right now.'

'I understand,' he says, sounding deflated. 'I can wait until you have more time.'

'That's not what I meant,' she hurries to explain. 'Everything's so hectic right now, and I don't have time to wait. I can meet this evening if that works for you?'

*　*　*

Saga pulls on a pair of jeans and a warm sweater, gets onto her motorcycle and drives over to Hornstull. As she crosses the Liljeholmen Bridge, she thinks about just how close Karl Speler came to avoiding her. It wasn't until the very last second that she realised he wanted to trade information for the chance to be close to her, to see her with his own eyes and ask about all the things he doesn't know.

Pale clouds drift slowly across the sky above the calm bay.

She takes the bridge over the motorway in Brännkyrka, past the fire station and on towards Långsjön.

The houses get bigger and bigger, surrounded by lush gardens, the lights from their windows flickering through the glossy leaves.

There is no one else out and about, no cars driving by; the world around her feels dark and dreamlike.

Saga hasn't quite managed to come up with a justification for what she is about to do. She is carrying out an operational mission, in secret, and knows full well it could ruin her chances of ever being given a permanent position with the NCU.

The sound of her engine rattles along the empty streets.

She slows down and turns off to the right, pulling up by the driveway of a large villa from the sixties.

She locks her motorcycle and peers in through the row of windows in the kitchen. Past the kitchen table and white marble worktops, there's a pale wooden screen, behind which sits the living room followed by a huge dining room with windows looking out onto the garden.

The lights are on, but there is no sign of anyone inside.

Karl Speler asked her to go to the back entrance rather than the front, so Saga cuts across the grass to the other side of the villa.

She can hear a dog barking somewhere in the distance.

The paving stones are mossy underfoot, and she notices an old jam jar stuffed with hundreds of cigarette butts.

Beside the kitchen door, a piece of tape with the name Speler scrawled on it has been stuck above a wireless doorbell.

Saga presses the button and takes a step back.

She hears a couple of heavy thuds inside, and a short, stocky, middle-aged man with a round face and pale brows opens the door. Other than his fringe, which is combed back, his blonde hair is cropped short.

'That was quick! Come in, come in,' Karl says with a smile, sharp canines poking out from beneath his lip.

He is wearing white socks, blue jeans and a Depeche Mode T-shirt beneath a crumpled jacket.

Saga follows him into a cramped hallway, where coats are hanging on hooks beneath the hat rack. The door to the kitchen is closed, but she can see a narrow staircase down to the basement up ahead.

'God, this is so cool,' he says as he locks the door behind her.

Karl starts making his way down the stairs, pausing and glancing back when he notices her hesitation.

'I rent the basement from the family who own the house,' he explains. 'We try not to bother each other unless it's absolutely necessary.'

'Are they home right now?'

'I don't think so, no.'

Saga steps over a pile of trainers and a pair of cowboy boots that have been kicked off on the hallway mat, following him down.

'Feel free to use the torch on your phone,' he says, eyes lingering on her. 'I've been having a bit of trouble with the electricity in my little museum; the circuit breakers keep tripping.'

She takes his advice and sees a glistening bead of sweat roll down his rounded cheek.

The stairs creak as they descend, Karl's shadow rocking from side to side in front of them. The light from her phone sways up towards the sloping ceiling and down to the pale plastic flooring.

Saga knows she shouldn't have come here alone, that she should have sent the address to Joona, but she just couldn't take the risk of being stopped.

She can hear a strange swishing sound through the walls, almost like someone skiing on crisp snow.

Karl grips the handrail with his right hand, the gold links of his wristwatch clinking against the wood. Saga notices a grubby-looking plaster on his thumb.

In a slightly manic tone, he says something incoherent about the people from his journalism class who have gone on to make names for themselves.

He trails off as they come out into a large, dark room. Karl takes a few steps forward, then turns around and squints back towards her.

'The real Saga Bauer . . . in my little museum,' he says.

She uses the torch on her phone to illuminate the space. Through the two small windows up by the ceiling, she can see tall grass and a plastic football. The walls are covered in framed photographs, all with some sort of link to Jurek: police reports, forensic documentation, copies of her and Joona's material.

Jurek's system of graves has been marked out on a large map on the ceiling, from the site in Lill-Jans forest to the last, unused spot by the motorway in Moraberg.

In the middle of the creamy-yellow floor there are three glass display cases, illuminated by the spotlights on the ceiling.

'This way,' says Karl, beckoning her in.

She follows him, pausing when she spots the spade from the chapel on Högmarsö inside one of the cabinets.

'Guess you recognise that. I bought it for next to nothing at the estate sale,' he tells her.

Saga's bloody slippers from the psychiatric bunker are in the next case, and in the last are three small, dark brown bottles containing the sedative Sevoflurane.

'OK, that's the tour,' he says.

17

Karl Speler opens the door to a brightly lit room, and Saga hears the same swishing sound as before, but closer now.

She switches off the torch on her phone and follows him into a windowless kitchen. On top of a long bar made from dark wood, she can see glasses, shakers, an ice bucket and a soda siphon. He has the South African flag hanging on the wall behind the counter, along with an almond-shaped shield decorated with what look like dogs' teeth.

'Kitchen and bar,' Karl says before he moves on, like an estate agent showing her around a property.

Saga brushes up against the vacuum cleaner as she passes, and she feels the heat radiating from the plastic. There is a slightly withered balloon in the shape of a hand grenade hovering just below the ceiling, and it bobs away in their wake.

They walk around an old-fashioned bubblegum dispenser, complete with glass bowl, turn-handle and slot underneath.

'And this is the living room, where I thought we could talk,' he says, pushing a door open.

Saga's heart starts racing when she sees that there are two other men inside, standing at opposite ends of an American shuffleboard table.

The swishing sound she heard earlier must have been from them sweeping the disc back and forth.

Both men stop and stare at her as she comes into the room.

The older of the two has a prominent nose, dark brows and long hair. There are silver rings on each of his fingers, and he is wearing a pair of tight leather trousers and a black T-shirt.

'Incredible,' he says with a grin, slowly moving closer without taking his eyes off her.

'The guy who can't stop staring is Dragan,' says Karl. 'And this is Rüssel, he's scared of germs.'

Rüssel, a boyish man in his mid-thirties gives her a nervous wave. He has slim shoulders and thick glasses, and the skin around his mouth looks red and chapped. He is wearing a pair of brown loafers, beige trousers and a checked pullover on top of a shirt.

As in the kitchen, there are no windows in the living room. A few brown leather armchairs have been positioned around a low coffee table with a scented candle on it, and in the soft light from a floor lamp Saga can see a television and a shelf full of game consoles and controllers, a candle shaped like the Statue of Liberty and a red tin.

The stairs up to the back door are the only way out, she thinks to herself, and the heavy bottle on the bar counter is probably the best weapon to hand.

'Sorry for staring, but I mean . . . Saga Bauer!' says Dragan. 'You're practically mythological to us . . . and just as beautiful in the flesh.'

'At least,' Karl adds.

'At least,' Dragan agrees.

'I'll get some wine,' says Karl.

He has a framed copy of his confiscated article on the wall, alongside the picture of Jurek taken immediately after his arrest in the forest. The short text describes the classified hunt for a serial killer on the loose. A representative from the Police Authority denies all knowledge of the case, and the lead investigator – Saga Bauer, of the Swedish Security Service – could not be reached.

Karl returns with a glass bowl of dill crisps, a box of Californian red and four glasses.

'Why don't you take a seat?' he says with a smile.

Saga, Karl and Dragan each take an armchair, Rüssel perching on a chair just behind Dragan. Karl pours the wine, and a few droplets spill onto the table.

Saga takes one of the glasses, joins in the toast and pretends to take a sip. She looks up at the men's eager faces and realises that they have made a real effort for her: they've vacuumed, lit a candle, bought wine and served crisps in a bowl – possibly even scrubbed the toilet and put the lid down.

'Before we get started . . .' says Karl. 'I just need to know. Am I paranoid, or was it the Security Service who got me fired from the paper?'

'Of course it was,' Saga replies.

'I knew it!' he shouts, nodding to the others.

'Those bastards.' Dragan grins.

There is a strange scent in the air, like burnt hair and ammonia. Karl drains his glass and refills it to the brim.

'I was wondering,' Saga begins. 'Since you've done so much . . . research.'

'It was mostly Karl,' Rüssel points out.

'I was wondering if you knew who might have met Jurek . . . someone who is still alive, who might have been influenced by him.'

'OK . . . I understand,' Karl sighs, giving her a hesitant glance.

'I don't want to know how you got hold of all the classified material,' she says in an attempt to reassure him.

'And I'm not going to ask how you got the green light to go back to operational duty,' he grins.

'I'm working with the NCU now.'

'We know,' says Dragan, tucking a lock of hair behind his ear with a trembling hand.

Rüssel gives Karl a stressed glance, and Karl slowly takes out a pack of cigarettes, peers inside and then sets it down on the table.

'OK, so . . . I might not have the most positive feelings towards the police,' he begins. 'But since it's you, and since you're here, I'm willing to come to some sort of agreement – an exchange, you might say.'

'What kind of exchange?' she asks.

'There are still a few gaps in my biography, and you can help fill them in,' he says with a smile, baring his pointy teeth again.

'Quid pro quo,' Rüssel adds, his voice flat.

'I don't want to talk about my dad or my sister,' Saga tells them.

'We understand,' says Dragan.

He is slumped back in his chair with his knees spread and a satisfied smile on his face. Karl scratches his ankle and meets her eye.

'My first question is an obvious one,' he says, leaning forward.

'I'm listening.'

'Are you here because Jurek Walter is still alive?'

'No.'

'I've seen the photographs from the Dutch police, I've read the autopsy report, but those could easily be faked.'

'He's dead,' she says, holding his eye.

'See, I told you,' Rüssel whispers.

'Rüssel said Jurek had to be dead because Joona Linna is out there living a normal life again,' Dragan explains.

'I still had to check, though,' Karl says with a grin. 'I mean, she's not here because she wants to hang out with us or because she thinks Jurek Walter is the coolest killer on earth.'

'So why *are* you here, after all these years?' asks Dragan.

Saga takes a deep breath. 'I received a threat from someone calling themselves Artur K. Jewel,' she says.

'And who's that?' Dragan presses her, giving Karl a confused look.

'Huh? How am I meant to know?' Karl replies, his face turning red.

'It's an anagram,' she explains.

'Of course.' Rüssel nods.

'What was it?' asks Dragan. 'Artur K. Jewel?'

'Yeah.'

'Woah,' he whispers. 'Got it . . . Crazy.'

'And since Jurek is dead . . .' Karl continues, a new intensity in his voice. 'And his family tree died out with him, that means it must be someone else . . . Some other connection.'

'Has this Artur K. Jewel . . . killed someone?' asks Dragan.

'I can't answer that; the investigation is still ongoing.'

'OK,' says Karl, biting a nail.

'Ugh, I've got goosebumps,' Rüssel says with a grin.

Dragan grabs the box of wine and tops up Saga's glass, despite the fact that she hasn't touched a drop, then does the same with his own. Rüssel is sitting on his hands, eyes downcast as he chews on his lip.

'I could really do with a smoke, but I feel like I don't have time,' says Karl, picking up the carton from the table and dropping it into his inner pocket.

'I can stay another forty minutes,' says Saga.

'OK, let's keep going.'

'Who could have reason to threaten me and Joona? And who might come up with the idea of calling themselves Artur K. Jewel?' she asks.

'No idea . . . Like you said, almost everyone who ever crossed Jurek's path is dead,' Karl replies.

'Which really narrows it down,' says Rüssel, pushing his glasses back onto the bridge of his nose.

'Once I worked out what Jurek was up to during the last few years of his life,' Karl continues, 'I started searching for anyone he might have been interested in.'

'Good idea.' Saga nods encouragingly.

'I made a top three list of people who might be somehow connected to him . . .'

His round face seems both solemn and anxious. His blond brows are creased, and his lips have lost all colour.

'Who?' Saga asks calmly.

'We don't know for sure whether Jurek ever actually met any of them, but my best guesses are Jakov Fauster, Alexander Pichushkin and Pedro Lopez Monsalve.'

'I know those names,' says Saga. 'The first two are in prison, and Monsalve is an old man, in pretty bad health. He lives in Colombia and doesn't have a passport.'

Karl has wolfed down half of the crisps and wipes his hands on his jeans.

'My turn now,' he says, looking Saga straight in the eye. 'I've always had trouble working out exactly what happened in the bunker under Löwenströmska Hospital.'

'It was an advanced infiltration mission,' she says.

He holds up a hand in the air to stop her. 'I already know the basics, I've listened to the recordings; what I want to know is what went on between you and Jurek, what you saw and felt.'

Saga grits her teeth and nods. 'My task was to get him to talk without letting him into my head,' she says flatly.

'As I see it, you're the closest Jurek ever came to love?'

'I doubt that,' she replies, looking away.

'He called you a siren. That means he must've been tempted,' Rüssel chimes in with his monotonous voice.

'He just wanted me to feel special.'

'But he didn't kill you when he got the chance,' Karl insists.

'Because he saw me as a future resource; he'd found a back door into my mind that even I didn't know about.'

'He was fucking incredible,' Karl nods.

'A proper old school strategist,' Rüssel blurts out. 'Objectives, means and methods.'

Saga picks up her glass and makes it look like she is about to take a drink, only to be waylaid by a sudden thought.

'To get back to the question at hand, who, out of everyone Jurek met, is still alive?' she asks.

'You, Joona, Lumi . . . The Beaver too, of course,' Karl says, draining his third glass. 'Reidar Kohler Frost is dead, but his kids are still alive. They both live in London these days, they've always politely turned down all requests for interviews.'

'Do you have their contact details?'

'I can send them.'

'Thanks.'

Karl gets up, takes a few steps and runs a hand over his slicked-back hair before turning back to Saga.

'God, I've just got so many questions,' he says. 'Jurek came to your apartment on Tavastgatan once. You were armed; why didn't you kill him?'

'Biggest mistake of my life . . . He made me believe I needed him alive,' Saga replies, trying to force back the anxiety she can feel welling up inside her.

'Despite Joona's warnings?'

'Yes,' she says, checking the time on her phone. 'It's getting late . . .'

'Can we take a picture together?' asks Rüssel, immediately blushing.

'OK, but . . . one more thing,' she says. 'Karl, you did a telephone interview with Susanne Hjälm in prison?'

'Right, I forgot about her, she's still alive,' he says, sitting down again.

'In the transcript on your website, it looks like she hung up?' says Saga.

'Yeah, I assumed there must've been some technical issue and called her back, but she just started screaming about how much she hates Joona Linna.'

'Did you get a sense of why?'

'No, I mean . . . I just assumed she blamed him for the fact that she shot an officer, but I don't know. I've been trying to get in touch with her again now that she's out, but I can't find an address or a phone number for her.'

Saga straightens up in her chair. 'She's been released?' she asks.

'Yeah, she got out three years ago, on September 1st.'

Saga's heart starts racing, and she rubs her mouth as she does a few quick calculations.

Susanne Hjälm was released from prison on September 1st, three years ago. That was two weeks before Saga received the postcard with the image of the cholera cemetery in Kapellskär on the front.

Jurek Walter got into Susanne Hjälm's head while she was working in the secure psychiatric unit. Before she was arrested at home, she had killed one police officer and attempted to kill two others.

'Thanks for this evening,' Saga says, getting to her feet. 'I'd love to stay longer, but . . .'

The three men leap up and pull out their mobile phones. One after the other, they move over to her and pose for selfies.

Their hands tremble, and when it's Karl Speler's turn to get up close, Saga can feel the damp heat radiating from his body.

18

Saga wakes to the sound of her letterbox rattling. She hears the mail fall to the floor with a thud and opens her eyes, blinking in the bright light. It's six thirty in the morning, and her bedroom is bathed in sunlight. She rolls over onto her side and closes her eyes. It was late by the time she got into bed last night, and she would have liked a few more hours' sleep.

Her thoughts turn to the three men in the basement. They hadn't wanted to stop taking pictures, and Karl had tried to buy something from her before she left – her socks, her hair tie, anything.

Saga reaches for her phone on the bedside table and realises that it is far too early for the mail carrier to have been making deliveries.

She immediately leaps out of bed, grabs her pistol from the chest of drawers and hurries out into the hallway in nothing but her underwear. She sees the squashed cardboard box on the mat, unlocks the door and runs down the stairs to the street.

Tavastgatan is deserted.

Barefoot, she runs to the crossing with Blektornsgränd. The steps down to Hornsgatan are empty.

On the pavement outside the café, an old man with a walker is staring at her with wide eyes.

Saga turns around and heads home, locking the door behind her and giving the apartment a quick once over before she puts down her gun, pulls on a pair of latex gloves and carries the grubby, damaged little box to the kitchen table. She contacts the rest of the investigation team over the radio.

'Morning, Saga,' says Manvir, his voice so bright and alert that it sounds like he has been up for hours.

'Everyone but Petter is on the line,' says Joona.

'OK. I think another figurine just arrived,' Saga tells them. 'Someone pushed a parcel through my letterbox a few minutes ago.'

'But you didn't see who—'

'No, I was still asleep, I wasn't quick enough.'

'You haven't opened the box yet, have you?' asks Greta.

'I've just put some gloves on, I—'

'Don't worry about fingerprints or DNA,' Joona interrupts her. 'Just open it. We don't have much time if we're going to get ahead of the killer.'

Saga tears the tape from the box, folds back the flaps and reaches inside. She takes out the small bundle and sets it down on the table. Working slowly, she opens the white handkerchief and unfolds a ball of newspaper to reveal a small tin man.

'It's a new figurine,' she confirms.

'OK, everyone, this is our chance to get one step ahead,' Manvir says breathlessly.

'Can you see who it is?' asks Joona.

'No, his face is flat . . . Hang on, I'll take a picture,' she says.

Saga places the little figure in a pool of sunlight on the table, takes a few photographs and enlarges the images. Other than a broad forehead, one ear and the curve of its skull, she can't make out many features on its damaged face.

She sends the photographs to her colleagues.

The man is slim, the model slightly taller than the previous figurines, perhaps two and a half centimetres this time. He is wearing a suit jacket and sturdy shoes and carries a briefcase in one hand.

'What's that on his back, Saga?' Joona asks after a moment.

She picks up the figurine and realises that what she initially thought were marks from the casting process is, in fact, a pattern on the back of his jacket.

'They've carved . . . it looks like a bunch of tiny clouds, I'm not sure. It's really faint . . . Let me try to get a better picture.'

'So, what do we think? Who's the next victim?' asks Greta.

'Impossible to say,' Saga replies.

'Damn it.'

'What about the wrapping?' asks Joona.

'We're running out of time,' Greta reminds them all.

'A crumpled newspaper article and a handkerchief, a cotton one,' Saga tells them.

'What's the article about?' asks Manvir.

'An abandoned metro station.'

'And on the other side?' Greta asks, sounding stressed.

'Algal blooms in the Stockholm archipelago . . .'

'Is there anything unusual about the handkerchief?' asks Joona.

'It's got a monogram or whatever it's called, an embroidered A in one corner.'

'Go back to the article about the water,' Joona tells her.

'I think we should focus on the metro station,' says Saga.

'Does it mention any specific locations where these algal blooms have taken place?'

'No, but there's a table with lots of places in it . . . Tyresö, Österåker, Värmdö, Nacka, Saltsjöbaden, Ingarö . . .'

'Let's focus on the metro station,' says Manvir.

'Is it Kymlinge?' asks Joona.

'Yes.'

'I'll let command know,' says Greta.

'Read through both articles carefully,' Joona reminds Saga. 'We need to know if anywhere else is mentioned or hinted at.'

As Saga tries to focus on the text, she hears Greta talking to command. Four cars in the vicinity immediately respond to her call.

Saga's heart is racing as she reads both sides of the newspaper cutting. The only specific location mentioned is the ghost station in Kymlinge, which was built back when there were plans to relocate a number of government departments out of central Stockholm. When the government later decided to move the authorities elsewhere, the building work ground to a halt – despite being nearly finished.

'Nowhere else,' she says.

'I'll head out to Kymlinge,' says Joona.

'See you there,' Saga tells him, ending the call before anyone has time to argue.

*   *   *

Verner Zandén puts on his glasses and tiptoes out of the bedroom, quietly pulling the door shut behind him to avoid waking his wife. He slowly makes his way down the stairs.

The large house is bathed in the dawn's soft glow, and the oak floors creak beneath his feet.

Everything to do with the Security Service is classified, he thinks. Everything but the boss. His name and image are everywhere.

Just yesterday, an unassuming little man with a pale face and small, round glasses followed him around the supermarket. Verner noticed the man surreptitiously taking photos of him several times.

That wasn't so unusual in and of itself, but there was just something about the man's behaviour that felt different. He didn't smile, didn't seem excited. If anything, he seemed more like a joyless collector.

'Of souls,' his wife Maja suggested when Verner told her about him.

The strange little man had reappeared in his dreams about Sebastian last night.

Verner often dreams about his younger brother, who was born with two spines. Sebastian died when he was just eleven years old, during one of his many operations. Some nights the dreams are incredibly sad. Verner and his father might be sitting in a small waiting room when the doctor comes out to explain that something went wrong during the operation. Verner usually drops to his knees in tears after that, overcome by grief. Either that or he watches his father trudge out into the first snow of the year, howling like a wounded animal.

Other times, the dreams are more like nightmares. Sebastian chases him through the house, his underdeveloped spine trailing after him like some sort of tail, thudding against the floor and swinging into doorframes.

In last night's dream, the colourless little man from the supermarket was there too. He operated on Sebastian with a kitchen knife, hacking at the tissue and membrane to reveal his two tailbones, wrapping paper towels around them and pulling them apart like the two halves of a zipper.

Verner woke with a start and lay gasping for air beside Maja for quite some time before he got up.

He is now making his way along the dark hallway, through their two lounges and out into the sunroom to check the weather, as he does every day. His eyes drift down to the bay between the big water-front houses, and he sees the choppy water glittering in the sunlight.

Verner likes to run five kilometres before breakfast every morning. He generally takes a route through the Svärdsö nature reserve, along

Älgövägen to the Grand Hôtel before heading back on one of the trails on the other side of the lake. But on Tuesdays, when he works from home, he always rounds off his run with a trip to the cold water bathing house, where he has a full hour to himself. Verner is on the board of the management association, but he still pays full price for membership – an obscene sum simply to use the sauna and swim in the sea. Still, he likes it there: the 1920s atmosphere, the peace and quiet, the solitude. Going there is his form of meditation, his moment of mindfulness ahead of the rest of the week.

After a session in the sauna, he usually gets changed and walks home to make Maja breakfast in bed.

The morning sun is so bright that Verner can barely see as he makes his way back through the unlit lounges.

He hears a loud thud from the boiler room in the basement, almost like someone tossing a rubber boot into a tumble dryer.

Verner isn't the most technically minded of men, but Maja always seems to like it when he goes down to the basement and tinkers with the boiler.

He walks down the dark hallway. The door to the family room is wide open, blocking his view.

Shouldn't he have noticed that earlier, when he was walking the other way?

He pauses and peers in to the dim room, sees the TV and the sofas, the Chinese tea service on a tray, his magnificent Lars Lerin watercolour on the wall.

Last night's whisky glass is still on the table.

Verner closes the door and has just decided to go down to the basement to make sure everything is OK when the thudding stops.

He pricks his ears, listening for footsteps. Maybe the noise woke Maja and she decided to take matters into her own hands.

But the house suddenly feels alarmingly quiet.

Verner makes his way to the utility room and takes his workout clothes from the drying cabinet. He gets changed, pulls on his running shoes and rucksack and steps out into the cool morning air, locking the door behind him and setting off across the lawn.

The whole family is coming over on Sunday afternoon. His daughters, their partners, the grandchildren and step-kids. Verner makes a mental note to clean the barbecue and practise his magic tricks on Saturday. A young man at the office has an uncle who works as a welder, and he has helped Verner build a contraption that will make it look like Maja is floating.

Verner walks down the driveway, pausing when he reaches the bottom. He lifts his right foot onto the edge of the planter and straightens the tongue of his shoe before jogging out onto the road.

Running is always hard work at first, but today his trainers feel like ski boots. He attempts to transfer more weight onto the balls of his feet, trying to loosen his toes, well aware that he probably looks like a weary elk on his long legs.

That was what one of their neighbours told him last spring. A neighbour who – worryingly – also happens to be a passionate amateur hunter.

Everything feels a little easier once he reaches the forest. The gravel track feels perfect underfoot.

The loud sound of a woodpecker cuts through the sleepy rustling of the pines.

Verner is still thinking about his dream, about the sound he heard when the strange little man pulled Sebastian's two spines apart.

He speeds up on the bend where the ground flattens out, and beneath the trees it feels like he is running through an enormous columned hall.

There is a black van parked up ahead. It doesn't have any registration plates, and the fenders are caked with mud.

A full rubbish bag has been dumped in the ditch just behind it. He can see the slow swaying of the trees mirrored in the van's dark surface.

19

Naomi Hallberg is driving along a paved footpath through Ursvik Forest. Her partner had to go home to look after a sick child an hour ago, and she has been alone in the patrol car since then.

She took the call from regional command while she was parked on a back street in Kista, around fifteen kilometres north of central Stockholm. She had been watching a young man leaning against the wall of a building beneath a damp set of stairs. His face was covered in sores, and his lips trembled as he heated his heroin on a bent spoon. By his feet, an older woman had nodded off on a flattened cardboard box.

The man burnt himself on the lighter and had just dropped it to the ground when the call came through. A priority one alert.

She responded and set off towards Kymlinge as the dispatcher briefed her on the strange details of the alert.

Naomi turns off onto a gravel track and speeds up. Trees race by outside.

In the rear-view mirror, she can see the cloud of dust swirling up into the air behind her.

The dispatcher told Naomi to take every precaution and to deploy a spike strip across the road on the other side of the abandoned metro station. Another four units are currently en route, but she would be first on the scene.

First and alone doesn't sound like the best of combinations, she thinks now.

Her mind drifts back to the day her football coach tugged her underwear down and she started shaking in fear. Who knows what might have happened if they hadn't heard the other girls outside a moment later.

She thinks back to her twentieth birthday, when she and her sister decided to go out to celebrate. She arrived early, and her sister's new boyfriend answered the door. He let her in, gave her a pill, and when she next woke up she was in intensive care.

Naomi switches off the siren, brakes and pulls over by the gate blocking the road. She gets out of the car and hurries over to it, unlocking the pin and lifting the bar. Naomi watches as it falls back against the green bins, then gets into the car and continues along the bumpy forest road running parallel to the metro tracks.

The suspension clanks and groans beneath her, bushes scraping against the doors.

When she gets her first glimpse of the concrete building between the trees up ahead, she comes to a halt and switches off the engine.

She has never used a spike strip before, but she thinks she more or less remembers what to do. First she needs to carry the heavy metal box over to the ditch and then pull the extendable strip of nails across the road.

Just do it, she tells herself.

With a knot of anxiety weighing in the pit of her stomach, Naomi gets out of the car, opens the boot and puts on her bulletproof vest. Only then does she realise that the box is missing.

Naomi reports back to command, and the operator tells her that it doesn't matter, that her colleagues are approaching from the other direction.

'Await backup,' the voice says.

Naomi adjusts the straps of her vest as she sets off along the forest road. Thin tendrils of mist swirl up from the vegetation in the morning sun, and multiple metro trains thunder through the station without stopping.

Nothing has changed since the builders dropped everything forty years ago: a bare concrete shell without any lifts, escalators or ticket barriers.

Only the dead get off in Kymlinge, that's what people say. A reference to the urban legend of a silver train of corpses that trundles through the Stockholm transport network at night. Most variations of the story involve a young girl accidentally boarding the silver train after a night out. She is later found at Kymlinge, either with her throat cut or worse.

Naomi stops and loosens her pistol from its holster. She holds it out in front of her, eyes on the gleaming metal, on her fingers around the grip and her pale nails.

The forest is quiet, fog curling up above the ferns, through the undergrowth and around the trunk of a birch tree.

The golden morning light washes over the raw concrete of the station building.

Naomi moves through the hole that has been cut in the tall barbed wire fence as though in a daze.

Her shift is due to end in thirty minutes, and as soon her colleagues show up, she will head home and get a few hours' sleep, then order pizza and eat it in bed while watching TV.

She pushes through the tall weeds, climbing up the embankment and crossing the tracks. She then climbs up onto the platform and peers through the covered section of the building.

It feels strange not to see any of the usual fixtures and fittings, information boards and advertisements.

Pools of rainwater glisten on the bare concrete floor.

All she can hear is a low electronic hum, some sort of clicking relay and the echo of her own footsteps bouncing off the walls.

Naomi makes her way towards the stairs up to the ticket hall. The doorway straight ahead is covered in graffiti, and reminds her of a ghost tunnel at a fairground.

She has almost forgotten why she was called out to the station when she notices movement further down the platform, almost entirely hidden behind a partition wall.

With trembling hands, she releases the safety catch on her pistol and steps to one side to get a better look around the corner.

The tracks to her left start to vibrate.

The water in the puddles begins to shake.

Dust and dirt swirl up from the ground.

Naomi steps back, onto the very edge of the platform, and raises her gun just as a train thunders past. A sheet of grey plastic rises up into the air behind the partition wall.

The breeze from the train blows Naomi's hair across her face, and she moves her finger to the trigger in sheer panic.

* * *

Verner Zandén is sitting on the top level of the sauna, skin slick with sweat and the hair on his head too hot to touch.

The van parked on the forest track belonged to a man who was busy setting out control points for an upcoming orienteering race. Verner stopped to exchange a few words with him, and noticed that the glade nearby was full of bloody feathers and scattered down.

The sauna is now so hot he can hardly breathe. Verner climbs down and opens the door. His body is enveloped in steam, his face and shoulders flushed red and sweat trickling down his chest and stomach. He puts his glasses on and checks the time, then pushes his wedding ring onto his finger and leaves the changing room.

He loves spending time alone in the bathhouse, drinking in the atmosphere, walking along the row of changing stalls that look out over the inner courtyard, down the stairs and through the pines and rhododendron below.

Still overheated, Verner emerges into the morning air and looks out at the calm surface of the bay. He stands there for a moment, taking it all in.

The wide staircase leading down to the water is sheltered from the elements by two blocky towers with vanilla-coloured panelling and diving boards.

He hears the gulls screeching over by the ladies' locker room.

According to the signs in the ticket office window, the water temperature was fifteen degrees yesterday.

Verner makes his way down the steps and into the water, rings rippling out from his legs before he ducks beneath the surface.

By the time he realises he is still wearing his glasses, it's too late. They swirl away, disappearing into the darkness among the bubbles.

Verner breaks the surface with a snort, swimming out to the white buoys before turning back.

He can feel the endorphins pulsing through him as he makes his way inside and locks the glass doors behind him.

Verner takes a shower and dries off, changing into a pair of casual trousers, a white cotton shirt and sandals. He is looking forward to his morning coffee and to eating breakfast with Maja.

The creaky door to the changing stall swings shut behind him, and he walks along the long row of blue doors, into the entrance hall, past the ticket office and to the locked door leading outside.

Without his glasses, finding the keyhole proves a little tricky at first.

The ground is littered with brown needles and pinecones, and between the trunks of the tall pines, the small boat harbour looks like nothing but a floating white shape.

Verner turns around and squints over towards a pickup at the far end of the car park. He hears a dry twig break somewhere nearby and peers towards the edge of the trees, trying to get his eyes to focus. He can make out a blurry figure standing by one of the trunks, and he finds himself thinking that it must be the strange little man from the supermarket again, the collector.

Verner has just started making his way towards the trail when he hears quick footsteps behind him. He wheels around at the exact moment a gunshot cracks through the air. He feels a searing pain in his arm and sees a hunched, blurry figure slink off to one side.

Somewhere behind his back, the pistol clicks. The next round must have caught in the barrel.

Blinking wildly, Verner tries to make sense of what is happening. The first shot hit his right upper arm, he realises. The pain is no worse than cramp, but he can feel the hot blood pulsing out onto his sandal-clad feet, and it makes him light-headed.

The pistol clicks again, and Verner quickly turns around and runs back towards the main entrance, fumbling with the key and unlocking the door with shaking hands.

The other person's footsteps quickly draw closer across the car park.

Verner manages to fling the door open, tearing the key from the lock and hurrying inside, locking it behind him.

There is a loud bang, and shards of wood fly across the floor as whoever is outside shoots the door to pieces.

Verner backs up into the old ticket kiosk, hitting his head against the glass. He turns and runs towards the gallery of changing stalls.

There is nowhere for him to hide.

His legs are trembling as he stops outside one of the far doors, slips inside and pulls it shut behind him.

Someone surely must have heard the shots?

He takes off his rucksack and lowers it to the bench, searching the pockets for his phone. Right then, he hears one of the doors further down the row open.

20

Joona has almost reached the abandoned metro station when command calls to let him know that neither the suspected killer nor any vehicles with electric winches have been found.

'Any blood?' he asks.

'We're still searching the area, but not yet . . .'

He pulls up by the police cordon. The blue lights from three of the five patrol cars sweep across the tree trunks and concrete.

Joona lifts the plastic tape, ducks underneath it and makes his way over to an officer in uniform. As he introduces himself, a train passes through the station at full speed. The trees along the tracks sway violently in the breeze.

The officer updates Joona on the situation and tells him that the forensic technicians likely won't arrive for another hour.

A motorcycle approaches and comes to a halt behind Joona's car. The driver takes off their helmet and hangs it on the handlebars.

The officer forgets what he was saying when he recognises Saga. She strides over to them in a pair of jeans and a thin leather jacket with wide lapels and a belt around the waist.

'We were wrong,' Joona tells her when she reaches them.

'How the hell is that possible?'

'The riddle must have had to do with the water and the handkerchief.'

A police officer in a bulletproof vest emerges from the station building. She squeezes through the hole in the fence and runs towards them. Her face is grey with exhaustion, but her eyes seem feverish.

'This is Naomi Hallberg, she was first on the scene,' the other officer explains. 'She went in and—'

'Saga Bauer,' Naomi interrupts him.

'That's me.'

Naomi studies her with a peculiar look on her face.

'Come this way.'

They follow her through the fence and over the tracks.

The sunlight filters through the leaves, causing bright ovals to sway anxiously across the ground, but inside the station building everything is dusty and dark.

Naomi takes them across the platform and up the stairs to the ticket hall. The floor is littered with empty wine bottles, dead rats, dirty mattresses and sooty scraps of foil, condoms, cigarette butts, a burnt out campfire, torn cardboard, crisp packets and broken glass.

The officer points to one of the graffiti-covered walls.

Alongside a mishmash of elaborately drawn names and crude skulls, dominated by the word YASH in large, bulging letters, there is a half-destroyed mural of a girl with rounded cheeks, a serious face and wide eyes.

Joona and Saga make their way over to the wall.

In the middle of one of the girl's pupils, almost as though her eye is glittering, is a piece of cardboard.

A postcard, with its image turned to the wall.

Joona shines his torch on the back of the card.

Saga Bauer,
There are five white bullets left in my red Makarov, and one of them
is reserved for Joona Linna. Do you still think you can save him?
She who fails to solve the mystery will be judged by the dead.
Jesu Fatvarok

Joona takes out an evidence bag and asks Saga to hold it while he pulls on a pair of latex gloves and reaches for the postcard. The glue crackles as it peels away from the concrete, and he reads the message again before turning the postcard over.

'This is endless,' Saga mutters, bracing herself against a fire extinguisher bracket on the wall.

*   *   *

Verner Zandén slumps down onto the bench in the changing stall and presses his hand to the bullet wound on his arm. His mobile phone isn't in his bag. It must have fallen out of the side pocket when he fled back into the bathhouse and stumbled up against the ticket kiosk.

He can hear door after door being pushed open, footsteps drawing closer.

The brass latches clatter against the wood.

For the first time, his thoughts turn to what happened to Margot.

Verner tries to keep his breathing steady, to think clearly.

If he can catch the shooter off guard, he might be able to knock him over and run to the entrance, find his phone and take cover among the trees while he calls for help.

But if there is more than one of them then they probably have someone standing guard at the front door.

Could he get down to the water and swim away?

He gets up without a sound, holding his breath and pricking his ears.

As the shooter goes into the fifth stall, Verner quietly opens the door out onto the gallery. He wipes up the blood from the floor with his workout pants and then throws his rucksack over the railing before closing the door again.

There is a thud on the grass in the inner courtyard as his bag hits the ground and rolls away beneath the rhododendrons. The shooter stops dead, then Verner hears him walking away towards the stairs.

The pistol in his hand knocks dully against the spindles of the handrail.

Verner starts thinking about his little brother again, about the way one of his spines was trailing behind him as he moved through the rooms in his nightmare.

His arm is now throbbing.

Verner stands with one ear to the door, trying to follow the shooter's movements and work out when he will be out of sight.

He knows he doesn't have long.

The blood has soaked through his shirt and started dripping to the floor from his fingers.

Verner thinks he can hear footsteps on the duckboards in the courtyard, and he slowly opens the door to his stall and peers out.

He can't see much without his glasses, but he is fairly confident there is no one there.

His heart is beating too fast, and he can feel his breathing getting shallower and shallower with every minute that passes. He knows he won't be able to swim or run very far, which means his only option is to take a chance on the front entrance being unguarded, to get outside and try to find help or a place to hide.

He feels increasingly dizzy, and his legs are shaking as he starts walking along the gallery past the cornflower blue doors.

Verner tries to keep a tight grip on his arm, but he can feel the hot blood pulsing out between his fingers.

He squints over to the stairs, but everything is blurry now; he can no longer even make out the pillars.

The blood is trickling down the fingers on his hand, leaving a trail of droplets behind him, falling between the boards beneath his feet.

Verner knows he will have to wipe up the blood behind him once he gets outside, maybe even leave a trail in the wrong direction in an attempt to mislead the shooter.

He pauses, stoops slightly and peers down the stairs to the inner courtyard.

He can make out a few dark green shapes against the pale yellow wood. Trees and bushes in the sunlight.

Everything is quiet.

Right then, something grey peels away from the background, moving towards the bottom step.

Verner turns and staggers towards the main entrance. He has lost so much blood he is starting to feel weak, and he stumbles as he opens the door to the foyer, bumping his shoulder on the frame as he makes his way through.

He tries to force his eyes to focus, and as he gets closer he realises that the broken door is open onto the sun-drenched parking area.

Fragments of wood and pieces of the lock are scattered across the floor.

Verner hurries forward and spots his phone on the floor beneath the ticket kiosk.

Something rattles across the floorboards on the gallery, almost like a ball bearing rolling towards him.

He lets go of his upper arm, bends down and grabs his phone. Everything goes black for a few seconds as he straightens up again.

His heart is really pounding now, and the thuds on the floor are drawing closer.

The phone is slippery in his bloody hand, and he has so much trouble seeing the buttons that he can't manage to unlock it.

He needs to get outside, to shout for help.

Verner has just started making his way towards the door on unsteady legs when he hears the sound of quick breathing behind him. He doesn't have time to turn around before a gunshot rings out through the air.

Blood sprays across the uneven paving stones in the bright sunlight.

The bullet has passed straight through.

Verner's phone clatters to the floor and skids away towards the restaurant, beneath a blue chair.

Coughing, he pushes through the turnstile and starts making his way back towards his phone.

He is struggling to think straight; the only thing going round and round in his head are the words 'I don't want to die, I don't want to die'.

The next shot hits him in the thigh, making him fall. He manages to get up onto all fours, bellowing in his deep baritone, and keeps moving towards the phone. Verner wraps his fingers around it and crawls towards the door into the restaurant.

21

Joona follows Saga along the forest road away from the abandoned metro station as the morning sun shines brightly across her bike.

Branches brush up against the sides of his car.

Joona is thinking about the message glued to the girl's pupil, the renewed threat and the closing words about the punishment for failing to solve the mystery.

A message signed by a new anagram.

He had turned the postcard over and studied the black and white image on the front. Judging by the bare branches and the pale sky, it was taken in spring. The image showed an open metal gate and a raked gravel path leading past a runestone and a whitewashed building, past graves and crosses to a small church with a steep roof.

In the bottom right-hand corner, the words 'Funbo Parish, 1879' were written in looping, old-fashioned handwriting.

Yet another cemetery, Joona thinks as an alert comes in over the radio.

The security guard at the open-air bathhouse in Saltsjöbaden called emergency services after arriving at work to find the door to the men's building in pieces and blood all over the floor.

Joona sees Saga sway on her bike as they hear that Verner Zandén had booked out the men's bathhouse for personal use that morning.

The whole investigation team immediately joins a call over the radio system.

'We don't know whether the blood is Verner's yet,' Petter points out. 'It's just guesswork, we—'

'But unfortunately—' Joona begins.

'We don't know anything,' Petter interrupts him.

'But unfortunately it fits neatly with—'

'Why do you always have to be so fucking negative?!'

'Calm down, Petter,' says Manvir.

'What do we know about the crime scene?' asks Joona.

'The first unit will give us an update as soon as they arrive. They should be there any minute now,' says Manvir.

'But Verner . . .' says Petter. 'I don't get it. Why Verner?'

'It makes no sense,' Greta agrees.

'Joona?' Manvir speaks up.

'With hindsight, isn't it actually pretty obvious that the figurine represents Verner? It's thin, taller than the others, and those little shapes on his back are oak leaves, not clouds.'

'Of course,' says Saga.

'Fuck,' Petter whispers.

Within the Swedish police force, the more oak leaves on a police officer's insignia, the higher their rank. And the central motif of the Security Service's coat of arms is a burning torch and four oak leaves.

'But that means our theory about the wrapping was wrong,' says Manvir. 'The killer can't possibly have expected us to search half the archipelago?'

'The only specific place mentioned was the metro station,' says Saga.

'He wanted us to go there first,' says Joona.

'To find the new postcard for Saga,' Greta concurs.

'One thing we do know is that we're still one step behind, because Verner wasn't attacked at the station.'

'The bathhouse,' says Manvir.

'The other side of the article was about algal blooms in the archipelago and—'

'But that's not enough, that's not fair!' Petter interrupts. 'We're talking about a huge area, thousands of islands, beaches and rocks.'

'We must be missing something,' says Joona.

'Saltsjöbaden is number five in the list of places affected by algae,' says Greta.

'Fucking shit,' Petter sighs.

Saga slows down as they approach the barrier, then turns right. Joona follows her, gravel crunching beneath his tyres.

'I think we have one of the officers at the bathhouse on the line,' says Manvir. 'This is Manvir Rai from the National Crime Unit, over.'

'Jörgen Karlsson, over.'

'Tell us what you've got.'

'Annika and I were over by the dump when the call came in, we just got here. We went inside and . . . Jesus, I don't know . . .'

He trails off. They hear the microphone crackle, followed by a few quick breaths.

'Are you still there?' asks Manvir.

'I don't know how to describe it. There's no sign of the victim, but we've got blood in the car park, all over the floor, everywhere. It's like a goddamn slaughterhouse by the entrance to the restaurant, and we've got drag marks by the main door, on the steps, God . . .'

'Any other observations?'

'No, I . . . We've found a few empty casings, including one that's white all over. I've never seen anything like it. We need to get forensics out here, the door's been shot to pieces . . . Which reminds me, there was one thing that . . . I don't understand it, but it's like they've sawed chunks out of the skirting boards and doorframes. There's wood shavings all over the floor.'

'Have you found anything to identify the victim?'

'A bloody phone, though we haven't touched it yet.'

'Good.'

'I'll call Verner's number,' says Greta.

'Cordon off the area and wait for forensics,' Manvir tells the officer.

'Hang on, Annika's coming . . . she's saying something.'

They hear an agitated voice in the background.

'The phone we found is ringing,' says Jörgen. 'It's ringing.'

'Don't touch it; wait for forensics,' Greta says, her tone resigned.

The forest around Saga and Joona opens out onto an area of low buildings, roads and overpasses.

Once the officer in Saltsjöbaden has left the call, the group is quiet for a moment.

'What's this about a fucking saw?' Petter mumbles.

'The winch,' says Joona. 'The killer dragged the cable inside and then winched the body back out, around corners and through doorways.'

'Can any of you make sense of this?' asks Manvir. 'What does he want? That's three of our colleagues now, two of them high ranking.'

'And an old priest,' Saga mumbles.

'It's fucking insane,' says Petter.

Joona overtakes Saga, pulling back in front and leading her onto the E4 towards Uppsala.

'I think he's choosing victims he knows will keep us engaged,' says Saga. 'Maybe it's as simple as that – letting us know that he really will kill Joona if we don't stop him.'

'That could well be it,' Joona says quietly.

'What did it say on the postcard?'

'She who fails to solve the mystery will be judged by the dead,' Joona replies.

'So he's putting the responsibility for stopping him on us.'

'On me,' says Saga.

'I'll talk to the protective unit and make sure they're guarding Joona closely,' says Manvir.

'No.'

'This is serious, Joona.'

'I'll be ready for him if he comes.'

'What a hero,' Petter mutters.

'I'm just ready, that's all.'

'OK, we can discuss this later,' says Manvir. 'Are you and Saga on your way to Saltsjöbaden?'

'No, that's—'

'I assumed you—'

'That's what he wants us to do,' Joona continues. 'But there's nothing for us to do there. We'll go to the cemetery on the front of the postcard.'

'Saga, I need to reiterate that you aren't cleared for operative duty,' says Manvir. 'We can call you an observer so long as you're with Joona, but that's as far as I can go.'

'OK, thanks.'

Saga follows Joona as he passes a bus and pulls back into the right-hand lane. Her leather jacket feels tight around her shoulders, the loose end of the belt flapping behind her.

It's almost ten o'clock in the morning, and the shadows from the clouds overhead drift slowly across the fields and meadows, like schools of fish beneath the surface of the sea.

Saga has told Joona that she shudders every time she passes Löwenströmska Hospital, and Joona himself always feels a dark maelstrom swirling inside him.

A red noise barrier races by on the left-hand side, and the power lines between the pylons glitter in the sun. A truck with a wide load kicks up dust at the side of the road.

So far, the killer has been in control of every step they take, thinks Joona. They're still dancing to his tune. He knows they will go out to the bathhouse and the cemetery, but none of this will help them to shorten his lead.

If anything, the opposite is probably true – unless, deep down, he actually has a strong desire to be caught.

Joona doesn't think the matter has been settled yet.

It's still in the balance.

Perhaps the decisions he and Saga make right now will shape the outcome of the case.

Or maybe this is all just a game.

Does the killer want them to turn around and drive over to Saltsjöbaden now, so that he has time to leave the bag containing Verner in the cemetery? Only to then claim they could have saved him if they hadn't been so busy chasing shadows?

Joona and Saga leave the motorway just north of the small hamlet of Danmark, by an industrial area surrounded by high fences. The road takes them across the fertile land surrounding Uppsala, past fields and wooded areas, a timber yard and numerous red cottages.

The white twelfth-century church is visible between the trees as they turn off towards Funbo.

Joona parks and gets out of his car as Saga pulls in behind him. The iron gate is identical to the one in the photograph, but the fence has been replaced by a low stone wall.

They hurry down the gravel path, past the runestone, splitting up to cover the rest of the churchyard.

Neat box hedges separate the rows of headstones and crosses.

There is no sign of anyone else, and the car park is empty.

Neither of them has said anything, but Joona and Saga are both hopeful that they will be able to save Verner's life if he has been left in the cemetery.

A flock of doves flaps up into the air as Saga hurries around the back of the vestry.

Joona keeps walking along the thick bushes growing by the wall. He spots something blue on the ground in the distance, and he runs over to check, but it's just a bag of compost.

He hears a series of thuds from behind the storage building, almost as though someone is attempting to flatten the earth on a grave with their hands.

Joona straightens up and steps to one side. He sees a large white sack hanging about a metre above the ground in the middle of the cluster of oaks at the far end of the cemetery.

He starts running and sees Saga approaching from the other direction.

The sack is wrapped in white cloth and silver tape, and several crossed ropes have been wound around the branches and trunks of the oaks.

There are no movements inside the bag, no sounds.

Saga calls command as Joona takes out his knife and starts sawing at the ropes.

As he hacks his way through them, the heavy sack drops slightly, making the remaining ropes creak under the weight.

In the treetops, the birds are singing.

The sack is soon hanging from a single rope looped twice around a thick branch and tied to the trunk. As Joona carefully unties the rope and lets out the excess, Saga attempts to guide it down.

Working together, they slowly lower the bundle to the ground, where it lands softly in the grass.

The bell in the red tower on the hill above the church starts ringing.

Joona crouches down over the bag and cuts a large cross in the fabric, folding back the layers of tape, fabric and thick rubber.

A sharp chemical smell makes their eyes water.

The body is surrounded by a foamy gunk, jelly-like and half translucent.

The man's facial features and hair are gone, but there is no doubt about it: They have just found the body of police officer Simon Bjerke.

22

In the large conference room at the station, Manvir, Greta, Joona, Saga and Petter have gathered for a hastily called meeting with Morgan Malmström, the acting head of the NCU.

Morgan is in his forties, with a boyish face, white teeth and a relaxed manner.

As Manvir matter-of-factly recaps everything they know about the scene at the bathhouse, the others listen quietly, eyes downcast. He keeps going until he hears Greta sob.

'Sorry, it's just so upsetting,' she says, drying her cheeks. 'I know Verner, I know Maja, I can't believe this is happening.'

'Maybe we should take a break?'

'No, not for my sake. Keep going, please,' she says, taking a tissue someone holds out to her.

Sunlight floods into the room through the row of low windows, giving Joona's solemn face a bright outline. He is sitting perfectly still with his hands clasped on the table, listening to Manvir.

'The riddle seemed impossible,' Saga says quietly. 'And it doesn't make any difference now, but Joona and I did some digging . . .'

'What?' asks Manvir.

'We solved the riddle,' says Joona.

'Really?'

'Viewed from above, the men's bathhouse in Saltsjöbaden looks like a big A. All we had to do was look at the satellite images,' he explains.

Torben Grut, the architect behind the Stockholm Olympic Stadium, designed the bathhouse so that the tip of the A pointed inland and its legs out into the water.

'That's what the handkerchief with the embroidered A was hinting at,' says Saga.

'So we were just too slow again?' says Manvir.

'Going forward, I think we should assume that all of the riddles can be solved,' Joona continues. 'But I don't know whether it's a good thing for us to do that.'

'Why, because it's almost like we're approving of the rules of the game if we do?' asks Greta.

'Just a thought,' he says.

'I looked into the material the second figurine was wrapped in,' Petter speaks up, clearing his throat. 'As we suspected, it comes from a christening gown belonging to Maria Magdalena Church, one they lend out.'

'Have you been over there?' asks Manvir.

'Just got back. The gown disappeared from the office on Sankt Paulsgatan last week. The road had just been swept, but I cordoned the whole place off and got forensics to come out.'

'Good,' says Joona.

'So far we've recovered one white casing and three regular ones from the bathhouse,' says Manvir.

'Which means we're either looking at two different pistols, or he has it loaded with one white round and the rest normal ones?'

'One white bullet for each victim,' says Manvir.

'So you think these four murders are the first in a series of nine?' Morgan sums up, scratching his forehead.

'Yes.'

'Why nine?'

* * *

Joona and Valeria are sitting at a small window table in Un Poco, an Italian restaurant on Karlavägen. The long curtains flutter as the waiter arrives with their starters of fresh truffle pasta.

'You aren't wearing your watch,' she says as she raises her fork to her mouth.

'No, I couldn't find it yesterday.'

'Strange.'

'It'll turn up.'

Valeria is wearing a plum-coloured dress, her curly hair gathered in a loose ponytail.

She takes a sip of her wine and wipes her mouth with the back of her hand.

As Joona studies her across the table, he thinks back to the meeting earlier, which ended with an exhortation from the acting boss: 'It's been a long day, so I want you all to go home and get some rest,' Morgan Malmström had said, gesturing to the photographs and the boxes on the table. 'Naturally we'll continue our investigation as best we can, but I don't think we're going to be able to stop the perpetrator before the next figurine arrives.'

'I think I'll keep going for a while,' said Saga.

'It's terrible, but there isn't really anything for you to do – aside from being well rested when he makes his next move,' said Morgan. 'The technicians, the lab and pathology will keep at it all night, and we've also got Saga's apartment, our mailroom and Saga's former workplace under surveillance.'

Joona knows that he and Saga are right where the killer wants them. The perpetrator is communicating with them, and they need to find a way to see around corners, to find whatever they aren't supposed to find.

After the meeting drew to a close, he called Valeria and they arranged to meet at Un Poco at eight.

He headed home to his apartment in the Corner House first, took a shower and pulled on a fresh pair of boxers. He then drank two glasses of fresh orange juice and stood in the window, gazing out at the city.

Joona got dressed and took out the ring he has been keeping in his gun cabinet, studying it for a moment: polished platinum and a perfect two carat diamond. He takes the ring with him whenever he sees Valeria, but so far he hasn't been able to bring himself to propose; he knows he needs to tell her about his secret first. It isn't often that he finds himself being pulled under, but since his first relapse after Jurek's death he has been to Laila's place to smoke opium at least ten times.

'What are you thinking about?' Valeria asks with a smile.

'Nothing,' he mumbles.

He can feel her seeking out his eyes, but he tries to resist; she always seems to read his mind, and he simply doesn't feel ready for that right now.

'Is it the case?'

'Sorry.'

'I think it's a good rule that you hold off on telling me about your cases until they're over,' she says. 'But don't feel you have to do that for my sake. If you want to talk, I'm happy to listen. You can tell me anything, you know that.'

'Thanks.'

She waits for him to go on as the waiter clears away their plates.

'It's all this stuff with Jurek Walter,' he says quietly. 'What happened on the roof when I . . .'

He trails off and stares down at the table. How is he supposed to explain that he is a different man now, that something dangerous seeped into him that day? That a darkness took root inside him?

'Have you had another argument with Lumi?' she asks softly.

'No, this is about me.'

'You think you crossed a line?' she says.

'But that I also did the right thing.'

'And that troubles you – not just that you crossed a line, but that you still think it was the right decision.'

'More or less . . .'

He falls silent again as the waiter sets down two bowls of asparagus risotto in front of them.

'And what do you think about that?' she asks once he has gone.

'Sorry for talking about such boring things, but . . .'

'It's not boring.'

'But that day, up on the roof . . . After the Nietzsche quote, which really wasn't anything other than a chalkboard he wanted to scribble his last words down on, he whispered something.'

'And you haven't stopped thinking about it since?' she fills in.

'No.'

'Tell me,' Valeria says softly.

'I can't, I don't want to repeat his words . . . He said them right after the impulse to push him over the edge came over me, just before I actually did it, so I wouldn't have time to change my mind.'

'I've got goosebumps.' Valeria's face has paled, and her dark eyes are serious.

Joona drinks a mouthful of wine. He has become part of Jurek's cruel orbit; there is no way to stop the transformation now, not after that whisper. He will end up like Jurek, someone who rejects life, who doesn't believe in the dignity of others, who only cares about his own dark plans.

'You stopped him, and he isn't in charge of you,' says Valeria, meeting his eye.

'No ...'

She puts down her glass, leans forward and touches his hand.

'I know his words got into your head,' she says, lowering her voice again. 'That you carry that moment with you, that it's the reason you choose to numb yourself whenever you feel trapped.'

Joona pulls away from her. 'What do you mean?' he asks in a cold voice.

'Are you upset?'

He ignores her question, eats another forkful of risotto and stares out through the window to avoid looking at her.

'Joona, what is it?'

'Nothing, I'm just tired.'

'You wanted to tell me, in your own way,' she says.

'I don't know what you're talking about.'

'You can't fool an old junkie. I noticed it right away. In the way you talk, your pupils, your sluggish gaze.'

'I take Topiramate for my migraines,' he snaps.

'That's what I would have said too,' she says with a smile.

'OK, but I was trying to tell you about something that's important to me,' he says, setting his cutlery down.

'I'm listening.'

Joona shakes his head and takes out his phone. He glances at the screen and then beckons to the waiter and asks for the bill.

'Don't be like this,' Valeria begs him.

'I have to get back to work.'

He can feel her eyes on him as he takes out his credit card and explains to the waiter that unfortunately something has come up at work, that his dining companion will finish her dinner at her own pace.

He then gets up and leaves the restaurant without another word, without even glancing back at Valeria, marching out onto the street and making his way to the closest metro station.

The pavement is dark and empty, and his footsteps echo between the tall buildings.

Joona doesn't know why it bothers him so much that Valeria has seen through his attempts to cover up his drug abuse and hasn't said anything. He was so ashamed he instinctively denied everything, like a child – which she also understood and forced him to confront.

He digs out his phone and calls Laila to tell her he will be there in half an hour. She tries to talk him out of it, warns him that he has been coming around too often, but he hangs up mid-sentence.

On a wall outside a shop, he notices an old poster telling people to maintain a two metre distance from one another.

Joona catches his reflection in a shop window as he passes, and he finds himself thinking back to Valeria's warm gaze as she begged him not to leave.

When he reaches the entrance to Rådmansgatan station, he pauses, turns around and runs back to the restaurant, taking out the ring as he strides through the dining room. Their table is now empty. He hurries back outside and calls Valeria, but she doesn't pick up. He tries once more, then gives up.

Joona walks home along Luntmakargatan, past the homeless people sleeping in every service entrance. By the gates at the back of Albert Bonniers Förlag, a man is smoking, the glowing tip of his cigarette illuminating the underside of his nose. A woman is rummaging through the glass recycling bin with a metal rod.

Joona pauses at his building, enters the code, opens the door and steps into the lift.

The machinery whirrs quietly as it carries him up to the eleventh floor.

When he emerges into the hallway, he sees that the door to his apartment is ajar and he feels a flicker of hope that Valeria might have come over, though deep down he knows that isn't the case.

There is a sucking sound behind him. The lift, making its way downstairs.

Joona loosens his Colt Combat from his shoulder holster, releases the safety, pulls the door open and listens carefully.

He can't hear a thing.

Joona steps inside, swinging his gun to the right. He locks the door behind him and makes his way into the bedroom, moving quickly around the bed to open the wardrobe doors, then returning to the hallway to check the bathroom.

He can hear a soft ticking sound.

Joona moves quickly through the living room, swinging around the corner to secure the kitchen.

He returns his pistol to the holster and walks over to the dining table.

His notepad is on the wrong side of his computer, the pages stirring gently in the warm air rising from the brass vents on the floor.

23

The scent of the oak flooring mixes with the tang of sweat in studio two at Dansens Hus, where the two children Saga supports take dance lessons.

She first got in touch with the Swedish National Down Syndrome Association two years ago, volunteering to help with various activities, and later became a designated support person for Astrid and Nick.

There is a large mirror covering one wall of the space, and along the other the barre runs beneath the row of windows.

Saga is on her knees in front of Astrid, helping her with her shoes and legwarmers. Both children have made real progress over the past year, but despite the fact that they are eleven – and most of the others in their group are between four and eight – they aren't yet ready to move up to the next level. Nick is the only boy in the class, but he loves ballet and frequently declares that he will be one of the Melodifestivalen backing dancers when he is older.

Saga usually manages to forget all about work while she is with the kids, but today she is finding it hard to think about anything other than Verner being dead. His death has shaken her much more deeply than she expected it to. Verner was someone she saw on a near daily basis while she worked for the Security Service, and in many respects he was her mentor.

If the killer's aim was to make things personal, then he definitely succeeded.

Nick tugs at the crotch of his black tights a few times before peering down inside the waistband.

'Back to front,' he says, his mouth curling into such a big grin that she can see his little teeth.

'Do you need me to help you?' Saga asks, getting to her feet.
'It's OK.'

'I'll go and wait outside, then,' she says.

'Don't you want to dance with us?' Astrid teases.

'Oh, I don't dare,' Saga replies, the way she always does.

'Noo,' Astrid laughs.

'It's way too hard,' Saga continues.

'We can show you ... Just do it like this, *grand-plié*.' Astrid demonstrates what to do.

'Like this?' Saga attempts to copy her.

'No, you have to bend your legs!' says Nick.

'*Demi-plié* ... and a pirouette.'

Saga spins around and Astrid claps her hands.

'You're really good!' the girl shouts.

'You think?'

'Super good,' says Nick, clamping his hands to his mouth as he laughs.

'One more time, *demi-plié* ...'

Their dance teacher comes into the room, crossing the floor with her chest puffed out and her head held high, dark hair gathered in a tight bun at the nape of her neck. She pauses in a pool of light by the windows, then turns around and studies the children with a brief smile before her face turns serious.

'Avant, avant!' she shouts.

The children fall silent and hurry over to her so that she can tick them off her list.

Saga leaves the studio and makes her way out to the waiting room, where she buys a bottle of water from the vending machine.

There are only a couple of other people in the waiting room: a wiry old man in an oversized jacket, busy peering down at his phone, and a young woman reading a thick library book.

Saga takes a seat opposite the woman, opens her bottle and gulps down the water.

'Are you a ballerina?' the young woman asks. Her voice sounds much older than she looks.

'No ... Are you?'

'I wish I had a flair for dancing, but I'm just waiting for my little sister.'

She is wearing a silver windbreaker, black jeans and silver trainers. On the floor between her feet, she has a grubby rucksack in the shape of a panda.

Saga scrolls through the latest emails on her phone, and her mind turns back to Verner. He was shot several times, fled into the bathhouse, and may have been dead before he was even winched out into the car park.

The old man mutters something to himself, presses a tissue to his nose and tips his head back. He has a shaved head, pronounced cheekbones and a deep scar on his throat, as though he has recently had an operation of some kind.

Saga knows she needs to pick up her things from the detective agency, but she doesn't want to risk bumping into Henry. Seeing him will only make her angry, largely because he hindered the investigation by intercepting her private mail.

The sound of laughter can be heard inside the studio.

A bumble bee thuds into the window and then continues on its way above the rooftops.

The young woman sitting opposite Saga has straight blonde hair, a broad forehead and pale blue eyes, lips pressed together as she reads.

After a few minutes, she closes the book, using her finger as a bookmark. She peers over to the old man, who is still sitting with his head tipped back.

'What are you reading?' asks Saga.

'Maths. Graph theory,' she replies, meeting Saga's eye.

The man lowers his chin, whispers to himself and squints down at the bright red blood on his tissue before folding it in two.

'Are you familiar with the problem known as the Seven Bridges of Königsberg?' the young woman asks in her old-fashioned manner.

'No, I don't think so.'

'It's not the easiest – do you want to give it a try?'

'Sure.'

'Königsberg was originally in Germany, but since World War II it's been part of Russia,' the young woman begins.

'Kaliningrad,' says Saga, noticing that the old man is now paying attention.

'In any case,' the young woman continues. 'In the eighteenth century, the beaches and the two islands in the river were linked by seven bridges, and the question is whether you can find a route that crosses each of the bridges only once.'

'Got it.'

'Let me draw it for you,' she says, digging an old receipt out of her bag. 'Have you got a pen?'

'No, sorry . . .'

The old man gets up and shuffles over to the young woman, handing her a pen without a word.

'Thanks.' She starts drawing.

Saga studies the girl's face: her taut lips and the frown between her pale brows. The cuffs of her windbreaker are slightly grubby, and her nails are bitten down to the quick. The pen is red, with the words *De Re Militari* printed in gold on one side.

'Back then, all the bridges had names,' says the young woman, looking up at Saga. 'Honey Bridge, Shopkeeper Bridge, Green Bridge, and so on.'

'But that has no bearing on the solution,' says Saga.

'Not to a mathematician, but try asking a quantum physicist,' the young woman says with a smirk. 'Some would probably transfer the problem to algebraic graphs and use algorithms to . . .'

She trails off as the old man abruptly gets back onto his feet. He drops his phone into his inside pocket and wanders off along the row of windows, turning his back on them and gazing outside for a moment before making his way towards the exit.

Right as he disappears from sight, Joona appears around the corner, waving when he spots Saga.

'Sorry, I need to talk to my colleague,' Saga tells the young woman. 'But I'll try to solve your problem.'

'Tell me what you've come up with next week,' the young woman replies, handing the drawing to her.

'OK.'

Saga and Joona move further down the corridor in order to talk in peace. They pause by the empty play area, with a clear line of sight back to the door for studio two.

'You called me,' says Joona. 'What did you want to talk about?'

'I have a possible lead that got lost in all the chaos around Verner,' Saga says quietly. 'I didn't want to bring it up in front of the others, because I've . . . overstepped a little.'

'What is it?'

'Do you remember Susanne Hjälm?'

'Yes.'

'You know she was convicted of killing one of our colleagues.'

'I testified twice, once in district court and once in the court of appeal,' he says.

'Well, she's been released. She's been out a while, apparently . . . and she seems to blame you for everything.'

'How do you know?' he asks.

Saga knows she can't tell him she went to see Karl Speler, that she acted as though she was on operational duty.

'I've got a source,' she says instead.

'Who is it?'

'I can't say. But Susanne fits our profile, and she was released just before the first postcard arrived.'

'She definitely has a strong connection to Jurek.'

'He's the one who broke her, we know that, but she doesn't seem able – or willing – to understand the link. It's easier just to blame you, the police force, the justice system.'

'Do you know where she lives?' Joona asks.

'No, she doesn't have a registered address, no bank cards, no phone contracts, nothing. Joona, I also wanted to ask you something . . . Have you put a surveillance unit on me?'

'No.'

'I just want to know if you have.'

'Of course.'

'There was a man in the waiting room, and . . .'

They hear excited voices and clapping through the door, and the children come streaming out into the corridor.

'What was it?' asked Joona.

'Nothing. Forget I said anything.'

Astrid and Nick run over to Saga and Joona. Both are rosy-cheeked and happy, Nick hopping up and down. Astrid grabs Joona's hand and studies his pink nails.

24

After dropping the kids off at school in Enskede, Saga and Joona make their way to Upplands Väsby, to the north of Stockholm. The knowledge that they might finally be closing in on the killer has left them both quiet and focused.

Following her dealings with Jurek Walter, Susanne Hjälm developed a form of aggressive paranoia and kept her family locked in their villa in Sätra. Her husband Mikael filed for divorce once she was arrested, but for several years he continued to take the children to visit her in Hinseberg Prison. That ultimately didn't work out, and he now has sole custody of the two girls, with Susanne subject to a far-reaching restraining order. She is no longer allowed anywhere near their home, Mikael's workplace or the kids' school.

Mikael and his daughters live in a terraced house in Runby, and he works as a lifeguard and wellness consultant at the local leisure centre.

Joona pulls up outside the large box-shaped building with huge expanses of glass and a green roof, and he and Saga make their way inside. They ask the woman behind the reception desk if she can direct them to Mikael Hjälm, and she tells them he is probably by the pool, where the senior aqua-fit class is due to start in forty minutes.

The large pool is virtually empty. The air is hot and humid, and there is a strong smell of chlorine rising from the water.

Pale light filters in through the blinds on the enormous windows.

At the far end of the pool, a man in white is busy loading an anti-wave rope onto a trolley. His short hair is peppered with grey, and he is frowning. He is wearing a white shell necklace, and the sleeves of his T-shirt are tight around his biceps.

The man looks up as Joona and Saga walk over to him. He clearly recognises Joona, because the colour drains from his face and he drops the rope, fumbling for support against the wall.

'Don't worry, nothing has happened,' Joona hurries to reassure him.

'So you're not here about Ellen and Anja?' Mikael whispers.

'No, but we need to talk to you about Susanne.'

Mikael slowly slumps down onto one of the starting blocks and tugs at his necklace.

'What has she done now?' he asks, his voice little more than a whisper.

'We need to speak to her, but she doesn't have a registered address,' Saga replies.

'Look, I don't want to get involved.' Mikael attempts a smile, but his face seems more sad than anything.

'When did you last hear from her?' asks Joona.

'I've got a restraining order.'

'We know, but she wouldn't be the first person to break one of those.'

'I think she lives at some yoga retreat or whatever it's called.'

'Do you know where?'

'Near Munkfors. Please don't tell her you spoke to me.'

'You're afraid of her,' says Saga.

Mikael looks down, lost in thought. The lane rope is dripping, the pool of water beneath it spreading across the tiles.

'Joona was there back then; we know what happened,' Saga continues. 'We know about the time she spent in prison, but what about since then, what has that been like?'

'What has it been like?' he replies, looking up at Saga through red-tinged eyes.

'I don't want anything to do with her ever again.'

The water laps against the overflow drain, and the dark blue markings on the bottom of the pool seem to dance in the ripples.

'We're police officers; we can help you.'

'I just don't want to talk about it,' he replies.

'She's threatened you, hasn't she?' says Joona.

'You saved our lives back then, I know that,' he says, looking up at Joona. 'And I really want to help you, so if that's what this is about then we can continue this conversation – but not for my sake, I don't want her to start thinking about me or the kids again.'

'We'll keep your names out of it.'

'Thank you,' says Mikael, taking a deep breath. 'I'll try to explain . . . When she first got out, she was different. She said she needed to get her life in order, to avoid losing all contact with the girls, so she started meditating and she went to therapy to help her accept her part in what happened. I told her I was happy for her, but then she moved into some sort of collective, she was doing lots of yoga. She started ringing the house more and more, talking about how the girls and I should visit her over Midsummer, just for the day . . . but we couldn't, because we were spending the summer with my parents in France.'

'How did she take that?'

'She started ringing the girls, telling them what she was going to do to me.'

'And what was that?' asks Saga.

'She said she'd come over to the house in the middle of the night, that she'd force me to beg for forgiveness and then castrate me in front of them and . . . she said she'd make them decide whether or not I bled out on the floor.'

* * *

Biondo Yoga, just west of Munkfors, offers an extensive range of courses for women.

'"We aim to inhabit ourselves completely and pool our strength to give a neglected world the love it deserves,"' Saga reads aloud from her phone.

'Sounds great,' says Joona.

'According to the website, their five-day retreat finishes today. Through guided flow, breathing, shaking, chanting and dance, it's meant to help participants find their primal female strength in their hearts, womb space and yoni.'

Manvir has already been in touch with the district of Bergslagen, who told him that Munkfors police have an ongoing case with links to Biondo Yoga. A couple of local officers are due to pay a visit to the retreat in order to speak to one of the residents there – a woman who refuses to appear in court to testify against the man who threatened and abused her after she left him – and Manvir has arranged to coordinate their visit with Saga and Joona's, enabling them to visit the facility without revealing their true aims. Meanwhile, an officer was stationed at Saga's place, waiting for any new packages that might arrive.

Saga and Joona drive through a small community, over the Klara River and along route 241 to the northern shore of Ransjön before turning off onto a private forest road.

Three kilometres later, they reach a locked boom barrier.

'Guess we're first,' says Saga.

A masonite arrow with the word PARKING on it has been tied to the fence. It is pointing towards an area of meadow beside the road, where the tall grass seems to have been cut back relatively recently.

The gravel clatters against the chassis as Joona reverses out of the way and parks the car in a suitable location for making a quick exit if necessary.

'Check whether there's anything you might need in the glove compartment,' he tells Saga.

She opens the hatch and takes out the holster inside, unclipping the weapon: a compact Glock 26. Saga presses the magazine release and lets it drop into her hand. There are eleven 9mm Luger cartridges inside. Out of habit, she checks the mechanics and the recoil spring before pushing the magazine back into place.

They get out into the warm air, insects buzzing in the tall lupins.

'Thanks,' Saga says as she puts the holster on.

Joona has just grabbed the radio unit when a patrol car appears on the forest track. The reflections of the treetops flow across its windscreen.

Saga waves and zips up her jacket as the car pulls right up to the barrier. The doors open, and she and Joona walk over to introduce themselves to the two officers who get out.

Magnus in his fifties, with a thick beard and a unibrow. Luke has a broad jaw, a dimpled chin and a blond moustache.

'You guys didn't need to drive all the way up from Stockholm, you know. If you need help in the future, all you've gotta do is ask,' Magnus tells them.

'Google the Munkfors police,' Luke says with a grin. 'We've only got one review to date.'

'One star out of five,' Magnus beams.

'Congratulations,' says Joona.

'Honestly, it feels great.' Magnus laughs.

Saga walks through the fireweed and cow parsley by the edge of the barrier as Luke ducks down beneath the rusty bar.

'Ow, shit . . .'

'Lucky Luke here's a bit sore,' Magnus explains.

'I got a tattoo yesterday.'

He loosens the compress on the inside of his forearm to reveal a child's sketch of two blob-shaped people holding hands on his pinkish skin.

'My daughter's first drawing of the two of us together.'

'Nice,' says Saga.

They start walking down the gravel track. The grass in the middle of the lane is tall, and a bird chirps a handful of notes over and over again. The forest around them is dark, the ground dry.

Magnus keeps talking, telling them that one star isn't as bad as it sounds; that they shouldn't forget that a star has five points.

The overgrown meadow to their right is surrounded by a sun-bleached wooden fence, and over by the edge of the forest there is a tree stand.

Luke says that Biondo Yoga has become a kind of informal safe zone for women who, for various reasons, need a bit of breathing space, and that there are also two families living on site.

After walking for ten minutes, they spot the lake glittering between the trees up ahead. The first few buildings appear not long after. Saga and Joona have studied aerial photographs of the site, and they know that there are two large buildings, a narrow row of houses and four small cabins. All have tiled roofs, red wooden cladding and white window frames.

'You do what you need to do, go and talk to Svetlana. We'll try to find Susanne Hjälm,' says Joona.

The forest opens out onto a grassy slope down to the water's edge.

There is no sign of anyone else around.

In the middle of the grass, a table has been set with plates and glasses. Two of the chairs have fallen over, and a yoga mat seems to have blown into the reeds by the jetty.

The officers make their way over to the biggest of the buildings, around the gable end and past a rainwater drum, stopping dead when they spot two women lying flat out on the porch facing the lake.

'What the hell,' Magnus mumbles.

They slowly continue down the slope, along the side of the wooden deck, where a sheet of tie-dyed fabric obscures their view. A black cat slinks into the dappled shade between the concrete pillars, and someone has lined up small mussel shells along the edge of the veranda.

There is a third woman lying in the long grass, her legs up on the stairs.

Inside, through the open patio doors, they can make out more bodies on the floor.

25

Saga moves slowly towards the house with the others just behind her. The whole scene is enchantingly quiet, the only sound coming from the insects buzzing above the weeds and the rowing boat bumping into the jetty.

The woman lying closest to them is flat out on her back with her mouth open and her eyes closed. Saga studies her calm face, her soft laughter lines and the freckles on her nose.

The sunlight shines across her chest, and her thin mustard yellow top strains with every calm breath she takes.

'They're asleep,' Saga whispers.

The four officers slowly make their way forward, down the slope by the side of the deck. The woman at the foot of the stairs squints up at them and then closes her eyes as they pass.

The boards squeak under their weight as they approach the doors into a large yoga studio.

'Oh, come on,' a woman sighs in disappointment.

She sits up, back straight and knees wide apart, the soles of her feet pressed together in front of her. Her black hair is neatly parted down the middle, and she has dark circles beneath her eyes, a large chip missing from one of her front teeth.

'What's going on here?' Magnus asks, gesturing to all of the other bodies around them.

'Yoga nidra. Yogic sleep,' she replies.

'Sorry to interrupt,' says Luke, 'but we need to talk to Svetlana Johnsson.'

'OK, everyone,' the woman calls to the others as she lithely gets to her feet. 'You can start the wake-up now, or keep going for as long as you like, but I want to say thanks . . . It's been a great experience getting to know you.'

She follows Magnus and Luke down the steps and out onto the grass by the lake. Joona and Saga remain where they are on the deck, searching for Susanne among the women still lying on the ground. There is no sign of her, so they turn into the yoga studio instead.

Their plan is to find and detain Susanne as discreetly as they can while their colleagues talk to Svetlana about her failure to testify.

A young woman appears on the twisting wooden staircase from the floor above. She is barefoot, wearing a see-through yellow dress. Her blonde hair is knotted and her lips are dry, and the skin on her cheeks looks slightly sunburnt.

'Can I help you?' she asks with a smile.

'Do you live here?' Joona replies.

'Do I live here? Our souls are free, aren't they? But yes, I came to the community on the spring equinox.'

'Could you tell us where we can find Susanne Hjälm?' asks Joona.

'Susanne? What do you want with her?'

'It's a private matter, to do with her children,' says Saga.

'And it's urgent,' Joona adds.

The woman crosses her fingers at him, as though she was trying to ward off a demon, and then she laughs.

'No, I understand, children are the true manifestation of the divine, aren't they? The womb and the child. I can see you're getting impatient with me. God, what a silly, difficult woman.'

'Something like that,' Saga mutters.

'Don't you see? I'm not the enemy,' she replies, her eyes fixed on Saga. 'There's nothing but love between us.'

'OK.'

A few of the other women sit up and squint over to them.

'Just tell us where we can find Susanne,' says Joona.

'Susanne,' the woman repeats, waving her hand vaguely. 'She took the buckets to the compost heap, should be back soon.'

'We can't wait,' says Saga. 'Where's the compost?'

'You have to understand . . . we're very particular about our food here, we follow the ayurvedic principles,' she says. 'And we're very particular about composting; only the residents of the ashram are allowed to go up there.'

'Where is it?' Saga repeats.

'In the forest, there's a trail behind the shed,' the woman replies, pointing out through a window at the rear of the building. 'But I urge you to respect our rules . . .'

They head back out onto the porch. The woman follows them down the stairs and round the house, pausing to watch them with an anxious look on her face.

Saga and Joona hurry up the grassy slope, past the shed, the firewood and chopping block. They manage to find the trail, and start making their way among the trees.

The forest quickly becomes much denser around them, the light softer and the air easier to breathe.

They pass an overturned pine, a dark burst of sprawling roots and rich earth torn up from the ground, leaving an opening like a portal to the underworld.

* * *

Down by the jetty, the yoga teacher tells Magnus and Luke that she has no idea where Svetlana is.

'We really do need to talk to her,' Luke tries again.

'I can't help you,' she snaps, her tone now much colder.

'Listen: we know that Svetlana is the victim in this trial, but the law says she has to appear in court when called; it isn't optional.'

'What if she can't?' the woman asks.

'Then she needs that in writing from a doctor.'

'There are other ways to testify,' Magnus explains. 'Via video link, for example. That way she can avoid having to come face to face with the accused. We'll find a solution that works for her, but in order to do that we need to talk to her.'

The yoga teacher gives them a dismissive look.

'You should have sent a female officer,' she mutters.

'We know, that would have been much better, but unfortunately it wasn't possible today,' says Luke.

'Men aren't forbidden here, but the idea is that it's a safe space for women.'

'We can wait here by the lake if that helps,' Magnus suggests.

'OK,' she says, glancing over to a small red building by the edge of the forest.

'Could you go and get her for us?' asks Luke.

'I'm not allowed inside the ashram, but I'll make sure she knows you're here when we sit down to eat.'

'Is it that building over there?' asks Luke, pointing to the red building.

'You can't—'

'Wait here,' Magnus interrupts her, moving to block her way.

'You don't know what you're doing,' the woman warns him, fear in her eyes.

'You and I are going to stay here and have a chat until my colleague comes back with Svetlana,' Magnus says softly.

'Don't go over there!' she calls after Luke.

'I'm going to have to ask you to be quiet,' says Magnus.

'This is private land!'

'Just relax, it's all going to be OK.'

'No.'

'I understand you have something very special here, but you have to adhere to the law, even if it feels awkward or intrusive.'

* * *

Luke follows the well-trodden path through a shady patch of weeds, heading towards a red building with white corner panels and window frames.

He hears the yoga teacher's anxious shouts behind him, and he finds himself thinking about the classes on how to avoid offending other cultures that all new recruits have to take.

Sadly there isn't a manual for anything like this.

A windchime made from bones and feathers clinks in a nearby tree.

Luke has no idea what an ashram is, but he has visions of some sort of temple full of images of God and offerings of fruit.

He notices a gap between the mustard yellow curtains in one of the windows, and he makes his way over to it through the ferns, pushing back the brush with one hand.

There is no sign of anyone inside, but he can see a heap of clothes on a chair. A pair of blue jeans, some black lacy underwear, a tie-dyed dress and some dirty socks, a large white bra.

The floor is covered in some sort of glossy red fabric, and there is a dark blue drape studded with small silver stars hanging over the doorway into the hall.

Three incense sticks have been pushed into a glass bowl of sand on a low table, and he can see the thin columns of smoke curling up into the air.

From the ceiling, a number of mirrors have been hung on lengths of string, all at different heights, and the lampshade is made from what looks like perforated copper, casting hundreds of tiny chinks of light across the saffron-coloured walls.

The back half of the room is hidden behind a folding screen featuring prints from a Hindu temple: a famous sculpture of four softly smiling women having sex.

Luke notices the three columns of smoke from the incense all bend sharply to one side, and the lampshade sways on the ceiling, making the flecks of light dance.

There must be someone in the room after all.

He uses his hands to shield his eyes and leans in close to the window, his hot breath making the glass fog up. One of the mirrors by the side of the screen has started turning slowly, and Luke watches as the reflection swings around. He sees a purple cushion with golden tassels, the edge of a bed, red sheets – and then a foot, toes splayed.

Another of the mirrors is spinning faster, and Luke sees the inside of the screen race by, followed by a glimpse of three naked bodies on the bed.

26

Joona and Saga follow the trail through the trees, breaking into a run as they round a boulder covered in moss.

All they can hear is the soft thudding of their feet on the ground.

A birch has fallen across the trail and hit the trees on the other side, creating a kind of entryway they have to duck through.

The ground slopes gently away, and they slow down when they reach the bottom of the dip.

'Did she just send us on a wild goose chase?' Saga asks as she catches her breath.

'I noticed a bit of spilled earth in a few places,' says Joona.

Someone has used three birch logs to make a kind of provisional bridge over a small stream, and the trunks bend beneath their weight as they cross, squelching down into the water.

They keep running along the sloping ground by a bare rockface.

The forest closes in around them again. There are strings of wiry lichen hanging from the branches overhead, and the ground between the trees is studded with brown needles and cones.

Pale light filters between the spruces up ahead.

As they emerge into a small glade, a wood pigeon flaps up from the ground.

There is no sign of anyone, though they do spot a spade and a pitchfork that have been left driven into a pile of earth.

The compost heaps, held in place by half-rotten boards, are full of decaying food waste, lettuce leaves, potato tops and withered apples.

The stench is almost unbearable.

Saga and Joona make their way around a heap of grass and leaves, stopping dead when they reach the other side.

Curled up on the muddy ground behind a rusty wheelbarrow is a child. A young girl with plaited blonde hair, dirty hands and a runny nose.

'Hi,' Saga says as she slowly moves over to her.

'Hi,' the girl replies, sitting up straight.

'Are you from Biondo Yoga?'

The girl nods and picks a dry leaf from her hair.

'Have you seen Susanne?'

'She emptied the buckets and left.'

'When was that?'

'Don't know.'

'Was it just before we got here?'

'Not really,' the girl says, getting up and brushing the dirt from her red dress.

'Are you allowed to come out here on your own?'

She shakes her head.

'But you do it anyway?' Saga says with a smile.

'Every day,' she replies, shaking off a fly that has landed on her hand.

'Why do you like coming out here?'

'So I can see Daddy,' she says softly.

'And where is he now?'

The girl turns to the tall heap of soil.

'Oh God,' Saga whispers.

* * *

In a round mirror hanging from a silver thread towards the back of the room, Luke catches a glimpse of a milky-white backside – all soft flesh and stretchmarks – just as the woman rolls onto her back.

His heart is pounding.

The biggest of the mirrors turns slowly on its string, glass streaked with fingerprints. Little by little, more of the bed comes into view.

Luke sees a younger woman with slim hips lying on her back with her head turned away from him. Her wrists are bound with red scarves.

The hair beneath her arms is dark, her stomach slick with sweat and her shoulder muscles tense.

His eyes dart between the different mirrors as fragmented images flicker by: a yellowing bruise on a calf, lips closing around a brown nipple, bitten nails stroking a cheek, rows of vertical scars on a flat bottom, rolls of flesh on a pale stomach.

In the biggest of the mirrors, the bound woman's face suddenly comes into view. She has her eyes squeezed tightly shut, and he can see tears clinging to her lashes.

She speaks, and Luke realises it is Svetlana. She lost her front teeth when her ex beat her up last year.

The mirror keeps spinning, revealing the sweaty back of a knee, pillows, a head of blonde curls, the inside of the screen and the walls. Right then, Luke finds himself staring at his own reflection in the window.

His face looks oddly absent and dark against the bright sky outside, and for the few seconds it takes him to tear himself out of the role of the spectator, time seems almost hypnotically slow.

He notices that there is someone behind him, but he remains perfectly still.

His eyes shift from the mirror inside to the reflection in the window in front of him, and he watches a figure raise a long axe in the air.

Adrenaline floods through Luke's veins, making every single hair stand on end. His brain tells him to grab his gun, turn around and shoot her in the shoulder.

He can hear his blood roaring in his ears.

He slowly lowers his hand from the windowsill, past his stomach to the holster on his belt. His fingers reach the fastening just as the woman lunges forward with a stifled whimper.

Luke's forehead hits the window with such force that the outer pane of glass breaks. He manages to pull his pistol free and disable the safety catch, and has just started turning towards her when everything comes to a halt.

Something is stopping him from moving, and he feels a strange pressure on his neck.

He tries again, but he can't turn around.

All of a sudden, he realises that the axe is buried deep in the back of his skull. The handle hitting the wall of the building was preventing him from turning.

His heart starts racing as hot blood trickles down his neck and back.

He doesn't have much time; he needs to find Magnus and call for an ambulance.

Luke staggers away from the building and wheels around, staring at a woman with brown plaits and a tattooed throat as she backs away from him with wide eyes.

He pulls the trigger and fires a bullet into the ferns.

The pistol snaps back in his hand, and the sound of the shot echoes off the rocks on the far side of the lake.

Blue and white circles of light have started dancing across his field of vision.

He follows the woman, but he can't manage to raise his weapon again. It feels as though there is an elastic band connecting it to the ground.

Luke finds himself thinking about his daughter's rubber frog toy that clambers down the wall as his knees give way and he slumps onto his hip among the ferns. He tries to crawl forward but ends up face down on the ground, gasping into the soil.

The earthy aroma of roots, plants and minerals fills his nose.

He thinks back to childhood, when he helped his mother plant peas at their place in the country. It felt like a miracle that those tiny peas could ever have emerged from such delicate little flowers.

27

When the gunshot shatters the silence, the yoga teacher with the dark hair tries to cling on to Magnus's arm, but he pulls himself free with such force that she stumbles forward.

'Just leave us alone!' she shouts after him.

Magnus unholsters his service weapon as he runs along the trampled path through the weeds, keeping the barrel low to the ground. He rounds a large rhododendron and sees the little red building by the edge of the forest.

There is no sign of his colleague.

Magnus slows down, breathing heavily as his eyes scan the windows. Everything is calm and quiet. All he can hear is the dry rattling of a windchime.

'Luke!'

He releases the safety catch, puts a finger on the trigger guard and moves forward towards the door.

'Police!' he shouts as he opens it. 'I'm coming in!'

Magnus steps forward into a cramped hallway with patterned paper on the walls. There are three pairs of shoes on the rug and a dark blue velvet drape over the doorway into the next room.

'Police!'

As he reaches out to push the drape back slightly, he realises his hand is shaking. He stops to listen.

'I'm coming in!' he shouts, his finger now hugging the trigger.

Magnus raises his pistol, ducks beneath the drape and moves through to the next room, quickly securing the space.

The air is thick with the scent of incense and sweat, and it feels like there isn't enough oxygen in the room.

He exhales through a narrow gap between his lips.

There are mirrors on strings everywhere, and with all of them in motion it feels as though the walls and décor are spinning too.

Half of the room is hidden behind a large screen featuring erotic motifs.

He notices some black underwear and blue jeans on a stool, and he slowly makes his way forward, pushing the mirrors out of his way as he passes.

The soft floor is lined with red fabric.

'Luke?'

Luke is more than just a colleague to him; he was the only person to stand up for Magnus when he came out. The others all refused to shower at the same time as him, refused to work the same shift or even to ride in the same car.

The mirrors behind him sway from side to side, casting bright flashes of light across the walls and ceiling.

The lamp on the low table flickers.

Magnus swings around the screen with his gun.

A naked woman is sprawled on the bed on the other side. Her front teeth are missing, and she is staring up at the ceiling with a blank look on her face.

Magnus lowers his pistol and realises that his palm is slick with sweat.

The woman's stomach rises and falls with each slow breath. Her legs are parted, and he can see red scratch marks on the insides of her thighs. She is bound by her wrists with scraps of fabric tied to a metal loop on the wall.

'Svetlana?' he whispers.

She turns her head and gives him a woozy smile.

A red silk sheet with golden embroidery has been hung over another doorway, and it billows softly in the breeze from the room on the other side.

'Are you on your own in here?' he asks as he unties her wrists.

'This isn't some fucking porno fantasy,' she slurs, crossing her legs.

'I need you to tell me whether there's anyone else in the building, through that doorway.'

'Only Death, who ... who's sitting in a little box. Open the lid and ...'

She trails off, licking her lips and closing her eyes. Magnus moves past the bed, accidentally knocking a mirror with a brass frame and setting it spinning.

He uses the barrel of his gun to push the red silk drape back, glancing over his shoulder at the mirrors and the woman on the bed before moving through into the narrow corridor.

There are doors on both sides, and the only light is coming from a rice paper shade.

The foul stench of sewage catches in Magnus's nose.

The floorboards creak beneath his feet.

At the far end of the corridor, he can see a wooden chest on the floor. It's roughly the size of a carry-on suitcase, with metal reinforcements.

The light barely stretches that far.

Magnus nudges one of the doors and peers in to what seems to be a small cell containing nothing but a narrow metal bed and a bare mattress.

He keeps going.

The key in the lock of the little chest glitters in the soft light.

He reaches a doorway into a pantry. There are two hotplates inside, a small fridge with a grubby handle and a shelf of groceries.

Up ahead, another of the doors slowly swings open.

'Luke?' he whispers.

From up on the ceiling, he can hear the whirring of a fan behind a yellowed plastic grille. The door closes, and he hears the lock click.

Magnus's shoulder is aching, and he lowers his pistol for a moment, thinking that he should wipe his sweaty palm on his trousers.

He is no more than five metres from the chest now.

It looks far too small for there to be anyone inside.

He takes a step forward and hears a rusty hinge creak softly.

Magnus blinks and tries to work out whether the lid is opening, but another door in front of him swings out into the corridor in the draught, blocking his view.

Magnus raises his pistol and moves closer.

He can hear the fan whirring again, and the door swings shut.

A large woman wearing a pair of glasses is now standing in front of the wooden chest. She has curly blonde hair, a broad forehead and a prominent underbite.

She is wearing a pair of red silk trousers and a white bra, and she is holding a small knife in one hand.

Magnus is just about to take aim at her feet and tell her to drop the knife when a loud crack overpowers everything else. The bullet passes clean through his leg just above his knee, sending a spray of blood across the wallpaper in front of him.

He drops his gun and braces himself against the wall, slumping to the floor.

The bullet has shattered his thigh, and there are shards of bone protruding from the exit wound. His blood spurts out in powerful throbs.

A red-haired woman wearing nothing but a pair of underwear is standing just behind him, aiming an elk rifle at him.

* * *

Joona and Saga run past the fallen tree with their pistols drawn, emerging from the forest just as the second shot rings out. It was caused by a different weapon this time, a rifle rather than a handgun, and it sounded more muffled than the first. They pass the shed, cut across the grassy slope and jump a low fence, continuing through the tall weeds towards the house.

One of the windows is broken.

Beneath it, the ferns are flattened, as though someone has tried to create a snow angel.

Saga runs over to Luke's body and drops to her knees beside him as Joona keeps an eye on the house and the edge of the forest, taking aim at one window after another.

The windchime in the tree nearby rattles softly.

Luke is dead.

Saga gets up and gives Joona a quick shake of the head.

'I'll take the back,' he says.

'Be careful.'

'You too.'

Saga makes her way into the hall. She tears down the drape and quickly scans the corners of the main room, ignoring the spinning mirrors. She marches over to the folding screen and knocks it to the floor.

On the bed behind it, a naked woman is lying with her hands behind her head, gazing up at Saga with weary eyes.

156

'Police,' Saga tells her, keeping her voice low.

She grabs the woman's ankle, drags her onto the floor and cuffs her hands behind her back.

Saga then tears the second drape from the doorway and strides into the corridor on the other side. She can hear thudding and screaming through the walls, and the air is thick with the scent of gunpowder. A red-haired woman wielding a rifle turns awkwardly towards her.

Saga darts forward and grabs the barrel of the gun in her free hand. She breaks the woman's collarbone using the butt of her pistol, then tears the rifle from her grip.

The far end of the corridor is almost entirely hidden behind an open door, but she can see that Magnus is lying on the floor with his trousers around his ankles.

As Saga forces the red-haired woman onto her stomach, she notices another woman straddling Magnus with a knife between her teeth.

'Don't do it,' he gasps as Saga stands up and raises her gun.

The woman grabs Magnus's penis and testicles in one hand and grips her knife in the other.

Right then, Joona appears in the doorway behind her. With three long strides, he kicks the woman in the ribs, hitting her so hard that she is thrown back onto the floor, still clutching the knife in her hand.

Saga reaches her a moment later, stamping on the woman's wrist and shooting her in the shoulder.

Joona makes his way down the corridor, opening every door to make sure the cells are empty. He finds Susanne Hjälm sitting on the little metal bed in the third room, with her hands clamped over her ears. Her brown hair is plaited, and her face and tattooed throat are both streaked with blood.

28

Two days have passed since the operation at the yoga retreat, but Joona and Saga are still at the police station in Örebro, helping the prosecutor with her enquiries and trying to get a better understanding of the place where Susanne Hjälm lived before they interview her.

Luke Larsson died almost immediately from the axe blow to the back of his head.

Magnus Wallman was airlifted to the hospital in Karlstad, where he remains in a serious but stable condition.

Joona and Saga have spent a total of fourteen hours interviewing the women from the retreat. So far, the prosecutor has notified three of the women that she suspects they are guilty of aiding and abetting a crime, and has filed charges against the four women from the ashram.

The image of the retreat that has emerged following their searches of the property and their interviews with the women is complex but clear. Biondo Yoga was conceived as a collective for alternative lifestyles and yoga, offering vulnerable women a safe space while raising money to fund its operation through seminars and courses.

The small group of women at the heart of the business originally bonded over their frustration with the prevailing gender power balance in society, but their deep wounds – mostly caused by male violence and oppression – spiralled into paranoia and extremism.

Their spiritual leader, Camilla Boman – also known as Guru Biondo – created a kind of sexual healing programme to help her followers move past what she called their 'heteronormative rapes'.

Svetlana likely wouldn't be alive today if it weren't for the safe haven Yoga Biondo had offered her, and she remained stubbornly loyal to her saviours during police interviews, refusing to accept that she had been abused or sexually exploited by the other women in the ashram.

'Before I came here, I was just a bunch of holes,' she explained. 'Men are obsessed with fucking; they're prepared to kill for it. A man would swim across a sea of shit if he thought there was a nice warm cunt waiting for him at the other side.'

So far, two bodies have been recovered from the compost heaps. One has been identified as Camilla's husband, and is thought to have been there for around five years. He is still registered as living at the retreat, and has continued to collect his pension every month.

The second body belongs to Ida Andersson's husband, Marcus. He was killed and buried much later, around Christmas last year, and the cause of death was likely severe injuries to his face and skull. Since his death, Marcus's benefits and child support payments have all been paid to the retreat.

Ida Andersson has now been charged with attempted murder. She declined legal representation and immediately confessed to shooting Magnus Wallman when questioned.

Saga has handled all the interviews with the women from the ashram, with Joona watching from a TV screen in another room.

Ida's red hair was loose, and she was breathing heavily, almost as though it took a real effort to sit in the chair in the interrogation room. She blushed intensely the moment the focus was on her.

'Who killed your husband?' asked Saga.

'He fell.'

'Where?'

'Tripped over a rock in the forest. Slipped on a branch.'

'The pathologist thinks he was beaten to death, with a weapon of some sort. Probably a claw hammer or a small sledgehammer,' said Saga.

'I don't know anything about that.'

Ida pushed out her lower lip like a stubborn child.

'So you didn't kill him?'

'Nope.'

'Who did, then?'

She pulled out several of her pale eyelashes, dropped them to the table and pushed them into a row with her index finger.

'All I'll say is, I'm Guru Biondo's disciple. She knows a lot ... what to do ... how to make sure the whole world survives.'

As she brought the interview to a close, Saga realised that Ida genuinely had no real idea of what went on at the retreat. She didn't seem to know who was responsible for killing her husband, but she did confess to moving his body in a wheelbarrow prior to burial.

And despite the fact that her own daughter was traumatised by the murder and visited her father's grave every day, Ida seemed completely nonplussed by their questions about the girl.

* * *

Saga is alone in the windowless interview room, sitting on a dark blue desk chair. The glare of the ceiling lights glitters in her blue eyes. Saga always used to wear her hair in plaits, securing them with different coloured elastics, but for the past few years she has let it hang loose down her shoulders and back instead.

By the microphones on the table, there are a few plastic bottles of mineral water, unbleached paper cups and a box of tissues for anyone who needs them.

Saga bends down and takes her phone from her bag. A receipt falls to the floor, and she picks it up and turns it over, studying the young woman's sketch of the seven bridges of Königsberg on the reverse.

While she waits, she attempts to find a route that crosses each bridge only once.

It proves much harder than she expected, and she has made at least fifty failed attempts by the time she hears footsteps in the corridor outside.

There is a knock at the door, and Saga tosses the receipt into the wastepaper basket as Camilla Boman, Guru Biondo, is led into the room by two guards.

Camilla has no legal representative, having forced her lawyer out during the remand hearing by claiming he was a biological accident, an abomination.

Saga has looked into Camilla's background and knows that she took her surname from Dorothy Marie Biondo, mother of Valerie Solonas, who is best known for writing the SCUM manifesto and attempting to murder Andy Warhol in 1968.

She nods to Camilla and briefly explains what will happen during the interview, what her rights are and that their conversation is being recorded.

Camera one is mounted on the wall behind Saga, recording Camilla's face straight on. Camera two covers them both from one side, and camera three is on the ceiling, providing a bird's eye view of the room. From the office next door, Joona can see more of Camilla than Saga can.

'Take a seat,' Saga tells her.

Camilla has a bandage on one shoulder and a deep bruise stretching from her chest to her throat. She is five foot nine, with broad shoulders and large hands, and flaking lilac polish on her nails.

The chair creaks as she sits down, leans back and spreads her knees.

The combination of her prominent underbite, crinkled nose and curly blonde hair makes her look like an angry doll.

'Your disciple Ida Andersson claims you know how to save the world,' Saga begins in a neutral tone, turning to a fresh page in her notepad.

'Does she?'

'Is it something to do with pollution?' Saga asks, deliberately playing dumb.

'Think bigger.'

'OK, bigger.'

'You don't have kids,' Camilla says, leaning forward.

'No.' Saga smiles, feigning surprise.

'A sperm provides one half of a foetus's chromosomes and an egg the other half,' Camilla explains. 'That's how it's always been, but several researchers have now managed to produce gametes from female cells that can fertilise another woman's eggs. That means two women can have a biological child together – but only daughters, because women don't carry the necessary genetic information to create a boy.'

'I understand.'

'Do you?' Camilla raises her eyebrows. 'It means we no longer need men for the survival of humankind. We don't need men to fertilise us. And we'll no longer have any sons.'

'A world without men or boys.'

'I'm not naive, but if a large percentage of women actually start families with other women and give birth only to daughters, that will cause the power balance to shift. All men will, in effect, be at risk of being excluded from the gene pool.'

'You could always just kill the men.'

'Nice thought.'

'You lured Ida's husband out to the retreat and killed him.'

'He'd taken her daughter,' Camilla replies, utterly indifferent to his fate.

'And what about your husband?'

Camilla leans back and gives Saga a dreamy smile. She then knocks on the table and gets to her feet.

29

Joona didn't have time to shave that morning, and he has a faint five o'clock shadow.

The sun drifts across the sky as he sits in the office beside the interrogation room, its light eventually spilling in through the dusty window and making the shadow of a pen in a plastic pot from Legoland twist across the desk.

He feels a flicker of pain stretch out from one eye, digging deep into his brain before fading away.

Years ago, Joona sustained a head injury when a car exploded beside him, which led to him developing atypical cluster migraines. When the pain is at its worst, it can be so intense that he loses consciousness.

It's been so long since his last serious episode that he has stopped taking his preventive medication – the epilepsy drug Topimax – because it makes him tired, but over the past few weeks the premonitory signs have been getting more and more frequent.

Joona gets up and closes the blinds, angling the slats to block out the light. The image on the TV screen becomes a little sharper, though the glare of the sun is still visible in the glass.

Through camera one, he can see the table, an empty chair and the wall behind it. Saga isn't in shot, but he can hear her pen scratching against the page in her notepad.

The scent of sesame oil is still lingering in the air after lunch.

The first interview with Susanne Hjälm – the reason they visited the retreat in the first place – is due to start any minute now. Joona has been waiting for this moment for almost twenty-two hours, and he has lost count of the number of times his eyes have drifted around the room, across the blue folders on the shelves, the desk and the landline, the computer and the stacks of case files; the grease-stained menu from a Thai restaurant on the noticeboard.

'She's coming,' Saga says into the microphone.

* * *

Two guards have brought Susanne Hjälm down from the break yard on the roof.

Saga and Joona discussed their strategy earlier, and they decided that there was no point wasting time trying to convince her to confess to killing Luke; Susanne will be convicted of his murder whether she admits to it or not.

Instead, their plan is to coax her into talking about Jurek Walter. Because if Susanne is involved in the murders of Margot, Severin, Simon and Verner then that makes Jurek Walter an unfinished chapter in her psyche, the key to understanding why she has done the things she has.

Neither of them is convinced that Susanne is the serial killer they have been hunting, but she could easily be his partner. She views the entire state as her enemy, feels persecuted by the police and hates Joona Linna above all else.

The guards lead Susanne into the interview room. The prison uniform she is wearing is loose, with baggy knees and fraying cuffs.

The duty officer asks Saga to sign a sheet of paper and then opens the door for Susanne's legal representative, a middle aged woman with a stubby nose, big glasses and a broad mouth.

Susanne slumps down with a sigh and then stares at her hands on the table. The tattooed skin on her throat is bluish green, her two plaits resting against her shoulders.

She has a pretty face, Saga thinks to herself. It isn't hard to imagine her in her school portraits as a child, all bright eyes and a sweet smile. One of the cutest girls in her class, with good grades and nice new clothes.

But the Susanne sitting opposite her today has a look of bitterness on her face, puffy bags beneath her pale brown eyes and flaky skin on her hairline.

When Joona arrested her for the second time, she was in one of the small cells in the ashram building. He cuffed and photographed her, documenting the blood on her face and the flaking paint from the handle of the axe on her right palm as she mumbled that she wasn't done with him yet.

'When you were thirty-five, you were a specialist doctor with two degrees,' Saga begins. 'You had a high-paying job, you'd been married to Mikael for fifteen years. You had two daughters together and lived in a nice big house. No criminal record, no defaults on your credit score, no parking fines, nothing.'

'Act one,' Susanne mutters without looking up.

'What about act two? You became a killer, you shot a police officer and spent years in prison . . . And now another policeman is dead, Luke Larsson. He died almost immediately from the axe wound to his head.'

'Susanne,' the lawyer says, raising a hand in the air. 'I'd just like to remind you that you don't have to answer any questions at this stage. Remember what I said over the phone, what you need to think about.'

'Just take your time and tell me what happened, in your own words,' Saga continues unperturbed.

'I'd gone to get the axe from the shed, to cut down a dead birch, and—'

'Susanne,' the lawyer warns her with a smile.

'What?' she snaps, giving the woman an irritated glance.

'We've talked about this. You shouldn't make any admissions or—'

'What difference does it make?'

'If you want me to defend you, I need you to listen to me.'

'I'll get life either way,' she says, turning back to Saga. 'I saw the policeman peering into our ashram, during one of our most intimate rituals . . . No respect, nothing. He shows up at our ashram and turns all our spirituality and love into a fucking peep show.'

'I understand,' says Saga.

'It was like a dark sheet of glass broke, right here behind my eyes, in my brain . . .'

'Susanne admits to being there, but not—'

'All I could think was that he had to die,' Susanne continues. 'Die, you fucker, die, you pig . . . After I did it, the only real disappointment was that it wasn't Joona Linna's skull I'd cracked in two.'

'Why is that?'

'Is he listening to this?'

'Of course.'

'Joona,' says Susanne, looking straight into the camera. 'I hope you die soon, that you and your family end up in hell.'

'Why do you hate him so much?'

'How is a woman supposed to forgive the person who tore her children away from her?'

'Have you really thought through what happened?' Saga asks calmly.

Susanne's mouth hardens. 'What do you think?'

'Tell me what happened, how you ended up losing custody.'

'Joona showed up and ruined everything.'

'You worked in the psychiatric unit at Löwenströmska Hospital,' Saga begins.

'Yes.'

The lawyer gives her a concerned glance.

'And you'd been responsible for a patient by the name of Jurek Walter when you requested some time off,' Saga continues.

'Yes.'

'Why did you do that? Why did you need time off?'

'Because I'd stopped trusting myself,' Susanne replies, looking down. 'I'd changed, I was no longer in control of my own thoughts.'

'And why was that?'

Susanne smiles to herself and shakes her head.

'Jurek got you to say things you didn't want to say, didn't he? He made you listen to things you didn't want to hear,' says Saga.

'More or less.'

'And what did he say to you?'

'All sorts of things, I can't remember.'

'I know you still think about some of the things he said. I believe you think about them every day.'

Susanne's breathing has grown heavier, and she looks queasy.

'They warned me about listening to the patient. Most of the others wore earplugs around him, but I don't know . . . that felt inhumane to me.'

'You were still in act one,' says Saga.

'Mmm, for another few weeks.'

'What did you hear?'

'Philosophical and moral deliberations. Things he wanted me to . . . think about.'

'Could you give any examples?' Saga pushes Susanne.

As though the memory was her own, Susanne starts telling her about a winter's night in a dilapidated mountain village in the Caucasus.

It was minus twenty, the snow crisp and glittering, so cold that it almost made people's hair freeze.

Susanne wrings her hands and stares straight ahead as she recounts how Jurek forced a mother and her adult son out into the garden in nothing but their pyjamas, tying them to an ice-covered pole by the well.

'Lyala and Ahmad, those were their names. Both had pale blue eyes . . .'

Jurek took out his knife and pushed it between Ahmad's ribs, a little more than half-way in, slanting upwards. The young man panted like a wounded animal, and his mother dropped to her knees and prayed for him. Jurek let go of the handle and saw the cold steel fog up in the heat of the man's body.

'He left them by the well and re-joined his unit,' says Susanne, closing her eyes for a moment before she goes on. 'Ahmad wouldn't bleed to death so long as the knife stayed where it was, but that meant they would both freeze to death. Lyala had no choice but to pull it out, cut herself free and try to find some warmth.'

As Susanne starts listing the victims buried in Lill-Jans Forest, the lawyer gets to her feet. Her face is pale, and she leaves the room without another word.

'Did he ever directly threaten you?' Saga asks once Susanne is finished.

'He told me about a Russian diplomat, a man who was planning to return to Sweden once he retired. He wanted to bring his whole family together to celebrate his seventy-fifth birthday,' Susanne says, looking up with her bloodshot eyes. 'Jurek said he would be waiting for him, that he'd get every last one of them, young and old alike; he said he was going to lock them in a bunker and then bury them alive, one by one . . . until the diplomat was left all alone.'

Susanne swallows and starts talking about a woman in a coffin, though she pauses after a few words and seems to have only just noticed that her lawyer is gone.

'You spent eight years in prison and were released three years ago. What did you do once you got out? What did you have planned for your third act, aside from killing your ex-husband and taking your kids back?'

Susanne lowers her eyes again. 'My lawyer thinks I should be careful about what I say.'

30

The large conference room is bright beneath the strip lights on the ceiling. Saga finishes her briefing, and Manvir then announces that the police chief's decision to refrain from talking to the press until the prosecutor has been brought on board still stands.

'Bergslagen District is holding a press conference tomorrow, but they won't mention our involvement,' he says.

Greta sips her black coffee with a frown. She is wearing a pair of pinstripe trousers and a silk shirt in the same icy shade of blue as her eyes.

Petter is in jeans and a navy T-shirt, slumped back in his chair with his chin to his chest and his arms folded.

'Shall we keep going?' asks Greta. 'Start from the part where you talked to the girl by the compost heap.'

'We were running back through the woods when we heard the first gunshot, and we'd just come out behind the shed when the rifle went off,' Joona says, rolling up his sleeves.

Saga takes over and describes the moment when they found their colleague dead among the ferns with an axe in the back of his head. Greta becomes visibly upset, and Manvir mumbles 'disaster' and moves over into the corner with his back to them.

'I went inside,' Saga continues, 'and found Ida Andersson with an elk rifle in the hallway. I managed to disarm her, got her onto the floor and cuffed her hands behind her back, and that's when I saw that another woman, Camilla Boman, was about to castrate our other colleague from Munkfors.'

'But that all worked out, didn't it?' Petter asks, clearing his throat.

'Joona came in from the other side,' Saga explains, restlessly boun-cing one of her legs.

'What happened?' Greta asks, turning to Joona.

Joona remembers that he ran along the edge of the building with his gun drawn, ducking beneath the windows and slowing down when he reached the corner.

All he could hear from the forest around them was the rustling of the treetops and the sad song of a blackbird.

A rusty drainpipe had fallen down and was lying in the grass beside the wall.

He glanced back over his shoulder and tiptoed forward without a sound.

The air smelled like petrol, damp earth and grass.

As he rounded the corner, an engine started spluttering.

The plastic handle on the end of the start cable clattered against the side of the lawnmower, which was shaking on the grass in front of him.

The cloud of exhaust fumes swirled off towards the bushes.

A young woman backed away from him in the long grass, moving through the brush and among saplings. She bent down and, with a dreamy look on her face, picked up a scythe from the ground.

Joona approached her, his gun still trained on the end of the house, on the back door with the creased curtain in the window.

'Put the scythe down,' he said, killing the engine on the spluttering lawnmower.

She stared at him, breathing heavily. It was the same woman he had spoken to earlier, the one with the tangled blonde hair.

'I'm going to come closer and take the scythe now,' he said, approaching her with his free hand raised in a calming gesture.

'Don't touch me,' she mumbled, eyes wide with panic.

'I promise I—'

Without warning, she lunged forward. The long blade followed her movement, swinging through the air at waist height. It sliced straight through the tops of the young saplings, and their thin trunks dropped to the ground in unison.

Joona leaned back and watched as the curved steel passed his stomach and severed a couple of vines beside him.

He darted forward and rammed his foot into her knee as the tip of the blade dug deep into a thick birch trunk.

With one hand on the back of her neck, he threw her to the ground, pointed his pistol towards the building and dragged her across the ground by her foot.

The slim blade of the scythe was still buried in the birch, handle quivering.

Joona cuffed her ankles to the lawnmower and then ran over to the back door. He could hear her screaming that he had assaulted her.

He opened the door and stepped inside, quickly scanning the bathroom. His eyes darted across the bathtub and the showerhead, the lidless toilet, the hand basin and a speckled mirror cabinet.

He stepped over a bloody towel on the floor, opened a narrow door and came out into a corridor with doors on both sides.

A large woman in a white bra was hunched over Magnus with a knife. The police officer was bleeding heavily from a bullet wound to his thigh, and Joona took aim at the woman's shoulder, though he quickly realised he couldn't shoot because Saga was in his line of fire behind her.

He didn't need time to think; his years of training in close combat instinctively told him that a clean kick was the only option available to him.

He ran forward, raising his right knee during the final step and pushing off from the floor, hitting her square in the middle of the chest with the sole of his foot.

The woman was thrown back, and she seemed to hang in the air for a moment before landing on her shoulder and skidding away across the floor.

The rice paper lampshade swayed overhead.

Saga was quickly on top of her, stamping on her wrist and firing her pistol.

The sound of the gunshot seared through the cramped space, and a pool of blood quickly blossomed across the floor beneath the woman's shoulder.

'Joona? How did it look from your point of view?' Greta presses him.

'I disarmed a woman with a scythe, entered the building via the back door and worked with Saga to arrest Camilla Boman and Susanne Hjälm,' he replies.

Manvir leaves his corner and returns to the table, unbuttoning his jacket and lifting his trouser legs slightly before he sits down.

'We no longer think Susanne has any direct link to our killer,' says Saga, anxiously crumpling an empty box of pills on the table.

'Once we had her in custody, her ex told us a little more about the threats Susanne had subjected him to,' Joona explains. 'And that gave her an alibi. Susanne has been harassing her ex-husband in many ways, including by standing in their garden for hours on end, staring in at them. She was there when both Verner and Margot were killed.'

'Have we managed to corroborate that?' asks Manvir.

'He took pictures and kept a record of every single incident,' Saga replies. 'Exact times, everything.'

'When Susanne was released from prison, she called him despite the restraining order and claimed she had changed,' Joona goes on. 'She begged him to let her see the children. She said she wanted him to bring them to the retreat, just for the day, for a few hours at first.'

'Wow,' Petter whispers.

Manvir smooths his slim black tie with one hand, and Petter leans back and scratches his belly.

A shadow passes over the creased curtains covering the glass wall onto the corridor, and the creaking of the wheels on a document trolley fades into the distance.

'Can I ask something?' Greta speaks up, taking a sip of water from her glass. 'I still don't really understand why you tracked down Susanne Hjälm . . . That wasn't something we'd discussed.'

'She's one of the few people who have been subjected to Jurek's influence and lived to tell the tale,' Joona explains.

'And I found out she'd been released from prison a few weeks before the first postcard arrived,' says Saga. 'She hates the police, blames us for ruining her life . . . And more than anything, she hates Joona.'

'But that doesn't answer my question. Why did you start looking into her in the first place?'

'I got a tip from a source I trust,' says Saga.

'Who?' asks Greta.

Saga holds her gaze.

'I can't say.'

'Joona?'

'I don't know who it is, I just thought the logic was sound enough for us to move forward with it.'

'Saga, you know you're not on operative duty, don't you? That you don't have police powers?'

'Of course.'

31

Manvir moves over to the whiteboard and rubs out some of the points, moves others, adds more information and then backs away with the marker to his mouth. The others stand up and gather around the board.

Serial killer with nine intended victims.
Studies his victims, knows their habits and routines.
Victim number 1: Margot Silverman, middle aged female, head of NCU.
Victim number 2: Severin Balderson, elderly male, priest at Maria Magdalena Church.
Victim number 3: Simon Bjerke, male, early middle age, Stockholm City police officer.
Victim number 4: Verner Zandén, male, late middle age, head of Security Service.

The ventilation shaft above their heads clanks and hisses, and a bright light flashes across the room as someone in the building opposite opens a window.

Greta's frown deepens as she stares at Manvir's list.

'How does the priest fit in?' she asks.

'Everyone on the list has a job that gives them authority over other people. That also applies to him,' Manvir suggests.

'Three police officers, one priest,' Greta continues. 'Three men, one woman.'

Joona seems concerned, with dark circles beneath his eyes. The back of his jacket is crumpled. He sighs and sits down on the edge of the table, eyes still on the board.

Tin figurines: sent to Saga, indicate next victim.
The wrapping predicts where the murder will take place.
Shoots victims from behind, at close range.
Ammunition: 9x18mm Makarov bullets, fine silver casings, Russian mercury primers.
Has a vehicle with an electric winch.
Material knowledge: casting tin, producing fine silver, using caustic soda.
Murder and discovery sites not the same.
The find sites are all cemeteries.
Two postcards with threats to Joona, placing responsibility for saving him on Saga.

Petter hooks a wad of tobacco from beneath his lip, throws it into the wastepaper bin and spits. The whiteboard marker has stained Manvir's lips blue, and Saga's eyes are focused on the overlapping lines the desk chairs have left on the linoleum floor.

'Are we being stupid?' asks Petter. 'What the hell are we not seeing?'

'We only see what he wants us to see,' says Joona.

'Do you have any better ideas?'

'I just mean that the clues might be hiding whatever we're actually looking for, that maybe we should try to see what's between these points.'

'Because they don't lead us anywhere,' Saga agrees.

'If you ask me,' says Greta, brushing a few crumbs from her blouse. 'If you ask me, the thing that stands out is the connection to the two of you, Saga and Joona. Because along with the fixation on Jurek Walter, that's hardly a coincidence.'

'Jurek is key here,' Joona says quietly.

They return to the table, pour themselves more coffee and start passing photographs and test results between themselves.

'Can I say something?' asks Saga. 'Before Jurek recruited the Beaver, he was in touch with a number of other criminals ... We tried to determine them all, but three names ended up dropping off our radar: Jakov Fauster, Alexander Pichushkin and Pedro Lopez Monsalve.'

Greta, Manvir and Petter all seem confused, unsure of where this is coming from.

'Fauster and Pichushkin are both in prison, and Monsalve is an old man,' says Joona.

'I still think it might be worth looking into them, just to make sure they haven't escaped or left the country.'

'OK,' says Greta.

'Is this from your secret source too?' Petter asks, a hint of scepticism in his voice.

Before she has time to answer, the five telephones in the room ping, buzz and ring as their owners all receive the same alert: the mail room has just taken delivery of a parcel addressed to Saga Bauer.

Everyone gets up and hurries out into the corridor.

'We're on our way down,' Manvir tells command. 'The bomb squad should be there in two minutes. Evacuate the large conference room and call for the technicians, make sure the tactical unit is ready.'

No one speaks during the lift ride down to the ground floor. They all know what they have to do, that this could be their chance to stop the killer.

The bomb squad has already run an ETD check on the parcel by the time they arrive and confirmed there are no explosives, and both the X-ray machine and their metal detector suggest a small metal figurine inside.

Joona marches over and grabs the parcel, running after the other members of the group and catching up with them just as they reach the conference room, where an operative command is in the process of being put together.

Two forensic technicians hurry over in their protective overalls and visors, but Joona simply sets the parcel down on the first table he reaches. Saga tears off the brown tape and tosses it to the floor. One of the technicians carefully retrieves it and lowers it into an evidence box.

Joona folds back the lid, lifts out a ball of foil and unwraps it. Inside is a small bundle of paper towel.

With deliberate, robotic movements, the technicians cover two tables with protective plastic and set out their equipment.

From the little paper bundle, Joona lifts up a photograph, rolled and tied with a red rubber band.

He tips the small figurine into his palm, and a butterfly wing comes fluttering out behind it, spiralling down to the table.

One of the technicians rushes over and grabs it with a pair of tweezers.

Joona holds the little figurine between his forefinger and thumb. He can see that it is a woman, but he can't make out any of her facial features.

Saga steps over the extension cord and tears the black PVC cover from the heavy digital microscope, tossing it to the floor and plugging the cable into the laptop on the table beside it.

Joona places the figurine on the slide and adjusts the light, focus and magnification.

The group gathers around the computer screen.

The little tin woman is wearing low shoes, a skirt and a sweater. She has a pronounced chin, a slim nose and pursed lips.

'That's Francesca Beckman, one of the psychologists at the Crisis and Trauma Centre,' says Saga, her voice raised.

'Are you sure?' asks Joona.

'Yes.'

'Did you catch that?' Petter asks over the conference call they've set up. 'It's our psychologist Francesca Beckman, from Crisis and Trauma.'

'I heard you,' Randy replies from the eighth floor.

'I've got her private number,' says Saga, taking out her phone and sharing the contact details with Manvir.

'Petter, tell Randy to find out where she lives,' says Joona.

'I'm calling her now,' Manvir says, his phone to his ear.

'She lives in Bromma,' says Petter. 'At Thaliavägen 9—'

He stops short as Manvir holds up a hand and switches his phone to loudspeaker.

'Francesca Beckman,' says a voice.

'This is Manvir Rai from the National Crime Unit. I need you to listen to me, there's a grave and immediate threat to your safety . . .'

'Ask her where she is,' Joona tells him.

'My phone has almost no—'

Francesca's voice is cut off mid-sentence.

'Hello? Francesca?'

Manvir tries calling her back, but her phone has clearly run out of battery.

'This can't be fucking happening,' says Petter.

'Was she at home or at work?' asks Saga.

'I don't know,' Manvir replies, staring back at her with tired eyes.

'Fuck,' Saga whispers, running a hand through her hair.

'Why don't we just send the tactical unit to her house?' asks Petter.

'I'll let command know,' says Greta, hurrying over to the group of officers by the furthest table.

'Can't they trace the call?' Saga asks Petter. 'Tell me they can trace her phone!'

'Can you give me a geolocation on Francesca's phone?' Petter asks.

'I don't know, we're trying,' Randy replies through the loudspeaker.

Petter rubs his eyes, hard. Dark patches of sweat have seeped through beneath the arms of his navy T-shirt.

'This is taking too long, I'm sending two patrol cars out to her house in Bromma,' says Joona.

He gets in touch with regional command while Manvir instructs the team on the eighth floor to call Francesca's employer, colleagues, family and friends in an effort to track her down.

'Her husband works at the court of appeal in Riddarholmen,' Manvir continues, peering down at his phone.

'I'll call him,' says Petter.

'They also have two adult sons who live in Täby. Her sister Jeanette lives in Hägersten and works in PR for Skanska. Both sons are students at the Royal Institute of Technology . . .'

'Have you tried calling her again?' asks Saga.

'I've been doing it this whole time, it just goes straight to voicemail.'

'Her husband is on a plane to Dallas,' Petter shouts.

'Her sons aren't picking up. No one is picking up,' says Greta.

'Try again, try again.'

At the other end of the room, the command group leader hits the table in frustration.

'We can't just let her die!' Saga cries.

'We'll find her,' Manvir reassures her.

'I think we have to solve the riddle,' says Joona.

'Quickly, clear the table . . . we need more space,' says Saga.

'Move that!' Petter points.

'Bring those chairs over here.'

One of the technicians comes running with a chair, tripping on the microscope cable. The heavy instrument crashes to the floor, sending shards of glass scattering around their feet.

'They're saying they can't trace the phone,' Randy announces over the loudspeaker.

'Shit!' Petter swears, so loudly that he sends a spray of saliva across the table.

'Quiet,' Saga tells him.

Greta comes over to join the others, her forehead creased in irritation.

'Four minutes,' Joona mutters to himself.

On the table in front of them, he lines up the crumpled aluminium foil, the paper towel, a plastic evidence tube containing the butterfly wing, the red rubber band and the photograph. The photo is curled up at each end, so he has to flatten it out with his fingers.

'We need to think,' says Saga, moving over to his side.

The forensic technician reappears with a broom and starts sweeping up the shards of glass around the broken microscope.

'Forget about that right now,' she snaps at him.

'Everyone shut up!' shouts Petter.

The little photograph – no bigger than a playing card – is an old hand-coloured image of a theatre, showing a man in what look like clothes from sixteenth century England: a velvet doublet, puffy breeches, white stockings and shoes with large buckles.

Other than his burgundy jacket and the gold rings on his fingers, the colours are all muted.

Manvir throws his tie back over his shoulder and leans in close.

'Are any of you getting anything out of this?' Greta asks, tucking a lock of greying hair behind her ear.

'Turn it over,' says Joona.

On the reverse of the image is a single line of text: *Victor Hugo's Marie Tudor, Stockholm Royal Dramatic Theatre, 1882.*

'Is he going to kill her at the theatre?' Greta asks, a note of scepticism in her voice.

'That seems too easy,' says Saga.

'He's tightening the screw with every victim; it's getting harder and harder,' Manvir points out, his forehead creased by his deep frown.

'Do any of you know the play?' asks Joona.

'No.'

'Come on, come on, we're running out of time,' Saga mumbles.

'Relax, we'll find her. We're going to find her,' says Petter.

'I just don't want her to die.'

Manvir bites on his lip and brings up an enlargement of the butterfly wing on his computer screen. It's brownish-orange, with a white stripe and a yellow oval by the tip.

'Foil, butterfly, theatre,' he says.

'We need to be more specific. What kind of butterfly is it, what species, where is it found?' asks Joona.

'This is too hard,' Greta whispers. 'It's taking too long . . .'

32

Francesca's legs are shaking as she climbs the stairs, holding her dead phone in one hand and gripping the handrail with the other.

The police officer's words about a grave and immediate threat to her life are still reverberating in her ears.

She reaches the landing, pushes the bead curtain to one side and makes her way into her sister's bedroom. There is a charger in the socket by the bed, and she walks straight over and plugs in her phone.

The plastic beads rattle behind her.

In the open drawer in the bedside table, she can see a pink massage device, a pack of painkillers and a plastic mouth guard.

Her little sister goes to her boyfriend's house on an island in Lake Mälaren every Friday. She takes the dog with her whenever she can but his kids are with him every other weekend and the youngest has allergies. That means Oki has to hang back, and Francesca usually volunteers to come over and look after him instead.

She takes him for walks and lets him out in the back garden, making herself a simple meal in the evening and then curling up on the sofa with a good book and a glass of wine before going to sleep in the guest room.

Her husband is currently headed to Dallas for work, but even when he is at home he does very little but watch TV, go to bed early and get up at 6 a.m. on Saturdays to listen to his favourite nature show on the radio.

Francesca feels pleasantly alienated in her sister's expensive home from the 1970s, all red brick, lacquered beech and cut glass.

The curtains are drawn in the dormer window.

She puts her phone down on the bedside table. The display is still dark.

She can't quite process what the man from the NCU was trying to say.

A grave and immediate threat?

It sounded as though he was about to offer her police protection.

As a psychologist, Francesca is fairly used to threats, and she rarely feels particularly anxious or afraid. Her line of work frequently brings her into contact with damaged individuals, and she knows how their minds work.

Despite all that, she got it wrong with Jonny, she thinks. She moves over to the window and cautiously pushes the curtain back to look down at the dark leaves on the roof of the car port, the tarmacked driveway and the mailbox on the narrow street.

Jonny Sylvan was a young man who had been traumatised by a bomb blast, and who went on to develop an obsession with her.

She thinks about his thin face, his reconstructed nose and jaw, the prosthetic eye that seemed to stare so intensely.

He had trouble understanding that his attention, which she had previously found flattering, suddenly felt intrusive and threatening.

Francesca hadn't reported him when he smashed the chair in her office; she simply handed his case over to one of her male colleagues. She knew he needed a second chance.

But a few weeks later, she realised that he was stalking her.

She turns back to the bedside table and tries to power up her phone, but it still won't switch on.

Maybe she should just go back downstairs, get into the car and drive over to the police station in Kungsholmen.

She realises the door isn't locked and Oki is still outside, and her heart begins to beat faster.

Francesca leaves the bedroom and makes her way down the creaking stairs. Between the banister on her right, she can see more and more of the hallway with each step she takes. The coat cupboard, the guest bathroom, the spare bedroom where she sleeps and, at the far end, the door to the porch.

The darkest part of the house.

She steps down onto the reddish-blonde parquet and stands perfectly still, listening.

The kitchen, with its brown tiles and copper accents, is off to her left.

Straight ahead, she can make out the living room through the reeded glass door.

She wondered what the call from the police might mean and whether it could wait until her mobile was charged. She'll call them back and get everything straightened out just as soon as it's working again.

Francesca opens the door to the living room and through the textured glass she studies the angular brick fireplace, the TV unit, the full bookshelves and the brown leather sofa.

Jonny Sylvan was on the street outside her house when the police finally arrested him. He was wearing an explosive belt, and he calmly told the officers that he and Francesca would die together in an embrace.

He was committed and placed in secure psychiatric care, but that was over two years ago now.

A shiver passes down Francesca's spine as she steps forward into the living room, and she has to stop herself from turning back into the dark hallway outside.

There is a cat flap in the door to the backyard, but she thinks her sister's dog might be too proud to actually use it. Oki is a two-year-old Chin – smaller than a cat, but a dog all the same – and his name means big in Japanese.

Francesca opens the door and pops her head out into the lush, shady garden, taking in the peeling furniture, the grid of green moss between the paving stones, the grass, the trees and bushes.

'Oki?' she shouts, her voice slightly subdued.

She steps outside and feels the chill of the paving stones beneath her bare feet, moving past the red kettle grill and looking down at a metal tray with an old mosquito-repelling spiral on it.

The row of gardens behind each house is separated by low fences, walls and hedges, and there is no sign of any of the neighbours, but she can smell the smoky scent of charcoal on the breeze.

Francesca moves forward onto the damp grass and looks up at the steep rocks, at the trees and dense greenery in the park.

She makes her way past the gnarled birch and over to the currant bushes, where she turns back to face the house. She studies the open door, the curtains in the living room windows, the dark kitchen and the potted plants on the windowsills.

Francesca realises that she is smiling when she finds herself thinking about the brief conversation she had with Erland on Thursday. They were sitting at the table after dinner, and she told him that she missed having sex, that it was her Christian upbringing that had made her pull away. She isn't sure she has ever seen him look happier than he did right then. Erland's cheeks flushed, and he tried to sound calm and mature when he replied that he had missed it too, that he would love to try again – at her pace.

Something rustles by the tarred wooden bathtub her sister insisted on buying but almost never uses. Francesca turns around and pushes back a few branches.

She hears the frantic thudding of paws, followed by a loud bark as Oki comes running from the house next door.

The old man who lives there often feeds him meatballs.

Francesca breathes a sigh of relief and walks back towards the house with the dog darting around her ankles. She locks the door behind them and takes the key out of the lock.

Oki runs off ahead of her, his claws clicking against the wooden floor in the hallway. He is already whimpering by his food bowls by the time she reaches the kitchen – but only half-heartedly, because he knows she isn't a pushover.

'What, didn't you get your meatballs today?' she asks, dropping the key onto a tray on the chest of drawers.

Oki runs over and starts scrabbling at the door to the carport.

'What are you up to?' she asks, pouring him some kibble and water. 'I'm in charge now. Jeanette is sick of you. She keeps waiting and waiting, but you never get any bigger.'

The dog bounds forward and starts wolfing down his food.

Francesca tries the door handle. It's locked, of course, and her car is parked so close to the wall outside that no one would be able to get in anyway.

Somewhere in the distance, she hears a man shout.

Her mind turns to the lifeless parts of Jonny's anxious face. The cloudy beads of sweat that dripped to the table. His thick, brushed hair hiding his hearing aid. He told her about how the initial shockwave blew out the match he was holding to his cigarette.

He said that he was the flame that ultimately went out; that he ceased to exist for a moment, resting in the incredible silence of absolute oblivion.

Francesca remembers that he clawed at his hairy forearms as he told her that he was blasted among the twisted car parts and rubble. He hit the ground and came back to life, wide awake and in terrible pain.

She often meets traumatised police officers in her line of work, people who have been injured, or have hurt someone, who have become aggressive and no longer recognise who they are. Men and women who have developed problems with addiction after digging the charred remains of children out of wreckage.

Through the door onto the carport, she hears a rattling engine grow louder and then die down abruptly.

Someone has just pulled up outside the house.

Could it be the police? A first patrol car?

Around seven minutes have passed since they called.

Francesca hurries down the hallway, past the stairs and the coat cupboard, the bathroom and the guest bedroom, opening the door to the porch.

They might already have arrested Jonny. They could have tried to reach her and sent a car when they couldn't get through.

She makes her way over to the little window in the front door, using her hands to block the light as she peers out.

An old pickup with a winch in the bed has reversed onto the driveway.

The driver's side door is open, the air is quivering above the hot bonnet.

The path up to the front door is hidden behind the thick bushes, which means she can't see whether the driver is heading her way.

Francesca takes a step back and reaches for the long key in the security lock, turning it without taking her eyes off the window.

She hears a click as the deadbolt slides into place, and as she pulls the key from the lock, the entire door shudders.

Francesca gasps and sees the key tumble among the shoes on the mat. She backs out of the porch and braces herself against the wall.

The door shakes again as another lorry passes down the street.

She is getting herself worked up over nothing; the pickup probably just belongs to a gardener.

She turns around and squints down the dark hallway, wondering how long it would take for help to arrive if she ran up the stairs and into her sister's bedroom, unplugged her phone and hid beneath the bed, pressed the power button, entered the passcode, opened her call list and phoned the National Crime Unit.

Her phone probably has enough charge to handle one call now, she thinks as she hears a clinking noise somewhere in the house.

She stops dead and holds her breath.

There is someone in the kitchen, opening the drawers and making the cutlery rattle.

Francesca tiptoes down the hallway, into the coat cupboard, pulling the door shut behind her. She knows there is no way she can sneak up the creaky stairs to grab her phone. She will simply have to get out somehow and make a run for it.

33

The conference room on the ground floor of the station is a hive of activity. The command group is in the process of devising a plan for the upcoming operation, running through the various decision-making protocol.

A number of maps have been pinned up on one wall, templates for risk assessments taken out, approaches planned.

Forensics still haven't managed to find any fingerprints, DNA or fibres on the packaging.

Joona checks the time and then holds the little plastic tube containing the butterfly wing up to the lamp, turning it over in the light. The back of the wing is the colour of old paper or tobacco, and the pattern reminds him of the web of veins in a leaf.

'Hello, anyone on the eighth floor?' Petter shouts into his phone. 'What's going on up there? Can we have some answers? Doesn't anyone know where the fuck she is?'

'We're working on it,' Randy replies through the speaker.

'That's great, but we need—'

'Take it easy, Petter,' Manvir interrupts him.

On the other side of the room, two of the technicians get into a heated argument.

'Does Francesca Beckman have any connection to the Royal Dramatic Theatre?' Greta asks, scratching her wrist.

'Well, does she?' Petter asks down the line.

'Not as far as we can see,' Randy replies.

Joona puts down the tube and picks up the photograph again. The colours have faded so much over the years that the actor's face looks like tin. He has just turned it over to study the back when a call comes in over the radio.

'Two units have just arrived at the address,' says the duty officer. 'Handing you over to the task force commander.'

'Should we go in?' a voice asks.

'Bullet proof vests on,' says Joona. 'One team at the rear, the other at the front door.'

Petter slumps down and uses the back of his hand to wipe the sweat from his upper lip.

'No answer,' the task force commander announces over the radio. 'No sign of a break in or—'

'Forced entry,' Joona tells him.

Petter holds up his phone to the others. His face is pale, his forehead beaded with sweat.

'Randy has an update,' he shouts.

'Francesca isn't at work. She left early, but she didn't say where she was going,' Randy's voice tells them through the speaker. 'She's not at the gym, not—'

'Ugh, I can't do this,' Petter groans. He looks like he might start crying at any moment.

Right then, the radio crackles and the task force commander says that they are now inside the property.

'We're in, checking the rooms . . . There's no one here, nothing to suggest a crime,' he says between breaths.

'She isn't home,' Joona repeats, loud enough for everyone to hear.

Randy tells them that they have just sent pictures of the photograph to the Museum of Performing Arts, to the theatre critic Leif Zern and the team at the Royal Dramatic Theatre.

'What about the butterfly?' asks Greta.

'There's a guy in Environmental Crimes who happens to be a butterfly expert,' Randy replies. 'He's on the national Butterfly Committee, wrote the *National Guide to Swedish Butterflies*.'

Saga's hands are shaking as she examines the tin foil inch by inch using a new microscope.

'The helicopter's in the air,' Greta tells the others.

In order to save time once they have worked out where the perpetrator plans to kill Francesca, the local police chief has issued an order to bring in the National Task Force.

'It's been eleven minutes,' Joona whispers.

'Think, think, think,' Saga says, her voice manic. 'We have everything we need, we know who the victim is, we just need to work out where the hell it's going to happen. It must be possible.'

One of the technicians steps away in an attempt to hold back his tears. He stands with his back to the others for a moment, pretending to study the map, then dries his eyes and gets back to work.

'Randy, what's going on?' Petter asks.

'This is taking too long!' Saga shouts to him.

'We're ringing around everyone who—'

'I've got a call,' Joona interrupts him, holding up his phone.

'Quiet!' shouts Petter.

'Joona Linna.'

'This is Nisse Hydén,' says a gruff voice.

'Have you had a chance to look at the picture of the butterfly wing?'

'I called you as soon as I got the message.'

'Can you tell us anything about it?' asks Joona.

'Yes, it's a Nymphalidae, no doubt about that. They're not found in the wild in Sweden, but ... just let me have a quick look ... It's a Limenitis ... archippus. No, Limenitis iphiclus, as documented by Carl Linnaeus. They're native to South and Central America, one of a number of species known as sister butterflies because of the white markings on their wings ... Sister in the sense of nuns, you understand.'

'OK, so where might you find a butterfly like this in Sweden?' Joona asks, checking the time again.

'Certainly not at the butterfly house in Haga, but possibly at the Museum of Natural History or with a collector ... I can do some ringing around.'

'It's incredibly urgent,' Joona replies, ending the call.

'Sisters, nuns? What convents are in Sweden?' asks Saga.

'There's the Sisters of Saint Francis in Sjövik, the monastery in Linköping, the Daughters of Mary in Enköping,' Manvir suggests, turning his computer towards the others.

'So we've got the Royal Dramatic Theatre, convents,' Greta begins. 'Butterflies, Victor Hugo, France, *The Hunchback of Notre-Dame, Marie Tudor* ...'

Her voice falters, and she trails off.

'Notre-Dame is Mary ... and we've got the Daughters of Mary convent in Enköping,' says Saga, tapping her pen against the table.

'I don't know if that gets us anywhere, but does Francesca Beckman have links to Enköping, to the convent?'

'Looking into it now,' says Randy.

Joona closes his eyes for a few seconds, trying to find the connection.

'The name of the butterfly is Limenitis iphiclus,' says Manvir. 'The Greek demigod Heracles, who was known as Hercules in Rome, had the same mother as Iphicles ... They were actually twins and half-brothers. It's really unusual, known as superfecundation, which is when—'

'Hold on, I've got an incoming call from the theatre critic.'

Joona answers the call and switches his phone to loudspeaker.

'I've never seen that picture before,' Leif Zern tells him, trying to hold back his enthusiasm. '*Marie Tudor* is about Mary I of England – better known as Bloody Mary, of course ...'

'Go on.'

'I can only assume that Victor Hugo, who was French, had a lot of fun giving the English queen a lover – fiction has a right to its own truths, after all. In any case, this lover, Fabiano Fabiani, he was executed by beheading, despite her love for him,' Zern continues, pausing to clear his throat. 'And in this image from Dramaten, of course, we have the actor Georg Dahlqvist, who was also an opera singer—'

'Thanks for your help,' Joona interrupts him, ending the call.

'Listen up, everyone. The actor in the photograph is Georg Dahlqvist, who has a park named after him in Hägersten, which is where Francesca Beckman's sister lives.'

'Sister butterflies,' says Saga.

'Petter, check whether the sister's house is anywhere near Georg Dahlqvist's Park.'

'Come on, come on,' Saga whispers.

'She lives in a villa on Sankt Mickelsgatan, one that backs right onto the park.'

34

Francesca is standing on a heap of shoes and umbrellas in the coat cupboard, huddled up between winter coats, collapsible chairs, bags of empty bottles, an ironing board and a stepladder. She grips the little porcelain handle tight, trying to hold the door shut.

The house is quiet again.

Her blood starts thundering in her ears as she cracks the door open slightly in order to hear better.

The intruder seems to leave the kitchen and pause in the hallway.

If he would just go upstairs to look for her, she could run down the hallway to the living room and out the back door, making her way between the gardens until she bumped into one of the neighbours.

'Help me, God,' she prays quietly. 'Come and save me, amen, amen. Maranatha! Come, Lord Jesus.'

She hears Oki's clicking paws in the hallway, followed by the intruder's heavier footsteps.

Francesca closes the door, clinging to the handle to stop it from swinging open again.

Oki stops outside the coat cupboard.

She holds her breath.

The heavy footsteps pass, and she catches a glimpse of the figure through the crack around the door, making his way towards the guest room.

Her bag and jacket are on the bed in there.

She takes a deep, quiet breath.

He turns into the bedroom and pauses.

He must know she is in the house now.

He checks behind the curtains, beneath the bed and in the wardrobe before turning back to the hallway and opening the bathroom door.

When Francesca ducked into the coat cupboard, her left foot ended up at a strange angle against a pair of sturdy boots, and it has now gone completely numb.

She needs to change position, but when she tries to move a couple of the empty bottles clink together.

The hallway outside is silent.

Her hand trembles on the doorknob.

Francesca finds herself thinking about Jonny. She needs to talk to him as a psychologist, she realises; there must be a way of getting through to him. In panic, she desperately tries to remember what used to calm him down when he was her patient.

The intruder starts moving again, past the coat cupboard.

The stairs creak under his weight, and Francesca recognises the rattling sound of the bead curtain upstairs.

She opens the door a little further and hears his footsteps continue.

Holding her breath, she peers out.

The hallway is quiet.

A grave and immediate threat, that was what the police officer said.

Were they trying to warn her that Jonny had a new suicide belt, that he was on his way over?

The plastic beads in the doorway to her sister's room fall silent.

The ironing board falls back against the coats as Francesca leaves the cupboard.

Her knees are weak, and she can feel the adrenaline pumping.

She runs over to the glass doors and skids into the living room, where she crashes straight into the footstool. As she reaches the patio door, she realises that it is locked, that she took the key into the kitchen earlier.

The bead curtain upstairs rattles again.

Francesca gets down onto her knees and pushes her fingers beneath the rubber seal around the edge of the cat flap, pulling it open.

Her entire body is shaking as she gets down onto her back, holds the flap open and uses her legs to push herself through the hole. Her head emerges into the cool air on the other side.

Clouds race overhead in the pale evening sky.

She can no longer see whether there is anyone in the living room, and she feels a wave of panic wash over her. This is just like playing hide and seek as a child, the feeling of almost being caught, that strange moment before it happened, when you wanted to give up but kept going anyway.

She manages to get her shoulders out, but her arms are still pinned by her sides.

Her back is stinging from where she has grazed it on the floor.

Oki is barking frantically by her legs.

She pushes as hard as she can and manages to pull her arms free.

She presses against the door with both hands, but something is holding her back.

The cat flap has fallen down and caught on the waistband of her jeans. She reaches back inside and lifts the flap, and has just started to wriggle out when someone grabs her foot.

Screaming, she feels herself being dragged back through the hole. Francesca braces herself with one hand and lashes out with her legs. The intruder lets go of her ankle, and she manages to pull away, hitting one knee on the edge of the flap and groaning in pain.

She crawls away across the paving stones and clambers up onto her feet. She has just started running when the crack of a gunshot rings out through the air. Shards of glass and wooden splinters scatter across the ground behind her.

Francesca leaps over the low fence into the neighbour's garden, running past a couple of lounge chairs and a parasol. She climbs over the hedge on the far side and hurries through the next yard, past a dark sun room full of rattan furniture.

She clambers over a low wall, scratching herself on the raspberry bushes and landing in the soft soil on the other side before stumbling forward onto the lawn.

Up ahead, a man is grilling chicken skewers as a couple of children bounce up and down on a trampoline.

Francesca is petrified, her thoughts chaotic, but she knows she can't ask the man for help. If Jonny detonates his suicide belt, the children will die.

The man stares at her in confusion, taking a step back with the tongs in his hand.

'Get inside, get inside!' she pants. 'And take the kids. Lock the doors! Call the police!'

She keeps running through the neighbours' gardens, crossing a narrow road and pushing through bushes, over patios and past two small greenhouses, all without seeing another soul.

When she spots the chapel in the distance, she stops dead, gasping for air. Her back is slick with sweat, and her legs feel like jelly as she starts moving again. The white paint is peeling from the woodwork on the facade. Francesca knows that the spare key is inside a hollow plastic stone between the strawberry plants by the steps.

35

The helicopter that was hovering in the air above the National Task Force building in Ulriksdal veered off to the south no more than twenty seconds after Joona solved the puzzle.

Joona himself ran towards the lifts, jumped into his car and sped through the tunnel towards Fridhemsplan.

The helicopter swept across the sprawling network of narrow roads obscured by the area's mature trees. The houses are so tightly packed together that there was nowhere obvious for it to land, and two operatives were winched down to the ground instead. They stopped the traffic on Hägerstensvägen, enabling the helicopter to land on the wide crossing and the rest of the task force to disembark.

The downwash from the rotor blades whips up dust from the ground, tearing leaves from the bushes in the gardens nearby.

A metal descender clatters to the tarmac as the other six operatives disembark and the rope is pulled in before take-off.

The operatives are all wearing ballistic helmets, ceramic body armour and are carrying assault rifles.

As they run towards the address, command supplies them with information about risk zones, individual approach routes and points of coordination with other units.

Road blocks will be put in place on all major roads out of Hägersten.

Joona has just left the motorway past Aspudden when the tactical unit reports that the house is empty, but that the door to the rear – backing onto the park – has been shot to pieces.

* * *

Francesca is standing outside the chapel when she hears a car approaching. Panic rises up inside her, and she pushes the key into the lock with shaking hands and manages to turn it.

The sound of the engine is getting closer.

She quickly opens the door, slips inside and pulls it shut behind her. Leaflets about music lessons and church services flutter on the noticeboard as she hurries through the porch and into the main hall.

The inner door swings shut behind her with a click, almost like someone cracking their knuckles.

The church is bathed in the dusk's soft light, spilling in through the tall, narrow windows.

Francesca has somehow compartmentalised her fear as she ran, and she carries it inside her like some sort of heavy urn, making her oddly tired and detached.

Maybe it's just the first rush of adrenaline fading from her body.

She hurries down the aisle, taking in the stirring shadows of the leaves cast on the wall up ahead, above the crucifix with its golden crown of thorns.

Francesca's family have been Baptists for generations, and she often comes here to pray when she is staying at her sister's house.

For the first time, it strikes her that it might have been a stupid idea to take refuge in the church; if Jonny has been stalking her, he probably knows that she comes here from time to time.

She passes the font and continues into the vestry. On the desk, between the notepads and psalm books, she can see a pale grey telephone.

The loud rattle of a helicopter passes over the church.

Her heart starts racing as she lifts the receiver and holds it to her ear. Nothing. She presses the switchhook a few times, then checks that the phone is actually plugged in.

She doesn't know what to do now.

Maybe she should just sit down to pray on one of the uncomfortable pews, wait until she feels safe enough to go out and look for someone who can call the police for her.

But as she turns and heads back out into the hall, she hears a vehicle pull up on the gravel outside.

Francesca stares at the door and realises the key is still in the lock.

She slowly moves to one side, in front of the first row of pews.

Flecks of dust start rolling towards her down the middle of the aisle.

She slumps to the floor as the door swings open and closed on its stiff hinges.

A strange drawn-out whine follows the slow footsteps through the church.

Francesca shuffles back and looks up at the font. She should have hidden beneath the font cover, she thinks, let the holy water protect her.

Outside, the sound of police sirens grows louder.

She hears something rattle, and the strange whining sound stops.

Three police cars race by, sirens fading.

The church is now silent again.

Francesca slowly gets to her feet.

There is a long metal cable on the floor in the middle of the aisle, and she hears something creak between the pews.

She turns around to see what it is, but can't localise the sound.

Her neck feels oddly stiff.

'Jonny, is that you?' she asks, swallowing hard.

Nothing. Francesca moves slowly along one wall towards the front, trying to work out where he could be hiding.

'Please don't do anything stupid,' she says, aware of just how unsteady her voice sounds.

Francesca realises he must be crawling across the floor between the pews, and her heart starts beating so hard that it makes her chest ache.

'Jonny, listen to me, I . . . I want you to know that I've never stopped thinking about you. I wish we could have continued our sessions, we had a great connection . . .'

Something metallic rattles between the pews to her right. Francesca tries to keep her breathing calm as she moves back, out into the aisle.

'I . . . I don't know why you're following me, or . . .'

She turns slowly towards the crucifix on the wall. Perhaps she could run through to the vestry, lock the door and climb out of the window.

'But Jonny, listen . . . Whatever's happened, we can fix it. We'll fix it together.'

She shudders as she hears him stand up between the pews behind her, his slow footsteps coming closer over the wooden floor.

'I'm going to leave now, and you're going to let me go,' she says, still not moving an inch. 'But I think you should come back to me, I want to help you, I just wanted—'

A sharp crack makes her ears ring, and she feels something slam into her back, as though he just threw a rock at her.

She feels like a bowl of warm milk is spilling into her lap as the blood spurts from her stomach and onto her thighs.

Both legs give way beneath her.

Francesca drops so suddenly that she doesn't have time to break her fall. Her face hits the floor, splitting her lip and snapping her front teeth.

She might even have lost consciousness for a few seconds.

The ringing in her ears gives way to a roaring wall of noise.

The pain in her back is agonising, and she realises she has been shot.

A white shell casing rolls away into the dust beneath one of the pews.

Her heart is racing, her breathing much too shallow.

Francesca has lost all feeling in lower body, but she can tell he is doing something to her feet and she feels a sudden wave of fear that he might rape her.

She tries to pray, but can't find the right words. All she can remember is the ending, the lines that they repeat over and over.

'Maranatha,' she pants. 'Come, Lord Jesus, come.'

She lies perfectly still, fully aware that she will die soon unless she finds help. She can hear the faint sound of sirens somewhere nearby.

Right then, she starts moving backwards. She is being dragged by her feet down the aisle. Her blood paints the floorboards red, and Francesca tries desperately to find something to hold onto, but it is impossible. She tumbles onto her back and stares up at the high ceiling, at the sloping boards where they meet in the middle. It looks like the bottom of a hull, she thinks, like the church is a boat and its keel is pointing towards heaven.

36

Joona pulls up behind a patrol car and runs towards the house. The blue lights on the roof of the vehicle sweep across the bushes, trees and walls.

There is a red Ford parked in the carport.

Two uniformed officers are in the process of setting up a police cordon across the road, and the blue and white tape flutters in the breeze.

An operative from the tactical unit is standing guard by the front door, clutching an assault rifle to his chest. The lock has been shattered, and one of the windows is broken following their forced entry into the property.

'Where's the CO?' Joona asks as he holds up his ID.

'Out back, I think.'

Joona makes his way into the house, through the porch and into the hallway. He notices that the door to the coat cupboard is ajar as he passes.

A framed photograph of Joan Baez picking up Bob Dylan is hanging askew on the wall.

On the floor in the kitchen up ahead, he can see the case of a stun grenade.

One of the operatives is sitting on the stairs up to the first floor, his helmet on the step beside him, and he wearily points off to one side.

Joona follows his direction into the living room and sees that the patio door at the rear of the house has been shot to pieces from the inside.

'We're in the right place and our perp was here, but there's no sign of any blood,' Joona reports back over the radio as he steps out onto the paving stones, which are covered in glittering shards of glass.

The commander of the tactical unit comes over, setting down a small dog before he introduces himself and explains that the house was empty when they arrived.

'You've got a helicopter in the air, right?' asks Joona.

'Yes, but—'

'Search the area, look for a pickup with a winch.'

'But command—'

'We don't have time to wait,' Joona says, interrupting him as a call comes over the radio.

'One of the neighbours called 112,' the duty officer at regional command tells Joona. 'Francesca ran across his garden at 83 Sankt Mickelsgatan. She told him to get inside and call the police.'

'Did he see the perpetrator?' Joona asks, setting off over the gardens himself.

'No, and he doesn't know where Francesca went.'

Joona jumps over a low hedge and sees himself reflected in the glass of a dark sun room.

He clambers over a stone wall and notices bare footprints in the vegetable patch, soil that has been kicked out onto the grass. In a black kettle grill, the charcoal is still red hot.

Joona pauses when he reaches a narrow road, eyes scanning in both directions. He continues through the garden up ahead, where the washing looks like it has been torn down from the line, pushes through the hedge and keeps running.

Regional command gets in touch to let him know that a woman has called 112 to report a loud bang inside the chapel.

Joona crosses the next garden and then turns, running along the edge of the house. He passes the garage and comes out onto Sankt Mickelsgatan, continuing to the left.

The roar of the helicopter fades into the distance towards Mälarhöjden.

Joona takes the first road on the right, grabbing his gun as he reaches the small wooden church building. As he makes his way inside, he realises that the gravel outside has been swept.

There is a trail of blood on the floor, stretching from the main hall to the porch. He makes his way forward. Up ahead, at the far end of the aisle, a dark pool of blood catches the light. Joona can smell gunpowder, but the scent is so faint that he realises he must have arrived several minutes too late. He slumps down onto the back row of pews and buries his face in his hands.

* * *

Despite forty police cars and a helicopter sweeping the area, officers knocking on doors, checking traffic cameras and manning road blocks, the pickup couldn't be found. The residential area is sprawling, with hundreds of escape routes through its smaller, unguarded roads.

* * *

The sky is white above the dirty yellow tower blocks in Vällingby, and a lone crow caws forlornly from the top of a lamp post.

In one of the windows on the ground floor, Joona catches a glimpse of a pale blue sculpture of Our Lady of Fátima through a crack in the net curtains. It reminds him of the figure in the photograph on the floor in Valeria's greenhouse. The three girls had waded out into the water with their own blue sculpture, though not of Mary; theirs was some sort of water goddess.

Joona turns his attention to the small barred windows level with the pavement and then takes out his phone and calls Valeria.

'Joona?' she says when she picks up, her voice little more than a whisper.

'Sorry . . . I'm sorry for being so stupid, I was just taken aback. It felt like I'd been caught red handed.'

'I know, but . . .'

She takes a deep breath but doesn't go on.

'Do you think you can forgive me?' he asks.

'Of course I can. But I'm still upset.'

'I understand. I was an idiot.'

The light shifts slightly behind the curtains in the little basement windows.

'Do you want to tell me about it, in your own words?' she asks.

'That sounds like something we'd say in an interrogation,' he replies in an attempt to lighten the mood.

Behind one of the tower blocks, a girl is skateboarding, trying to perfect her kick-flip, but her board repeatedly clatters against the ground.

'I don't have a drug problem, if that's what you're thinking,' he says.

'Good.'

Joona moves back onto the grass as two women with strollers walk by on the pavement.

'What do you want me to say?' he asks.

'The truth would be good, once you're ready for it.'

'Are you trying to say that I'm lying?'

'First a man takes drugs, then the drugs take drugs . . . and ultimately, the drugs take the man.'

'I'm not the addict here, Valeria.'

'It sounds that way, it really does.'

A young man wearing a football kit and carrying a bag over one shoulder emerges from the stairwell and disappears around the corner.

'I take them in a controlled manner,' Joona explains. 'The same way I take my medication.'

'Look, I'm not going to get angry with you,' Valeria snaps. 'Because I know that was the last thing I needed when I was struggling. But if you're going to lie to me then—'

'You just don't get it,' he interrupts her.

'Except I do.'

'You were at rock bottom, it was completely different. You ended up in prison . . .'

'I'm going to hang up now, Joona. Go back to your drugs. Who knows, maybe I'll be waiting for you once you're done.'

Joona drops his phone into his pocket and walks over to the building, passing an overturned shopping cart. He presses the button on the intercom and leans forward when he hears the speaker crackle.

'It's Joona,' he says quietly into the microphone.

When the lock clicks, he opens the door and makes his way into the stairwell. The lift doors are covered in graffiti, the glass in the little window scratched.

Joona follows the stairs down to the basement, where the door has been propped open with a bag of rubbish. He steps inside and pushes the bag back with one foot, letting the heavy door swing shut behind him as he heads down into Laila's dark space.

The floor is covered with a thick layer of industrial plastic, and a tattooed man is lying with his eyes shut on the sofa bed.

On the little table beside him, a tall oil lamp flickers, its light dancing over his muscular arms and relaxed hands.

Joona slowly moves through the room.

He finds Laila in the pantry, standing beneath the oven hood with a set of scales and a small cellophane packet. She is in her seventies, in blue jeans and a black polo shirt. Her short grey hair is spiked with gel, and the wrinkles on her cheeks look like they were carved with a knife. Her veiny hands are covered in liver spots.

'Tell him to leave,' says Joona.

'He does what he wants,' she replies without looking up.

The man's head is propped up on a corduroy cushion, his chin against his chest.

'I need to be alone,' Joona insists.

Laila scrapes the inside of a pipe with a spatula and deftly taps out the oily ash – something she will reuse later – into a plastic tub.

'Then you'll either have to sit on the floor or come back another time.'

37

The oil lamp casts a splintered glow around the room, small chinks of light swaying across the concrete walls and plastic flooring. The air is heavy with the scent of opium and vomit. Laila presses the lid onto the tub and puts it in the fridge.

Joona marches over to the man on the sofa bed, looks down at his calm face and gives him a gentle nudge.

'You need to leave.'

'Huh?' the man mumbles.

'You need to leave, right now,' says Joona, shoving him harder this time.

'Go fuck yourself.'

The man blinks wearily and then closes his eyes. Joona grabs his upper arm in one hand and his neck with the other, dragging him to his feet.

'Hey, man, what the fuck're you doing?'

His legs are about to give way, but Joona keeps him upright.

'I'm a police officer, but I'll let you off with a warning if you clear out right now.'

Joona drags him across the room. The man is unsteady on his feet, and he pauses, grabs his stomach and spits onto the floor.

'I just need a minute,' he groans.

Joona ignores him and keeps going, over to the door, opening it and shoving the man out. The man stumbles over the rubbish bag and slumps down onto the stairs.

'Seriously, what the fuck's your problem?'

Joona snatches his jacket from the hook, tosses it over to him and then slams the door, making his way back over to the sofa bed.

Laila takes off her glasses, turns around and studies him with her calm eyes. 'So this is how it's going to be now, is it?' she asks.

'Sorry, I just need to think, I've got so much to think about.'

'What, and you really think the vapour helps with that?'

Joona grabs a towel from the floor and wipes up the vomit from the tarpaulin, then turns the damp corduroy cushion over and lies down.

Laila empties the bucket from the floor beside the bed and brings it back over. 'You have an important job,' she says.

'I don't know anymore. I can't do it, I feel like I don't know anything . . .'

'Don't you have anyone who can comfort you?'

When he fails to answer, Laila shuffles over to the fridge and takes out a small package. She pushes her desk chair over to the bed and sits down. In the flickering glow of the oil lamp, she unwraps the plastic from around the dark raw opium and pinches off a small piece.

'You're still on your way down,' she says as she rolls a sticky ball of opium between her thumb and finger.

'I think of it like an hourglass.'

'That's good . . . but only if you're able to turn it over yourself when the sand runs out.'

She pushes the ball onto a sooty needle and holds it in the heat above the top of the lamp. Right as it is about to melt, she spreads it like a film over the hole in the bowl of the pipe. She then attaches the mouthpiece, leans forward and hands it to Joona.

'You've painted your nails,' she says.

The opium starts to crackle as Joona holds it over the heat, and there is a bubbling sound as he inhales the warm vapour.

The sense of pleasure is so immediate, so all-consuming, that it makes his eyes well up.

He feels himself relax, and Laila's stern face transforms, suddenly becoming much more beautiful. Right there and then, he knows that his conflict with Valeria will work out just fine.

A wisp of smoke curls up towards the ceiling in the soft light.

Joona holds the bowl over the lamp again, fills his lungs and grins.

Laila is watching him.

He finds himself thinking about Valeria's eyes in the restaurant, and he inhales the last of the sweet smoke, closes his eyes and leans back against the cushion.

The silver necklace one of her sons gave her had ended up outside on top of her dress, and she gripped it between her slim fingers and dropped it back inside, between her breasts. Joona feels Laila taking the pipe from his weak hands and lowering it to the side table as she rolls a new ball of opium.

At first he doesn't understand where the thoughts of Jakov Fauster have come from, but then he remembers the manic look in Saga's eye as she repeated the names of the three serial killers.

Before the German was arrested, the press christened him 'the Silversmith of Berlin'. His first known victim was found on a railway track on the outskirts of the city, his eyes burned out with molten silver.

Joona doesn't have the energy to get up, but he knows he should get back to the station and investigate whether there could be a link between the Silversmith and their killer's use of tin figurines.

Laila heats the next ball of opium above the lamp.

'Wait,' he whispers.

She smooths it over the hole, carefully pulls the needle out and hands him the pipe. He takes it from her and holds it in the heat, pushing the mouthpiece between his lips and inhaling the smoke.

As the rush spreads through him, he sits up and gazes out across the dark room.

Squinting, Joona thinks that the splintered glow of the lamp looks like hundreds of golden butterflies.

He can no longer remember why he needs to leave, but he hands the pipe back to Laila and gets up on unsteady legs.

The sheet of plastic on the floor shimmers like water beneath him, and Joona makes his way over to the door through the swarm of flapping butterflies, swatting them away from his face, staggering to one side and knocking over an ironing board.

He bends down and grabs a scarf from the lost property box, knows he will start shivering soon.

Laila opens the door and lets him out into the stairwell without another word.

Joona clings onto the handrail, pausing for a moment with his eyes shut before he makes his way up the stairs and out into the cool evening air.

He is still clutching the pink and gold scarf in one hand, and he doesn't notice that it is trailing behind him.

As he walks, the ground seems to start spinning like a carousel. The tower blocks race by and away before he has time to focus on any of them.

The effects of the opium are still building.

By the time he reaches the pedestrian square next to the supermarket and jewellery shop, the tiredness is almost overwhelming.

Vague thoughts of tin figurines and the Silversmith of Berlin are now all that is driving him forward.

Gulls screech in the air above the entrance to the metro station.

Joona pauses, bracing himself against a rubbish bin. He could do with a quick lie down by the wall, he thinks.

Moving slowly, he sets off again, sitting down to compose himself when he reaches a bench outside a McDonald's. He slumps down on his side, pulls the scarf over him and closes his eyes.

In his dreams, he and Valeria are getting ready to celebrate Midsummer in her garden, setting the table with the good china, wildflowers and delicate little schnapps glasses.

The sound of voices and laughter drag him back to the surface, but he doesn't have the energy to open his eyes. He feels someone snatch the scarf from him, saying something about how sexy it is.

'Man, check out his nails.'

'I heard about some kid getting groped by an old perve like this last week, over by Vällingby School.'

'Hey? You awake? You want to suck some dick?'

Joona feels one of the men press the sole of his shoe to his cheek.

'Clear off! Hey, old lady? Get lost!'

He feels a searing pain across his thigh, and when he opens his eyes he sees a young man with a silver baseball bat raised in the air, but he still doesn't have the energy to get up.

One of the other men steps forward and pours beer in his face.

Joona manages to sit up and sees the man with the baseball bat getting closer. He should use his arms to protect himself, he thinks, though he doesn't have time to do anything before the bat strikes his cheek and he tumbles to the ground in front of the bench.

He feels them kicking and hitting him, hears an agitated woman shouting that she has called the police.

The men run away, laughing among themselves.

The woman helps Joona up. She can't be much older than twenty, with thick black brows and a red bindi on her forehead.

'Do you need me to call an ambulance?' she asks.

'No, I'm fine, but thanks,' he replies, wiping the blood and beer from his face.

'Sure?'

'Yes.'

'I hate those idiots,' she mutters, glancing over towards the church.

38

Once it dawned on Saga that they had failed to save Francesca, she locked herself in a toilet stall at the station and sat there for some time with her arms wrapped around herself and her eyes closed.

She really had thought they would be able to turn things around this time.

In the end she made her way home with a sense of numbness deep down inside, feeling lost and anxious. She was in no state to eat or sit still, she realised, and so she headed out again, to her old boxing club, despite the fact that she is no longer a member.

*   *   *

The reception desk at Narva Boxing Club is unmanned, and the vending machine casts a cold glow across the wall of framed photographs of successful members and posters from various championships.

The main training space is laden with the scent of sweat, liniment and cleaning products, and a series of loud thuds echoes between the walls as a muscular man darts around the punching bag, delivering hook after hook. Two younger men are taking turns on the bench press, and a woman in a red hoodie is doing push-ups by the side of the ring.

Saga picks up a rope and starts skipping at a fast pace while she practises her footwork, trying to find her way back to the flexibility and lightness she once had.

Her old coach used to say that her feet should barely touch the ground. The feet are key to making unpredictable moves and winning a match.

As she lay awake in bed last night, she found herself thinking about the Seven Bridges of Königsberg again, unable to find a solution.

She needs to gather her thoughts, find her focus.

The team is now moving faster on every level, but the riddles are also becoming increasingly complex.

The perpetrator is killing people around her in order to pile the pressure on her, to make the hunt personal and raise the stakes even further.

But Saga has no family left for him to hurt.

Earlier that afternoon, she got in touch with the National Down Syndrome Association and explained that she needed to take a break from being Astrid and Nick's support person. The victims all seem to be people she has been in conflict with, but she simply can't take any risks when it comes to the kids.

The ninth bullet is reserved for Joona, and only she can save him.

He is her friend, she knows that, though she still doesn't understand how he could have left her alone with Jurek.

Behind her, someone starts pummelling the speed ball.

A woman with a shaved head and a look of determination on her face, practising upper cuts.

Saga glances up at the clock, which has a strip of sports tape plastered over a crack in the glass, and realises she has been skipping for sixty-five minutes. She stops, and her breathing quickly slows to its usual rate. She tosses the rope to the floor beside her training bag and takes a few tentative steps. Her legs feel heavy, her calves tight, and she braces herself against her thighs with both hands.

Sweat drips from her face onto the peeling plastic mat, and her damp T-shirt is clinging to her back.

Saga stopped boxing competitively several years ago, but she decides to start training again then and there. Boxing helps her to focus, to empty her mind of all unnecessary thoughts.

She digs her phone out of her bag and reads through Randy's summary report, hesitating for a few seconds before dialling his private number.

'How are you?' she asks.

'OK, I think. It's good to hear your voice.'

'Sorry for snapping at you earlier.'

'Don't worry, it was a high pressure situation . . .'

'I just can't bear the thought that we could've saved her but didn't,' she whispers.

'I know.'

The glare from the ceiling lights bounces off the white plastic floor in the ring. Saga's old coach used to point down at the dark scuff marks left by people's shoes to demonstrate which areas were rarely used.

'What are you up to?' she asks in an attempt to break the silence.

'Just hanging out at home, need to do a load of washing . . . Linda will be back soon.'

'Can we talk a little longer?'

'You know, it's not so easy for her.'

'She's really attractive.'

'I know, but she doesn't feel that way after seeing you.'

'Stop it. You know what I think about—'

'That's how it is, though,' he interrupts her. 'She says I would leave her, that I'd forget about our future and everything we've planned and go running to you if you gave me the word.'

'Would you?' Saga asks, suddenly serious.

The woman with the shaved head massages her shoulder for a moment before launching another attack on the punchbag.

'I never understood why you ended things, Saga, why you didn't just let me help you. I was there for you, it would've done us both good . . . You said it was over, but I waited. Did you know that? I waited a couple of years.'

'You shouldn't have.'

Saga sees that Rick is in the ring with Sasha Smedberg, one of the coaches, and she watches as they pull on their head guards and start sparring.

The coach picks up the pace, shoving Rick into one corner and delivering a hard body blow.

Someone has left a mop leaning against the ropes on the outside of the ring, and it clatters to the ground.

Rick ducks away, jabbing with his left hand and landing two rapid hooks.

'I'm happy with Linda. We've actually started talking about kids,' says Randy, his tone sad.

'Good . . . I'm happy for you.'

'But I'd go out into the hallway right this second, I'd grab my jacket and shoes and never look back if you said you wanted to give me another chance.'

'I know you don't mean that.'

'Maybe not.'

Rick takes a straight right to the head and staggers back, rolling his body away from the coach and delivering a left hook of his own as he takes another fist to the ribs.

'I can't make anyone happy, Randy. I'll never be able to.' Saga feels like her heart is falling into a bottomless pit. 'There's something wrong with me, something—'

His doorbell rings.

'Is that her?'

'Yeah.'

'Go and answer it,' says Saga, ending the call.

She swallows hard and drops her phone into her bag, swigs a mouthful of water from her bottle and picks up a pair of boxing gloves. She pulls them on and uses her mouth to fasten the Velcro around her wrists.

Quick footsteps thud across the ring. Rick lowers his elbows to defend himself, drawing an upper cut and managing to hit the coach in the face with a combination of blows.

Sasha Smedberg holds up his left hand, takes off his head guard and sways slightly, leaning back against the ropes and breathing heavily.

'Sorry,' Rick chuckles.

Rick Santos is twenty-three, one of the club's regular competitors. There is already talk that he might be selected for the next Olympics.

Saga remembers when he first joined the club. He was a shy, lanky kid who showed up barefoot in a pair of cut-off jeans.

She walks over to the heaviest of the punchbags, which has been wound with silver tape, and starts practising snappy left hooks. Her coach always used to say that they should come out of nowhere.

After a while she switches to different combinations, thinking about the messages Stefan Broman has left her. He wants her to go over to his apartment in Solna tonight; he's having a party, a belated birthday celebration. Stefan has never invited her to a party before. In fact, he has never asked her to go anywhere.

Saga knows what his repeated calls are really about, and she tries to convince herself that she shouldn't be upset.

On multiple occasions over the past month, he has mentioned the idea of making a film of him and his friends having sex with her.

211

She laughed him off each time, said it was never going to happen, but she can tell from his tone that he has invited his pals over anyway and promised that tonight is the night.

Saga turns her attention to the force of her hooks. Her hair lashes against her face as she twists her hips, and the bag makes a sucking sound with each blow, chains clinking. She loses track of time, punching harder and harder. The ceiling mount creaks, small flakes of concrete falling to the floor.

When she notices Rick watching her with a smile, she stops to catch her breath. He has already showered and changed. The woman with the shaved head is gone, and a young man is busy reorganising the hand weights and kettlebells.

'Saga Bauer,' Rick says as he approaches her.

'It's Rick, right?'

'You know my name,' he says with a grin.

'I've heard it's going well for you.'

'Yeah, but Sasha doesn't think I've been training hard enough . . .'

'Always the way.'

'He told me to let you know the women's showers aren't working.'

'Bit late,' she says, tugging at her sweaty T-shirt.

'I know.'

'Well, it is what it is,' she says, grabbing her bag from the floor.

'You know, you can always jump in the shower at my place if you want,' he says.

'Thanks, but I'll just head home,' she replies, though as the words leave her mouth she realises that she doesn't actually want to be alone right now. 'Or . . . I mean, if it's not a problem?'

'No, for God's sake, it's totally cool.'

'OK, then sure.'

She makes her way towards the changing rooms. From the men's, she can hear laughter and the drumming of the shower on the tiled floor. In the women's room, someone has taped off the doorway into the showers.

Saga pulls her jacket on over her workout clothes and shoves the rest into her bag. When she comes out into reception, Rick drops his phone into his pocket. She follows him out into the cool evening air, and they set off towards Odenplan together.

'I saw one of your matches,' he tells her. 'I can't remember your opponent's name, she was from Hungary . . .'

'How'd it go?'

'You knocked her out in, like, ten seconds or something,' he says with a grin.

'Good.'

'It was a sick combination. I've been trying to copy it ever since.'

39

They spend most of the train ride in silence, staring down at their phones or letting their eyes drift across their fellow passengers' weary faces and the buildings racing by outside.

When they get to Barkarby, they take the escalator up to the ticket hall and come out onto the bridge. Saga and Rick cross the railway tracks and motorway, then cut over a lawn and into a residential area. The apartment blocks are clad in rough yellow plaster, with small windows and balcony screens made from corrugated iron.

They head for the third building and take the stairs to the second floor. Rick unlocks the door, opens it, picks up the mail from the mat and lets her in ahead of him.

'Nice,' Saga says as they move through the living room.

'It's a bit big, really. My ex moved to Höganäs last year, I got my ass dumped,' he says.

Rick hands Saga a clean towel from the wardrobe in the bedroom, and she takes it into the bathroom along with her sports bag, locking the door behind her.

The toilet seat and lid are both up, she can see a couple of stray beard hairs clinging to the edge of the sink. There is only one toothbrush in the glass.

She instinctively scans the room for hidden cameras and then opens the cabinet. No makeup or tampons, no pink razors or women's perfume. Saga is a little sick of always being so suspicious, but it wouldn't be the first time a man had claimed to be single in order to sleep with her.

She peels off her damp clothes, drops them to the floor by her bag and studies herself in the mirror. Her muscles are still pumped with blood after her workout, the skin on her chest dimpled from her tight sports bra.

She opens the frosted plastic shower screen, turns the tap and waits until the water is running hot before stepping underneath it. She squeezes a blob of Pro Sport soap into her palm and lathers herself up, watching as the foam runs across the floor by her feet.

Saga stands beneath the hot jets for a moment, feeling the muscles in her neck and back start to relax before she turns it off and rubs herself down.

Her body is still a little damp as she pulls on her clean clothes, and though she has squeeze-dried her hair several times, it's still dripping as she comes out into the kitchen.

'Thanks for letting me use the shower, that was really nice of you,' she says.

'Can I get you anything? Tea, juice? I don't actually have much.'

'No, I'm fine, thanks.'

'We can make toasties . . . if you're hungry?'

She shakes her head and meets his big brown eyes, then turns towards the hallway and mumbles something about how she should probably head home.

'I noticed you from day one . . . but you stopped coming,' he says. 'I never, like, found the nerve to actually come over and talk to you.'

Saga smiles, but she can't think of anything to say. His boxing success has made him braver, and she decides she wouldn't mind sleeping with him after all.

'Your top's wet.'

'Happens every time. I never have the patience to dry my hair properly,' she says.

'I can lend you another T-shirt.'

She follows him into the bedroom, where his big bed is neatly made with a pale blue blanket folded at the foot. On the nightstand, he has a small lamp with a glossy porcelain base and a white paper shade.

Rick opens a drawer and grabs a T-shirt with the Nike logo on the front, holding it out to her.

'Thanks.'

Saga peels off her vest and stands in front of him in her see-through white bra.

'You're so hot,' he blurts out, swallowing hard.

Rick reaches out and pushes a few damp locks of hair back from her face, looking her straight in the eye.

Her fingertips dance over the bump on his nose, and he leans in and kisses her. His lips are warm and soft, and Saga smiles and kisses him back. She lets him guide her over to the bed, lets him kiss her throat and suck her nipples through the thin fabric, then lies still as he unbuttons her jeans with shaking hands, tugging them down along with her underwear.

Rick tears off his top and drapes it over the open drawer. His body is muscular yet boyish, with a tattoo of a red heart wound with thorns on one shoulder, a dark bruise above his ribs and a yellowing one on his left upper arm.

He takes off his trousers but keeps his boxers on, then crawls on top of her on the soft bed. Saga lies still as he kisses her and reaches beneath her bra. He gently squeezes her breast, kissing her on the tip of her chin before pulling back and studying her with anxious eyes.

'Do you want to keep going?' he asks.

'If you do.'

Rick moves downwards, kissing her stomach, her pubic mound and groin before slowly pushing her legs apart. Saga had assumed he would be eager, that he would be the kind of man who wanted to get it over and done with as quickly as possible. But instead he lowers his head and she feels his hot breath on the inside of her thigh.

'You don't have to,' she whispers as he starts licking her.

She closes her eyes and tries to ignore the way it feels, but she knows she is getting wet. His tongue moves upwards, circling her clitoris and sucking gently.

She reaches out and puts one hand on his head, digging her fingers into his short hair, powerless to resist the pleasure for a second longer.

His hot tongue slips inside her.

Saga groans and thinks about warm clay: tactile, moist and silky smooth. Push a finger into it and you can feel the suck of the earth; make a small hole and you can see the water rising up from within.

She tenses her thighs and buttocks for a moment, making herself relax and then tensing again.

His tongue follows her grooves, circling round and back.

She wants him to keep going a little longer, and she holds his head in place with both hands.

Her toes are tingling, and her thighs begin to shake. Saga's breathing quickens and she tenses again, pushing him away before she climaxes.

She sits up, sees her underwear and jeans on the floor and feels a pulsing heat between her legs.

'What is it?' he asks cautiously.

'Nothing,' she replies, cheeks flushing. 'I just need to . . .'

Rick seems worried, and Saga realises she should go, that Stefan and his friends are waiting for her, but she changes her mind and attempts a smile.

'Do you have any condoms?' she whispers.

He nods and opens the drawer in the nightstand. With trembling hands, he pulls out a small, shiny wrapper. Saga lies down again, gazing up at him and his big, dark eyes. She holds out a hand and whispers for him to come closer.

'Are you sure?'

'Yes.'

He climbs on top of her, heat radiating from his heavy body. She parts her thighs and lets him push inside her.

She squeezes him once he is inside, clinging on as he pulls back and then letting go and groaning into his ear.

She wraps her arms around his back as he thrusts into her, stroking his backside, keeping up with him as he increases the pace.

The bed creaks beneath them, and tiny flecks of dust swirl through the air.

Their shapes are reflected in the base of the lamp on the bedside table, like some sort of erotic sketch.

Rick's breathing shallows, and his back gets sweaty. He lets out a low moan as he comes, then slumps down on top of her, gasping for air.

Saga feels his heart pounding in his chest, feels his muscles relaxing.

He grips the top of the condom with his right hand and pulls out before he goes completely limp, rolling over onto his back and then shuffling closer and kissing her on the head.

They lie like that for some time, eventually breaking into chat. Rick sounds cheery, relaxed.

'I don't even know what you do for work,' he says.

'Same.'

'I'm a carpenter . . . work for ABC Building. It's a small construction firm.'

'Very imaginative name.'

'I know.'

Through the Venetian blinds, the evening sun paints a number of bright lines onto the wall.

'I do bits and pieces,' she says.

'You don't have to tell me.'

'I've been on sick leave for a pretty long time. Burnt out, I guess you could call it,' she says, sitting up.

'Listen, if you need work, I can talk to my uncle. He has a couple of restaurants, they always need people.'

'Thanks,' she says as she starts to get dressed.

'I've done it plenty of times – washing dishes, chopping onions. It's not great, and the pay is fucking terrible, but . . . it's better than nothing, and he can pay you some of the money under the table, if you want.'

'I've got something on at the minute, so I'll see how that goes,' she says as she pulls on her vest.

'OK, well at least you know.'

'Thanks.'

'No worries.'

She smiles to herself as she folds his T-shirt and puts it back in the drawer, then walks over to the bed, kisses him on the lips and says goodbye.

As she steps out into the evening air and starts making her way back towards Barkarby station, she hears him shout 'Saga!' behind her. She turns around and sees him waving to her from the balcony, still stark naked.

Saga blows him a kiss and keeps walking. Her heart is fluttering in a way it hasn't in a long time. She might not be ready to be happy, and she might not deserve Rick or Randy, but she should stop punishing herself, stop hurting herself.

She takes out her phone and blocks Stefan Broman's number, then calls the police and makes an anonymous report against him for buying sex.

40

It's twenty past eleven in the evening, and the parking area outside Lillkyrka School is deserted.

A gust of wind blows through the bushes every now and again, over towards the bicycle racks.

Ali is sitting on the fire escape at one end of the athletic centre. The metal structure seems to produce a different note every time he moves, each one soft and wavering.

An empty plastic bag has blown up against the red brick facade, and his bike is lying on its side on the tarmac in front of him, torn meadow grass clinging to the front mudflap.

Ali has just taken out his phone to ask Martin whether the bell ringer has caught him when he hears the steady clanking of his friend's pedal against the dented chainguard.

He gets up from the fire escape, grabs his bike and balances the spade over the handlebars just as Martin turns off into the car park and cycles beneath a street lamp, cruising over with a big grin on his face.

Ali and Martin are in their last year of middle school, and are both due to move up to the high school in Enköping come autumn.

They ride down to the crossroads, through the residential area and left onto Kyrkvägen. The metal detector sticking out of Martin's rucksack makes it look like he has a second head.

The boys often go hunting for treasure at night and have done since they were eleven, when they found out that the church silver stolen in 1858 had never been recovered. Back then, their theory was that the bell ringer had hidden it somewhere and claimed it had been stolen, only to die before he got round to digging it up.

Ali and Martin started by searching the fields around the church, beneath the clusters of trees that were like dense islands in a sea of ploughed earth.

They moved a little closer to the cemetery this year, along the outside of the wall where the suicides and criminals were once buried.

They have never discussed it seriously, but their jokes have already taken them over the wall and into the cemetery itself.

The burial vault in the church once belonged to the Eka Estate, owned by King Gustav I, and the boys like to fantasise about uncovering a huge pile of gold.

'Once we're rich I'm gonna buy some Lil Nas trainers,' Ali says, pedalling harder.

'And I'm gonna date Cardi B!'

Laughing, they ride side by side. The landscape around them grows darker as they leave the last of the houses behind, and the boys fall silent, only their heavy breathing and the rhythmic scraping from Martin's bike are audible in the silence.

They pause for a moment when they see the headlights of a large vehicle approaching at the crossroads. It's a lorry with a trailer, illuminating the bushes around them in a dry white glow. The ground shakes as it passes, and the lights sweep away. The lorry kicks up a cloud of dust in its wake, making their hair blow across their faces.

Between the trees to their right, they can see a flock of anxious jackdaws above the roof of the church. They look like lumps of tar that have peeled away and swirled up into the sky.

Ali and Martin cycle on, cutting across the road and into the small parking area.

The double metal gates into the cemetery are open.

They pull up and wheel their bikes through the tyre tracks in the strip of grass by the wall. All they can hear is the screeching, unhappy cries of the jackdaws.

Once they are no longer visible from the main road, they drop their bikes into the long grass. Ali's bell rings softly as it hits the ground.

They follow the mossy wall to a spot where the ground has started to subside, then switch on the metal detector and begin sweeping the area.

The jackdaws flap around the dark tower before returning to the roof of the church.

The clicking sound of the detector dies down abruptly.

Martin has switched it off, and he crouches down and points into the churchyard. There is a pickup parked on the gravel in front of the bell tower, engine running.

'Must be the groundskeeper,' Martin whispers.

'Did he see us?'

'Dunno, I don't think so.'

They hear a piercing mechanical screech, followed by a low buzzing sound. Something wooden creaks ominously, and there is a little more buzzing, then the churchyard falls silent.

The two boys stare at each other in the darkness, unsure whether to stay where they are or run back over to their bikes.

They hear a couple of loud thuds, followed by a sudden rattling noise, then a car door slams and the pickup rolls away, tyres crunching on the gravel.

The boys lie perfectly still for a moment before peeping over the top of the wall.

The churchyard is quiet.

The dragon-shaped weathervanes on the ends of the church building creak softly in the breeze.

Martin grins at Ali and is just about to switch the metal detector back on when they hear a low, guttural groan.

'What the hell was that?' Ali whispers.

'Sounded like a deer that's hurt or something.'

'What?'

'Let's have a look.'

They leave their spade and detector, climbing over the wall onto the neat lawn on the other side. Moving slowly, they creep forward between the gravestones. When they reach one of the tall oak trees, they stop to listen.

It sounds like something is thumping against the walls inside the bell tower, trying to force the door open.

They start moving just as the three dragons' heads on the roof turn in unison, almost as though they have spotted the boys down below.

The thudding and moaning sound is coming from inside the bell tower. The door is closed, but it looks like someone has sawed a deep nick in the top of the doorframe.

'What are you doing?' Martin whispers as Ali makes his way over to the door and knocks. Above the treetops, the jackdaws start screeching.

With a shaking hand, Ali reaches out and tries the handle. An acrid chemical smell hits him as the door swings open.

'Hello?' he says in a feeble voice.

'Come on, let's go,' Martin whispers.

Ali switches on the torch on his phone and shines it inside. The wooden stairs are wet, and he can see some sort of red-streaked slime on the bottom step.

'Shit, look at that.'

A series of loud thuds make Ali look up. Several metres above him is what looks like an enormous cocoon made from sheets, grey plastic and tape. It is swinging back and forth, and there is some sort of murky liquid trickling from a hole in the fabric. A droplet hits Ali's hand, and he cries out in pain as it burns his skin, wiping it on his trousers, backing up and bumping into Martin.

* * *

Joona drives slowly along Greiders väg, past one red brick building after another. He turns the corner when he reaches the National Board of Forensic Medicine and its faded blue awnings, pulling up in a parking space outside.

It feels as though the entire team is on the verge of suffocating. With heavy hearts, they had sat down together that morning to analyse everything that had happened since the arrival of the latest figurine.

Was there anything they could have done better?

How should they proceed from here?

They were forced to admit that they still had nothing – absolutely nothing – that brought them even a step closer to their killer, the Predator.

Manvir muttered the word 'disaster' and then got up and stood in his corner.

Greta's face had turned grey, the creases deepening around her mouth; Petter chewed his nails, and Saga got a dark, dangerous look in her eye.

A sense of apathy seemed to settle upon them.

Joona sat with his face in his hands, trying to remember what he had been thinking about when he left Laila's sofa bed. He knew he had some sort of insight linked to the killer, but he no longer had any sense of whether it was important or even fully formed as an idea.

He scoured his phone for any messages or notes he might have made – he even emptied his pockets and wallet of all receipts and money – but he hadn't jotted his thoughts down anywhere.

Now, Joona gets out of the car, locks the doors and walks past a white Porsche Taycan taking up three spaces. Its charging cable has been stretched across the grass and plugged in to an extension cord snaking through the bushes and up to an open window.

He finds The Needle and Chaya Abdouela sitting in white plastic chairs at an outdoor table by the concrete ramp up to the main entrance, drinking coffee from metal cups.

The Needle is a professor at the Institute of Forensic Medicine, Chaya is his assistant.

'New car?' Joona asks, unable to muster a smile.

'Fossil fuels are over, or so I've heard,' says The Needle.

'Nice nails,' says Chaya.

'Thanks.'

'And nice eyeshadow.'

She points to the bruised skin above his eye.

'I know . . . Close combat practice with . . .'

He breaks off his lie as Saga rolls in to the parking area on her black motorcycle. The powerful twin engines sound like machine gun fire between the brick walls.

She wheels around The Needle's car, pulling right up to the table before switching off the engine and taking off her helmet, hanging it on one of the handlebars.

'This is Doctor Abdouela,' says Joona, gesturing to Chaya.

'Saga Bauer. I'm working with Joona at the NCU,' she replies, holding out a hand.

'Call me Chaya,' she says as she gets up from her chair.

She and The Needle empty their cups into the flowerbed and then head up the stairs to the main door.

'This is really hard,' Saga mumbles.

'You should prepare yourself for the possibility that it could be Verner,' Joona tells her.

'I know.' Saga sighs.

'Shall we go in?'

'We've got five dead bodies now, Joona. That means there are only four bullets left,' says Saga, fixing her eyes on him. 'Maybe you should consider letting them give you protection after all.'

'Never,' Joona replies with a smile.

'But everything the killer has said has come true so far.'

'Then maybe we should start asking ourselves why you're the only one who can stop him.'

'I don't understand,' she says. 'Why does it have to be me?'

'Let's bring it up with the others this afternoon.'

They head inside, past the reception desk and down the corridor, following the sound of classic rock to the examination rooms. Joona holds the door for Saga and follows her in to the brightly lit space.

The music stops abruptly as Chaya pulls the plug on the cassette player.

'Thanks,' says Joona.

'*And we walk the earth with our heads held high,*' The Needle continues, singing to himself.

'Please,' Joona begs him.

'Sorry,' he says, turning to Saga.

'It's fine.'

'Frippe sent us a mixtape,' Chaya explains as she puts on a plastic apron.

On one of the stainless steel benches, several thousand pieces of bone have been lined up, everything from tiny fragments to an entire elk skull.

'We were in the process of sorting through the bones they found when they drained the lake in Sandakärret when . . . we got the delivery from Enköping.'

'He's in room two,' says Chaya, gesturing to another set of doors.

'So it is Verner?' Saga asks, the colour draining from her face.

'Yes.'

'Condolences,' says Chaya, tucking the elastic ear loops of her face mask beneath her pink hijab.

'Thank you,' Saga whispers.

'I don't usually offer, but this time . . .' says The Needle, holding out a blue container of VapoRub. 'We've already documented the smell. As with the previous cases, it's caused by the chemical reaction between the sodium hydroxide and the body.'

'OK,' says Joona, rubbing a little of the salve beneath his nose before passing it to Saga.

They follow The Needle and Chaya through the door into the next room. Despite the powerful menthol scent, strong enough to make their noses sting and their eyes water, the chemical stench is noticeable.

Above the large autopsy table with a drainage hole and two sinks, a low-hanging lamp is switched on. The mouth of the hose is dripping. The strainer from a collection vessel has been laid on a sheet of plastic, and there is a shower scraper leaning against the wall by the floor drain.

'Just a quick word of warning,' says The Needle, stopping them before they get any closer. 'The arms and head have come loose from the body. You won't be able to make a visual ID. The decomposition process kept going until we got him here and rinsed off the corrosive substance.'

'We understand,' says Joona.

'He was still alive when he was found, but by that stage he was in such bad shape that he probably wasn't conscious . . .'

'Or at least we hope not,' Chaya mutters to herself.

41

Joona brakes and gently turns the wheel, pulling up by the kerb outside Verner's spacious home in Saltsjöbaden. He turns off the engine but can't quite bring himself to get out. Over the lingering scent of menthol, he can still smell the terrible stench of chemicals and dissolved tissue.

He closes his eyes and tries to compose himself.

The identification process is complete. The DNA was a clear match.

Joona has known Verner his entire working life. The last time he saw him was the day Verner showed up at the station and asked whether anyone knew any magic tricks, because he had promised his grandkids he would make Maja float.

In truth, he probably just wanted to see Saga.

Joona thinks about Verner's deep voice, the way he rubbed his nose as he thought, how, judging by his gait and gestures, it often seemed as though he had never really learned how to master his long limbs.

A blue butterfly flutters over the bonnet, its reflection almost black in the dark paintwork.

Joona gets out of the car and walks along the supporting wall at the edge of the lawn, past the driveway leading to the garage and over to the front door.

He hasn't seen Maja since the police ball five years ago. She was wearing a forest green dress that evening, and she joked that the Security Service had created a couture collection that doubled as camouflage in the Swedish countryside.

He rings the bell, and as he listens to the chime he thinks that there is nothing harder than what he is about to do. Breaking news of this sort is merciless, bringing all hopes of a happy ending to a close and wiping out any notions of salvation.

A tall woman in her thirties opens the door. She must be Verner's eldest daughter, Veronica, Joona realises.

'Hello, my name is Joona Linna. Is Maja home?' he asks, swallowing hard.

'What's this about?' she asks, blinking quickly.

'I'm from the National Crime Unit.'

'Is it about Dad?' she asks, a couple of tears spilling down her cheeks.

'I'd really like to speak to Maja.'

'It's just . . . Sorry,' she says, wiping her face. 'She's not doing so well, and . . .'

Joona hears the footsteps of two people approaching down the hallway.

Maja and her youngest daughter Mikaela appear in the doorway. When Maja sees Joona, all colour drains from her face. She stops dead and fumbles for something to hold onto, knocking a wooden shoehorn to the floor.

'Mum?' Mikaela sounds frightened.

She tries to pull Maja back in to the kitchen, but Maja shakes her head and looks up.

'Joona, please . . . Don't say it,' she begs him.

'I wish I didn't have to, Maja.'

'No, no, no,' she whispers, clamping her hand to her mouth.

Mikaela's face is red, and she whispers 'it's OK, it'll be OK,' as she pulls her mother away.

Veronica watches them go, then she hangs up the shoehorn and turns back to Joona.

'I think she might need to hear it again,' she says, taking a few steps to one side.

She shows Joona in to the kitchen and asks whether he wants anything to drink before they make their way into the sunroom.

Maja is hunched over at the dining table, clutching a piece of paper towel in her hands.

Mikaela is standing behind her, with her arms wrapped around her mother.

Beyond the rooftops, the bay glitters in the sunlight. Verner's reading glasses are folded on top of an unfinished crossword on the windowsill, and there is an unused coffee cup by his place at the head of the table.

'I'm so sorry, Maja, I really am,' says Joona.

Maja slowly looks up and stares at him as though she had forgotten he was there. Her tears drip down onto her cardigan, glistening for a second before soaking into the fabric.

'Why? I just can't understand it,' she says, her voice completely flat.

'The investigation is still ongoing . . .'

Mikaela whimpers and buries her face in her mother's shoulder, shaking as she sobs quietly.

'But you said he wasn't dead, that there was a chance you'd find him,' says Veronica.

'We failed.'

'You failed?' Veronica repeats. 'So is there going to be an enquiry into what went wrong?'

'Stop it,' Mikaela whispers to her sister, taking a seat.

'How did Dad die? Don't we have a right to know?'

'He was shot, several times,' says Joona.

Maja starts to shake.

'Shot,' she mumbles, drying her cheeks with the paper towel. 'Was that the cause of death?'

'Did he suffer?' asks Veronica.

'Stop it!' her younger sister shouts. 'I don't want to know!'

Someone's mobile phone starts ringing, though no one has the energy to answer the call or even react to the sound. They just sit quietly, waiting for it to stop.

'And the person who did this . . . I'm guessing we would know if you'd caught them?' Veronica says after a moment or two.

'Like I said, it's an ongoing investigation,' says Joona.

'I'll show you out,' says Maja, pressing both palms to the table and forcing herself up.

Her daughters remain where they are, eyes downcast and faces pale, and Joona reiterates his condolences and leaves the sunroom with Maja.

When they reach the dark hallway, they stand quietly for a moment. Verner's trench coat is hanging on the coat rack, his huge shoes neatly lined up on the floor.

'I'm sorry about Veronica,' Maja says, swallowing hard. 'I know Verner respected you, possibly more than anyone else . . .'

'The feeling was mutual.'

'I just thought I'd get to have him around for years to come, you know?' she says, lips trembling. 'We loved our life together, and not everyone can say that.'

She breaks down in tears again, and Joona wraps his arms around her. Her shoulders shake with grief. After a few moments, when her breathing settles down, he takes a step back.

'It's my job to look after our girls now,' she says.

The sheet of paper towel in her hand is now nothing but a small, hard ball.

'You know how this works, Maja. If you think of anything, no matter how insignificant it might seem, let us know,' says Joona, moving to open the door.

'There was actually one thing,' she says. 'Everything has been so chaotic that I forgot all about it, but Verner mentioned a pale man taking pictures of him in the supermarket a few weeks ago . . .'

'You don't happen to know where and when, do you?'

'No, I . . . I have no idea.'

'If you could check his receipts or his bank account and see whether that jogs your memory, that would be great.'

'I've also had the sense that someone has been in the house, several times over the past . . . six months, it must be.'

'Has anything gone missing?'

'No, but things have moved,' she says, her voice little more than a whisper.

42

The core investigative team needed to meet, but no one could bring themselves to go back to the station. The thought of being there made them feel like insects trapped under a glass, and so they decided to meet at someone's house instead. Petter drew the short straw.

Saga pulls up on a hill outside a nondescript apartment building in Lilla Essingen. The ochre-coloured facade is blotchy, and the paint on the underside of the balconies seems to be coming away in large sheets.

The rubbish bin has come loose from its post and is now leaning against it on the ground, overflowing with dog waste bags.

She walks over to the lacquered oak door, enters the code and takes the stairs to the second floor, where she rings the bell.

Petter welcomes her in.

He is wearing a dark grey flannel shirt, hanging loose over his faded jeans.

Twelve years ago, he was a muscular man who shaved his head to hide the fact that he was going bald, and who frequently made sexist remarks. These days he is a divorced forty-seven-year-old who has stopped exercising and climbing the ranks at work, and weighs a little more with every year that passes.

He sets the coffee machine running in the kitchen and carries two chairs to the living room.

In the sloping afternoon light, the rows of small nail holes left behind when he removed the vinyl flooring are visible on the wooden floorboards.

'I sleep on the sofa when the boys are here,' he tells Saga.

'How old are they now?'

'Time flies . . . Milo is sixteen, about to start his first year of upper secondary, and Nelson is fourteen. They're both about this much taller than me now,' he says with a smile, holding his thumb and index finger around ten centimetres apart.

'Do you have them every other week?'

'Not much pans out the way we think it will, does it,' he says, slumping down onto the sofa.

Saga peers over to the window. There is a cactus on the black stone sill. The blinds are open, and the stained cords are full of knots.

'I know,' she says.

Someone rings the buzzer, and Saga goes to the hallway to let them in. Greta and Manvir don't even have time to take their shoes off before Joona arrives.

Petter sets out a box of biscuits, grabs the coffee pot from the kitchen and starts filling their cups.

'Did you just brush your teeth too?' Petter asks as he leans in towards Joona.

Neither Saga nor Joona feel like explaining the reason for the menthol scent as they tell the others about their trip to Forensics. Their words create a heavy atmosphere, but no one has anything to say; the pattern is exactly the same as in the previous murders.

Manvir lowers his cup to the saucer, and his forehead creases before he looks up at each of them in turn.

'We've lost every round to date, and that's something we'll have to live with for the rest of our lives,' he says. 'But we need to turn things around. The killer has to be stopped.'

'My assumption so far was that the killer picked his victims to put pressure on me,' says Saga. 'He's been following a set pattern, and everything has happened just like he said it would. It's like a clock that can't be stopped, but—'

'We can't think like that,' says Greta.

'But today Joona said something really interesting,' Saga continues. 'He said that if everything the killer says is true, then we should be asking why I'm the only one who can stop him.'

'And how,' Joona adds.

'I always thought he picked Saga at random,' says Petter, rubbing his stubbly chin, 'and then he raised the stakes by making it personal.'

'I think we all did,' says Saga. 'But maybe there's a concrete reason why I'm the only one who can stop him.'

'OK, let's run with that thought . . . What's special about you?' asks Manvir. 'What is it that's special about Saga?'

'She worked for the Security Service for years,' Petter begins.

'She's beautiful,' Greta adds.

'No other officer has suffered such great personal loss,' says Joona.

'I have a family history of mental illness,' Saga says quietly.

'You have an anonymous source that provides you with information,' Manvir continues, deep in thought.

'Yes.' Saga nods.

'Is that really true?' asks Greta.

'Yes, it is.'

'Could your source be the reason you're the only one able to stop the killer?'

'No, I really don't think so . . .'

'Anything else?' asks Manvir.

'She survived her interactions with Jurek,' says Joona.

'I don't know about that,' Saga mutters.

'What do you mean?' Greta asks with a smile.

'I fell into a deep depression after my sister died,' she replies, her lips and cheeks turning pale. 'I couldn't cope with the idea of her being alone and afraid during the last few days of her life.'

'Valeria was with her the whole time, she talked to her,' Joona says comfortingly.

'Valeria? Come on,' Saga snorts.

'I'm just saying . . .'

'What the hell did she do?' Saga asks, raising her voice slightly.

'She talked to her, kept her calm and—'

'Kept her calm until she died? She could've saved Pellerina if she'd just—'

'I think she tried,' Joona interrupts her.

'She was there, for fuck's sake. Clearly she didn't try hard enough,' Saga shouts, getting up from the sofa. 'My sister is dead and Valeria is still alive. My sister is in a fucking grave, nothing but a pile of bones.'

'You know that Valeria was a victim too,' Joona replies, remaining composed.

'What, like you? Everyone's a victim, everyone's had a tough time . . . Go fuck yourself.'

Saga leaves the room, storming out into the hallway and slamming the front door behind her. Joona gets up and goes out onto the balcony Petter shares with his neighbour. He leans back against the corrugated metal wall dividing the space and gazes down at the street, towards the corner shop. Above a row of small basement windows at pavement level, there are a number of posters advertising grocery store sales.

Joona catches the scent of old cigarette butts from a can on the floor and finds himself being carried back to Laila's opium den.

The warm vapour filled his lungs and she rolled the next ball and his thoughts drifted along like a sluggish river, flowing around rocks and low-hanging branches.

When Joona remembers thinking about Valeria's glittering silver necklace, he finally manages to grab hold of the thought that has been evading him ever since, and he makes his way back into the living room.

'What's going on?' Greta asks when she sees his face.

'Saga's list, the alternative list of serial killers Jurek Walter might have been interested in,' he says. 'It's just a thought, but Jakov Fauster was known as the Silversmith of Berlin in the press.'

'I didn't know that,' says Greta.

'Am I missing something?' asks Petter.

'You're making a connection between Fauster's nickname and the fact that our killer makes metal figurines?' Greta continues.

'Yes.'

'We're just trying to find a link to the killer that isn't intentional, that's not part of his plan, his game,' Joona attempts to explain. 'I never bothered looking into Fauster while Jurek was still alive, he'd been in prison for decades and had never been granted leave.'

'But Jurek could have visited him . . . and our killer, the Predator, he could have visited him too,' says Greta.

'Why was he known as the Silversmith?' asks Manvir.

'He blinded his victims with molten silver and then left them on the train tracks around Berlin,' says Joona.

'But silver and tin figurines?' Manvir sounds sceptical.

'It's too much of a stretch,' Petter agrees.

'Too flimsy,' Manvir sighs. 'Let's focus on the killer's logic in terms of—'

'The name on postcard number two,' Joona cuts him off. 'It was . . .'

'Jesu Fatvarok?' says Petter.

'That's an anagram of Jakov Fauster.'

'Shit,' Petter whispers.

'Where is Fauster in prison?' asks Greta.

'Santa Fu,' replies Joona. 'Fuhlsbüttel.'

'Which is near Hamburg,' Manvir fills in.

'I need to speak to him,' says Joona, getting to his feet.

43

Valeria leaves the greenhouse and pushes the wheelbarrow over to the root cellar. Her shoulders and back feel weary after a hard day's work. She just needs to grab a few bags of potatoes, then she will call it a day and head inside to shower and make dinner.

The root cellar has been dug out of a natural hump in the ground, with meadow grasses and slender birches growing overhead. For some reason, the cool space has always reminded her of the story of King Sveigðir from the Old Norse *Ynglinga Saga*. King Sveigðir was on his way home after a party when a strange little man turned up and told him he could meet Odin. The man opened a door in an enormous rock, and the king peered in to a great hall on the other side. The table was laden with heaping plates of food, and there were huge chandeliers hanging from the ceiling. But the minute he set foot inside, the door swung shut behind him and he disappeared without a trace.

Valeria opens the heavy door, grabs the gardening basket and starts making her way down the steep set of stairs.

A few strands of hair shimmer like copper in her ponytail as she moves through the last patch of sunlight and into the darkness.

She hasn't been down to the root cellar for a long time. She just hasn't been able to bring herself to do it since her encounter with Jurek. The stairs feel much more cramped than she remembers.

A completely different kind of silence seems take over no more than a couple of metres below the ground.

Valeria feels a bead of sweat trickle down her back, and the sweet scent of earth and old leaves fills her nose.

The ceiling light is switched on, glinting off the bottles of elder-flower cordial. A little dry sand falls from the crack between two of the stones lining the roof.

The weight of the ground above must have pushed the walls inward over the winter, making the stairs narrower.

She feels her legs shake as she continues.

The air is completely still.

The vents must be overgrown.

Valeria has almost reached the bottom of the steps when the ground above her shakes. The ceiling seems to drop by around ten centimetres, and dry sand rains down to the floor.

Someone must be standing right above her.

A couple of small pebbles clatter against the bottom step, and her blood starts roaring in her ears.

The stale air has left her light-headed, and she decides she should turn around and head back up.

Valeria knows it is just the weak light, but the steps now look about as wide as a rabbit's burrow.

At the top, the doorway gleams like brass. She hears the hinges creak, sees the sliver of light narrow, and the door swings shut.

Valeria drops the basket and tries to hold back the walls with both hands.

Her breathing is quick.

Her vision goes dark, and she slumps to the floor.

The door opens again, and she hears a man's voice say something. She peers up and sees a slim silhouette.

'Hello?'

The figure comes down the stairs towards her.

'Are you hurt?'

He helps her onto her feet and practically carries her up the stairs; her gloves fall off at some point along the way.

The stranger helps her sit down on the grassy slope, and Valeria takes a deep breath, raising her face to the pale sky overhead as she rubs her mouth.

'I don't know what happened, I just got a bit dizzy,' she says.

The man holds out a large bouquet of flowers and a shiny heart-shaped balloon on a string.

'Interflora. I'd just pulled up,' he says, pointing over to a van in the turning circle, 'and I saw you go down there.'

'Thanks.'

'Are you going to be OK?'

'Absolutely.'

'If you're sure. I'll be off, then.'

Valeria remains where she is with the flowers and the balloon, watching as the man drives away.

She knows she should probably seek help for her claustrophobia, but her feelings of guilt for what happened always get in the way. Joona has brought it up on a number of occasions, told her that she is traumatised to such a degree that she needs professional help, but she refuses to feel sorry for herself.

The red glow of the sunset is reflected in the glass on the greenhouses, making it seem as though they are full of lava.

Valeria's legs are still shaking as she gets up and makes her way over to the house. She hangs her work clothes up in the mud room, lathers her hands and rinses them clean in the big metal sink.

The string of the balloon is tied to a weight, preventing it from floating up to the ceiling when she lets go of it. Now wearing nothing but her underwear, she carries everything to the kitchen and puts the flowers down on the bench. She tears off the paper and puts it on the stack of newspapers and flyers beside the woodpile.

Joona has sent her twenty-five red roses.

On the card, the shop assistant has written the words 'Forgive me, darling Valeria' in rounded letters.

She trims the roses with a kitchen knife and puts them into a vase on the dining table.

Valeria then heads upstairs and gets into the shower, standing under the hot jets until she is warm again. She dries herself off and pulls on some clean clothes.

She makes her way back down to the kitchen and gets to work making potato soup. Once it is simmering away, she grabs her phone and sits down at the table, gazing out through the window for a moment before dialling Joona's number.

'Thank you for the flowers, they're beautiful,' she says.

'I'm sorry. I've been such an idiot,' he says. 'I've hurt you and made a mess of things just because I didn't want to seem weak.'

'You can be weak around me.'

'But I don't want to, I want to be strong.'

'We all do.'

'That's why I convinced myself that I'm in control of the drugs, but it's not true.'

'I know, I've been there.'

She hears him take a deep breath.

'I realised today that I'd let the drugs hinder the investigation, that I'd forgotten all about a key insight I'd had. I just had to admit it to myself . . . and then I also realised what I'd done to you, to us.'

'Good,' she says, drying her tears.

'I have to fly to Germany as soon as they've given me the green light, but can I call you after I get back?'

'I'm not going anywhere, Joona.'

* * *

Joona looks down at the phone in his hand and whispers 'thank you' before turning back to the kitchen table where he has all the material about the Silversmith of Berlin spread out in front of him: court transcripts, photographs, newspaper cuttings and maps marking out the crime scenes.

He knows he needs to eat if he is going to be able to focus, but he just doesn't have the energy to cook. Joona opens the fridge and finds half a sandwich on a plate. He eats it standing, then rinses off the plate and turns his attention back to the material.

He needs to try to find out whether there is any connection between the German serial killer and his Swedish counterpart. Fauster could be their perpetrator's link to both Jurek and the tin figurines.

Twenty-eight years ago, the hunt for the killer known as der Silberschmied aus Berlin entered a new and intensive phase, and Jakov Fauster was ultimately arrested at his home in eastern Berlin. During the trial, he refused to answer any questions unless addressed as 'Master', but once that demand was met he went into great detail about the ten young men he had murdered.

Using personal ads, Master Fauster got in touch with a number of men, the majority of whom were also sex workers. He claimed to be rich and generous, and arranged to meet them in empty car parks, where he drugged them in his van and used molten silver to burn out their eyes. After blinding his victims, he took them to various rail lines around the city and then watched from a distance as they were hit by trains.

Fauster was sentenced to life in prison, and spent two years in Moabit before being transferred to a new specialist unit at Fuhlsbüttel Prison in northern Hamburg.

Joona drinks a glass of water and has just started skimming through a psychiatric evaluation of Fauster when Manvir calls.

'We're in luck – if that's the right word. Sabine Stern, the governor of Fuhlsbüttel, knew Verner . . . She was extremely upset when I told her what had happened and she said you were welcome to visit. You'll have an opportunity to speak to Fauster, though there are no guarantees he'll actually answer any of your questions . . . or talk to you at all.'

'I'll book the tickets now,' says Joona.

'There was one more thing that I . . . that I feel I need to bring up. Are you alone?' asks Manvir, breathing heavily through his nose.

'Yes.'

Joona moves over to the window and gazes out at the city. A grid of pale grey, silver, black and light green rooftops. The sound of people and traffic on the streets down below doesn't reach this high.

'Greta and I were talking and we . . . We've been wondering about Saga's role in all this,' he continues.

'She loses her temper sometimes, but it'll pass.'

'That's not what I meant.'

'OK . . .?'

'She's a very good police officer,' says Manvir, pausing to clear his throat.

'Yes.'

'Maybe even a bit *too* good . . . She's always one step ahead, and she has that "secret contact". The entire case revolves around her, as we discussed at the last meeting.'

'Yes, because the killer has been communicating with her.'

'She knows all the victims, has actually been in conflict with every single one of them . . . I wouldn't be doing my job if I didn't ask whether she might be involved.'

'In the murders?'

'Not physically, of course – she has an alibi for each of them, but . . . She could be working with someone, which might explain why we're always playing catch up. The game is rigged.'

'It's a good thought. Brave. But there's no way.'

'How can you be so sure?'

'I can't, but—'

'She has a motive. If Valeria isn't to blame for her sister dying, then the police are, Verner and Margot. And, ultimately, you.'

'But I know Saga and—'

'It's good that you're so loyal, Joona,' Manvir interrupts him. 'But we've begun an investigation into her – classified, of course. Just so you know.'

44

Joona catches the first flight of the day to Hamburg. The plane was almost fully booked, but he managed to find a seat at the very rear, where the engines are at their loudest and he is last to be served.

A blanket of sun-kissed clouds blocks out the cities, forests, fields and lakes down below.

He has gone through all of the material on Master Fauster and is now thinking about the Predator, about the way the little tin figurines in their makeshift wrappers are a kind of precursor to the bodies in rubber bags.

Once they land, Joona clears passport control and catches a taxi straight to the prison complex. His car pulls up outside the entrance just fifteen minutes later.

The sky is bright and the air cool as he makes his way inside and reports to the desk.

Low planes thunder constantly overhead.

Fuhlsbüttel is a mix of handsome nineteenth century brick and more modern, sterile buildings, complete with high walls, barbed wire, secure zones and electric fencing. The oldest parts of the complex were first brought into use towards the end of the nineteenth century, and later became both a Nazi concentration camp and a Gestapo prison.

Today, Santa Fu is a modern facility for men serving long-term sentences.

Joona passes through security and a short woman in a grey suit comes out to meet Joona. She looks somewhere around fifty, with a pretty but sad face, heavy eyelids and short blonde hair.

'Good morning. I'm the warden, Sabine Stern,' she says in English, holding out her hand.

'Joona Linna.'

'Did you know Verner well?'

'Yes, I did.'

'He was a wonderful man.'

She opens a secure door and they take a set of stairs down to the underground walkway connecting the various parts of the prison.

'I'll be sitting in on your interview; I've blocked out the whole morning,' Sabine tells him as they walk.

'Thank you, but that isn't necessary.'

She flashes him a brief smile.

'You don't know Master Fauster. He'll start negotiating before he even agrees to talk to you. He never gives up anything for free.'

'What does he want?'

'Things you can't offer him, most likely.'

'But you can?'

'I'm prepared to make certain concessions if it will help you catch Verner's killer.'

Their footsteps echo between the bare concrete walls. The air is cool and the glow of the inset light fixtures every three or so metres paints a viper-like pattern on the floor.

'His sentence also stipulates the high level of security here at Fuhlsbüttel, which is incredibly rare in Germany. That's why he is in our wing for extremely dangerous prisoners who are likely to try to escape – even though our experts all agree that he has responded well to prison and could be capable of readjusting to life in society.'

'Really?'

'Yes, but considering the nature and extent of his crimes, his life sentence hasn't yet been commuted to a specific time-limited period . . . which gives us the upper hand in any negotiations.'

They pause by a barrier and wait for the central security office to let them through. The door whirrs and swings open, allowing them to move forward into the space on the other side. Once the door behind them is locked, a door to their right opens and they turn the corner.

'The level of security is clearly high, but if I've understood correctly Fauster isn't in isolation?' says Joona.

'He's allowed to interact with the other inmates, but he chooses to spend most of his time alone. He has never been granted leave, but he can send letters, book slots to use the phone – all under supervision, of course – and he is also allowed visitors.'

'Does he ever get any?'

'Quite regularly, yes. Most are journalists, criminologists and representatives from various religious groups . . . When he was younger he actually used to get a lot of visits from women wanting to start a relationship with him.'

Sabine Stern explains that, to date, there haven't been any escape or rescue attempts on the secure unit. All doors are controlled from a central office, and in the event of a hostage situation the protocol is to keep them locked regardless of whose life is at stake.

The entire unit is fifteen metres below ground and has its own separate break yard in an internal courtyard, separated from the outside world by three layers of bars and fencing.

They continue down a staircase and along another corridor.

On the bare concrete wall, the words HEISSE WARE AUS DEM KNAST are written in large red letters.

They pause in front of another door marked ABTEILUNG 9.

The lock whirrs, and they move forward into another corridor, passing a staff room, a pantry kitchen and a surveillance room full of TV monitors.

The walls are pale yellow, the plastic flooring speckled like granite and the furniture all varnished pine.

The steel doors to the inmates' rooms are painted white, with hatches and peep holes.

Sabine pauses and pushes back the sleeve of her jacket to check the time.

'Master Fauster is already waiting in the visitors' room, but I thought you might like to see his cell first,' she says, opening a door.

Joona enters the cramped space. The curtains are drawn over a nook where the light comes from a lamp rather than a window. The toilet has armrests, the table is bolted to the floor, and the bed has been adapted for someone with limited mobility.

'He speaks eight languages,' the warden says, nodding to a bookshelf full of classical literature and philosophy.

They head back out into the corridor, past the showers and over to a man standing guard outside a blue door.

He says hello and then lets them inside, locking the door behind them once they are on the other side.

It's hard to believe that the man in prison issue clothing sitting at the table inside is the same one known as the Silversmith of Berlin during his active phase almost thirty years ago.

His plump hands and thick fingers are resting on the table in front of him, handcuffs looped beneath a metal bar on the table.

A red line has been painted on the floor, indicating a safe distance from the prisoner.

On the near side of the line, two chairs are tucked beneath a smaller table fitted with an alarm button and a plexiglass screen.

Jakov Fauster is severely overweight, with thick bottle glasses, a broad forehead, light brown hair and short sideburns. His double chin obscures his entire neck, and he has rounded shoulders, fat arms and an enormous stomach.

'Master Fauster,' says Sabine.

'Frau Stern,' he replies, gesturing to one of the chairs.

'This is Detective Superintendent Linna,' she says in English.

'Who is trying to catch a serial killer in Sweden. I may be able to help you with that, but what are you going to give me in return? How much are those Swedish lives worth?' he asks, turning his attention to Joona for the first time.

Sabine's clothes give off a soft lavender scent as she takes a seat. Master Fauster leans back slowly, and the reflection of the ceiling light in his glasses obscures his eyes.

'You'll have to negotiate with me,' says Sabine.

Fauster's narrow mouth curls into a smile, and he points one of his chubby fingers at her.

'So this is personal,' he says.

244

45

Joona pulls out a chair and sits down beside Sabine. The small plexiglass screen is streaked where someone has rubbed it with a damp cloth. Master Fauster is breathing heavily through his open mouth, his tongue glistening behind his small, gapped teeth.

'What can I do for you?' asks Sabine.

The handcuffs clink as Fauster places both palms on the table and leans forward.

'The shock of everything being laid bare in the courtroom led the judge to talk about a particularly heinous crime,' he replies in a neutral voice. 'They found me guilty of more crimes than might have been expected. I can understand that, the witness testimony was extremely powerful, but the words "sexually deviant tendencies" suggest notions of purity that I find old fashioned.'

He pauses, his eyes locked onto her, breathing through his half-open mouth as though he is short of breath.

'I think,' says Sabine, clearing her throat. 'I think we could discuss a recommendation to have your sentence commuted to a fixed term.'

Fauster is still staring straight at her.

'I want it changed to five years' probation followed by complete release, in line with Section 57a of the penal code.'

'That would be a rather big step,' she replies, failing to manage a smile. 'But I've read all of the assessments around your progress, and I think it could be time.'

Master Fauster stretches his right hand as far as the clinking cuffs will allow. Sabine gets up, glances over to Joona and then slowly crosses the red line. Fauster's face is focused, expectant. She pauses, leans in over his table and gives him her hand.

'Cold fingers, high heart rate,' he says as he lets go.

His eyes follow Sabine as she makes her way back over to her chair and sits down with her ankles crossed and her hands in her lap.

'What do you have to say, Detective Superintendent Linna?' Fauster continues, turning to Joona. 'If I'm going to help you, I want a written statement confirming that what I have done for the Swedish police reinforces Frau Stern's opinion that my sentence should be reduced to probation.'

'Does that mean you can help me?' Joona asks, holding Fauster's blue-eyed gaze. He can see the man searching for weaknesses in him.

'Yes.'

'Then I'll write your statement.'

'Did you hear that, Frau Stern?'

'I did.'

'That's worth five questions,' Fauster says with what almost looks like a jovial smile.

'Good,' Joona replies.

Fauster sits up straight, spreads his knees and places both feet squarely on the floor. His green trousers ride up a little. He is wearing a pair of grey orthopaedic slippers and compression socks, which are tight around his powerful calves.

'A detective from Astrid Lindgren country,' he says. 'Do you have any idea what you've got yourself into by coming to see me?'

'What do you mean?' asks Joona.

'Do you know anything about me? Who I am. Do you? Have you read my file?'

'Yes.'

'So, what is my psyche like? What do you see? I want to know who I'm talking to.'

'I see sexually motivated violence without any direct sexual abuse,' Joona begins. 'The files described someone with a narcissistic person-ality, delusions of grandeur, but I also see someone who creates rules and sticks to them in an attempt to avoid feeling lost.'

'Why should my deeds have been sexually motivated?'

'The victims were almost all male sex workers, and the violence centred around the anus, genitals and face.'

'Did it?' Fauster asks, his face cracking into such a wide grin that his stubby little teeth are visible again.

'According to the forensic report,' Joona replies.

'But they weren't there when it happened, were they? Isn't that the case, that everyone but me is simply guessing?'

'Of course,' Sabine attempts to chip in.

The corners of Master Fauster's mouth curl downwards, and his eyes harden behind his thick lenses.

'I have no sexual feelings towards boys.'

'He didn't say you—'

'Just look at my first, Kemal. What can we say about him? He was ugly and stupid, spoke terrible German. He had a snotty nose, dirt under his nails and around his throat, behind his ears . . . His body started shaking and he promised me all sorts of things, said he would suck my penis . . . I couldn't help but laugh, because I'd already poured silver into one of his eyes by that point; it shrivelled and disappeared as though it had never been there in the first place. He shat himself and pulled so hard on the ropes that there was blood trickling down his arms, almost like he was Jesus.'

Fauster leans back in his chair with a smile, though his fists are still tightly clenched. Sabine's face has turned pale, and her pupils have widened.

'I distance myself from all that today, of course. I'm a changed man,' he explains in a soft voice.

'That's good,' says Joona.

'I've had a lot of help over the years.'

Joona has studied the map of Fauster's ten murders around Berlin. The first victim, Kemal Ünver, was only nineteen when he died. Drugged and blind, he was left on S2 line between Karow and Buch, right at the point where the tracks pass beneath the A10 ring road. He was conscious at the time, crying out for help, and had sat up as the train approached.

'It was interesting, what you said earlier,' Fauster says, looking Joona straight in the eye. 'About me creating rules and sticking to them in order to avoid feeling lost.'

'Isn't that the case?'

'I've only ever thought of it as evening out the odds a little through a distinctive modus operandi. Keeping the excitement alive even when I felt utterly superior.'

'And yet here you are.'

'I was arrested by chance, which is slightly ironic,' says Fauster. 'I gave away all the pieces of the puzzle, but no one solved my riddle.'

'Why don't you tell us the answer now?'

'Because it no longer matters. And because I don't want anything to do with the person I was back then. What I did was terrible, but I wasn't well; I thought they were staring at me, I saw things.'

'Let's move on,' says Joona. 'Because the case I want to talk about still matters, and it's incredibly urgent.'

'I hope you're right that I can help.'

Joona pulls his chair across the red line on the floor, right over to Master Fauster's table, then sits down and starts telling him about their ongoing hunt for the killer in Sweden. He makes no mention of the find sites and lies that all of the victims have been women, but otherwise sticks to the truth and brings up the tin figurines that reveal who the next victim will be.

'Allow me to be perfectly honest,' Fauster says once Joona stops speaking. 'I don't know much, but I know much more than you.'

'What?'

'You suspect there might be a link between the Silversmith and the figurines?'

'Among other theories,' Joona replies.

'It's the Spider's way of saying thank you,' says Fauster.

'The Spider?'

'The little spider,' he replies with a restrained smile. 'I only receive visitors who pay their way, but when I discovered the Spider had just been released from the psychiatric unit in Ytterö, claiming she needed me as a mentor . . . well, naturally I was curious. She came to see me, pulled her chair over just like you have, and explained that she was planning nine murders and wanted to learn the craft from the foremost living serial killer in Europe. I asked her whether she considered Gilles de Rais to be the greatest of all time.'

'But she said Jurek Walter,' says Joona.

'Precisely, because his darkness is unparalleled. But it was me who taught her how the police think, how forensic technology works. How to avoid mistakes and how to shape the game. We aren't pyromaniacs; we don't let the fire burn out of control. We are the fire.'

'Do you know her name?'

'Yes, but you've already had your five questions.'

'I've only asked two,' Joona replies, though he knows it is futile.

'You started by asking what I meant when I wondered whether a detective from the land of Astrid Lindgren knew what he was getting into by coming to see me, and four more followed,' Fauster says, turning to Sabine. 'I'm done here, I'd like to go back to my cell now.'

'Give him the name,' she says.

Joona is still sitting right in front of Fauster, so close that he can smell his breath and the musty scent of old fabric.

'This conversation is being recorded, and he promised me a letter in which he acknowledges my help.'

'You'll get your letter,' says Joona.

'You should write that you think my sentence should be commuted to probation.'

'I can't do that.'

'What?' Fauster smiles.

'Because you're going to kill again.'

'You can't do this!' Fauster protests, raising his voice. 'Frau Stern, he can't break a binding agreement.'

'I've solved your riddle,' Joona says calmly.

Fauster immediately calms down, slumping back in his chair and meeting the detective's grey eyes.

'You can't have,' he says.

'You still have two murders left.'

'Stop it,' Fauster mumbles, swallowing hard.

'I've studied the maps. The tracks where you left Kemal, between Karow and Buch, lead north-north east,' Joona begins. 'Victim two was left on a north-eastern stretch between Babelsberg and Griebnitzsee, victim three on a track heading due east . . .'

'I don't understand,' Sabine whispers.

Master Fauster sighs and closes his eyes, sweat trickling down his cheeks.

'The various tracks correspond to the numbers on a clock, and you'd only made it to ten o'clock when the police stormed your apartment.'

'Oh God,' says Sabine.

'And the reason you want to be released is so that you can finish the sequence with numbers eleven and twelve,' Joona rounds off.

Fauster opens his eyes and stares straight at Joona. 'Who are you?' he mumbles.

46

Saga is sitting at one of the high tables in the lunch room on the eighth floor of the station. The noodles in the plastic bowl in front of her have no flavour whatsoever, but she still finishes them off and sips the warm stock.

At the bottom of the pot, the flavouring has formed a sticky paste, and she pushes the end of one of her chopsticks into it. She lifts it to her mouth and gets a sense of what the noodles were supposed to taste like at last: lemongrass, Szechuan pepper and salt.

Saga tosses the bowl into the bin, wipes the table and hangs the dishcloth over the tap, then glances up at the clock. Forcing back her unease about the meeting, she makes her way over to Manvir's office, knocks and opens the door.

'Come in, take a seat,' he says. 'Greta is on her way. Sit wherever you like.'

'Have you heard from Joona?'

'Not yet,' Manvir replies, typing something on his keyboard.

Saga takes a seat in one of the floral armchairs.

She has no idea why she has been called in to a meeting, but she hopes it could be something to do with her application. Deep down, she is praying that Manvir will grant her operative clearance. That would mean she could tell the rest of the team about Karl Speler and his friends; she could bring them in for a formal interview.

A dead potted plant with a small greeting card hanging from one of its dry stalks has been left in a recycling box on the floor.

Greta comes into the room and closes the door behind her.

'Sorry I'm late,' she says as she sits down in the other armchair.

'Do you know why we've called this meeting today?' Manvir asks, turning to Saga.

'No.'

'OK. We have a few questions we . . .'

He trails off and rolls back in his desk chair, studying her with a frown as he continues.

'You're on the verge of being given a permanent position here, as an operative detective inspector,' he continues.

'I can hardly believe it,' Saga says with a smile.

'But despite the fact that you aren't currently employed here, you're at the very centre of the biggest murder investigation we've ever worked.'

'Yes.'

'How can that be?'

'I don't understand the question,' Saga tells him. 'Before I officially work here, you mean?'

'Yes,' Manvir nods.

'Because the killer has been communicating directly with me.'

'And why is that?' Greta asks, leaning forward.

'We've already talked about this,' Saga replies, trying to read their faces.

'Yes, but it's not just the fact that he only communicates with you,' Greta continues. 'You also have an anonymous source who gives you, and only you, information.'

'Would you mind telling me what this is about?' asks Saga.

'You've been incredibly observant as an investigator,' says Manvir. 'You've managed to see through the killer's riddles at lightning speed, and—'

'Not like Joona,' Saga butts in.

'But his logic, his thought processes, they always make sense to me afterwards,' says Manvir.

'Whereas with you, it's as though you suddenly just know the answer,' Greta fills in.

'No, I . . . You know what it's like,' Saga attempts to explain. 'Sometimes I just guess based on what I've seen. Sometimes it's more logical, and sometimes I've had help from a source I promised to keep anonymous.'

'You're often right, down to the last detail, and yet we still haven't managed to catch the killer . . .' says Manvir.

'Don't you think that's strange?' asks Greta.

'I'm going to leave if you don't tell me what you're getting at. What the hell are you trying to suggest? Just say what you want to say!'

A number of red, agitated blotches have started to flare up on her forehead.

'Your fingerprints were found on the platform at Kymlinge station,' says Manvir, pushing a report over to her.

'Am I suspected of something here?' Saga asks, ignoring the file.

'We're just wondering if there's anything you want to tell us,' says Greta, right as Manvir's phone starts ringing.

'It's Joona,' he says, answering the call and switching to loudspeaker. 'Hi, Joona. I've got Greta and Saga with me here.'

'I'm on the plane home. It all happened so fast,' says Joona. 'They gave me a police escort back to the airport to make sure I didn't miss the next flight.'

His voice grows faint, and they hear the mechanical roar of the engines in the background.

'They probably just wanted to see the back of you,' Greta jokes.

'The captain gave me permission to make one call before we come in for landing.'

'Did you speak to Jakov Fauster?' asks Manvir.

'Yes, I did, and Saga was right, but—'

'What a surprise,' Manvir mutters.

'What was that?'

'Nothing.'

'In any case, we've got a breakthrough,' says Joona. 'Our killer is a woman who went to visit Fauster. She used a false ID, but he called her the Spider, said she'd been a patient at the secure psychiatric unit in Ytterö and that . . . she went to see him to learn how to carry out nine murders without being stopped. I think the way she strings up her victims in rubber bags is supposed to represent the way a spider dissolves its prey in its web.'

Saga leaps up from the armchair.

'But we still don't have a name?' asks Greta.

'No, but . . . OK, sorry, I have to go. I'll call you back as soon as I can.'

The room is silent once he hangs up. Manvir lowers his phone to the desk and then looks up at Saga.

'Sit down,' he says.

'But we need to look into this,' she protests.

'And we will, soon.'

She sits down in the armchair, sighs and turns her attention to the pine filing cabinet, studying the pattern of fingerprints around the lock.

'We still need answers from you,' says Greta.

'About what?' Saga snaps, meeting her eye. 'I happened to touch a bracket on the wall in Kymlinge, I was about to pass out . . . I'm pretty sure Joona saw me do it, he probably just forgot to say anything.'

'We're not accusing you of anything, Saga, but . . . we're just doing our due diligence,' says Greta. 'We need to know if you've helped the killer in any way.'

Saga stares at Greta and her blood runs cold. 'What?'

'The killer seems to know a lot about the way we work, about crime scene technology and so on,' says Greta.

'Have you supported the killer in any way?' asks Manvir.

'What are you talking about? Joona just said—'

'You might have tried some sort of infiltration on your own, for example, and been forced to give up information?'

'No,' Saga snaps.

'OK, well, now we know.'

Saga gets up again, and she realises her back is damp with sweat.

'Joona said that our killer is a woman,' says Greta, looking up at her.

'Seems that way,' Saga replies, unable to stop herself from smirking at the bizarre situation.

'Do you know who the woman is?'

'It's not me, if that's what you're asking.'

'No, we know that, but were you responsible for picking out the victims?' asks Manvir.

'What?'

'Each one of them is someone you knew, someone whom you had some reason to dislike.'

'Enough,' says Saga, her voice dark, attempting to keep her breathing steady.

'Try and see this from our point of view,' says Manvir.

'Why aren't you asking Joona these questions?' asks Saga. 'He had issues with both Margot and Verner, he works things out on his own.

He was the one who linked the tin figurines to the Silversmith, who solved the anagram and—'

'Because we're not talking about Joona right now,' Greta interrupts her.

'I just think this is really fucking stupid, honestly.'

'But is it, really?'

'It's our job to ask these questions,' says Manvir.

'OK, but I don't care if—'

'And since you don't seem to understand the gravity of this, I'm suspending your temporary position with us,' he says.

'I'm trying to answer your questions, but it feels like you've already made up your minds. You know what? Go fuck yourselves,' Saga shouts, marching out of the room.

47

Joona hurries through the arrivals hall, over the bridge and into the parking garage. When he gets to his car, he jumps behind the wheel and tears off towards Ytterö.

His phone starts ringing, and he presses a button on the console to answer. It is the director of the prison, Sabine Stern. She thanks Joona for his visit, and he thanks her for giving him the opportunity to speak to Jakov Fauster.

They both fall silent.

'I'd heard a lot about you before your visit,' she eventually tells him. 'And I want you to know that Fauster will never be released.'

'It's hard to believe he'll ever change,' says Joona.

'No. I did a little digging after you left, and I spoke to Herbert, who was the warden here before me. Once I came out and asked him directly about Fauster, he told me about an incident that had been hushed up the year before he retired. During a private conversation, one of the guards apparently confessed to being pressured into helping Fauster escape . . .'

'Pressured by who?'

'I don't have any names, but the guard said it was a terrible man . . . that he was like death itself.'

Joona thanks her and ends the call. He tries to get through to Saga, but she doesn't pick up.

He drives through central Stockholm, heading south towards Farsta.

The sky is pale, a light rain falling.

Joona calls Manvir and takes him through his meeting in Germany in detail, telling him that Sabine Stern hadn't found any Swedish women in their visitor records, which means that their perpetrator used a fake ID.

He rounds off by mentioning the conversation he just had with Sabine, in which she told him that Jurek really had tried to help Fauster escape from prison.

'Just like Saga said,' says Manvir.

'I'm on my way to the psychiatric unit in Ytterö now.'

'And we'll finally find out the Spider's name.'

Joona finds himself thinking that they started calling the killer the Predator because of the way in which victims are approached and attacked. It feels almost menacingly accurate, because spiders are incredibly effective predators.

Forty-five minutes later, Joona is driving through the forest on the shore of Lake Magelungen, past two red tennis courts and into the parking area outside a large brick complex.

The psychiatric unit in Ytterö is a secure facility with space for twenty-eight adults.

Joona gets out of the car and walks over to the main entrance, pressing the buzzer and explaining through the intercom that he needs to speak to the presiding doctor in charge.

Around ten minutes later, a man in loose clothing and well-worn clogs appears on the other side of the door. He cracks it open slightly.

'You wanted to speak to someone, was that right?'

Joona pulls the door open and moves past the man, into the deserted reception area with its empty armchairs and glossy pamphlets on the tables.

'Do you have an appointment?'

Joona turns around, takes out his ID and holds it up.

'Who's the attending doctor here?' he asks.

'I don't actually know. Jensen has gone home for the day, but we've got a psychologist, an occupational therapist and a physiotherapist.'

'I'll try the psychologist.'

'Good choice,' says the man, turning and walking away.

Joona tries calling Saga again. He moves over to the fire escape chart as he listens to the phone ring. The complex seems to consist of four interlinked buildings, laid out in a horseshoe around a small park.

Joona glances up at the clock as a lock clicks and a thin haired man with pockmarked cheeks comes over to him. He is wearing brown corduroy trousers and a blue cardigan, with a small personal alarm on a plastic chain around his neck. The name badge on his chest reads *Bror Jansson, Practitioner Psychologist.*

'Sorry about the wait, I got held up with an anxious patient.'

'No problem,' says Joona, handing over his ID card.

'I'm afraid we don't have any free beds at the moment,' Bror jokes.

'Not even for a weary detective?'

'We might be able to make an exception, just this once,' says the psychologist, handing Joona's ID back to him.

'I need your help with some information about a former patient.'

'We have strict rules about patient safety and confidentiality here, though I'm assuming you already know that?'

'We're way past that point.'

Bror opens a door and shows Joona into the secure unit.

They walk down a corridor with large windows out onto an enclosed garden. The raindrops seem to be swarming beneath the glowing lamps, dripping from the leaves. Bror unlocks the door to the psychologists' spacious office.

'Coffee, tea, water?'

'No, thank you.'

Bror takes a seat behind the desk, and Joona pulls out the visitor's chair and sits down opposite him.

'A former patient, you said?' says Bror, putting on his glasses.

'I don't know her name, but she was likely discharged around three years ago,' says Joona.

'OK, that's before my time. But the majority of our patients are men, so we should be able to find her.'

'She may have called herself the Spider.'

'Doesn't ring any bells, but let me see what we've got,' Bror replies, logging in to the computer. 'We transitioned to a new patient record system last year . . . We still have copies of all the old files, of course, but it's a bit messy.'

Joona gazes out the window to the grey water of the lake. A kayak glides by, leaving a perfect arrowhead wake.

'We discharged five female patients three years ago,' he says. 'Katarina Nordin, Jeanette Vogel, Anna-Maria Gomez, Mara Makarov, and Gerd Andersson—'

'Makarov,' Joona interrupts him.

'OK, let's see. She was nineteen when the police dropped her off at the hospital in Huddinge, undernourished and confused. They thought she must be undocumented. When she came to us, she was given a diagnosis of paranoid psychosis and . . . discharged two years later.'

'I need her entire file,' says Joona, convinced there is no way that the message on the postcard and the patient's surname can be a coincidence.

'That's everything. Other than the medication she was taking,' says Bror, clicking away.

'But she was here for almost two years, surely there must—'

'Hold on, it says here that . . . Oh, interesting. Sorry, it's just that she was part of the Sven-Ove Krantz group. That probably doesn't mean much to you, but it means all her sessions would have been filmed. Doctor Krantz got a huge research grant from the Karolinska Institute.'

'Is he here?'

'On leave. But the films are, they're filed here,' Bror says, gesturing to the fireproof cabinet by the bookshelf.

'Could you dig them out for me?'

'Of course.'

Bror pushes his glasses back onto the top of his head, gets up and moves over to the lead grey cabinet. He enters a long code, turns the knob and opens the door.

Joona gets up and follows him over. Every shelf inside the cabinet is divided into three smaller sections, with metal boxes bearing the patients' names and ID numbers on the edges.

'Here's Makarov,' says Bror.

He pulls out the box and lifts the lid. The corners of his mouth curl downwards oddly, and he turns to Joona and shows him that there is nothing inside.

'Check the others,' says Joona.

Bror opens box after box, comparing the ID number on the front with the hard drives and handwritten journals inside.

'They're all fine,' he says once he is done. 'It's just hers . . . Let me call my colleague, we split responsibilities.'

Bror heads back over to the desk, brings up a contact on his phone and pushes an earbud into one ear.

'Hi, it's Bror. Sorry for bothering you, but . . . OK, that's great. It's just that I've got a police officer here, and he wants to check some patient files, one of Krantz's patients . . . Hang on, how did you know that?'

He listens quietly for a moment, his face completely blank, and then he nods.

'I see . . . Thanks.'

'What did he say?' asks Joona.

Bror Jansson turns to Joona with a thoughtful look in his eyes.

'He says one of your colleagues was already here. A woman from the National Crime Unit turned up an hour ago, someone who "looked like a fairy tale princess". She took all the material on Mara Makarov.'

48

Standing in front of the silvery grey projection screen, Saga almost feels as though she is in the same room as the patient in the film.

The young woman is hunched up in the corner by the foot of the bed, both hands clamped over her ears. Every now and again, a slight shudder seems to pass through her.

She is wearing grey tracksuit bottoms with muddy knees and a T-shirt with the cover of ABBA's *Arrival* on the front. Her face is gaunt, and her dark, apathetic eyes are staring straight ahead. Her knotted hair looks dusty and her skin lifeless, the colour of concrete.

The ceiling light has a pink fabric shade, casting a warm glow around the little room. There is a mustard coloured rag rug on the pale yellow vinyl floor, the wallpaper has a subtle lily-of-the-valley print, and the little wooden bed is neatly made.

The sound of a chair being dragged across the floor makes the young woman shrink back away from the camera.

'Welcome to Ytterö, Mara,' a man's voice says from somewhere out of shot. 'My name is Sven-Ove Krantz, I'm a psychologist here. My colleague von Fersen, the one who admitted you, has diagnosed you as psychotic, code F60.0 in the ICD-10. But I don't care about any of that, I don't think of you as sick; I think you're misunderstood ... We're going to be seeing quite a lot of each other while you're here, and I hope we can work together to turn "misunderstood" into "understood".'

A shimmering string of saliva trickles from Mara's mouth.

The material Saga took from the psychiatric unit in Ytterö consists of three slim hard drives containing a number of high-resolution videos and a folder of handwritten notes.

The forms and journals describe her ongoing therapy, but not the content of her conversations with the psychologist. For the most part, they cover daily notes on medication, conversations about side effects and interactions, her weight curve and her relationships with the other patients.

The films consist of a number of relatively short sessions, recorded at one-month intervals: a kind of CBT conversation therapy between the psychologist and his assigned patient, Mara Makarov.

According to the handwritten journals, Sven-Ove Krantz's method is to listen to the patient and take their version of reality seriously, rather than questioning it or trying to talk them out of it.

If one of his patients is convinced that someone is listening in on everything they say, for example, Krantz would suggest playing loud music, sitting close together and chatting in hushed tones.

Saga's phone starts ringing. Glancing down at the screen, she sees that it is Joona and rejects the call.

In the video, the lights of a car passing by outside swing across the shot just as the second session begins.

The camera films Mara Makarov through the hatch in her door as she attempts to smash the window with the base of the floor lamp. She is stark naked, and her thin body is covered in cuts and bruises.

One of the walls behind her is streaked with spaghetti and tomato sauce.

Mara seems incredibly anxious, her body trembling as she shouts in Russian, her voice breaking over and over again.

There are two nurses in the room with her, trying to calm her down. She turns to them and her eyes widen, urine streaming down her slim thighs.

As they move closer, she lashes out with the lamp, but the two men manage to overpower her. They lower her to the floor and give her an intramuscular injection in one of her buttocks.

The recording stops abruptly, and when the footage starts again the camera is back on its tripod in Mara's room. Mara is tucked up in bed with a white bandage over one eye, staring blankly ahead through the other.

The food has been wiped from the wall, but the red sauce is still visible on the pale wallpaper.

'I know you want to get out of here, Mara, that you're afraid of being poisoned,' Sven-Ove Krantz begins. 'If it helps, we can taste your food before you start eating, I can do it, or one of the nurses ... but I'm afraid we can't discharge you. That has to be done in consultation with my colleague, you see, and he still considers you to be psychotic. Do you understand what I'm saying? It's going to be a little while before you're released, but until then you can talk to me. Let me know if there's anything I can do for you. I know you're tired right now. That's because you were given a sedative called Haldol. It isn't dangerous, but it will make you feel drowsy. I'll leave you to get some sleep.'

Saga hits pause and takes the psychologist's journal to the kitchen, flicking forward to the end of the document, to his comments after their final session and his notes on her discharge, attempting to work out where Mara could have gone.

The person Krantz describes towards the end is a composed young woman who is reconciled with her life story and her self image. She takes pride in her appearance, dresses properly and has plans to study mathematics.

'Who are you?' Saga whispers. 'Where did you go after you were discharged? And where are you now?'

* * *

Standing at the bench in her workshop, Mara Makarov rubs her face with both hands and flicks through a book on abstract algebra, circling a section on complex numbers with a red pen.

Hands shaking, she opens a tin of sweetcorn and scoops the kernels into her mouth with her fingers, drinking the murky liquid. She feels her stomach contract almost immediately, and gets down onto her knees to throw it all up into a bucket.

The woman on the concrete ramp by the loading bay has regained consciousness. She shouted and begged at first, but then she tried to compose herself and force back any hint of emotion from her voice.

'Listen to me,' she says now. 'I don't know why you're doing this ...'

Mara spits a gob of mucus and reaches into the bucket to pick out the pieces of corn, popping them into her mouth and chewing slowly.

'What happened to you?' the woman asks.

Mara pushes another few kernels into her mouth and gets to her feet, still chewing.

'Could I have some water? I'm really thirsty.'

The woman trails off, gasping as a wave of pain and anxiety overwhelms her.

Mara uses her arm to sweep the book and pens from the workbench, then picks up a blue plastic bottle and pours chlorine onto the surface, using a cloth to wipe it down.

'God,' the woman groans, panting for a moment before she attempts to go on. 'You hurt me. Do you want to talk about that? I've been shot . . . You shot me, a fellow human. I'm bleeding. I'm in a lot of pain.'

Mara opens a pack of sterile overalls and pulls them on along with a pair of latex gloves and a face mask. She then opens a drawer and takes out a plastic folder full of pages torn from library books. Using a scalpel, she cuts out a section of Botticelli's *Birth of Venus* and sets it down beside an old map of Roslagtull's fever hospital. She rummages through the folder and finds a text about the strength of spherical buildings, placing it third in her row.

'Have you noticed that my pain and fear have no bearing on your own pain and fear?' the woman asks between shallow breaths. 'But I think . . . I think that if you help me, if you take me to hospital, everything will change for the better, you'll feel a sense of relief. Don't you agree?'

Mara moves over to one side and tosses the scalpel, gloves and overalls into the drum for combustible waste.

'Because if you help someone, you also open yourself up to help. Are you listening? Everyone needs help. None of us is alone, even if it feels that way sometimes . . . It's not too late for you to change direction.'

Mara bends down and picks up the scalpel again. She presses the blade to the nail of her left index finger, cutting a deep gash and allowing the pain to fill her.

For the first time, Mara turns to the woman on the ramp. She is lying flat on her back, looking up at the overhead crane on the ceiling. Her breathing is shallow, fitful. The bullet missed her spine, passing straight through her gut and exiting by her navel. Her blood trickles down the ramp beneath her, past her feet and into the drain down below.

Mara climbs up onto the heavy tool cabinet, crouches down and studies the material on the workbench. She shakes the blood from her hand and watches as the droplets fly through the air and land on the floor.

It's time to put on the mask and protective gloves, she thinks. Open the bag of sodium hydroxide, scoop out fifteen litres of pellets and dissolve them in a small amount of water.

'Please, listen to me,' says the woman, no longer capable of hiding the fear in her voice. 'I don't want to die, I don't deserve to die, regardless of what you've been through.'

Mara climbs back down to the floor and takes the pistol from the tool cabinet. She stares at it, presses the barrel to her temple and then takes aim at the woman on the ramp. She pulls the trigger until she hears a bang, and the woman's thigh jolts.

Blood sprays across the concrete and the railing, and the woman screams until her voice breaks. She then lies there, desperately praying to herself.

'Maranatha, come. Lord Jesus, come . . .'

49

Joona is in the car on the way back to the station. Using the personal ID number the psychologist gave him, he has managed to establish that the Spider was born Mara Ivanova Makarovina, and that government documents list her name as Mara Makarov.

She has no current address, telephone number or place of employment, but as a child she lived in Lidingö, to the east of Stockholm, with her sister and parents. Her mother Tatiana was a famous mathematician.

Seven years ago, her entire family died in a boat accident.

The rescue services launched an extensive search effort, but the only body ever recovered belonged to the captain.

Joona has looked into the incident, but there was no suggestion a crime had been committed.

The traffic builds as he approaches Hornstull, slowing to a crawl on the bridge over Långholmen. By the time he reaches the mid-point of the bridge, it comes to a complete standstill. Joona switches off his engine and watches as several drivers up ahead get out of their cars and gawk down the road, taking out their phones.

On the radio, the news reports that two buses have crashed outside the National Archives and that both sides of the road are blocked.

The water and the buildings along Norr Mälarstrand are all bathed in golden afternoon light.

People from different cars have started chatting among themselves, others gazing across to the city or pointing out various landmarks to their children.

An older man leans back against the bonnet of his car and lights a pipe. He looks as though this is the best thing that could have possibly happened to him.

Joona's phone starts ringing, and he takes it from his pocket and answers the call.

'You need to come in,' Manvir tells him, sounding stressed. 'A new parcel just arrived for Saga. We've got the bomb squad examining it as we speak.'

'I'm stuck in the middle of Västerbron. The traffic's not moving.'

'Right, the buses. It'll be at least an hour before they—'

'Is it possible to get past on a motorcycle?'

'No, both sides are blocked. We'll send a helicopter,' Manvir tells him before ending the call.

Joona peers through the railings on the side of the bridge. From where he is standing, he can see the green copper roof of City Hall and the spire on top of the Police Authority building.

When he hears the roar of a helicopter approaching, he gets out of the car, locks the doors and clambers up onto the roof.

The police helicopter flies in from the north, swinging around before coming to hover over the bridge.

The pilot slowly dips down above the traffic.

People instinctively move back.

Joona buttons his jacket and presses one hand to his hair.

A harness on a cable swings down towards him, blowing in the violent downwash. The other people on the bridge have started filming Joona on their phones.

The breeze tugs at his clothes, and the deafening whirr is like an assault on his eardrums.

The light blinks between the rotor blades.

Joona catches the harness in his free hand, climbs into it and checks everything is secure. The helicopter then swings out over the railing in a dizzying arc.

He glances down at the stationary cars, the upturned faces, the hulking metal structure of the bridge and the glittering water down below, swinging back as the helicopter climbs into the air.

Långholmen drops away beneath him.

The cable shudders as he is winched up and pulled inside, and an officer helps him into an empty seat.

Joona fastens his seatbelt and takes the pair of ear protectors someone holds out to him.

The pilot increases the angle of attack, and the helicopter tilts forward and gains speed. They fly in across Kungsholmen and are soon given the green light to land, swaying down towards the helipad on the roof of the station.

Joona ducks and runs over to the waiting lift.

As the doors ping and roll shut, no more than three minutes have passed since he caught the harness in his hand as he stood on top of his car.

He heads down to the ground floor and runs through the glass-roofed hall. The forensic technicians have just started delicately cutting the tape with a scalpel when Joona bursts into the conference room.

Manvir, Greta and Petter are already standing around the table, and the temporary command group is busy getting their gear ready in silence.

'Just open it,' Joona tells them.

He grabs the box and tears off the remaining tape, folding back the bath towel inside and lifting out a ball of crumpled paper. He unwraps it, unwinds a glossy sweet wrapper and picks up the small tin figurine inside.

This time, it is a two-centimetre tall man in a light jacket.

Joona sets it down on the microscope and adjusts the focus and magnification. A greyish white face appears on the computer screen.

'Who is it?'

'No idea.'

'Shit, shit, shit,' Petter whispers, rubbing his chin.

The little tin man has a straight nose, deep-set eyes and a certain tautness around the mouth. His coat is smooth, but his trousers are creased around the ankles. Beneath his slippers, there is a cone-shaped lump of tin, its surface porous from the casting process.

'Share the picture over the network,' says Manvir.

'We need to speak to Saga,' says Joona.

'She's suspended,' Manvir replies.

Joona turns to him. 'You've suspended her from the investigation?'

'Until we've straightened a few things out, yes.'

'But we need her,' says Joona.

'Be that as it may, my decision is—'

'I don't care about that right now,' Joona interrupts him, sending a picture of the figurine's face to Saga.

'Did you just share that picture with her?' Manvir asks in disbelief. 'Yes.'

He lines up the three pieces of wrapping from the box and takes a picture.

A shiny, crinkled sweet wrapper, silver on one side and with a drawing of a dark skinned mermaid on the other.

A small towel.

And a black and white photograph of what seems to be some sort of tall, woven vase.

50

Saga gets up from the kitchen table, turns on the cold tap and takes a glass out of the cupboard.

In his journal on Mara Makarov, Sven-Ove Krantz writes that his patient has difficulty sleeping in a bed. More often than not, she simply curls up in a corner of the floor. She has stopped binge eating and throwing up at mealtimes and now hoards her food instead, stashing it in various places around her room.

Saga fills the glass, takes a sip of water and goes back through to her home cinema.

She hits play, and the projector fan whirrs to life behind her.

She moves closer to the screen, only stopping when the shadow of her head appears at the bottom of the image.

Mara is sitting in a chair, wearing pale blue sweatpants and a soft sweater with sleeves that are much too long for her. Her messy grey-blonde hair is loose over her shoulders, and the compress over her eye looks grubby.

'Would you like to tell me why you ended up here?' Sven-Ove Krantz asks. 'The police found you near Skärholmen, asleep on the strip of grass between the two lanes of the motorway. That's no good, is it? Not only is it dangerous, it's also illegal.'

'I felt safer,' Mara replies, folding her arms.

'Why?'

'It's not easy to snatch someone from there, with all the cars everywhere.'

'I understand. Smart. But . . . who do you think might want to snatch you?'

'The KGB.'

'The Soviet intelligence agency?'

'They're called the FSB now,' she mutters impatiently.

'Why would they want to snatch you?'

'Because I ran away from them, *shlyukha*,' she replies, bouncing one leg up and down.

'Here in Sweden?'

'I don't know, but I think so. This is where I am, where I was born and raised.'

'We haven't been able to find any relatives who—'

'Well, what the hell did you expect?' she interrupts him. 'They took everyone. My family, the whole family, every . . .'

Her voice falters, and she looks down at her knee.

'Can you tell me about it?' Krantz asks hesitantly.

'I don't remember,' she mumbles.

'Try.'

'Why?' she asks. Her knee stops bouncing.

'To help me understand what—'

'You're one of them,' she snaps.

'I'm a psychologist here at Ytterö . . .'

'I knew it, I fucking knew it!'

'Would you like to see my ID or—'

'*Blyad, zayebal*,' she shouts, knocking her chair over as she leaps to her feet. '*Yobanyy khuyesos!*'

'Mara,' he says in a calm voice. 'If you think I—'

Saga's phone pings with a message from Joona.

She pauses the video, unlocks her phone and realises that another figurine has arrived at the station. When she enlarges the image, she immediately recognises the next victim.

51

The glassy facades of the tall buildings in Kista Business Park mirror the grey sky overhead as a silver Lexus races by on the motorway.

The car is quiet, but Stefan Broman's head is ringing after a long shift at the hospital. He has spent all day running back and forth between the theatre and intensive care. Being an anaesthetist means facing a never-ending torrent of stress, maintaining a general overview of his patients while remaining utterly focused on the details.

He needs to relax. For the next few hours, he doesn't need to worry about saving any lives and can think about himself for a change.

He phoned Saga as he made his way down to the parking garage, but she hasn't answered any of his calls since he tried to convince her to come to his party. That was a mistake, he realises now. He had assumed she was unstable enough to be receptive to an arrangement like that.

Stefan turns off towards Risingeplan and drives between the tower blocks that look like drab gravestones lined up in a row.

He pulls up outside a pale yellow building with traces of old graffiti still visible on the walls. The two basement windows are the only ones on that side of the block, and behind the bars and the filthy glass, the blinds are closed in both.

He sends a message to his wife Jessica to let her know he won't be home in time for dinner, then gets out of the car, opens the boot and takes out his big carry-on case. He locks the car and wheels the bag over to a set of damp concrete steps.

On the blue metal door at the bottom, the plastic sign reads YEMOJA MASSAGE.

He took two Viagra three hours ago – a total of 100 milligrams of Sildenafil – and his head is aching, his face hot.

Since Stefan first gave in to his unusual urges, he has tried around ten different escort girls, visiting at least thirty massage parlours before he found this one through an anonymous recommendation online. He started with requests the women couldn't disagree with, like keeping quiet, lying perfectly still and not using any oils or lubricant. He was friendly, polite and generous with his tips.

It wasn't until his third visit that he introduced his real request, telling them how much he was willing to pay if they accepted his terms.

The women were tempted by the large sums of money, and they asked him for more information. He answered all of their questions, but they just couldn't get over the fact that they would be entirely defenceless, and in the end they said no. Stefan then offered to let one of them stay awake, watching what happened to make sure it really was just regular sex.

Last week they finally agreed to let him put them both under at the same time.

He hasn't been able to stop thinking about it since, knew right away that he needed to do it again.

It was as though another universe opened up to him during that hour when he had two unconscious women at his disposal. Their limp bodies couldn't make any demands of him, couldn't make comparisons or stress him out. Gone were all thoughts of his bored, unhappy wife. There was no one watching the clock, waiting for him to finish. No one thinking about themselves and masturbating instead.

This country puts official rainbow flags on public transportation and loves to claim that anything goes, everything is accepted, yet the minute a couple of grown adults come to an agreement that involves sex and money, the police have to get involved and the feminists want to cancel you, Stefan thinks, shaking his head in disgust.

His heart starts racing as he opens the door and walks down the hallway, past a fake potted orchid.

He enters a small waiting area with two armchairs and a copy of *Health* magazine on the table. There are a couple of scented tealights floating in a bowl of water.

On one wall, there is a small picture of a woman in a shimmering dress made of pearls and shells.

He hears someone toss a towel into a wash basket in one of the other rooms.

Stefan stands still, gripping the handle of his suitcase as his headache eases. His face still feels hot after the double dose of Viagra, and his vision keeps blurring, as though he is looking through a sheet of cellophane.

A toilet flushes, and he hears water surging through the pipes in the ceiling.

Somewhere nearby, a telephone pings.

Pooh comes out into the waiting room and dries her hands on the back of her denim skirt. The straps of her red bra are visible beneath her black vest. Her real name is Mapula, but she calls herself Pooh – 'like the bear'.

'Hi,' he says.

'Steffe . . .'

'Is Nina here?'

'In the shower.'

Stefan knows that their parlour is controlled by the Ramon X gang, which means that Pooh and Nina find it difficult to send any money home to their families.

'Have you had a good day?' he asks.

'Good?'

Pooh never smiles. Her gaze always seems empty, drained of all life. She is slim, with delicate limbs, and her shoulder-length hair is gathered in thirty or so thin plaits with gold beads at the tips.

'Will Nina be ready soon?' he asks.

'We need to talk. What the hell did you do last time?' Pooh asks.

'Do? I did what we agreed on,' he replies with a confused smile.

'Really?'

Nina comes out into the waiting area in a pair of pink sweatpants, sliders and a T-shirt with a glittery heart on the front. She is only four foot nine, with next to no breasts and no waist to speak of. Her black hair is shoulder length, with a blunt fringe cut just above her brows. Unlike Pooh she often smiles, but there is always a hint of something anxious in her eyes.

'I pay ten times more than anyone else,' he says with a shrug.

'We know, but . . . but Nina was bleeding,' Pooh says in a flat voice.

'Nina, I swear I—'

'She was bleeding after,' Pooh repeats in the same calm tone.

'No, seriously, I'm always careful, I've told you. I'm a doctor, it's my responsibility, I take care of you. It's just that this is my thing – everyone has their own thing. I don't need to tell you two that, but this is my thing.'

The muscles in her left shoulder tense as she raises her hand and tucks a couple of plaits behind her ear.

'But no funny business or I'll have to talk to Ramon,' she says with a frown.

In actual fact, Stefan had given them both a water enema with added laxative while they were out cold. He had extremely rough sex with both of them without a condom and took a series of pictures.

'Fine. Do you want me to go?' he asks carefully.

'I had bruises on my thighs after,' says Pooh.

'Not because of me.'

'You have to promise to be careful,' she says.

'Of course, I always am.'

'And not do anything weird.'

'You can trust me.'

'You think?'

'Yes, I do . . . I pay extremely well and you can send the money home . . . I'm a gentle guy. I'm clean, careful, a specialist doctor . . . and you only need to be asleep for a short time.'

'What do you think, Nhung?' asks Pooh.

'I'll do it if you will,' Nina replies without enthusiasm.

'OK, Stefan. This time, since you're here . . .'

'Thank you.'

'But any funny business, and that's it,' says Pooh.

52

The two women follow Stefan as he wheels his suitcase through to one of the other rooms and drops it to the floor.

He notices that the black fabric is streaked with pale dust, and realises he must have bumped up against the car as he was getting it out of the boot.

Their movements cause a poster of a woman lying on a massage table, skin slick with oil, to bulge out from the wall with a rustling sound.

Stefan's sedative of choice is Midazolam. The solution is meant to be given intravenously, but it can also be administered orally – even if it is slightly slower-acting that way.

He unpacks his equipment onto the bedside table and then gets up and holds out two fat envelopes. Pooh's gaze is still utterly devoid of all life as she takes them from him. She peers down into both envelopes, carries them over to the safe in the cleaning cupboard and locks them inside before making her way back into the room.

'Ready?' he asks.

Pooh has her arms wrapped around herself, and she seems tense, sweat glistening on her face. Nina looks like she might start crying.

Stefan has already prepared two bottles of iced coffee laced with both the sedative and morphine, to help numb any pain and to make them relax. He has upped the dose slightly since last time, and has also brought the antidote, Flumazenil, just in case anything goes wrong.

'Start by drinking this,' he says, handing them each a bottle. 'It doesn't taste great, but it's tried and tested.'

Nina's eyes are downcast, fixed on the bottle in her hands, and her breathing is quick and anxious.

Pooh pushes her plaits back from her face.

'I can do this,' she mumbles, swigging a big mouthful.

'Nina?' Stefan says with a smile.

She takes a deep breath and sips from the bottle. She coughs, drinks a little more and then dries the tears from her cheeks.

'Ugh,' Pooh mutters after draining the last of the liquid.

Once Nina is done, Stefan takes back the bottles, puts them into his suitcase and says something about the worst part being over.

His cheeks still feel hot, and the blurry film over his eyes seems to be getting thicker. He has to blink repeatedly just to make out the hands on his watch.

Pooh moves over to Nina and gives her a hug to calm her down. She stands with Nina's cheek to her chest, stroking her hair and gazing over to Stefan with a blank face.

'My feet are cold,' Nina says, her voice full of regret.

Stefan has brought a carbon dioxide monitor, a blood pressure monitor and oxygen monitor, plus an EKG – though he doubts he will need any of them.

'Why don't you ladies get comfortable on the bed?' he suggests when he notices the morphine starting to take effect. 'It'll take a while before you feel anything, but I'll be right here the whole time . . .'

Nina smiles as she struggles to kick off her sliders.

The two women lie down together with their legs crossed and their eyes on the ceiling.

It won't be long before the sedative takes effect, giving him unrestricted access to their bodies.

He checks the time as he hears their breathing slow, becoming heavy and regular.

Nina twitches once before drifting off into deep anaesthesia, and her phone clatters to the floor beside the bed. Behind its protective plastic case, she has a couple of small photographs of her family.

Stefan moves closer and takes Nina's small hand in his. It's warm and lifeless, dry flakes of skin around her nails.

Her pulse is already worryingly low, and he knows he should probably check their oxygen levels.

The room is so quiet.

Stefan looks up and studies the two women, their calm bodies and their absent faces.

They are beyond all performance or power games now.

His hands shake as he pushes Nina's T-shirt up and studies her.

Her pale lips are parted slightly.

He can feel her hot breath on the back of his hand and see the thin red veins on her rounded eyelids.

Stefan pinches her nipple hard and gazes down at her slack face.

They no longer have any free will, are no longer capable of resistance; they no longer feel any pain at all.

He pulls down her pants and underwear and studies her flattened pubic hair. Then he rolls her over onto her stomach.

Stefan turns his attention to Pooh.

Her pride and her rage are both gone from her face. He reaches out and pushes her lips into a smile.

That's better, he thinks, tugging down her tight skirt and tossing it to the floor. Her black vest gets caught on her plaits as he pulls it up over her head, and as he tears it free one of the little beads bounces away across the floor.

They have no idea what he is planning to do to them; they'll never know. Both will just feel slightly tender and remorseful afterwards.

Stefan takes off his pale brown trousers and underpants and drapes them over the back of a chair. He then unbuttons his shirt and moves over to Pooh, pressing his half-limp penis to her full lips. He rubs it across her face and jabs it into her eye.

He yanks her underwear down.

She is clean shaven, but her thighs feel a little prickly. He bends her left knee, angling her thigh to one side so that he can study her between the legs, the folds of her skin the colour of clay.

He soaks a cotton pad in alcohol, then wipes her down.

His heart is really racing now.

Pooh's hips crack as he pushes her legs as far apart as he can and climbs on top of her.

He should give her a muscle relaxant, he thinks.

As he thrusts away, he glances over to Nina, who is rocking in time with his movements.

He can feel the sweat running down both sides of his torso.

His heart is pounding, his erection almost painful now.

Right then, he hears a loud thud against the front door, not unlike a bird flying into a window.

Stefan holds Pooh down, gripping her throat as hard as he can as he ploughs away.

The poster of the woman on the massage table seems to be clinging back against the wall, and clumps of dust start dancing across the floor.

As he continues to thrust into Pooh, he hears light footsteps in the waiting area. He pauses and glances back over his shoulder. His immediate thought is that it must be Ramon X, but then he sees a young woman.

She is grey like an insect under a rock, and she moves quickly.

Stefan mumbles an irritated 'what the fuck' just as a loud crack deafens him.

He feels a sudden burning sensation, as though the young woman has just thrown a pot of boiling water over him, and before he has time to work out what is going on he falls from the bed and lands shoulder first on the floor.

His legs tumble after him like cooked spaghetti.

He can hear a loud ringing in his ears and realises he has been shot in the back, in one of his upper ribs. His spinal cord is damaged; he'll be paralysed.

Blood pumps out onto the floor.

His vertebra need to be immobilised. He needs surgery – and now.

'I'll pay,' he gasps, coughing up blood from his punctured lung.

Stefan is lying on his side, his open shirt twisted around his torso. He glances down at his naked lower half, surrounded by a pool of blood, and sees that his penis has shrunk to nothing but a tiny nub above his testicles.

The woman aims a glossy red pistol at Pooh's face, but rather than shooting her she turns and hurries out of the room.

Using his arms, Stefan manages to roll over onto his stomach and pull himself forward. His body is heavy, his heart suddenly beating unnaturally fast. He has no feeling below the waist, and has to drag his lifeless legs behind him.

Stefan tries desperately to get to the chair, where his phone is in his trouser pocket.

He pauses, gasping for air and spitting out a mouthful of blood. He reaches out, but the chair is too far away. He tries to find something he can grip on the plastic flooring and manages to drag himself another few centimetres.

His field of vision has started to shrink.

It feels as though he is looking through the wrong end of a pair of binoculars, and he watches his hand reach out and brush the chair leg with his fingertips.

The young woman comes back into the room.

She is carrying a metal cable, and she winds it around his ankles and secures it with a winch hook.

'What do you want?' he pants.

She ignores his question and makes her way over to the chair, patting down his clothes, taking his phone and then leaving the room.

Stefan lowers his cheek to the floor and closes his eyes.

53

Saga accelerates hard, reaching 190 kilometres an hour as she races past Mariehäll. Above the vines growing over the noise barrier, she can see the trees and grand rooftops of the big houses on the other side.

She has no idea what Manvir and Greta are thinking, but she knows she can't stop working on the case just because they have suspended her.

Saga is on her own now, and she needs to do this even if it means ending up on the wrong side of the law.

The others are too slow.

A minute or so after the first image of the new figurine came through, Joona sent a picture of the wrapping.

The moment she saw the mermaid, Saga knew exactly where Stefan would be killed. She has seen his chat threads with other men who like to buy sex, and she didn't even need to try to decipher the woven vase.

She took her Glock 17 from her gun cabinet, grabbed her bullet-proof vest and helmet, pulled on her trainers and ran down the stairs.

She turns off onto the E18 after Ursvik, taking the next exit and following the curving bridge over the motorway before continuing straight ahead at a roundabout with yellowing grass in the middle.

Two blonde girls are sitting on the bench at the bus shelter, looking down at their phones.

Saga sees that Joona has tried to reach her again, from a landline at the station this time.

She accelerates down a straight stretch between an avenue of tall chestnut trees and drab grey apartment buildings. Dry leaves and garbage swirl up into the air behind her.

She turns off, driving a few hundred metres down the wrong side of the road before pulling up in front of Stefan's silver Lexus.

Saga takes off her helmet, struggles into her bulletproof vest and tightens the straps.

The ground by the steps down to the basement property looks like it has been swept, and Saga realises she is probably too late.

The lock on the steel door is broken, shards of metal lying on the step outside.

Hooking her finger around the trigger, she opens the door and points her gun at the narrow corridor inside.

A bloody mop has been left lying in a dark pool on the floor.

The plastic flooring is still damp, and a fake potted orchid has been knocked over, scattering the clay pebbles across the floor.

The air smells like scented candles and soap.

Saga steps over the mop and moves down the corridor without a sound. She sticks to the right wall, lowering her gun for a second to give the muscles in her shoulder a rest.

There is a table blocking the doorway into a small waiting room up ahead.

The massage parlour is silent, the shadows unmoving.

She raises her pistol and swings around the corner, scanning past a couple of armchairs to the two doorways inside.

There is no sign of anyone.

A glass bowl of candles has shattered on the floor, and a framed photograph of Beyoncé as an African goddess is hanging askew on one wall.

Saga flinches when water starts rushing through the pipes in the ceiling.

The hastily mopped up blood is like some sort of smeared arrow, pointing through to the room straight ahead where the door is ajar. The light is on inside.

She aims at the crack around the door and pauses to listen for a moment before slowly making her way over.

The faux-wood strip on the threshold is bloody, the air heavy with the acrid stench of gunpowder, blood and excrement.

Saga slowly pushes the door open using the barrel of her gun and sees two lifeless women on the bloody bed inside.

One is completely naked, lying flat out on her stomach. The other is on her back, thighs parted, wearing nothing but a red bra.

Saga moves forward through the doorway, quickly checking the rest of the room and securing the blind spots before she hurries around the bed.

Stefan is gone, but there is blood everywhere. Mara has only bothered mopping the floor to get rid of her own footprints. A heap of clothes has been left on the dusty floor beneath the bed.

Something rattles out in the waiting room, and Saga wheels around, drops to one knee and braces herself with one foot against the wall.

It's just the pipes again.

The sound continues for a moment or two before fading away.

Saga gets up and moves over to the two women. She checks their pulses, notices the medical supplies in the suitcase, and realises Stefan must have anaesthetised them. He asked her to do it once, but quickly dropped the idea when he saw her reaction.

As she rolls the two women into the recovery position, she notices that they are both in the process of waking up.

A white bullet casing clatters to the floor from the bed.

'God,' one of the women pants.

She pushes her plaits back from her face and attempts to raise her head.

'He's gone,' says Saga. 'Just lie there and rest for a moment.'

'What's going on?' the woman mumbles.

'You've both been drugged and assaulted. I'd like to call an ambulance, if that's OK.'

'No, no ambulance, please,' the woman begs her.

'I think it would be good to—'

'No ambulance.'

'OK, I hear you, I'm listening, but I still think it would be a good idea for someone to check you over. Do you understand what I'm saying?' Saga quickly scribbles down the number for a confidential walk-in clinic.

'I feel sick,' the other woman mumbles.

'It'll pass. Just lie still, drink some water,' Saga tells her.

'God,' the first one whispers again.

'Call this number,' says Saga, handing it to the woman along with her own card.

'OK.'

'I'm serious, they can help you. The whole thing is confidential, they're on your side. It's free, and it can be anonymous if you want it to be . . . Do you understand?'

'OK.'

'Call them.'

'We will.'

'I don't want to worry you, and there's no need to panic, but I think the police might be here pretty soon . . . Maybe you should grab your things and go?'

'OK, thanks.'

'But you have time to rest for five minutes.'

Saga backs up and studies the blood on the floor, the spatter on the bed and walls. It appears that Stefan – probably while he was in the process of assaulting the two women – was shot in the back with a bullet that expanded and stayed inside his body, like the rest of the victims.

He fell to the floor and attempted to use his arms to drag himself to safety while Mara brought the winch inside.

His blood, marrow and excrement then ended up being smeared across the floor beneath him as she winched him out. He put up a fight, clung on to the table, but ultimately wasn't strong enough.

Saga notices her own footprints in the sticky blood, and she realises she needs to clean them up before she leaves.

'Hello?' a man's voice shouts.

'Get dressed,' Saga tells the two women.

Holding her pistol behind her back, she steps out into the waiting room just as a man in his sixties appears in the corridor.

54

Since the arrival of the last figurine, the team has had the large conference room on the ground floor booked out around the clock, ready for the next one.

The temporary command group is in place, a direct line to regional command open, and a team from the National Task Force is primed to be in the air almost immediately after being given the order.

On the other side of the row of windows, clumps of white seeds like dandelions float through a shaft of evening sunlight against the grey concrete wall.

When Joona sent the images of the latest figurine to Saga, Manvir got up and moved over to his usual place in the corner. Eighteen minutes have now passed, and he is still standing with his face to the wall.

The next victim's identity remains a mystery, but it might not yet be too late to work out where he will be killed.

They have to work on the assumption that stopping Makarov is possible.

Joona is standing by the large table in the middle of the room. The overhead lights are bright on the lacquered surface, and he can see rings of dried coffee beside Petter's writing pad.

They have studied every last millimetre of the little figurine through the digital microscope hooked up to a computer with two extra screens.

'OK, let's solve this. We know how Makarov constructs her riddles, how everything fits together to point to a specific location,' says Greta.

Otis, one of the forensic technicians, pauses by the table in his wheelchair. His bow tie is slightly crooked, his eyes tired and the lenses of his glasses flecked with dandruff.

'Do you need any help?' he asks.

'Yes,' says Joona.

Greta straightens her pearl necklace so that the clasp is sitting in the right place.

'This is getting harder and harder,' Petter mutters, trying to hold back the stress from his voice.

'Think, look. What do we see? We need a location, an address,' says Joona.

'Let's start with the towel,' Greta suggests, turning it over. 'White, no sign of a monogram, brand or washing label.'

'No visible stains, either,' says Petter.

'Otis,' says Joona. 'Could you check whether there are any fibres on it? Any traces of DNA or hidden messages?'

'Is it urgent?' he jokes, pulling on a pair of latex gloves.

He carefully picks up the towel, lowers it into an evidence box and rolls off towards the other technicians.

'Let's look at the black and white image next,' says Greta. 'I'm guessing it's from a catalogue of some kind – possibly from an auction, a museum, an exhibition or a folk archive . . .'

They lean in and study the image of the woven object, some sort of tall vessel, and then read the text printed beneath:

INDEX TERM:
Fishing

TEXT:
Inscription: AC

DIMENSIONS:
Height: 113.0 cm

MATERIAL:
Wood: Juniper, spruce root

The sheet of paper is torn down the middle, making it impossible to tell whether any more information was given below.

'We know it has something to do with fishing, in any case,' Greta begins.

'A net of some kind?' says Petter. 'Or a lobster pot?'

'A trap,' says Joona.

'It must be possible to work this out,' Greta mumbles, sitting down at her computer.

Petter picks up the shiny, crumpled sweet wrapper. One side features a cartoon of a dark skinned mermaid, and the other is silver.

'A mermaid and some sort of fishing gear . . . So it has to do with water, in other words?' says Petter.

'Maybe,' Joona replies, trying to get through to Saga yet again.

The acting head of the National Crime Unit, Morgan Malmström, is deep in conversation with the comms group. The gravity of the situation has caused his true age to shine through the boyish veneer, and his face seems tense, with dark rings beneath both eyes and a tautness around his downturned mouth.

'Joona,' he says, pausing to clear his throat. 'It's been twenty-four minutes since the parcel arrived.'

'I know.'

'It's taking way too long to—'

'I agree.'

Joona moves past the command group and over to Manvir, who is still standing in the corner. His face is no more than twenty centimetres from the point where the two walls meet.

'I'm sorry, Manvir, but this isn't about the chain of command,' Joona tells him. 'Because if you really do think Saga is involved then it makes no difference that she got to see the latest package. But until we have any solid evidence against her, until a prosecutor has been brought in, we need her help – even if you don't want her here . . . The killer has been communicating with her, turning to her . . .'

'Saga is suspended,' Manvir mutters into the wall.

'We haven't found a single connection between her and Mara Makarov. That's not to say there isn't one, but—'

'She has a motive.'

'You've said that before, but I know Saga.'

'You *knew* her, but because of you her life also fell apart. It wasn't your fault, but it fell apart all the same,' Manvir replies into the wall, checking that his tie is straight. 'I mean, do you really think she's still the same person, after everything she's been through? That she's the Saga you used to know?'

'Yes,' Joona tells him, turning away and heading back over to Petter and Greta.

He picks up the silver sweet wrapper and holds it up to the light, turning it over and focusing on the colourful cartoon.

The water dispenser bubbles softly. Petter's eyes are locked on his computer screen, one hand resting on his stomach beneath his T-shirt.

'I just thought of something,' Joona says, looking up. 'It might be nothing, but I feel like I recognise this mermaid.'

'From where?' Petter asks, closing the lid of his computer.

'It's not exactly the same, but it reminds me of a photograph of a religious sculpture I found in one of Valeria's greenhouses. Mãe d'Água.'

'OK . . .' Petter smiles.

'I think it has something to do with a religion known as Candomblé in Brazil, a mix of Catholicism and various African religions.'

'Look into it,' says Manvir.

He turns around and returns to his seat at the table without another word.

No one ever remarks on his periods in the corner; the team just gets on with their work as though he has been participating the whole time.

'This shit is taking way too long,' Petter mutters. 'It's taking way—'

'Hang on a minute, listen to this,' Greta interrupts him. 'I've found it. The black and white image, it's something called a tena.'

'A tena?' Petter repeats, anxiously biting his lip.

'That's its name, an old-fashioned fish trap,' she says, turning her computer towards the others.

'Do they come from somewhere specific?' asks Manvir.

'Not that I can see,' Greta replies, catching her foot on the makeshift cable strip on the floor.

'Do we have any idea what Mara Makarov is up to with these riddles?' asks Manvir. 'Why she's giving us a chance to get there before her?'

'Is she?' Petter sighs.

He gets up, grabs a red marker from the shelf and adds 'tena' to the whiteboard.

Joona is at his computer, his eyes calm and focused. An eyelash has caught on his cheek, and it almost looks like a small smiling mouth.

'I've found it,' he says with a nod towards the mermaid. 'If I've understood it right, she's a deity, an Orixá – also known as an Orisha in West Africa. A protector of rivers, of women. There are multiple variations of her name, but the original one seems to be Yemọja.'

'Yemọja,' Petter repeats.

'It's Yoruba.'

'Which I've never heard of . . .'

'It has five times as many speakers as Swedish,' says Joona.

'Yemọja and tena,' Manvir speaks up. 'What does that tell us?'

'Thirty minutes . . . We're probably too late already,' says Petter, scratching his throat.

Otis wheels over to them, bumping into the edge of the table. He purses his lips and blinks behind his glasses.

'Semen and massage oil on the towel,' he says.

'Lovely,' Greta sighs.

'No DNA matches in our databases, no hits in—'

'I think this should be enough,' Joona interrupts him. 'Search the words tena, Mãe d'Água, Yemọja, Yemanjá, Orisha, Orixá and Candomblé in combination with massage parlours also selling sex.'

His blue shirt strains against his left shoulder as he adds the new search terms to the board.

Around the table, everyone is quiet.

Manvir opens various police databases and registers, and the others scour both the dark net and the open internet.

'Got it!' Greta leaps up from her chair. 'There's . . . there's a place called Yemọja Massage. It's not a registered business, but there are people discussing and rating it in a creepy little forum that—'

'Where is it?' asks Joona.

'Risingeplan in Tensta,' she replies.

55

Joona's pistol swings heavily against his torso as he hurries down the steps towards the blue metal door with a sign for Yemoja Massage.

The first documented references to the area of Tensta were made in the sixteenth century, and the name likely derives from the tena fishing trap.

Joona hesitates for a second or two, searching for the inner calm he needs in order to be as receptive to every single detail of the crime scene as he can be.

He takes a deep breath, opens the door and peers into the hallway on the other side. The floor is streaked with blood.

There is a mop lying just inside the door, and its head is dark red, slick with semi-congealed blood.

Joona switches on the ceiling light.

He can see a number of fresher footprints on the floor, suggesting that two people have left the premises since the floor was mopped.

Joona steps forward, over the crushed clay pellets from an overturned plant pot. The deep gash in the doorframe tells him that the steel cable changed direction in the next room.

He hears a sudden rattling sound, moving closer. It rushes across the ceiling, following the waste pipe and disappearing through the wall.

A soft roar, then silence.

Joona follows Mara's sloppily mopped-up footprints into the waiting room.

The whole place gives him the impression that someone made a hasty exit.

The coffee table has been moved from its original position, and a glass bowl has shattered on the floor.

The drag marks left by the victim's body turn sharply to the right, into a dark room.

The stench of blood and excrement is overwhelming.

Joona reaches into the room and switches on the light. There is a bed in the middle of the space, and the sheet on top is bloody. The victim must have been shot in the back and then fallen to the floor, because that is where the majority of the viscera seems to be.

He notices a fan-shaped spray of droplets that looks like it has been coughed across the floor, suggesting that the bullet passed straight through the man's spine and came to a halt in his lung.

In a small suitcase, Joona can see various pieces of medical equipment, enough to knock someone out and perform an operation.

His gaze lingers on the strange criss-cross of mop marks, and he notices a half shoeprint in the blood on the wall, just above the socket.

There was a fifth person in the room.

Joona realises it must be Saga.

She stepped in the blood after it began to coagulate, and then for some reason dropped to one knee and accidentally pressed her foot to the wall.

Saga mopped up her prints before she left the parlour, but she missed this one.

Joona heads back to the waiting area and makes his way into the other massage room, switching on the light in the bathroom. There is a telephone in the toilet.

He looks into a cleaning cupboard, where the safe is standing wide open.

The people who worked here won't be coming back, he thinks, turning to leave the premises.

Greta is outside, talking to a couple of technicians who are busy examining a parked Lexus. She has attempted to stop a ladder in her tights using clear nail varnish. One of the technicians tugs at her diamond earring and looks up.

'You can go in now,' Joona tells her.

'Anything in particular you want us to look at?'

'There's a phone in the toilet,' Joona tells her, hesitating for a moment before he continues. 'And there's a shoe print on the right-hand wall in the room with the bloody bed.'

'OK.'

Joona pauses, turns around and scans the area for CCTV cameras or windows looking out onto the basement property.

'According to our witness, they heard a pistol shot from the basement property at 19.39,' says Greta. 'The victim's name is Stefan Broman. He's an anaesthetist at the Karolinska Institute, lives in Djursholm, married with two kids . . . No connection to Saga as yet.'

Joona's team arrived sixteen minutes too late to stop the murder, but they might have made it in time if Saga had still been with them.

56

A naked boy runs across a high concrete beam with a rusty rebar protruding from one end. He reaches an opening in the floor, glances all around and then starts making his way down the stairs.

The boy is transparent, as though he is made from pale blue glass.

He keeps going down the stairs, but he gets caught, pulled down, and grazes his knuckles before an icy rag is pulled over his face.

Another boy, made from pale pink glass this time, comes running down the same stairs. He too is caught, pulled down, and grazes his knuckles before an icy rag is pulled over his face.

Stefan Broman opens his eyes and realises he was dreaming; he lost consciousness when the young woman pushed a gauze into the bullet wound on his back.

He remembers being in the back of a pickup truck earlier, beneath a muddy tarpaulin, mouth taped shut and with tight straps across his torso and throat.

The graze on his knuckles stings.

His hand got caught beneath him as she dragged him across the workshop floor.

Stefan is confused, but he knows he won't be able to last much longer.

He is lying flat on his back on a concrete ramp, looking up at the metal roof and the overhead crane with its thick rope and pulley system.

He repeats to himself that the young woman must have mistaken him for someone from a rival criminal gang.

The air in the workshop smells like chemicals, and he can see a number of large plastic drums lined up along one wall.

The young woman slaps her cheeks several times before she comes over and rolls him into a thick rubber sack, like some sort of oversized pea pod with sturdy grommets at both ends.

He sees her lifting his legs and shoving them inside, though he has no feeling in them whatsoever.

When she comes back, she's wearing a protective mask, a thick apron and a pair of black rubber gloves.

Using the overhead crane, she lifts one of the heavy plastic drums over him and connects a hose to a valve on the rubber bag.

A sharp, concentrated scent makes his nose burn, and his heart starts racing.

Stefan hears a soft glugging sound as the lower section of the bag slowly fills up, and he whimpers in pain when a few splashes of the liquid hit the back of his hand.

Panic and disbelief rush through his head as he realises that his lower body is dissolving.

The woman uses the crane to lift another drum over.

The pulleys creak under its weight as she hoists the heavy load over him.

She mumbles anxiously to herself and then connects the hose to the valve at the top of the bag with trembling hands.

For the first time, Stefan understands what is about to happen.

He must be in hell.

The woman throws up into a bucket and then comes back with the kind of heat welding gun used on wet room floors. She closes the opening over his torso and face and then melts the rubber and seals the bag.

Everything goes dark, and Stefan sees the transparent boy from his dream again. His naked body is made from yellow glass this time. The boy's feet patter across the concrete floor, and as he reaches the bottom of the stairs, Stefan is enveloped in a terrible inferno.

57

Saga takes her shoes off the minute she gets home, carrying them to the kitchen to scrub them with chlorine. Stefan is probably in the process of dying right now, she thinks.

She makes a mental note to delete any footage of her cleaning her shoes and jacket from the security cameras, and, with a feverish feeling inside, takes off all her clothes and shoves them into the washing machine, starting a long cycle before getting into the shower.

The hot water thunders down onto her head, spilling over her ears.

As Saga lathers herself up, she realises she might have overreacted when she saw the man in the waiting room.

His bald head was flecked with liver spots, his full beard yellow around the mouth and his T-shirt from the Byggmax building depot tight over his pot belly.

'Hi! I've got an appointment with Nina at eight,' he said with a cautious smile.

'Did you see the blood in the hallway?'

'Yeah, I thought—'

'What, you thought it was fine because you want to buy sex?' she said, pointing her gun at his face.

'Sorry, I—'

'Do you want to see what I did to the last john?' she shouted.

'I'll go,' he whispered, turning and stumbling out into the hallway.

'Stop exploiting women! I'll be keeping an eye on you, I know where you live,' she called after him.

Saga gets out of the shower and dries herself off as she goes to the bedroom to get dressed.

She needs to figure this out.

Mara Makarov is fixated on her for some reason, but why?

Saga goes to the living room, switches on the projector and waits until the rectangle on the screen has reached full brightness. She then pulls a chair into the middle of the floor, as close to the screen as she can get, and hits play on the next recording from Sven-Ove Krantz's sessions in Ytterö.

On this occasion, Mara Makarov seems to have showered and brushed her hair. She is no longer wearing a bandage, and though the skin around her eye looks yellow, the swelling has gone down. She tries to keep her anxious hands clasped in her lap, but keeps reaching up to push an invisible lock of hair back from her face.

Saga's blood runs cold when she realises that she has met Mara, in the waiting room outside Astrid and Nick's dance class.

Mara was the young woman in the silver jacket, reading a book about mathematics. The one who mentioned a problem involving the bridges of Königsberg.

There is a scraping sound as the psychologist drags his chair across the floor. Mara's eyes follow him, and she waits until he is sitting down before she speaks.

'You say you want to help me. In fact you've said that quite a few times,' she says, sucking on her lips.

'And I stand by that – if I can.'

'You can start by listening to me. Other than my grandmother, they're all still alive, waiting for me to bring help.'

'Why is that your responsibility?'

'Because I escaped from the cell when they brought us food. I was so dirty and grey that the guard didn't notice me . . . When he came in, everyone huddled up in the far corner like usual, quiet and afraid, but I was waiting by the wall beside the door. I slipped out as he put the box down on the floor, and I found my way out . . . It's tricky for me to remember everything, but somehow I managed to get out. I think I climbed up a long metal ladder and opened a trapdoor . . . What I know for sure is that I crossed a meadow full of dandelions, walked past huge houses and came out onto a road. All I could think about was making it home and trying to get in touch with the Swedish police so they could save my family. Their lives depend on me, do you understand?'

'Of course,' the psychologist replies calmly.

Mara rubs her forehead repeatedly.

'It's just so hard to remember,' she says. 'Maybe you know how that feels. I'm not sure I can find my way back to them . . . No, hang on, I saw a sign when I came up onto the road . . . It said *Moyaveyab*.'

'What's that?'

'I don't know, a name, it doesn't mean anything, but I know what I saw.'

'OK, good, you saw a sign.'

'*Moyaveyab, Moyaveyab*,' she whispers, as though to memorise the name.

'Did the guard speak Russian?' he asks.

'Of course.'

'So you escaped from that prison,' he says. 'But how did you end up here? The police found you on a motorway outside of Stockholm.'

'I don't know, maybe it wasn't in Russia, I don't know how it works. Maybe the Russian security services have secret prisons in Sweden too.'

Mara sits quietly for a moment, her hands covering her face, then she looks up at the psychologist again.

'What do you want me to do?' he asks.

'Contact the Security Service and tell them what I've been through,' she says. 'Tell them that my family are being held prisoner and that they'll starve to death soon.'

'I'll do that, but it might be helpful if you could remember any other details.'

'I've been trying, that's all I ever do.'

Once Sven-Ove Krantz leaves Mara's room, Saga presses pause and turns to the handwritten journals. She flicks through to the psychologist's notes following that session.

I reached out to the Security Service and shared everything Mara told me, without mentioning that she was being treated for paranoid psychosis. I received a standard response in reply, saying that they would be taking over the case going forward.

Saga smiles to herself at the doctor's unorthodox, yet really quite obvious and humane methods. She turns to look out of the window, feels the water from her damp hair soaking through the back of her T-shirt, and then keeps reading.

Mara seems to have been much calmer after that session. The doctors lowered her medication slightly, and she started interacting with the other patients, watching television in the day room. Everything seemed fairly stable until she read an article in *Expressen* one evening.

58

Joona and Greta meet outside one of the interrogation rooms in the Stockholm Police Station. They are there because a man walked in earlier and said he wanted to report a murder at a massage parlour in Tensta.

The man already has a lawyer, and claims he is only willing to speak in return for police protection.

'You should sort that out,' says Greta, nodding at Joona's chipped nail polish.

'I know, I need to book an appointment,' he says, knocking on the door before they head inside.

The man is middle aged, with a bald head and a full beard, and he is slumped behind the table with his hands in his lap. His lawyer is a woman with shoulder length blonde hair and a smear of lipstick on one of her front teeth. She is young, around thirty, wearing a dark grey skirt, a short suit jacket and a white blouse. She is perched on the very edge of her chair, and she waits until they have come in and closed the door before getting up and shaking their hands.

'My client wants a guarantee of witness protection,' she says.

'Of course, if there are grounds for that. Our witness protection unit will look into it if there are,' Greta replies. 'But any decisions of that nature are taken independently of the nature of the witness testimony. It's purely a matter of need.'

'Then I'm not saying a word,' says the man.

'Would you mind explaining to your client that, under Swedish law, he has a duty to give evidence?' Greta asks the lawyer.

'Let's skip that,' says Joona, sitting down beside the man. 'I need answers. What's the name of the massage parlour where you go to buy sex?'

'My client denies paying for sex,' the lawyer interjects.

'Yemoja,' the man mumbles.

'He was there for a massage, on a referral from his doctor. He has back trouble,' the lawyer explains.

'I'd just come into the waiting room when some psychopath started waving a gun about, saying she'd kill me just like she killed the other customer. She said she knew where I lived.'

'I understand that must have been frightening,' says Joona.

'What am I meant to do? That's a clear death threat, you have to protect me.'

'Could you describe the woman with the pistol?'

'Blonde, angry . . .'

Joona finds a picture of Saga on his phone and holds it up to the man.

'What, have you already arrested her or something?'

'Did she say she had killed a man?' asks Joona.

'Yeah.'

'Shot him?'

'I can't remember.'

'But she said she'd killed a man at the massage parlour and then she threatened to kill you?' he asks.

'Yeah.'

'Why would she want to kill you?'

'I don't know.'

'If you had to hazard a guess?'

'You don't have to answer that,' the man's lawyer reminds him.

'Did you see anyone else in the massage parlour?' asks Greta.

'No.'

'What about outside?'

'Nope.'

'And did you notice anything else unusual?' asks Joona.

'Don't think so, no.'

'You didn't see the pool of blood or the mop just inside the door?' Joona presses him.

'What?'

'Is that what the massage parlours where you go to get help with your back usually look like?'

'My client won't be answering any more questions,' says the lawyer.

'Please let him know that he'll be charged with soliciting sex,' says Greta.

* * *

The sunlight filters through the net curtains, spilling across the cashmere rug and the burgundy sofas. An aroma of ginger and cardamom drifts over from the modern samovar on the table.

Francesca Beckman's remains were found by a group of scouts in Sandtorpet yesterday. The bundle had been left in the overgrown ruins of a former orphanage that once belonged to Västerlövsta Church.

As a result of the latest murder and the discovery of Francesca's body, Manvir called a meeting at his house in Lidingö. He told Joona and Greta to look out for a villa on Riddarvägen that looks like two yellow shoeboxes stacked on top of one another.

Joona is busy setting out the teacups on delicate little saucers when a girl in a navy blue dress comes into the room. She is probably around six, with tightly plaited hair. There is something of Manvir in her eyes and cheekbones, but otherwise she doesn't look much like her father.

'Hi,' says Joona.

She approaches him with a look of curiosity, carrying a quarter-size violin in her left hand. It has a piece of foam instead of a chin rest, and there are a number of small stickers marking out three positions on the fingerboard.

'Why have you got pink dots on your nails?' she asks.

'Because I'm part of the circus.'

'No, you're not,' she says with a grin.

'True, but when I was your age I was good at tightrope walking, and I really thought a ringmaster might cycle past one day and discover me.'

'I'd be a clown who frightens all the stupid kids,' she says.

Manvir comes into the room with a plate of biscuits. Greta and Petter follow him in with the warm milk and sugar.

'This is my daughter, Miranda.'

'Hi,' says Greta.

'Hi.'

'And this is Greta, Petter and Joona,' says Manvir.

'OK,' she says.

'Why don't you run off to your room, Miranda?'

'Can I have a biscuit first?'

'Once you've finished practising.'

'I have.'

'It didn't sound that way – you forgot your half rests.'

'No, I didn't.'

The little girl's face darkens, and she puts her violin down on the table and marches over to the corner of the room, where she stands with her back to them. Joona catches Greta's eye and feels the corners of his mouth twitching.

'OK, shall we get started?' asks Manvir.

Keeping his voice low, Joona tells the others about his observations from the massage parlour and their interview with the witness. Manvir sighs and gets up from his chair.

He goes over to Miranda, crouches down behind her and whispers sorry.

'Take a biscuit,' he says.

'No.'

'You can practise again tomorrow.'

She turns around and hugs him, then walks over to the table, grabs her violin and a biscuit, and leaves the room without giving any of them a second glance.

Manvir sits back down and sips his tea as Greta adds to Joona's observations with a summary of the forensic technicians' initial finds.

'Do any of us seriously think Saga is a serial killer?' Joona asks. 'I mean, she might not always follow the rules, and she sometimes loses her temper, but . . .'

'I know,' Petter whispers.

'We can't afford to be naive,' says Manvir. 'It isn't unheard of for officers to go over to the other side. They have all sorts of contacts, they've seen how unjust the system is, seen the money involved.'

'This isn't about money, though,' says Greta.

'The other group of people who change sides are those who are disappointed or traumatised; the ones who find it increasingly difficult to leave the darkness, who know how easy it would be to—'

'But we're talking about Saga here,' Joona interrupts him.

'Yes, and she has a motive for each of the murders.'

'Revenge, you mean?' asks Greta.

Manvir sets down his cup, brushes a few crumbs from his fingers and then turns to Joona.

'My gut feeling says that Saga recruited Mara Makarov to carry out these killings,' he explains. 'Mara is mentally ill and easily led. Saga has the anger and the knowledge, she might have been misleading us, cleaning the crime scenes . . . always making sure she has a solid alibi.'

The sound of a violin seeps through the walls of the house, stopping abruptly before starting again.

'But do we actually have anything concrete to back that up?' asks Petter.

'The bloody print at the massage parlour is a match for Saga's shoes,' Manvir replies.

'She's still working the case. She was quicker and got there before us,' says Joona.

'If that's the case, why would she try to remove any trace of herself?'

'But you suspect she—'

'She threatened a man and claimed to have killed Stefan Broman,' Manvir cuts him off.

'That does sound like Saga, but I think—'

'You don't have to defend her, Joona.'

'I just think she was angry and she wanted to scare him,' Joona continues.

'I agree,' says Greta.

'Her fingerprints were also found at the station in Kymlinge,' says Manvir.

'I was there with her.'

'And did you see her touch a fire extinguisher bracket?'

'Manvir,' says Joona. 'I understand how it looks, but this is nothing.'

'There's more . . . She accused Verner of being responsible for everything that happened to her, and she also had issues with the priest. She wrote threatening letters to the parish, turned up late to Margot's funeral, in trainers; she—'

'We don't have time to—'

'Joona,' Manvir ignores his protests. 'We have the lab analysis of the samples taken from the chapel where Francesca Beckman was killed. I'm sorry to be the one to tell you this, but they found a clear match for Saga's DNA.'

'Oh God,' Greta whispers.

'And she had no reason to visit the church,' Manvir continues.

'No,' Joona admits, his voice subdued.

'I'm going to put out an alert. Saga Bauer is now our primary suspect.'

302

59

Saga is in her kitchen, eating pizza in her underwear. Strings of melted cheese stretch between the slice of pizza and the box, and she uses the back of her hand to wipe the grease from her lips.

Mara must have shown up outside the kids' dance session with the specific intention of giving her the Seven Bridges of Königsberg problem, she realises. Saga runs a quick search online and quickly discovers that there is no solution. A mathematician called Leonhard Euler proved that back in the eighteenth century.

So what was Mara trying to say?

Saga rereads Sven-Ove Krantz's journal, in which he writes that Mara was doing much better until she read an article in a tabloid one evening.

Mara spends a lot of time with her clay sculptures. Each is distinctive, with specific, individual features. Today I saw that she was working on a model of a woman carrying a sleeping baby, and when I — slightly tactlessly — asked whether it was for a nativity scene, she simply gave me a confused glance and continued her work. Mara spent another two hours in the hobby room before she took off her apron, washed her hands and took a newspaper to the day room.

Saga can hear the sound of a TV through the wall, the fridge is whirring, and she notices a patch of sunlight quivering on the wall behind the dining table.

She gets up and moves over to the window, gazing across to the apartment on the other side of the street.

The windows are probably around a metre higher than hers. One has been covered in paper, and through the other she can see tins of paint and brushes on a stepladder.

The metal catches the light as the sun comes out from behind a cloud.

Saga turns back to the table and keeps eating.

The neighbour's dog starts barking at the letterbox.

She knows she should start watching the next session with Mara Makarov, but she feels a powerful sense of anxiety growing inside her.

Something is unsettling her. What has she missed?

Saga gets up from the table and makes her way through to the bedroom, where she pulls on a pair of socks, her black cargo pants and a forest green T-shirt.

She shoves her phone into her back pocket and realises that she needs to be prepared in case a new parcel arrives, that she doesn't have a second to lose.

Mind whirring, she pulls on her trainers and unlocks the front door. She leaves her keyring and her gun in its holster on the chest of drawers, then turns back into the living room and starts the projector.

She opens the lid of her computer, plugs in the last of the hard drives containing the psychologist's sessions with Mara, and hits play.

The blackout curtains are closed, and the image on the grey pull-out screen is bright and sharp.

Following her earlier outbursts, Mara Makarov is now calm, standing in front of her chair with her dark gaze focused somewhere beside the camera, likely on Sven-Ove Krantz. Her hair is glossy and neat, clipped back at one side.

'I read about a serial killer in the paper,' says Mara, her voice tense. 'He killed two people while he was trying to kidnap a child from a nursery in Gamla Enskede.'

'A serial killer?'

'*Ty durak?*'

'Mara, I'm trying to understand what you're saying.'

Saga's heart starts racing. She knows exactly what Mara is talking about.

'I'm getting to it. There were pictures in the paper. Of the killer, you know? In profile and straight on.'

'So he's in prison now?'

'He escaped, I think. I'm not sure, but he's out in any case ... I know how it sounds, but I recognised him. I know it was him. I saw the picture of the serial killer in the paper and it was the captain of our boat,' says Mara, sitting down without taking her eyes off the psychologist.

Saga shudders when she realises that this was what Susanne Hjälm mentioned. Jurek spent his time in isolation at the secure psychiatric unit planning what he would do six years later. He waited until the diplomat gathered his entire family in Sweden, then he kidnapped them and took them to a bunker, where he buried them alive.

'What boat?' the psychologist asks kindly.

'I hadn't thought about it before, how it all started,' says Mara. 'But it started on my grandfather's birthday, when he came to Sweden with the rest of the family. We were supposed to go out on a boat and then have dinner at the Grand Hôtel ...'

'OK?'

'The captain was a wrinkly man who spoke Russian, and it's his picture in the paper, Jurek Walter. The last thing I remember is drinking strawberry juice on deck, from little frosted schnapps glasses ... and then we woke up in a cell.'

'So the person who imprisoned you and your family was a serial killer?' Sven-Ove asks, his voice patient.

'I'm sure it was the man in the picture, but I don't know if he's part of the Russian security service.'

'And it wasn't the same man that brought you food from time to time?'

'No,' Mara replies, restlessly getting up again.

Saga studies the young woman's grey face and realises there was no accident in the archipelago. Jurek sank the boat to hide the kidnapping. His helper, the Beaver, was likely tasked with keeping watch over the family until it was time to bury them alive, but when Joona killed Jurek, the Beaver abandoned his post like a defeated soldier, leaving Mara's family locked in their cell without anyone to bring them food or water. The Beaver fled the country, and is now serving a long prison sentence in Belarus.

'Was it even a prison, the place where you were held?' the psychologist asks.

'I don't know.' Mara claws at her arms.

'Were you taken to Russia?'

'I don't know, I've told you. We had so little food it's hard to remember, but we could've been in Sweden the whole time.'

'OK.'

'You don't have to do that, you don't have to keep saying OK all the time; I know I sound crazy. I told you it was the FSB, that they took us to a prison near Moyaveyab, and now, all of a sudden . . . It's just that when I saw his picture, I remembered all sorts of things.'

'That's not unusual at all; that's how memory works.'

'You have to help me,' Mara begs him. 'It says in the paper that a police officer called Saga Bauer is leading the investigation. You have to talk to her, tell her everything I've just told you: that my family was locked up by this serial killer, that she has to save them.'

'I'll try.'

A chink of light darts across the wall behind Mara, possibly the reflection from a watch or a camera lens.

'It's incredibly urgent,' she continues. 'You have to tell her that—'

Saga turns away, yanking out the cables and taking her computer and the last of the hard drives through to the kitchen table, where she sets them down on top of the journals.

She has finally worked out why she felt so anxious earlier.

The step ladder in the apartment opposite didn't have a single fleck of paint on it. It could be a coincidence, and the decorator might just be using it for the first time, but then it wasn't a painter who left it there.

If not, there might be a sharpshooter on the other side of the road, she thinks. Someone watching her through the scope of a rifle, waiting for the task force to kick down her door.

Saga moves calmly over to the counter, picks up the watering can and makes her way over to the window. As she waters her fern, she gazes down at the street.

It's deserted.

No cars, no cyclists, no people at all. It must have been cordoned off.

Adrenaline surges through her. It feels as though every single hair is standing on end, as though a freezing fog has just settled around her.

Her mind is racing, a voice screaming at her to run.

Heart pounding, Saga walks slowly over to the table, picks up a slice of pizza and bites off the end. She then grabs her computer and the rest of the material in her other hand and saunters out of the kitchen.

It is only once she is no longer visible through any of the windows that she starts moving quickly. She hurries out into the hallway and puts the slice of pizza down on the chest of drawers. She drops her laptop and the hard drive into a rucksack, grabs her gun and keys and a black windbreaker, and heads out into the stairwell. She closes the door behind her, but doesn't bother stopping to lock it.

She can hear quick footsteps on the stairs down below.

Without a sound, Saga turns and runs up to the top floor. She unlocks the steel door and lets it silently swing shut behind her.

Steep roof trusses and naked beams rise around four metres above the uneven tiled floor, and the warm, stale air smells like old wood and stone.

Saga quickly pulls on her holster and jacket, swings the rucksack onto her left shoulder and hurries through the storage space, over to a wooden ladder. She climbs up to the metal hatch used by snow clearers and chimney sweeps, carefully opening it and peering out as the wind lashes her face.

As far as she can see, the roof is deserted.

She pulls herself up through the hatch, closes it behind her and grips the railing tightly with one hand.

Her eyes automatically drift down the steep metal roof, black paint peeling, to the yellow plaster facade opposite, the rows of windows on each floor and the street twenty-five metres below.

She slowly makes her way up the ladder to the ledge, clinging on to a sturdy metal eyelet meant for safety lines as she straightens up.

Saga can see right across Södermalm, over the rooftops and courtyards; she can see Maria Magdalena Church, Götgatan and, in the distance, the Globe Arena.

Her hair whips across her face.

There is only one way she can go.

Crouching down, Saga hurries along the narrow gangway on the ridge of the roof, the metal clanking dully beneath her feet. She reaches the gable end. The buildings on her street are all joined, but the copper roof of the neighbouring building is much steeper and lower than her own. She jumps down, landing around a metre to the side of the ridge, swaying and holding out her arms to steady herself.

Her keys fall out of her pocket, clattering against the copper and getting caught on the eaves railing.

A gull soars overhead on an upward air current.

For a brief, dizzying moment, it seems as though the street down below has vanished into a deep ravine.

Saga crawls up onto the next gangway and follows it along the ridge to the connecting building.

There is a rusty ladder onto the neighbouring rooftop, and she reaches for the ridge railing and grips it tight, pulling herself up.

She slips and hits her hip, but manages to hold on and gets back onto her feet.

The wind tugs at her clothes.

Her legs are shaking as she shuffles over to a chimney, clinging on to the cleaning platform as she makes her way around it and clambers down to a dormer window below.

She can't see anything through the single-glazed window, and she uses her elbow to break the glass, knocking out the shards and climbing into a dark attic space.

The ceiling is so low that she can't stand up straight, and the space is full of dusty doors stacked on the rough wooden floor.

Saga sits down on a flooring joist, takes out her phone and opens her security camera app.

It doesn't seem to be working at first, but then she sees several beams of light swing through the smoke-filled rooms. She switches to HD mode and enlarges the image of the living room, where black-clad officers wearing helmets and protective masks are moving through the space with assault rifles mounted with torches.

Saga gets up, opens a low iron door and makes her way down a narrow set of steps to the top floor of apartments. A delivery driver has left six bags of food against the wall by the lift.

She runs down the stairs, past bicycles and flowerpots.

There are two strollers in the entrance hall, and Saga grabs one of them, releasing the brake and opening the door. She turns right.

Bastugatan is deserted.

Thirty metres up ahead, the police tape is flapping in the breeze, and she can see a black van with a flashing blue light just before the crossing.

She will have to get past it if she wants to escape.

Moving as calmly as she can, she pushes the stroller along the pavement. She pauses after a few metres, using the canopy to hide what she is doing as she loads a round into the chamber and tucks the gun beneath the little pink cushion.

There is no one else out and about.

Saga attempts to empty her mind, to avoid thinking about the operation going on up in her flat.

If she can just manage to get herself out of this then she will find out what is going on and come up with a plan.

She hears barking behind her as she lifts the police tape, ducks underneath it and continues towards the van.

Saga passes it on the left-hand side. She keeps her eyes fixed up ahead, but she can see the blue lights flashing in the chrome accents on the stroller.

If she can just get around the corner, she'll run down to Slussen and disappear among the crowds at the metro station, board a train.

She has almost made it past the van when a police officer steps forward with a coffee in his hand.

Saga glances down at the gun in the stroller and tries to make it look like she is checking on her baby.

She catches a waft of coffee as she passes.

Right as she moves past him, she hears the officer take a step forward. The gravel crunches beneath his boots. Saga shudders, but she keeps going, reaching beneath the cushion for the pistol.

A message comes in over the radio, and the officer turns back towards the van. Saga lets go of the gun and smooths the little blanket over the top.

60

Saga parks the stroller in a doorway, grabs her gun and pushes it into the holster beneath her jacket. She then hurries across Södermalmstorg and in through the shaky glass doors of Slussen station. She doesn't dare look back to check whether anyone is following her. There are people everywhere, streaming towards and past her. A young man is right behind her as she makes her way through the barriers, but he hurries down the stairs to the platform and disappears into the crowd.

A train pulls in to the station, causing the rubbish on the tracks and the dirty brown floor to dance in the breeze.

Saga keeps her head low and her eyes on the ground.

The brakes screech as the train comes to a halt.

She follows the throng onto the train, lingering by the doors in case she needs to make a quick escape.

A middle aged man with stubble and a blue sports jacket is standing at the other end of the carriage, and he glances at her before looking away.

The train sets off, and an older woman holding a bunch of flowers comes close to losing her balance.

Saga is used to being stared at, and it bothers her that the man with the stubble hasn't looked her way again.

She takes out her mobile and rings Randy.

He rejects her call, but as the train approaches Rådmansgatan he phones her back.

'I can't talk to you,' he says in a stressed-sounding voice.

Judging by the acoustics, she would guess he is in a toilet cubicle.

'Seriously, what the hell's going on?' she asks.

The train thunders into the next station.

'Saga, you have to hand yourself in and—'

'What the hell is going on?' she repeats.

'They're trying to work out whether you're involved in the killings.'

'Do you think I'm involved?'

'It doesn't matter what I think.'

'It might to me.'

'Why?'

'Because . . .'

The doors open with a hiss, and Saga studies everyone getting onto the train, the handful of people still on the platform.

'I have to go,' he says. This time, he sounds sad.

'Randy, I need somewhere to hide, somewhere to—'

He ends the call, and Saga leaves the train just before the doors close. The man with the stubble meets her eye through the door as the train sets off.

Saga crosses the platform and gets onto the next southbound train.

The doors close, and the train pulls away.

A middle aged woman sits down with her back to Saga, eating an apple and watching her in the dark screen of her phone.

The carriages sway as the train passes a switch, and they slow into Central Station.

Saga gets off the train, pushing her way through the other passengers to reach the stairs. On the next floor up, she jumps onto the train already waiting at the platform.

A piercing warning signal rings out, and the doors remain open. The departure is repeated over the tannoy.

The woman with the apple reappears, taking a seat at the far end of the carriage as she talks to someone on her phone.

The doors close, and the train sets off.

Saga's mind is racing. The National Task Force just stormed her apartment. They think she is directly involved in the murders.

She is standing with her face to the window, and though her heart is beating at a normal rate, her body is prickly with sweat.

Grey concrete walls race by outside.

They pass stations and neighbourhoods, and the train slowly empties out. The woman is still sitting at the other end of the carriage, now with her apple core in a napkin.

Saga leaves the train in Fruängen, running up the escalator and out of the building, cutting across the square between the fruit stands.

She glances back over her shoulder and then turns off onto the main road, following it to the right.

A white van overtakes her and pulls up by the kerb a few hundred metres ahead.

She passes a removal van, four cardboard boxes waiting to be loaded into the back stacked on the pavement beside it.

Saga drops her phone into one of them and turns off onto a narrow side street.

Twenty minutes later, when she reaches the sixties' villa with the huge windows, she cuts across the paving slabs by the front door and makes her way over to the side entrance. She rings the bell and then steps back into the shadows, pressed up against a warped fence entangled with weeds.

She hears a series of heavy thuds on the stairs, and the door opens.

'Saga?' Karl Speler seems surprised to see her.

He is wearing a brown T-shirt with the words 'Gentlemen Take Polaroids' printed across the chest, plus a pair of upturned black jeans. The brass buckle on his belt is barely visible beneath his bulging stomach.

'Are you alone?' she asks.

'Yeah, I—'

'Can I come in?'

'Sure, I just need to sort—'

She barges past him and closes the door behind her, turning the lock and switching off the ceiling light.

'Are you being followed?'

'No,' she replies, making her way down the stairs.

Saga hears him hurrying after her as she reaches the basement. As on her previous visit, the spotlights on the ceiling are focused on the most important objects in his little museum. The case displaying her bloody slippers glitters in the light, and she notices a replica of Jurek's old-fashioned prosthetic arm on a sideboard.

She continues into the dark kitchen, behind the bar counter, and pours herself a glass of water.

Karl comes in after her and perches on one of the tall bar stools, breathing heavily through a half-open mouth. His face is flushed.

'Can I stay here for a few days?' Saga asks him.

'Afraid not,' he replies, though a moment later he grins, his pointy teeth gleaming. 'What do you think? Of course you can.'

'Thanks,' she says, refilling her glass.

'What's going on?' he asks, pushing his long hair back.

'I just need to lie low for a while.'

'Because . . .?'

'It doesn't matter, I don't want to get you mixed up in this.'

'I *want* to get mixed up in this,' he replies.

61

Karl shakes his wrist to set the winding mechanism in his black Rolex in motion, then calmly studies Saga. She takes another sip of water, puts down her glass and dries her mouth with the back of her hand before meeting his eye.

'You can't write about anything I tell you.'

'OK,' he says, chewing on a nail.

'Do you understand what I just said?'

'Yes, I do,' he nods. 'What's going on?'

Saga sits down on the bar stool opposite him and takes a deep breath. 'I've been trying to stop a serial killer, but in the process I've somehow managed to become . . . a suspect myself.'

'In the murders?'

'I think so.' She sighs.

'What makes you think that? What have they said?'

'I'm suspended from work and the National Task Force stormed my apartment earlier.'

'Seriously?'

'Yup.'

A crumpled jacket with a worn lining is hanging on a hook beneath the counter. The sound of the TV seeps through the ceiling from the family home above.

'Why do they think you're involved?' asks Karl.

'They'll realise they're wrong soon enough, but I guess it's because I've been working on my own quite a bit . . . and I might have overstepped a few boundaries.'

'But you're not involved in the murders?'

'Are you seriously asking me that?'

'Yes.'

'I'm not involved.'

Saga peers through to the room next door. There is a plastic cover over the shuffleboard, and the armchairs, table and floor are strewn with empty beer cans, energy drinks, food wrappers and an empty bag from McDonald's.

'The NCU know who the killer is,' she tells him. 'But they seem to think I've been working with her.'

'So it's a woman?'

'Her name is Mara Makarov. It was actually thanks to you that we managed to find her – she went to see Jakov Fauster in prison several times.'

'Woah, really?' he says, his face cracking into an involuntary smile.

Saga takes off her windbreaker, rolls it up and puts it down on the bar counter. Her green T-shirt is inside out, the strap of her holster twisted.

'So is Fauster the link between her and Jurek?' Karl asks.

'One of them.'

She loosens her pistol from the holster, pops the magazine into her left hand and clears the round from the chamber.

'What else?' he asks.

'It seems as though Jurek Walter killed her entire family.'

'First I've heard of that.'

Saga pushes the cartridge into the magazine, slots it back into place and returns the gun to the holster.

'What I do know is that she was a patient at the secure psychiatric clinic in Ytterö when you wrote your article about Jurek,' she explains, nodding to the framed cutting on the wall. 'One of the copies that were sold before the rest of the edition was seized and destroyed must have ended up in the dayroom there, because Mara immediately recognised Jurek as the man who drugged and kidnapped her family. She was utterly convinced it was him, and she begged her psychologist to get in touch with me.'

'But he thought she was psychotic?'

'Well, yes and no. He did actually call me, he told me all about his patient and what she'd said.'

Saga trails off, returning to that conversation in her mind. She remembers listening to Sven-Ove Krantz, asking a few follow-up questions and then jotting everything down. The problem was that it all came too late, because by that point she was already lost in Jurek's dark labyrinth.

'Did you believe her story?'

'I mean, I didn't doubt for a second that Jurek had taken her family, but at the same time . . . She said she'd escaped from somewhere called Moyaveyab, and that didn't throw up any hits. What were we supposed to do? Scour the whole of Sweden and Russia with sniffer dogs?'

She falls silent again, staring straight ahead as her hand moves slowly back and forth across the bar counter.

'So what happened?' asks Karl.

'What can I say? You know what happened. I didn't manage to save anyone, I failed miserably, which is probably why my colleagues think I'm helping Mara Makarov get revenge now.'

'How is she getting revenge?'

'She's been killing people close to me and Joona, several of our colleagues. She hates the police because we didn't save her family. She's fixated on me, but she hates Joona most of all.'

'Why?'

'Because he ran when he could have stopped Jurek, because he chose to save his daughter over everyone else.'

'Sounds like a human reaction.'

'Yeah, but those of us left behind paid a price.'

'You're angry with him?'

'Yeah, I am . . . And I don't care that it's unfair of me.'

She picks up her rucksack from the floor and takes out her laptop and the journals.

'You should hand yourself in and tell them everything.'

'I don't have time,' she says, starting the computer.

'It's the only sensible thing to do.'

'What is?'

'Handing yourself in, getting a lawyer and—'

'I can't.'

'Why can't you—'

'No more questions,' she cuts him off. 'Sorry, but I need to think.'

She opens Sven-Ove Krantz's journal and reads his notes from the session after Mara begged him to get in touch with Saga, hoping she would be able to save her family.

The psychologist briefly describes how he went into the day room and found the paper, flicking through it until he found the article with the big headline and the photographs.

In my opinion, the text is rather speculative and irresponsible. There is no evidence for the existence of a classified serial killer, though the murders and attempted kidnapping outside the nursery must have taken place. At the same time, if detective superintendent Saga Bauer really is investigating the case alongside the National Crime Unit, then the matter is probably more complex than a simple custody dispute.

The next entry covers Sven-Ove telling Mara that he shared her information with the detective she mentioned, and it's clear that Mara experienced a manic episode after that. All she could think about was leaving the clinic to help the police save her family.

Saga finds her thoughts turning back to the psychologist's phone call once again. He came across as warm, empathetic and articulate as he told her about an unspecified patient who had shared frightening details that seemed to be linked to Saga's case.

Saga had made a note of the details and archived a recording of the call, but she has a clear memory of thinking that the information here felt more like a psychotic delusion than anything – especially given the detail about Jurek working for the KGB.

'Did your patient mention where this man took her family?' Saga asked him.

'No, she can't remember, just that there was a sign with the name Moyaveyab on it . . . Somewhere in Russia, perhaps? Or Sweden?'

Saga had realised that it was an impossible task, even if the family did exist and were still alive. By that point, she was already in an extreme situation – one that would soon escalate and culminate in utter disaster.

62

After the rain in the uplands, the mossy landscape looks almost unnaturally green. The Kaldakvísl River has carved a deep, winding canyon through the volcanic rock, and the water pushes Sven-Ove Krantz's waders against his thighs and hips, the steady stream trying to pull him forward and off to one side.

With a few slight tugs, he reels in the little fly with its shimmering peacock and goose feathers, silver hook and bluish-black hackle.

He slowly moves to one side and attempts a new underhand cast. Tiny droplets of water spray across his right hand as the line shoots out and rolls over the surface of the water. The leader catches the light, and the fly lands perfectly in the calm middle channel.

The meltwater from the glacier is so cold that Sven-Ove's feet are numb, but he can't stop now.

The fly ends up in the choppy water around a rock. It disappears beneath the surface, and he raises his rod and immediately feels the tug of a catch. The reel whirrs as the char darts away across the river, into the shady water by the sheer rockface on the far side.

Sven-Ove allows his rod to bend so much that the bamboo creaks.

In his rucksack, his phone starts buzzing.

The char rushes downstream, pausing deep in the dark river. The taut line starts to hum as the fast water pulses against it.

Sven-Ove waits, letting the fish wear itself out as he reads the crystal clear water.

Its snow-white abdomen bursts into sight as the fish veers sharply to one side, straight towards the seething, frothing water in the fastest section of the river.

Sven-Ove tries to hold on, knows there is a risk that the surging water will pull the hook out of its mouth.

The char is still struggling slowly towards the rapids, and he uses the brake, watches the line cut through the surging water.

He straightens his arm and lifts the rod; it bends, creaking, almost forming a semi-circle.

The fish stops abruptly, tugging on the line and turning back towards the steep bank.

Sven-Ove won't give in to any more escape attempts; he plans to leave the big char to work against the unyielding elasticity of the rod until it is so tired he can calmly reel it in.

Just five minutes later, the fish breaks the surface, rolling onto its side and throwing up a cascade of water.

Sven-Ove carefully brings it in, making sure to keep the char just beneath the surface to prevent it getting tangled up in the thin leader and pulling it loose.

He guides it towards him, letting it glide through the top layer of water, carefully gripping it just above the gills and unhooking the fly. He lifts the char from the water, studying its perfect body, its silver-flecked sides and lead grey back, kissing it on its rounded nose before letting it swim away.

Sven-Ove wades back upstream. He can no longer feel his feet, and he stumbles on the smooth rocks, though he manages to keep his balance and to clamber up onto dry land.

The pale clouds seem to be closing in on the dark grey mountaintops.

He lowers his rod to the moss and has just taken off his rucksack when his phone starts buzzing again.

'Krantz,' he answers the call, catching a whiff of fish from his hand.

'My name is Joona Linna,' says a man with a Finnish accent. 'I'm a detective with the National Crime Squad.'

'I'm actually on leave at the moment, what is this regarding?'

'It's to do with one of your former patients,' the man explains. 'Do you have time to meet?'

'Absolutely. I'm currently 150 kilometres east of Reykjavik.'

'Do you tie the flies yourself?'

'Yes,' Krantz replies in surprise, looking around. 'You could call it a hobby.'

'Do you remember a patient by the name of Mara Makarov?' asks Joona.

'I assume that . . . that a detective with the National Crime Unit is aware of the relevant laws surrounding confidentiality, which must mean that Mara has done something particularly stupid.'

'She's suspected of six murders.'

'Could you be mistaken?'

'What was she like as a patient?'

'Incredibly anxious to begin with, though she responded well to treatment. We reduced her medication to a stable minimum and eventually discharged her to outpatient care.'

Sven-Ove sits down on a rock and tells the detective everything he remembers about getting to know Mara and her traumas, and he then describes his method of treating a patient's psychotic statements as true.

'That was why I did what seemed appropriate,' he explains. 'I recorded Mara's recollections and got in touch with the officer in charge of the case.'

'Do you remember their name?'

'Saga Bauer.'

'How did she react?'

'She listened to what I had to say and thanked me for my help. I'm afraid I don't know what happened after that.'

'Do you remember what you told Saga?'

'Not in detail, though it's all recorded in Mara's journals. It was something to do with the KGB or a serial killer having kidnapped her family and locked them away somewhere near to . . . she mentioned the name of a place that didn't exist.'

'You don't happen to remember the name, do you?'

'Just that it sounded Russian, Dayaveyab or something similar? No, I'm not sure . . . In any case, Mara claimed she had escaped from the killer and that the police wouldn't listen to her, that they simply brought her to the emergency psychiatric ward . . . She claimed she would have been able to find and save her family if it weren't for that.'

Sven-Ove gets to his feet and gazes out across the surging water, overcome with a sudden rush of happiness at the prospect of having the river to himself for another four days.

320

'Did you ever get an update of any kind from Saga Bauer?' asks Joona.

'No, but nor did I expect one.'

'Did Mara change her story over time?'

'She dropped the part about the KGB.'

'And did she ever ask you to contact anyone other than Saga Bauer?'

'No, though she often asked me whether Bauer had been in touch.'

'Did she talk about anyone else?'

'The captain of the boat, mostly – she was convinced he was the same person as the serial killer Saga Bauer was hunting. She also talked about her family, her parents Ivan and Tatiana, her sister, Natasha. Natasha's young son, Ilya.'

'And the prison guard?'

'Yes, though never by name.'

'Any other patients from Ytterö?'

'She mentioned them from time to time.'

'Anyone by the name of Jakov Fauster, Master Fauster?'

'No.'

'Jurek Walter?'

'I'm not sure, but I'll be back in Stockholm next week, I can check the journals if you like.'

'One last question,' Joona says calmly. 'Someone referred to Mara as "the Spider". What do you make of that?'

Sven-Ove gazes out at the water again, though in his mind he can see Mara, hear her breathless way of talking.

'I remember that she often used to talk about the spiders she saw while she was being held prisoner. Tiny hunters that paralysed their victims and spun webs around them, injecting them with poison and dissolving them whole.'

* * *

Joona puts his phone down and gazes out at Adolf Fredrik's Church, across the rooftops to City Hall and the elaborate spire of the old Police Authority building.

He suspects he knows what happened after the psychologist got in touch with Saga on Mara Makarov's behalf: Saga became so important to Mara that she is still turning to her now, even though she has stepped into the role of the killer herself.

Joona needs to talk to Saga, and urgently. He doesn't believe she has been helping Mara in any way, but even if she has it would be best for her to hand herself in as soon as possible.

There haven't been any police conferences yet, but the media has already begun to speculate and the atmosphere at the NCU is dangerously fraught.

Saga's telephone was traced to Säffle, to the back of a moving van that was being unloaded.

It has also emerged that she does, in fact, have a link to Stefan Broman: she filed a police report on Saturday, accusing him of regularly buying sex.

On top of that, forensics have found traces of caustic soda on her motorcycle and horse hair in one of her rucksacks.

Manvir ordered a search of Saga's apartment, and the situation could easily escalate to a nationwide alarm and, ultimately, an armed response.

Joona tries to imagine everything that has happened from Saga's perspective, and he is sure she must understand why the suspicion has fallen on her. As soon as she swallows her pride, he is confident she will get in touch.

Joona picks up his phone and calls Morgan Malmström to share his thoughts.

'I understand what you're saying,' Morgan replies after a brief pause, 'but the fact of the matter is that Saga is now one of our main suspects.'

'Yes, and that's a mistake. She has a lot of questions to answer,' says Joona, 'but she does actually have an alibi for almost all the murders.'

'I know, but I—'

'She hasn't shot anyone.'

'And we're not saying she has. But she is involved, Manvir has proof of that . . . Besides, you don't have to actually fire the gun to be guilty of murder.'

Joona closes his eyes for a few seconds, sits down and takes a deep breath.

'All I'm saying is that if . . . if I'm going to try to convince Saga to hand herself in, I need to be able to guarantee that it'll just be me who meets her to bring her in, no one else.'

'Will she trust you?'

'I think so, but the whole thing needs to be discreet. No formal booking, no prosecutors, no press statements or—'

'Two days,' Morgan interrupts him.

'What?'

'I'll give you two days.'

'And do I have your word that I can do this on my terms?'

'Yes.'

'If I hear from her, I'll call you and you can arrange for her to bypass the booking process in custody.'

'If you think that's for the best,' the boss replies.

63

Saga has just cleared Karl Speler's coffee table to make room for her laptop and the last of the hard drives when he tells her he is going for a shower.

'Could I borrow your phone to make a call?'

'The code's 915837,' he says as he hands it to her.

Karl leaves the room, and Saga perches on the arm of the chair to call Randy's private number.

'Randy,' he answers, a note of surprise in his voice.

'Can you talk?' she asks quietly.

'Saga, what's going on?'

'I didn't do any of the things they're saying.'

'You don't need to tell me,' he says. 'I already know. You need to hand yourself in before—'

'We'll never catch the Spider if I do that.'

'That's not your responsibility, you're not even an officer anymore.'

Saga peers up at Karl's cluttered shelves, at the game console, the bong, the candle in the shape of the Statue of Liberty and the jack-in-the-box featuring a clown in a red and yellow silk costume.

'Has anything else come to light?' she asks.

'No, I don't think so.'

'No new figurines?'

'No.'

All around her on the floor, there are discarded crisp packets, sweet wrappers, game counters and LPs from the eighties.

'The National Task Force stormed my apartment,' she tells him.

'I just heard they were planning to search the place.'

'With assault rifles, snipers, stun grenades . . .'

'This whole thing is fucking insane,' Randy whispers.

'I really don't get it,' she replies, almost inaudibly.

'You said you needed somewhere to hide. I might—'

'I don't want to get you any more involved than you already are.'

'I don't care anymore.'

'In case I die, I just wanted to let you know that you were the one,' she says, ending the call before he has time to reply.

Saga takes a deep breath, wipes a few tears from her cheek and then slumps down in front of her computer to watch Krantz's final few sessions with Mara Makarov. Their conversations span more than a year, but she is always incredibly consistent in every detail.

Karl Speler emerges from the bathroom, hair standing on end and a towel around his shoulders. He moves a stack of newspapers and sits down in the armchair to watch the therapy session.

Mara Makarov has put down her book, Archimedes' *On the Equilibrium of Planes*, and her hair is neatly combed and sleek, her face composed, her gaze intelligent.

She calmly explains that she needs to leave the secure unit in order to save her family. Sven-Ove replies that she has made great progress, that they have reduced her level of medication and that he will talk to his colleague about discharging her that autumn.

Mara keeps talking about Saga Bauer, asking whether she has been in touch, whether the killer has been arrested.

'I haven't heard from her,' Krantz replies.

'Strange,' she whispers.

Six months later, Mara is pacing her room like a caged animal that refuses to admit defeat. She seems almost catatonic, mumbling anxiously to herself in Russian.

It's clear that she can't stand how long it is taking for her to be discharged into outpatient care. The minute the psychologist says something, she interrupts him by shouting '*Idi v Moyaveyab! Idi v Moyaveyab!*' over and over before falling silent and walking in circles again.

Almost fifteen months pass before the next session, and she is completely transformed yet again: quiet and weighed down this time.

'How do you imagine the future?' Sven-Ove Krantz asks towards the end of the final recording.

'Mine?'

'Yes.'

'Do I have one?'

'Try to give me at least one sentence describing the future as you see it.'

'I saw a little farm once, on the outskirts of Västerhaninge, I think,' Mara says, getting lost in thought for a moment before she goes on. 'I imagine being there with my family, on a hot summer's day. The meadows are dusty, the grass is yellow, the leaves on the trees have all curled up ... And I'm sitting on a chair in the shade by the tractor, eating a cinnamon bun in a greaseproof paper case, watching Vadim and Aglaya's kids play croquet. That's how I imagine my death.'

Saga closes the lid of her computer once the final recording comes to an end and she turns to Karl, who is sitting with his arms folded.

'That was that,' she says.

'Interesting,' he replies, getting to his feet.

As Saga reads through Sven-Ove Krantz's last journal, she hears Karl changing the sheets on the bed.

The psychologist explains that he believes Mara's therapy is complete, that she is now reconciled with her life story and her self image. He then notes that at each weekly meeting going forward, he will recommend that the senior physician discharges Mara Makarov.

Saga gets up as Karl comes back into the room and makes up the sofa with his old sheets. She looks up at his framed article about Jurek Walter and realises that he was right about most of it – though in reality the killer was far worse than he could ever have imagined.

'Could I use your shower?' she asks.

'There are clean towels in the cupboard just outside.'

Saga heads through to the bathroom, closes the door and notices that the lock is missing. She hangs a towel from the Grand Hôtel in Oslo on a hook.

The pale blue flooring is bumpy, there are yellow disposable razors on the edge of the sink, and the toilet doesn't have a lid. The black mould has climbed almost a metre up the wall in the far corner behind the washing machine.

Saga double checks to make sure there are no hidden cameras, then she gets undressed.

The showerhead has come loose from the wall, and is hanging from a piece of wire tied to a pipe on the ceiling. She carefully turns the knob, waits a few seconds and then steps beneath the hot water.

The shower curtain rattles loudly.

As Saga washes her hair, she thinks about what Sven-Ove Krantz wrote about Mara being reconciled with her life story. Those words suggested the psychologist had changed more than his patient over the years. He had treated her as though she was telling the truth, and had eventually come to believe that her words really did correspond with reality.

When Saga leaves the shower, she notices a large pool of soapy water on the floor beneath the washing machine in the far corner.

She pulls her dirty clothes back on and leaves the bathroom. The mouth-watering aroma of fried bacon hits her, and she notices that the air around the bar counter is hazy. From the stereo, a solemn pop song from the eighties is booming. Karl has set two places on the bar counter, and has filled a jug with water.

'You didn't have to cook,' she says.

'Pff.'

'Though I am hungry.'

He lifts the frying pan from the stove and sets it down on a cork mat.

'I've got other cutlery, but in my experience this is a dish best eaten with a spoon,' he explains.

'A spoon is fine.'

'OK, Bon appétit,' he says with a grin, adding a squirt of ketchup to his plate.

It could just be her hunger, but the combination of quick-cook macaroni, fried onion, bacon, salt and pepper is surprisingly delicious.

As they eat, Karl tells Saga that the world of journalism increasingly seems to be about nothing other than getting clicks to increase ad revenue.

'But what really worries me is the journalists' lack of independence,' he continues. 'That they're no longer allowed to give their own opinion, they're just expected to take the owner's line on everything.' He dabs his lips.

'Do you really think so?' she asks, helping herself to more food from the pan.

'Not really, but I'm bitter and it's nice to whine every once in a while,' he replies with a grin, baring his pointy teeth.

'You're from South Africa, right?' she asks, nodding to the flag on the wall.

'Yeah, but my mum and I moved here when I was fifteen. I just kept my dad's surname. It means player or gamer in Afrikaans.'

'Did you already speak Swedish?'

'Yeah, Mum is from Småland.'

'What was it like, moving here?'

'Nice, quiet, cold ... I'd gone to private school, sat all the high school exams here in the space of one year, got top marks and enrolled on a journalism course. And now here I am!'

Saga takes a sip of water and lowers the glass to the counter, watching the light as it refracts on the swaying surface.

'Seems like you've got an issue with the drain in the shower,' she says.

'The floor slopes the wrong way,' he replies. 'The showerhead is broken, the sink has a crack in it ... It's not exactly my dream home, but what can I say? It matches me and my career.'

'You just had a bit of bad luck.'

'I suppose it is unlucky to be in such a crappy location, shut in, with thin walls. I can hear the owners whenever they have sex up there, which I guess is a bonus ... There are no windows, no locks, there's no extractor fan ... No cinnamon buns in greaseproof paper or—'

'I have to go,' she interrupts him, hopping down from her stool.

'Sorry if I—'

'No, I just need to check something,' she explains, wiping her lips with a piece of paper towel.

His mention of cinnamon buns hit her with crystalline precision.

'Can I come?'

'If you've got a car,' she replies, strapping her holster over her shoulder.

'Do I look like the kind of person who has a car?'

'You've got a nice watch,' she says as she pulls on her shoes.

'My dad wanted to give me his Rolex when I turned eighteen, but I refused to take it. I was too proud ... So I bought this at auction when I turned fifty.'

'I'll be back in a few hours,' she says, turning to leave.

'Where are you going?'

'Västerhaninge.'

Karl grabs his jacket and hurries after her through his little museum. The display case containing Saga's bloody slippers shakes as they pass.

'You think that's where Mara is, because of what she said about her own death?'

'She needs somewhere spacious and quiet enough to store all her chemicals.'

'I'll get us a car,' he says.

64

Sitting in her dimly-lit kitchen, Mara Makarov bites the cuticle on her thumb. There are three photographs laid out on the table in front of her, and she picks one of them up and tears it in two, then gets to her feet. The empty tins on the floor clink together as she walks across to the stove. She turns the knob for the smallest ring to its highest setting and moves back over to the table, sweeps the remaining photographs to the floor and hits the tabletop several times.

'*Idi v Moyaveyab!*' she shouts, gripping her throat with both hands.

Mara squeezes until she can no longer breathe, staring at her reflection in the window.

She lets go and peers out at the maypole in the garden. The birch leaves are brown and crisp, the wildflowers wilted and dead.

On the ground around the pole, she can see a ring of pale bones: skulls and ribs, thigh and pelvis bones.

That last part is all in her mind.

She hears a clicking sound, and Mara spins around and pulls the pistol from her holster.

She had forgotten about the burner.

The ring is glowing red.

White bones and red blood, she thinks. White and red, white and red.

Mara sculpted a figure in clay earlier, studying the photographs and using the tip of her knife to carve its facial features before casting a silicone mould around it.

She moves over to the stove and places the crucible containing the lumps of pure tin into the indentation in the middle of the ring.

She used the overhead crane to lift the heavy rubber sack onto the pallet truck earlier that morning. His legs were hanging over the edge of the pallet as she hauled him over to the garage doors, and he started screaming and shaking in pain when she tipped him down onto the gravel. The base had already eaten away his skin and face by that point, his minor extremities.

When she got into the pickup and reversed over to the garage, she accidentally drove over his head. The sack burst, causing blood and grey matter to spray across the gravel. She pulled forward and got out of the car, lowered the tailgate and winched the sack up beside the drums that were strapped down in the bed. His body was limp, though every so often a nerve spasm shot through him like a shudder.

Mara mended the hole in the sack, shovelled gravel over the blood, parked her car by the edge of the trees and pulled a tarpaulin over the top. She then headed back inside and ate half a tin of tuna in olive oil before throwing up.

She is now standing at the stove, watching the lumps of tin melt into a mirror-like pool.

She grabs a match, breaks off the head and dips it into the liquid metal. A pale grey coil of smoke curls into the air.

Mara switches off the hob, lifts the crucible from the ring and gently tips it into the silicone mould. She can feel the heat of the molten metal inside, and she adds a little more and shudders.

A small bead of the silver liquid lands on her index finger. She feels a brief burning sensation, followed by searing pain.

Mara turns her shaking hand palm up and pours the last of the molten tin into it.

The metal hisses when it meets her skin, and the pain makes her legs give way. She slumps to the floor with her back against a cupboard door, clutching her right wrist and watching as the metal hardens and loses its sheen on her palm.

After a few minutes, she gets up on shaking legs, picks off the small crust of metal and hears it clatter into the sink.

Now wide awake, Mara takes out her schedule – complete with timeline, parameters and mathematical equations – and checks it for the thousandth time.

Her heart is still racing as she sits down at the table.

Despite the fact that she has had to adjust her plans several times, the past is near-perfect.

On the other side of the present, she has each key moment circled in red.

She studies the branching options the future may hold.

Time and time again, she calculates the probability and chance, working out stochastic variables and setting them against psychological likelihood.

65

In the amber glow of the street lamps, the shadows of the pillars dance back across Saga's determined face and her left hand on the wheel.

Karl is in the passenger seat beside her, trying his hardest not to glance over too often.

They have just passed Söderhagen in their stolen black Porsche, but twenty minutes ago Saga was standing on the street outside the large villa where Karl rents the basement apartment. She watched as he moved through the owners' kitchen in the blue light of the TV in the living room. He didn't say a word, didn't make a sound, didn't switch on any lights; he just snuck through to the hallway and took the key from the cabinet.

A few seconds later, the garage door swung open.

Saga got behind the wheel, and Karl followed her instructions and began searching for farms close to Västerhaninge.

He quickly found fifteen, but none with any links to the surname Makarov. It wasn't until he expanded the search to include the other names Mara had mentioned – Vadim and Aglaya – that they finally found a match.

A man by the name of Vadim Gurkin had bought a farm on Ormstavägen just one year before the accident in the Stockholm archipelago. The Russian relative who inherited the property once Vadim was declared dead hasn't yet applied for new title deeds from the National Land Survey, and as a result the farm remains in a kind of limbo.

At the Fors intersection, Saga leaves the motorway and drives past a dark quarry, beneath a bridge and onto road 560.

'This is all very exciting,' says Karl, 'but don't you think . . . Wouldn't it be best to, you know, hand yourself in and tell the police about this place instead?'

'There's no time; I'm the only one who can save Joona.'

She accelerates down the narrow gravel track that curves around a handful of blue industrial buildings.

'Why are you the only one?' Karl asks hesitantly.

'Because she said so, because she hates him more than anyone else.'

'Has Makarov said that—'

'If I don't stop Mara, she'll kill him.'

'You need to talk to Joona.'

'Maybe,' she whispers.

They leave the industrial buildings and their empty parking spaces and row upon row of rubbish containers behind, and the countryside opens up around them.

Saga drives along the bumpy gravel track, past fields with electric fences and into the dense woodland. Branches scrape against the side of the car, and the half-light forms a narrow avenue up ahead.

She slows down the minute she spots the deep potholes, but the car still shakes as she drives over them.

'We're getting close,' Karl says quietly.

It is almost impossible to make out the ground between the trunks, but suddenly the woods open out onto a pale, flat grey landscape. The fields have been left fallow, and they look dry and dusty in the gloom.

Anxious jays circle a clump of trees, and a few deer are grazing beneath the power lines in the distance.

'It must be somewhere around here,' she says.

They follow the road around the bend and catch a glimpse of a dark farm through the dense brush.

A cluster of dilapidated red buildings off to one side.

There are no cars parked outside, no lights in any of the cracked windows.

They pass the turn off to the farm and continue for another couple of hundred metres before turning around at the first opportunity. Saga drives back along the track and pulls over behind a cluster of trees where they can't be seen from the farm.

'I'm going to go and have a look around,' she tells Karl. 'No matter what happens, don't get out of the car.'

'So what am I supposed to do? Just sit here?'

'If you see any cars driving by – a pickup, most likely – I want you to duck down and call Joona the minute it's out of sight.'

'You want me to talk to Joona Linna?'

'Tell him you're calling on my orders, that Ormstavägen needs to be immediately cordoned off by the Fors exit.'

'OK, sure . . .'

She takes his phone from the compartment between the seats and adds Joona as a contact.

'In thirty minutes, I want you to get in touch with Joona and tell him what's going on – but don't leave the car,' she says as she opens the door.

'Got it.'

'Do you have a torch?'

'No . . . I mean, I've got one of these,' he replies, holding up a small Maglite keyring.

'Perfect,' she says, taking it from him.

The little torch is pink, so small it would probably fit inside a matchbox.

'Be careful,' he says as she gets out of the car.

Saga quietly closes the door and starts walking towards the farm. The tightly packed gravel crunches beneath her feet.

The wind sweeps through the brush and weeds.

Saga pauses and pulls her pistol from the holster, holding it close to her body as she leaves the track.

The buildings are packed tightly together, barns, garages and storage spaces that seem to have been knocked through to form one large interconnected space. Their roofs vary in height and pitch, and most seem to be made from corrugated metal or black zinc.

On the ground off to one side there are a few tractor tyres, excavator buckets and stacks of logs beneath a green tarpaulin, and Saga catches a glimpse of a cylindrical diesel tank at the edge of the forest. It is probably around four metres in length, painted a rusty red colour.

She crosses the gravel in the pale evening light.

There are five green plastic bins by one wall of the garage, the dark red wood rotten at the lower edge.

The paint on the window frames and transoms is peeling, some of the panes are missing, and there are shards of glass in the weeds.

She opens the lids of the plastic bins and sees that they are all empty.

A flock of starlings sweeps in over the rooftops, briefly landing in an old apple tree before taking off again.

Saga moves past the tall garage door and over to a smaller side door, slowly pushing the heavy black latch to one side and nudging it open.

She peers in to the dark space. The air smells like metal and oil, and when she switches on Karl's little torch she can make out a rusty tractor with a seed drill and a baler with flat tyres.

Saga steps inside and closes the door behind her, moving past the tractor and stepping over a harrow full of dry grass.

She stops to listen, lowering her Glock, the weight of the gun still lingering in her shoulder muscles.

There is a sturdy metal chain on the floor between the loading forks and bulldozer blades.

Saga reaches the end of the garage, and she opens a narrow door onto a cramped passageway with a sandy floor. She can see the yard outside through the gaps in the wall.

Something rustles in the darkness up ahead.

Saga raises her pistol. There is a large rat at the far end of the passageway, and it slinks away as she makes her way over to the door into the next building. Saga turns off the torch, plunging herself into darkness again. She is just about to lift the latch on the door when she hears a shuffling sound behind her.

It sounds like someone just brushed their hand across the bonnet of the tractor.

She holds her breath and moves her finger to the trigger, squeezing it roughly half way.

Every one of her senses is primed and focused on the darkness around her.

Saga hears cautious steps in the sand behind her, and she slowly turns around, aiming in the direction of the sound.

66

Karl Speler is sitting in the dark car, his phone in one hand and his eyes fixed on the turn off up ahead. Using the wing mirror, he checks the road behind him at regular intervals. It looks like nothing but a faint trail through the meadow grass, trees and bushes, disappearing into the forest around fifty metres away.

He pushes his hair back and checks the time.

Saga has been gone five minutes.

Following his conversation with Saga earlier, Karl thinks back to his eighteenth birthday, when his father travelled to Sweden from Cape Town. He wanted to take his son out to lunch, and Karl's mother convinced him to go.

He remembers that his father seemed so much older than he expected, and that he was wearing a short-sleeved shirt, khaki trousers and brown shoes. That the hair on his tanned arms was white.

As they were eating dessert, he pushed a present across the table towards Karl. He had tied a pale blue ribbon around the original box from the sixties.

'Do you really think giving me your old Rolex will make everything OK?' asked Karl. 'If you don't take that back, I'm leaving.'

Karl will never forget the look on his father's face then, his faltering smile. At the time he had thought it was a sign of irritation and miscalculation, but he later came to realise that his old man was probably just fighting back the tears.

'It's a piece of junk anyway,' his father said as he shoved the gift back into his bag.

Karl stares out through the windshield at the gravel track and the turn off to the farm, and he realises he hasn't checked the road behind him in a while. With a shudder, he glances over to the wing mirror and tilts his head slightly.

The road is still pale and deserted, but he can't see if there is anyone right behind the car.

He slowly reaches out and adjusts the rear-view mirror.

The back windscreen is nothing but a black rectangle.

He blinks and tries to get his eyes to focus.

Some sort of dark grey cloud appears at the lower edge of the window.

Karl has just turned to the wing mirror again when he hears a sound.

It's just a branch moving in the wind, he tells himself. Leaves hitting the back mudguard.

Karl rubs his forehead and tips his head back, staring out through the windscreen.

He notices a flickering light through the bushes straight ahead, like a flame struggling in the wind, but it disappears before he has time to focus on it.

His heartrate has picked up, and he grins to himself as he considers the absurdity of the situation: he and Saga Bauer are hunting a serial killer.

Rüssel and Dragan will never believe him.

Karl opens the door and gets out into the cool night air. He checks behind the car and then moves forward until he has a clear view of the farm buildings.

The whole place is dark and quiet.

He is just about to turn back when he sees another flash of light between the planks of wood on the wall of a small lean-to connecting the garage to a larger building.

The splintered glow spills out onto the ground, between the birch trees, making two red reflectors flash.

It's like a pair of eyes opening and closing.

A moment later, the farm is dark again.

Two red reflectors can mean only one thing: the rear lights of a vehicle.

He should go over and check whether they are on Mara's pickup, he thinks, though he quickly realises that is precisely what Saga told him not to do.

She probably spotted the pickup at the edge of the trees as she was approaching the farm.

Karl hesitates for a moment, then hurries back into the Porsche and locks the doors behind him.

He stares out at the road and the turn off to the farm, then checks the rear-view mirror.

The branches sway slowly in the wind.

In the distance, the forest looks almost black.

Karl forces back the thoughts of stacked meat that always used to terrify him as a boy, and he checks the time again. Saga has now been gone for twelve minutes.

He unlocks his phone to make sure he still has battery, but the light from the display makes the car worryingly bright, and Karl immediately switches it off again. He must have been visible from several hundred metres, he thinks.

He drops his phone into the compartment by the gearstick and thinks back to when he was thirty-two, when he got the news that his father had died after a long illness. After the funeral, he told his mother about the time his old man had tried to buy his forgiveness with the Rolex. Karl explained that he had always been on her side, that his father had never understood that loyalty wasn't something you could buy.

'I'm sorry to hear that,' she said, slumping down into a chair.

'What?'

'Your dad always said he'd give you that watch when you turned eighteen,' she said. 'Long before he and I had our problems.'

For the first time, Karl realised that it hadn't been a bribe or an attempt to win him over. There was no ulterior motive to it whatsoever. His father had been thinking about Karl when he first bought the watch – and every time he wore it since.

Sitting in the car, Karl pictures his father's aged face, his tanned arms and the white mark around his left wrist.

He doesn't know why all these thoughts of his father have come back to him now. Was one question from Saga all it took, or is it just because he is scared?

67

Saga moves slowly through what seems to be a utility room. There are five metal cabinets along one wall, dried flypapers hanging in the window, a large zinc tub and stacks of paper napkins on the cement floor.

The powerful adrenaline rush from earlier has started to fade.

She was convinced she had heard someone in the sandy passageway, so sure that she could have fired her gun into the darkness, but when she switched on the torch there was no one there.

Her finger trembled on the trigger.

The sound of creeping footsteps was gone.

She now pauses in front of a narrow door with a small pane of frosted glass above a laminated sign listing all the safety regulations for the workshop.

This is Mara's domain, Saga thinks, raising her Glock before she opens the door.

The soft light from the sky in the west spills in through the row of high windows.

Beneath the bare metal roof, there are a number of sturdy overhead cranes, a lifting system of some kind.

Saga stands quietly for a moment before taking a step forward, securing both sides and hurrying over to a steel workbench, ducking down beneath it.

In a plastic tub to one side, she notices a protective mask and a pair of stained chemical-safe gloves.

There is a faint hint of decomposition in the stale air, a number of large plastic drums lined up against one wall.

She peers over from where she is crouching beside the bench.

Directly beneath the overhead crane, there is a sheet of plywood covered in dried blood that seems to have trickled down into the drain below.

A concrete ramp leads up to a loading dock with an opening hidden behind a thick, yellowing plastic curtain.

Saga decides she will have to search the entire building and then find somewhere to wait for Mara. Rather than trying to solve her riddles, she will call Joona and work alongside him to set a trap for Mara right here at the farm.

She gets up, sweeping the room with her pistol.

Saga stands perfectly still, watching the doors. She focuses on the one out into the utility room and the sandy passageway first, then spins 180 degrees and stares at the tarred wooden door on the other side. It probably leads into the main house, she thinks.

She tears her eyes away from the doors and cuts across the floor towards the plastic curtain hanging over the opening to the more modern part of the farm.

She steps over a roll of thick rubber sheeting and climbs the ramp to the loading dock.

On the other side of the plastic, she can make out a bright room with a number of aluminium ventilation pipes.

She leans against the curtain, and the plastic flaps peel apart with a sticky sound. Saga glances back into the workshop and then slips through the gap, dropping to one knee and shifting her aim from the tall grain dryer outside to a half-open door into a grain storage room.

Time is running out. She only has nine minutes before Karl calls Joona.

Saga makes her way over to the open steel door.

There is a sturdy crossbar hanging against one side of the frame.

The storage room on the other side is empty, with high, metal-lined walls and a dusty floor scattered with grain.

There is a huge stack of pallets in the very middle of the space.

Saga is just about to turn around and head back when she spots something unexpected. On the floor around five metres from the door is a *matryoshka*, a set of Russian nesting dolls.

* * *

For the third time, Karl checks that the car doors are locked. He glances back in the wing mirror and sees the wind ripple through the treetops, making the dark branches sway against the night sky.

He can barely see the road behind him now. The light is so weak that the gravel almost seems to be floating, like a river flowing by, stretching out into a narrow channel.

He stares through the windscreen.

The potholes in the road merge together.

What if Saga didn't see the car, if it was hidden? That would mean she has no idea that Mara is home.

He glances down at the side mirror and then up at the rear-view mirror again.

Through the back window, the road just behind the car is still more or less visible. A root has caused the ground to buckle, pushing up through the gravel like a knee.

He slowly adjusts the mirror to check the ditch behind the car.

The weeds shake, and the white flowers on the ground elder bend slowly to one side.

Karl quickly checks the wing mirror and then turns back to the rear-view mirror.

For a few seconds, everything is still, but then the first row of oxeye daisies starts to move. Between the stalks and the meadow grass, he catches a glimpse of a large hand.

He blinks.

It's all just in his mind, a fantasy.

He had encephalitis when he was twelve, an inflammation of the brain that caused delirium and epileptic fits. The things he experienced during the peak of his fever, before the ambulance got to the little summerhouse in Småland, have never really left him.

It was late evening, and he was sitting alone outside the house.

In the pale light of the moon, he noticed a figure standing at the edge of the wood. A man made from stacked meat, scraps of different animals piled on top of human body parts.

He had a thick neck, a bull's head and human arms that were slick with blood.

The man came closer, stroking the tanned leather of his butcher's apron as he squinted at the house and cocked his head to listen.

Karl didn't dare get up and run inside. He was frozen in fear, and he held his breath until his body began to shake.

When he regained consciousness the next day, he was in the hospital.

Karl glances towards the turn off through the windscreen and then looks up at the wing mirror. He reaches out and adjusts the angle.

There is something in the ditch, wrapped in shiny black fabric.

Whatever it is is moving slowly, making the weeds bend forward.

Karl slumps down in his seat and tries to keep his breathing under control.

He never should have got out of the car, he thinks irrationally, those are the rules.

He hears something scrape against the body of the car, like long nails clawing at the paintwork.

Karl holds his breath.

He isn't sure anymore whether there was something moving in the ditch. Maybe it was just the wind in the weeds.

He clamps a hand to his mouth and tries to breathe quietly between his fingers.

Something thuds against the roof of the car.

He manages to stop himself from crying out.

There is a scraping sound, and a wood pigeon skids down the windscreen, wings flapping in an attempt to regain its balance. It struts across the bonnet.

Karl looks up at the rear-view mirror again.

There is nothing in the ditch after all.

He tries to compose himself.

He is sweating profusely, droplets running down his torso from his armpits.

There's no one here, he thinks as he opens the door. The pigeon flaps away.

Karl's heart is racing as he gets out. He moves around the car, checking the ditch and kicking the weeds. There is a black bin bag lying on the ground in the brush, and he grabs it and peers inside. It is full of old clothes and mismatched shoes.

Karl leaves the bag where it is and starts making his way along the gravel track towards the farm. It isn't often that he is afraid of the dark these days, but the sense of unease is still lingering inside him, making him watchful.

He knows he needs to sabotage Mara's car so that she can't escape.

He turns off onto the narrow track with a strip of grass growing in the middle.

The red buildings are dark, close together, interlinked.

Karl slows down and tries to remember where he saw the light earlier. It must have come from Saga's torch as she made her way from the garage into the main building.

He studies the planks of wood on the wall, the gaps between them, then turns his attention to the cluster of birch trees. He can make out a large tank, and he moves closer.

Right then, he spots the red rear lights.

Karl's eyes scan the ground, and he finds a shard of glass beside the green rubbish bins. He picks it up and starts making his way over to the car.

A number of cracked roof tiles have been stacked against a tree stump.

He passes the diesel cistern and realises that a camouflage net has been draped over the car.

It's an old Ford pickup.

Karl attempts to puncture the back tyre using the piece of glass, but the rubber is too thick.

There might be a knife or a screwdriver in the bed of the truck, he thinks, bending down to loosen one of the straps around a large rock.

He folds back one corner of the net, and hundreds of flies swarm into the air.

Karl's heart starts racing.

He can smell burnt hair and something powerful and chemical.

There is a huge sack of some kind in the bed of the truck. Karl takes a step back. He thinks he can see something quivering beneath the black rubber.

68

The plastic curtain swings back into place behind Saga as she heads through to the workshop and down the concrete ramp.

In the dark, sticky blood around the drain, she notices a few squirming white fly larvae.

Saga studies the two doors and then makes her way over to the furthest one, leading through to the main farmhouse. There is a grooved sheet of metal covering some sort of hole in the floor, and her footsteps take on a strange clang as she walks across it.

Saga steps over a toolbox and reaches the door. It smells like tar.

She hears a shuffling sound through the walls.

Saga dries her right palm on her trousers and then clenches her fist a few times to loosen up her fingers. She raises her gun and takes a deep breath, turning the handle, opening the door and stepping into a dark hallway with a rag rug on the sagging wooden floor.

She should have put her personal issues to one side and reached out to Joona right away, she thinks.

Why is she always so angry?

It's not good that she is doing this alone; it's too dangerous.

The Russian doll seemed to be staring at her earlier, and she imagines all the smaller dolls inside it were staring at her too.

When she reaches an opening that looks like it has been cut into the red woodwork with a chainsaw, she switches on Karl's little torch. The edges are splintered and rough.

The hole leads into a small kitchen with a low ceiling and transom windows looking out onto the yard, where she can see a withered maypole.

Saga keeps her eyes on the door for a moment or two and then lowers her pistol.

The air smells rancid, like rubbish and rotten food, and the floor is strewn with empty tins: ravioli, hotdogs, goulash, tuna, sweetcorn, apricots, mussels, fish balls and sauerkraut.

There is a yellow lampshade on the ceiling, and in the middle of the grey laminate table, there is an open tin of beans beside a book on algorithms.

Saga's eye is drawn to two photographs on the floor beneath the radiator: one of Joona and another, torn in two, of Margot.

A bloody axe has been left in the sink.

There is a stove with a brown tiled splashback, and Saga holds out a hand above the rings. Her heart starts racing when she feels the heat coming off one of them.

The empty tins on the floor clink together as she leaves the kitchen and heads through into a small hallway.

One of the doors leads into the bathroom, and she shines the torch inside.

The floor, walls, basin and toilet are all filthy and grey.

Saga feels a cold draught around her legs, and she wheels around, aiming her gun at the hallway, the main door and the opening into the kitchen, but the house is quiet, no sign of any movement.

With her finger on the trigger, she swings back and makes her way into the bedroom. The roller blind is open, and she can see a thick layer of dust on the bedside table.

Saga catches sight of herself in the glass of a framed wall hanging.

The bed is made, the tightly tucked bedspread studded with dead flies. No one has been sleeping here, that much is obvious. The wardrobe door is ajar, and a dry wasp on the windowsill trembles in the breeze.

Saga looks up at the wall hanging again and feels a wave of adrenaline course through her veins, the hair on her arms standing on end.

Mara is in the doorway right behind her. A slight, colourless figure, with grey hair and a dirty face.

Saga hurls herself to one side, swings around and shoots, but Mara has already gone, her rapid footsteps thudding away down the hallway.

Saga runs after her, firing her pistol again, but she is too slow. The bullet hits the doorframe into the kitchen, sending shards of wood and dust flying through the air.

She races down the hallway and hears the cans on the kitchen floor slamming into one another.

She trains her weapon on the doorway just as Mara disappears through the hole sawn into the wall, her red pistol catching the light.

Saga quickly crosses the kitchen and hears the tarred door swing open.

She rushes out through the hole in the wall and reaches the hallway just as the black door slams shut with a thud.

The floorboards shudder beneath Saga's feet as she fires off three bullets straight through the door.

She hears Mara's footsteps echo across the metal plate in the workshop, and she runs forward and tears the door open.

Mara has almost reached the loading dock.

Saga should shout that she is a police officer, she thinks, tell Mara to stop and lower her weapon, but she just can't bring herself to do it.

Mara ducks down behind a large engine block, turns around and raises her pistol.

Saga throws herself to one side and hits her head on the toolbox. As she scrambles back behind a plastic drum of sodium hydroxide, she manages to knock over a bucket of rancid blood. It slops out across the floor, trickling down into the gap around the metal plate.

The stench is unbelievable.

Saga scrambles to one side and gets to her feet, taking aim when she spots Mara crawling up the concrete ramp.

With her free hand she tries to steady her Glock, but her hands are shaking so much that the sight is still trembling. The pulleys are in the way, and she takes a step to one side and pulls the trigger the minute Mara's right foot comes into view.

The bullet hits the metal railing around the loading bay and ricochets back into the workshop.

Mara darts away, hunched over, and Saga takes aim between her shoulder blades before firing again.

The recoil slams into her shoulder.

Mara drops her pistol, but she is already on the other side of the curtain.

Saga keeps shooting as she rushes after her, and the bullets make a sucking sound as they pass through the thick plastic.

She runs straight across the workshop and up the ramp to the swaying curtain.

Saga takes aim again, trying to read Mara's movements on the other side.

She sees a shadow dart across the floor, through the open metal door into the storage room on the other side, and she pushes through the curtain. She can hear Mara's quick footsteps in the large room up ahead.

Without a single moment's hesitation, Saga runs in after her, through the open metal door. She scans the space and secures both sides and the corners.

The Russian doll has fallen over, and is staring up at her.

Saga points her Glock at the stack of pallets in the middle of the floor. There is nowhere else to hide, no other doors; Mara has nowhere left to run.

She is slowly making her way towards the pallets in a wide arc, prepared to fire again, when the metal door swings shut behind her and she hears the crossbar being slotted into place on the other side.

Someone has just locked her in.

Her heart is beating so hard that she can hear her blood roaring in her ears, but Saga keeps moving around the pallets.

There is no one here.

She looks all around, unable to make sense of what just happened. She heard Mara's footsteps, saw her come through the doorway. She was right behind her, and she knows that she secured both sides of the room.

There was nowhere for her to hide.

The storeroom is nothing but bare floor and smooth walls.

Saga strides around the pallets, checking again.

It makes no sense.

Mara must somehow have climbed up and balanced on the thin rail above the door.

Saga tries to slow her breathing, wiping her mouth with her sleeve.

Karl should make the call to Joona one minute from now.

There are no other doors, no hatches in the floor.

She looks up.

Beneath the ceiling, probably around twelve metres up, she can see a row of windows. They are half-hidden behind a layer of cobwebs, so thick that it almost looks like dirty tulle.

Saga pushes her gun back into the holster and turns to the mountain of pallets.

There is a grubby towel spread out on the floor to one side of them.

Beside a rolled-up jacket, a plastic bottle of water.

This must be where Mara sleeps.

Saga remembers the psychologist's observation that Mara preferred
to sleep on the floor.

In a plastic bucket, she sees a number of dead spiders with crooked
legs.

Intricate systems of web glitter between the pallets.

Some are white with flour dust.

Saga gets down onto her knees and reaches in between the pallets.
Her hand finds a red gingerbread tin, and the delicate spiderwebs
collapse as she pulls it out.

A shudder passes through her when she hears the crack of a pistol
outside.

69

Saga tries to resist the wave of panic that washes over her. She knows that the gunshot she just heard may mean that Karl is dead, but if he is still alive then he should have called Joona by now.

That means they will find her here, arrest her and take her into custody, and the Prosecution Authority will begin its inquiries.

Saga sits down on the floor with Mara's biscuit tin. She opens the lid and puts it to one side. There is a single page inside, torn from a notepad, and she lifts it out and turns it over.

With a trembling hand, Mara has drawn a pile of skulls and bones and written the words 'My Family' underneath.

As Saga returns the sheet to the tin, she realises she can smell smoke.

She turns around and sees a greyish-blue haze seeping in around the bottom of the door, curling up the wall towards the ceiling.

She gets to her feet and takes a few steps back, looking up.

If the fire spreads, she won't have many options.

She needs to stack the pallets in such a way that she can reach the roof trusses and climb up to the row of windows before too much smoke collects up there.

Saga could break a window and crawl out onto the roof, make her way over to the grain dryer and climb down the frame.

She moves over to the pallets and starts dragging them across the floor.

They weigh around twenty-five kilos apiece, and she knows she will have to build some kind of staircase in order to be able to lift the top pallets into place.

The smoke is now billowing into the room at such speed that that she wonders whether she has enough time, and Saga quickly pulls more pallets across the floor, trying to calculate how much of the original pile she can keep intact if she wants to reach the ceiling.

Each pallet adds no more than twenty centimetres, which means five per metre. She isn't sure she will have enough.

She starts dragging, lifting and stacking, constructing the first level of her staircase.

She works quickly and methodically, and sweat soon starts trickling down her chest, her muscles already shaking from the effort.

Saga drags a pallet up the first four steps, swinging it on top of the pile and then running back down to get the next one.

She groans in pain. A splinter of wood from a broken board has buried itself deep in her hand, and she drops the pallet, causing a cloud of dust to swirl up into the air.

The sliver of wood is on the inside of her right index finger, around five centimetres in length and just beneath the skin. She pulls it out, shakes off the blood and puts pressure on the wound.

The smoke has started to gather by the ceiling.

Saga continues to move pallets. She needs more before she can start building the next level.

She freezes when she hears the steel door creak. Her immediate thought is that it is probably just the fire growing hotter on the other side, but then she hears someone lift the crossbar away.

Saga grabs her pistol and ducks down behind the stack of pallets as the door swings open. She is pointing her gun straight at Karl's bare chest, she realises. He has taken off his shirt and wound it around his face.

'Hurry!' he shouts.

Saga runs over to him and pushes her gun back into the holster. Outside, the grain dryer is like a flaming torch, and the wooden frame collapses into a heap of glowing cinders.

'I've been looking for you,' Karl splutters.

His cheeks are sooty, and he is staring at her with wild, bloodshot eyes. A wall of heat hits them, jet black smoke billowing in through the conveyor tube.

'We need to get out,' she says.

The plastic curtain sways in the breeze feeding the flames.

'I know a way,' Karl pants.

They push through the yellowed plastic and pause on the loading dock on the other side.

'God.'

The fire has consumed almost the entire farm, emitting a low roar like some sort of distant thunder storm. The timber walls in the workshop are all ablaze, and one of the high windows shatters in the heat, sending a shower of glass raining down to the floor.

'I came from over there,' he shouts, pointing back towards the old farmhouse.

They clamber down from the dock and run towards the tarred door. Overhead, the metal roof groans. A rope in the pulley system catches fire, and the heavy block begins to spin.

They hear a series of loud bangs up ahead, the sound of more shattering glass and falling timbers.

The soles of their shoes begin to melt as they cross the large metal plate.

Right then, the tarred black door swings open in a ball of flames, and the rush of air causes the fire to surge towards them.

'Only one way out,' says Saga, dragging him back with her.

The roof trusses in the workshop now look like they are floating in a sea of fire, and a beam comes crashing down right in front of them, landing on the workbench and snapping in two in a cascade of sparks.

Sheets of roofing tumble to the floor, burning joists clattering down after them.

They keep going.

Saga coughs, her throat raw.

Karl loses his balance and pauses, bracing himself against his thighs and spitting out black saliva.

'Cover your mouth and nose again,' Saga shouts.

The fire seems to sigh as it sucks up more oxygen, and it is getting harder to breathe with every second that passes. One side of the workshop has begun to buckle in the flames, creaking inwards.

Glowing flecks of soot swirl upwards in the hot air.

Saga feels the heat of the air in her lungs, and she pulls her T-shirt up over her mouth.

The pane of glass on the door into the utility room is murky, and she opens the door and realises the room is full of smoke. She drags Karl in behind her and closes the door.

There is a real risk of an explosion at any moment.

They hold their breath, eyes stinging, barely able to see a single thing.

Saga bumps into a bench and turns off to the right.

The heat of the fire feels intense on her face. The flypapers start shrivelling up into tiny balls, and the metal cabinets groan.

In the workshop behind them, the drums of chemicals begin to explode. Each blast is like a battering ram to the door.

Saga's heart is now racing faster than ever. She needs to breathe, to get out through the garage.

The door into the sandy passageway is closed.

Karl drops to his hands and knees behind her.

Saga reaches out, but the handle burns her palm.

Her lungs are straining.

She takes a step back and kicks the door, well aware of how dangerous it could be.

The far end of the sandy passageway is already ablaze, but within a few seconds, once the gases catch fire, the utility room behind them will become a crematorium.

They need to make their way out to the garage through the burning tunnel before it's too late.

Karl staggers after her.

Saga fights the urge to breathe, her throat tightening and the pressure in her head building.

There is a sudden roar, and the door up ahead bursts open, torn from its hinges by a ball of fire from the garage.

They stumble back, burning shards of wood raining down on them.

The farming equipment creaks and warps in the inferno.

There is a loud sucking sound behind them and the utility room goes up in flames.

Before the last of her strength deserts her, Saga throws herself at the burning wall of the passageway, slamming her shoulder into the boards.

Surrounded by burning wood and glowing embers, she crashes out into the yard, hitting the ground and rolling away.

Karl lumbers out after her, his hair on fire.

His face is sooty, his nostrils black.

Saga beats out the flames on her legs and then gets to her feet, coughing and gasping for air.

The last of the windows in the garage crack and shatter.

Karl rubs a black hand over his head, drops to his knees and throws up.

The green plastic rubbish bins have melted in the heat.

One of the barn doors comes loose, falling to the ground and igniting the tall meadow grass just as the entire passageway collapses.

Glowing embers swirl up into the night sky.

Saga tries to pull Karl onto his feet.

The powerful stench of smoke mixes with the smell of diesel.

The fire illuminates the edge of the forest, causing the shadows of the birch trees to tremble.

Right then, she notices the bullet hole in the rust-coloured cistern. A large pool of diesel has spilled onto the ground in front of it.

'Karl! We need to get out of here,' she shouts, dragging him after her.

Without looking back, they run away from the farm buildings. They reach the gravel track just as one of the embers ignites the diesel fumes. In less than a second, the fire seems to be sucked down into the puddle of fuel and up into the tank.

The explosion is deafening, and shards of warped metal fly through the air.

The shock wave knocks them back and forces them to the ground as a fiery mushroom billows into the sky.

The broken trees are engulfed by flames, flaring as they fall.

Saga's ears are ringing as she crawls over the track and pulls Karl down into the ditch.

The garage and workshop both come crashing down, smoke and flames filling the air, beams snapping and corrugated metal being torn in two. The metal storage building is the only one still standing. Black smoke surges up into the dark sky, and the burning maypole in the yard topples to the ground.

70

Joona ejects the hard drive from his computer and unplugs the cable. He gets up from the desk, opens the blinds in his office and gazes out at the park. The dense leaves on the trees obscure the footpaths and buildings down below.

When he spoke to Manvir earlier, Joona got the sense that his colleague was either lying or holding something back when he told him about the search of Saga's apartment.

They found two of the three hard drives she had unlawfully taken from the psychiatric clinic in Ytterö. But what they didn't find, along with the third hard drive, were the psychologist's handwritten journals.

Joona has just finished watching the films they seized, and he rubs his mouth.

When she was first admitted to the clinic, Mara Makarov was incredibly confused, agitated and incoherent, but she became increasingly consistent with every session.

She initially claimed that the KGB was behind the kidnapping and imprisonment of her family, but after coming across the only image of Jurek Walter ever printed, she realised that he was the captain of the boat.

The last session on the second of the hard drives ended with Mara leaning forward and looking Sven-Ove Krantz straight in the eye. In a calm, composed voice, she said:

'If you're not going to let me go, you need to make sure Saga Bauer knows that this is serious, that my entire family will die . . .'

Joona leans back and remembers Saga's interview with Susanne Hjälm after the incident at Biondo Yoga. Using fear to break Susanne's psyche, Jurek went into great detail about the way he tracked down those who betrayed him and wiped out their families as punishment.

Saga had asked whether he ever directly threatened her, and Susanne simply repeated what he had said about a Russian diplomat who was planning to return to Sweden after he retired, getting the family together to celebrate his seventy-fifth birthday. Jurek would be waiting for them, he would lock them all in a bunker and then bury them alive, one after another.

A Russian diplomat, that was what Susanne had said.

Joona takes a sip of water, sits down on the edge of his desk, takes out his mobile phone and calls his friend Nikita Karpin.

The room is silent as he listens to it ring.

Karpin spent thirty years working for the KGB, making a name for himself as the Russians' leading expert in serial killers. Formally, he left the agency, but he was subjected to a secret probe and became an incredibly cautious person.

Russia may seem as though it is governed from the top down, defiantly unchanging, but in actual fact there is a simmering power struggle being waged beneath the surface. Sworn enemies and false friends trade places, unholy alliances are broken, and the balance of power shifts abruptly, time and time again.

Nikita is now seventy-five, and has finally come in from the cold. He has just been named the new head of the FSB, the federal security service.

'You again?' Karpin grunts, not bothering with any niceties.

'It's been a decade.'

'So what do you want this time?'

'Congratulations on the promotion.'

'Congratulations on the pink nails.'

'Your agents are thorough.' Joona smiles.

'Thank you.'

'I thought you might be able to talk on the phone now that you're head of the FSB.'

'Don't people talk on the phone in Sweden?'

'I'm assuming you already know that I'm hunting a serial killer, Mara Makarov.'

'Yes, I've been looking into it. She's Alexey Fyodorovich Gurkin's granddaughter. He was a diplomat at our embassy in Stockholm for many years, and he returned to Sweden to celebrate his birthday with his family.'

'There was a boat accident.'

'After a little diplomatic pressure, the investigation was handed over to Russia and the identities of our citizens were classified.'

'But nine passengers died,' says Joona, shuddering at his own realisation.

'Excellent deduction.'

'Go on, please.'

'This isn't information the NCU or the Swedish Security Service has access to, but Alexey Gurkin visited Jurek Walter in Löwenströmska Hospital.'

'I suspected something along those lines,' says Joona.

'They had a long, friendly chat that ended in Jurek asking for Russia to put pressure on Sweden to take him out of isolation. He claimed it went against his human rights and so on. But rather than helping Jurek, Alexey Gurkin recommended that the ambassador bury the case – fittingly enough.'

The two men end their phone call as unsentimentally as it began, with Nikita moaning about people wasting his time.

Joona sits down at his desk to think about Mara. She wasn't mentally ill. She was telling the truth all along, but since everything to do with Jurek was classified it seemed as though she was suffering from paranoid delusions.

The media reported on the tragic accident in the Stockholm archipelago, writing that all five Swedish members of the Makarov family were feared dead, but no one ever mentioned the Russian passengers because they were part of the classified material surrounding the case.

In actual fact, nine people died. That is why Mara's gun contained nine bullets when she first began her killing spree.

The grandfather who organised the trip to celebrate his seventy-fifth birthday didn't end up going out on the boat that day. He had recently been diagnosed with Parkinson's disease, and the rocking motion worsened his symptoms. The plan was for the whole family to meet for dinner that evening, at the Grand Hôtel in Stockholm.

Shortly after the boat accident, Alexey Fyodorovich Gurkin returned to Russia, where he lived alone for almost a year before going out into the forest and turning a gun on himself.

The pattern is all too familiar.

Joona runs a search on the name Gurkin. It turns up an unexpected result, and he gets up from his desk and leaves the room. He marches down the corridor, past the new break room and into the large meeting room where all the material relating to the case is kept. Alongside the images of Mara, photographs of Saga have now been pinned to the wall.

'Did you get anything from the films?' asks Greta.

'I know why Mara hates the police.'

'And you in particular?' says Petter.

'The same reason Saga hates both you and the police,' Manvir speaks up, glancing back down at his computer screen.

'Though I don't think she does,' Joona replies.

'We already know that Saga has an unresolved trauma linked to Jurek Walter, but what's Mara Makarov's connection?' asks Greta. 'Mara read the article about Jurek in *Expressen*, and suddenly the KGB weren't responsible for kidnapping her family after all, he was. It all sounds like some crazy fantasy.'

'I was just getting to that. I've spoken to one of my sources, and he—'

'What, have you got a secret source now, too?' Petter asks with a grin.

'And he gave me information suggesting that Jurek had a powerful motive to kidnap Mara's entire family.'

'OK . . .' Manvir sighs.

'Jurek wanted to take revenge on Mara's grandfather, Alexey Fyodorovich Gurkin, who was a diplomat with the Russian embassy in Stockholm while Jurek was in isolation in the Löwenströmska bunker.'

'Why, what did he do?' asks Greta.

'That's not important right now. I've just found a farm that belonged to his son Vadim before he died alongside Mara's family in the boat accident.'

'Where is it?' asks Manvir.

'On the outskirts of Västerhaninge.'

'There was a huge fire down that way last night,' says Petter.

'Then I think we've just found Mara's hiding place,' says Joona, turning and leaving the room.

* * *

Saga has borrowed a T-shirt with a picture of Duran Duran on the front, and she is wearing it as a dress as her dirty clothes tumble round and round in Karl Speler's washing machine. She has sterile dressings on her shoulder and hand, plasters on the cuts on her knees and right thigh, and her arms and lower legs are covered in scrapes and bruises.

She is drinking coffee and reading about the blaze on the outskirts of Västerhaninge on Karl's phone.

Her ears were ringing as they ran towards the car following the explosion. A rock had landed on the bonnet, leaving a deep crater in the metal.

They heard the first sirens just a few minutes after they set off, and Saga found herself wondering whether she would still be alive if she hadn't escaped the room full of pallets when she did.

She wanted to take Karl to the emergency room, but he refused, convinced they would link him to the fire on the farm.

The car stunk of smoke and burnt hair.

Karl explained that he had spotted the reflection of two rear lights at the edge of the trees and that when he went over to take a closer look he found Mara's pickup beneath a camouflage net.

'I don't know whether I was just imagining things,' he said with a cough. 'But I'm pretty sure there was a huge sack in the back, and I thought it was moving. I thought there might be someone inside . . . you know, like you mentioned . . . and then I panicked. I told myself that I had to call Joona, but then I realised my phone was still in the car, and I was running back over when I heard a shot. I couldn't find the keys, of course – it was like some horror film from the eighties, you know? I was searching every pocket when Mara's pickup pulled onto the road, and I started running back, saw that the air seemed bright above the farm. That's when I realised it was on fire and that I had to find you . . .'

They drove to a twenty-four hour pharmacy and bought sterile compresses and gel for treating burns, then headed back to Karl's place, returned the damaged Porsche to the garage and made their way down to the basement, where they carefully got themselves cleaned up and helped each other to dress the worst of their wounds and burns.

At three in the morning, they poured two whiskies, knocked back a couple of painkillers, said goodnight and went to bed.

Saga puts her coffee cup down and dabs her mouth with a napkin from a takeaway. Karl is wearing a burgundy silk-lined dressing gown, and he hums to himself as he fries eggs and makes toast. He has only a few strands of hair left on his singed scalp, and the glass on his Rolex is broken.

She continues to scour the internet and finds an article that has just been published on the *Aftonbladet* website. In it, the journalist writes about the hunt for a serial killer, making reference to trusted sources within the police force and adding that an unnamed former Security Service agent is the main suspect. Someone clearly gave him a genuine tip, but he then failed to dig up any more information. The journalist tries to imply that a detective superintendent from the NCU agreed to an interview, but it's obvious that whoever it was actually refused to comment. For want of any real details, the article provides a brief history of Swedish serial killers, with a series of links to similar pieces from the past.

This is nothing, Saga thinks to herself, though she knows the news will soon break. Before long, her name and picture will be everywhere.

Once they have eaten, Saga loads the washing into the tumble dryer and then helps Karl to shave the rest of the hair from his head.

'I'm sorry about your Rolex,' she says.

'It doesn't matter, I hated that thing anyway. But my hair . . . I had good hair.'

'This looks good too,' she lies.

He sweeps up the last of his locks, empties the dustpan into the toilet and flushes. They head back over to the bar and pour more coffee.

'So, what happens now?' Karl asks.

'I don't know. I had the chance to stop Mara, but I failed,' Saga replies. 'She was so quick, I don't get it.'

'Don't you think we're done with all this, maybe?'

'With what?'

'Isn't it time to call Joona and turn yourself in?' he asks, his voice serious.

'I don't know . . .'

'I really think it is.'

She takes Karl's phone through to the museum and pauses in front of a display case. Inside, she can see the form from when she was admitted to the secure unit at Löwenströmska Hospital, and she takes a deep breath before she makes the call.

Saga holds the phone to her ear as she waits, standing in a pool of light from one of the high windows by the ceiling.

'Joona Linna.'

'It's me, it's Saga.'

'I'm glad you called.'

She can hear wind crackling down the line as he crosses some sort of crunching surface.

'I didn't do any of the things you're saying, I'm not involved in the murders.'

'I never thought you were.'

Saga's eyes well up, and she swallows hard. She hears the soundscape around him change, a car door slamming.

'I'm out in Västerhaninge,' Joona continues. 'There was a fire on a farm, and Forensics have found bullet casings that could have come from your Glock.'

'Joona, I . . . I was just trying to stop Mara. I tried, but I failed.'

'You need to hand yourself in, Saga. I've spoken to Morgan, we came to an agreement on how it'll work. I told him you'd hand yourself in to me and no one else . . . I'll drive you to custody and take you in through the staff entrance, and then we can sit down in an interview room without your name ever ending up in the system.'

'OK.'

'You'll have to lay all your cards on the table,' he explains. 'There are a lot of questions, but everyone is willing to listen. It'll be fine.'

'If you say so.'

'And once we've got it all straightened out, you and I can keep investigating together.'

'Thank you,' she whispers.

'I really do think this is the best thing you can do right now.'

'I'll let you know the time and place,' she tells him, ending the call.

71

On the hill behind the Royal Institute of Technology, the AlbaNova University Centre is a joint initiative focused on the study of physics, astronomy and biotechnology. The modern campus was built on the site of the former Roslagstull Isolation Hospital, and several of the old hospital buildings were incorporated into the plans and remain in use.

The long, low buildings are organised in symmetrical blocks around a network of narrow roads, with ochre yellow facades, saffron-coloured eaves, tall brick chimneys and blind windows at both ends.

A light rain is falling from the leaden sky, dark clouds looming over the area.

Manvir gets out of the car and opens the back door to unfasten his daughter's seatbelt. His wife is on-call today, and had to respond to an emergency at the heart clinic at Sankt Göran's Hospital earlier.

Strictly speaking, the bay where Manvir is parked is reserved for university staff, but he will have the car in his sights the whole time.

'Do you want an umbrella?' he asks.

'Don't need one,' Miranda replies.

She buttons her little trench coat and untucks her plaits, letting them fall down over her shoulders as they walk.

The campus is deserted at this time of day.

The tarmac glistens between the buildings, the grass and the trees.

At just six years of age, Miranda is the youngest member of the summer course at the House of Science, where young people are able to conduct experiments, attend lectures and discuss technology and the natural sciences.

'We're designing weird things for the 3D printer today,' she tells him. 'And then we're going to make esters in the lab.'

'What do you know about esters?'

'You get them when alcohol reacts with acid,' she replies.

'More or less. And where do you find them?'

'In sweets that taste like pineapple and banana.'

'And in the bonds holding DNA together,' he says.

'Oh yeah, I knew that.'

They pass a small park with a handful of benches and pause outside the building.

'Listen to what your lecturer says, be careful in the lab, and don't leave the building if you can't see me,' Manvir tells his daughter, bending down to give her a kiss on the forehead.

'Don't smoke while you're waiting for me, Dad,' she says, looking up at him through the raindrops on her glasses.

'I won't. That only happened once. I'm going to go home.'

The course leader unlocks the door, says hello to Miranda and lets her inside. Through the glass, Manvir watches his daughter disappear down the corridor.

He starts making his way back to the car, footsteps echoing softly between the buildings. The rain has eased off slightly.

Other than Joona, everyone at the NCU is now convinced that Saga Bauer is directly involved in the murders. They no longer have any doubt that she has been working with Mara Makarov, yet for some reason Morgan Malmström is still reluctant to put out a nationwide alert.

He's probably just worried it would be bad PR. But what exactly is holding Joona back, Manvir asks himself.

Saga claims she is the only one who can save him, but in actual fact she is planning to kill him and anyone else who bears even the slightest responsibility for what happened to her family.

The evidence against her is overwhelming. Her fingerprints were found at Kymlinge station, her hair in the chapel, traces of caustic soda were recovered from her motorcycle, and hair matching Margot's horse from one of her bags.

Saga also made an anonymous report against Stefan Broman, and according to the crime scene analysts she attempted to remove any trace of herself from the massage parlour where he was attacked, only to forget about a bloody shoe print on the wall. She confessed to his murder to another john, and there were bullets and casings matching her service weapon among the wreckage of the burnt-out farm linked to Mara Makarov's family.

Why can't Joona see what everyone else sees? Why did he help her and send pictures of the latest figurine, breaking a direct order to do so?

Is he in love with her? Is he being blackmailed? Could he be involved too?

72

Joona is in his apartment at the top of the Corner House, and the sky above Stockholm's rain-slicked rooftops is uniformly grey.

Randy called from his private number earlier and told Joona that he had found a note from the NCU's old security division, made two months after Mara Makarov was discharged from Ytterö.

A temp at a cleaning firm hired by the security division had entered the archive to clean, despite the fact that it wasn't part of her work duties, scrubbing the floors and shelves in the vault where all the material on Jurek Walter was kept. The case was handed over to the Security Service, but they hadn't been able to trace her. The woman's boss at the cleaning firm couldn't explain why they had never formally hired her, nor why he had no idea what she looked like.

A sudden migraine flare up knocks out his vision for a few seconds, and he holds his breath and sits perfectly still.

By the time his vision returns and the pain shrinks to a pinprick and disappears, Joona's forehead is clammy.

He supports himself against the wall as he staggers through to the bathroom, opens the top drawer and takes out a blister pack of Topimax with a shaking hand.

It was only a brief flare up, and he can't afford for his mind to be even slightly dulled right now.

Joona puts the pack back in the drawer and heads through to the kitchen to make dinner instead. The plan is to fry salami, mangetout, cherry tomatoes, garlic and chilli, then mix it with spaghetti, rocket and fresh basil.

He wishes Valeria was here, that he hadn't let her down, that she was sitting at the dinner table, talking to him with a slight smile as he cooked.

He takes out his phone and dials her number, unease rising with every ring before she finally picks up.

'It's me,' he says.

'Love?' she replies, almost whispering.

Joona's eyes well up. It's the first time she has called him that since he abandoned her in the restaurant.

'Were you asleep?' he asks, swallowing hard.

'No, I was listening to an audiobook.'

'How are you?'

'Good, just a slight backache. I planted twenty-five thuja over in Moraberg today . . . It was a bit of a drive, all the way over by Södertälje, by—'

'I know where Moraberg is.'

Joona hears her get up move through to the kitchen, and though he knows he should ask her over for dinner he just can't bring himself to do it.

'Did everything go well in Germany?' she asks.

'Yes, it did, actually.'

'How are you doing?'

'I'm OK,' he replies.

'Have you eaten?'

'I was just about to make dinner.'

There is a popping sound as she pulls a cork from a half-empty wine bottle, followed by a soft glugging as she fills a glass.

'I wanted to say sorry again,' he says.

'There's no need.'

'I haven't touched the drugs since we last spoke, haven't felt the urge . . .'

'Good.'

'And I promise I—'

'Joona,' she interrupts him, her voice soft.

'You were right.'

'I know this need of yours to feel like your personal darkness is connected to Jurek,' she says. 'To what he said to you on the roof, his last words . . .'

'It's hard to explain.'

'If you really want to break free, maybe you need to let what he said out into the light.'

'I've always felt like I can't bring myself to repeat it,' he says, taking a deep breath. 'But I constantly hear him whispering in my ear.'

'You know that Jurek can't define you, don't you?'

Joona wanders through to the bedroom, over to the window, gazing out at the dark street below.

'Lately I've started to feel like I want to keep his words inside me for a while longer,' he admits.

'That doesn't sound healthy.'

'Possibly because it gives me a hardness that I'm going to need in the days to come.'

Joona hears her take a sip and lower her glass to the table.

'You've got wine, I've got pasta . . .'

'We should meet,' she says.

'Why don't you come over?'

Through the wall, the lift whirrs faintly.

'I can tell this case is asking a lot of you, so you don't need to worry about me, I'll be just fine,' she says. 'Do what you have to do, but remember that you need your heart, not hardness.'

'Hold on,' he says as he hears the lift ping on his floor.

'Be careful, I can't lose you,' she continues.

'Never.'

'Do you hear me?'

'I'll call you back soon,' Joona says when he hears someone outside his door.

He puts down his phone, grabs his pistol from the table and hurries through the living room. He reaches the hallway just as the buzzer rings, and Joona releases the safety on his gun and lowers it to his side as he opens the door.

He catches a glimpse of a man in a delivery uniform as the lift doors roll shut.

The little parcel has been left on the floor just outside his apartment.

He carries it to the kitchen table and calls command. As he tears the tape from the cardboard, he hears the speaker crackle.

'Rosanna Björn,' says the duty officer.

'This is Joona Linna, we've got a new parcel. It arrived at my apartment about twenty seconds ago.'

'Do you need us to send the bomb squad?'

'No, I'm opening it now.'

'We're on standby.'

He hears her contacting regional command on another line.

Joona folds back the lid of the box and unwraps the first layer of crumpled newsprint, followed by a ball of thicker paper inside.

He holds up the little figurine between his index finger and thumb, studying its face.

'It's Manvir Rai, the figurine is Manvir Rai,' Joona tells the officer. 'I'll call him now. Send all cars in the area to his house; this is urgent.'

He ends the call and dials Manvir's number, flattening out the inner sheet of paper from the box as he listens to it ring.

It's a page torn from a book, an archaic text on Nordic mythology written by a bishop called Olaus Magnus. In the middle of the page, there is a woodcut of Odin and his wife Frigg, queen of the gods, wearing a long dress, a hood, and carrying a sword and a bow.

Just as the call is about to go to voicemail, he hears a click.

'Joona?' Manvir answers.

'Where are you? I need to know where you are right now.'

'At home . . .'

'You're the next victim. Lock the doors, we're on our way.'

'Hang on a second, what did you just say?'

'Do you have your service weapon with you?'

'Of course,' says Manvir. 'Are Greta and Petter there too?'

'No, I'm in my apartment, the parcel was delivered here,' Joona explains, thinking to himself that Manvir's voice sounds strange.

'And you're sure it's me?' he asks.

'Yes, I am – have you locked the doors?'

'Yes, but wait. What's the wrapping like? Tell me about the riddle?'

There is some sort of interference over the line, and Joona hears a pumping, rushing sound, followed by a few rapid clicks.

'I'm looking at it now,' says Joona, smoothing out the crumpled newspaper. 'One is a page from a newspaper, a short article about the Globe Arena changing its name to the Avicii Arena.'

'I've only been there once, for a Lucia concert, but not—'

'Moving on,' Joona interrupts him. 'Avicii grew up in Östermalm and is buried in the cemetery outside Hedvig Eleonora Church. He—'

'It's not that, it's not that.'

'OK, on the other side is part of an article about Colonial Pipeline paying five million dollars to a hacker collective called Darkside,' Joona continues, making his way out into the hall.

'Means nothing to me.'

'You have a bathroom upstairs, don't you?' Joona asks, struggling into his holster and jacket. 'Go up there and get into the bath. Lie as low as you possibly can, with your gun trained on the door, and stay there until—'

'OK, got it,' says Manvir.

Joona grabs his keys and dashes out of the apartment, locking the door before he sets off down the stairs, still clutching the phone to his ear.

73

Manvir lifts the cigarette to his lips and hears the tobacco crackle as he takes a deep drag. His heart is racing as he stands beneath the overhanging roof to the back of the lab building, listening to Joona's quick footsteps in the stairwell over the phone. The light drizzle forms hazy spheres in the glow of the few street lamps, and the drips from the roof thud against an old plastic bag on the ground.

'What's happening?' he asks.

'We're on our way to you.'

'Who?'

'Everyone we've got. I should warn you that the call might drop out while I'm in the parking garage.'

Convinced that Joona has been helping Saga, Manvir automatically found himself lying when his colleague asked where he was, and after that he had no choice but to keep it up. He never goes home while Miranda is at her course, because he hates the man he becomes when he is home alone; he can never stop himself from searching his wife's computer, bags and clothing for any sign of infidelity. He is afraid that his irrational, jealous side will destroy their marriage, and yet it just keeps getting worse and worse.

'What else was in the box?' he asks, swallowing hard.

'A page from *A Description of the Northern Peoples* by Olaus Magnus,' Joona replies. 'It's all about Old Norse mythology, and there's a picture of Odin and Frigg.'

'Does the text mention anywhere specific?' asks Manvir, growing increasingly uneasy.

'No.'

'There must be something . . .'

'Hang on, hang on, I'm starting to understand her way of thinking,' Joona replies. 'I think Mara Makarov is planning to kill you outside the House of Science.'

'What makes you think that?' Manvir asks quietly.

'It adds up . . . According to Norse mythology, Venus was Frigg's star, and there's a statue of Venus right there, part of a scale model dotted around the country, the Sweden Solar System.'

Manvir's eyes scan the wet tarmac, stopping when they reach the concrete-grey sphere on a pedestal in the middle of the little park.

* * *

The heavy metal door swings shut with a thud that echoes behind Joona as he hurries down the stairs to the parking garage.

'Miranda is at a summer course at the House of Science right now,' says Manvir.

'OK, we'll arrange for—'

'Hello? Joona? I'm actually—'

'I'll call you back,' Joona tells him, realising that the connection is about to drop.

He runs over to his car, jumps in behind the wheel and reverses out of the bay. The tyres screech as he swings up onto the ramp, coming to a halt while he waits for the doors to open. A moment later, he pulls out across the pavement, ignoring the stop light, and turns right onto Sveavägen.

He tries phoning Manvir, but the call goes through to voicemail after eight rings.

Manvir will be safe at home, he thinks. The first patrol cars should be there in the next few minutes.

Joona is really speeding now.

The hunt could soon be over.

He is almost certain he has solved the riddle.

The first piece of the puzzle was the Globe – or Avicii – Arena, which represents the sun in the Sweden Solar System, the largest scale model of its kind on earth.

The model of the earth is in the Naturhistoriska Museum, Jupiter at Arlanda Airport and Sedna in a park in Luleå, 810 kilometres away.

The second part of the puzzle was the woodcut of the Norse goddess Frigg.

The planet Venus was considered her star, and the model of Venus is outside the House of Science.

Joona turns right, into the bus lane, stepping on the accelerator. Tiny raindrops patter against the windscreen like thumb tacks.

Everyone else is en route to Manvir's house, but Joona decides to head to the place where Mara is planning to kill him instead.

* * *

Manvir couldn't quite follow Joona's logic, but he understood enough to know that Mara Makarov has picked out his current location to kill him.

He drops his cigarette by the wall and hurries across the strip of grass to the House of Science to pick up Miranda and drive home.

The door is locked. He raps on the glass and peers inside, knocking harder and moving along the row of large windows.

He turns around and feels a jolt of panic when he notices a rusty pickup with an electric winch parked behind one of the old hospital buildings to the right.

'Oh God,' he whispers, turning the other way.

Manvir continues around the edge of the House of Science, breaking into a run when he reaches the grass at the end of the building, across the narrow road and over to the Nordic Institute for Theoretical Physics.

He pauses, short of breath, with his back to the wall.

His legs are shaking, his breathing rapid through his nose.

Further down the street, a number of cardboard boxes have been left out in the rain outside the school.

Manvir tries to think clearly and realises that he either needs to hide or get away.

The wet tarmac on the intersecting roads glistens between the tall oaks.

He looks straight ahead, past the next low building, and sees a green plastic sand bin at the edge of the road at the top of the steep slope.

The rainwater is trickling through the grate over a drain.

Manvir draws his service weapon, moves to one side and glances around the corner, back towards the main road leading from the roundabout to the AlbaNova building.

The area is quiet, shrouded in heavy drizzle.

He turns around and walks along the end of the building to the next corner. As he glances back, he notices a sudden movement to his right.

There is someone in the shadows behind one of the low yellow buildings.

A girl, with drab clothing and grey skin.

And she is moving quickly towards him.

Manvir panics and aims his gun at her, but his hands are shaking so much that he knows he won't be able to hit her from this distance.

He runs past the corner and across the narrow road, slipping when he reaches the wet grass on the other side. He throws an arm out to steady himself and hears his wedding band clink against the facade, then hurries around the corner of the Department of Theoretical Physics and pauses, heart racing.

His breathing is ragged, and the knuckles on his left hand are bleeding.

His legs feel like jelly as he moves back towards the corner. Manvir steels himself and peers around the edge, aiming his gun between the trees, but there is no sign of Mara.

'Mara, can you hear me? Backup will be here any minute now,' he shouts. 'Give up, it's over; you're not going to get away this time.'

He turns around and runs along the row of dark, gleaming windows. The AlbaNova building is to his right, the observatory and its domed roof. Two students are walking across the footbridge from the main entrance, but they turn and run back into the building when they notice him.

The glass doors glitter in the light.

Manvir keeps running. He has the sense that Mara is right behind him, and he jumps over an upturned electric scooter and hurries out into the turning circle with the big bronze sculpture. He spins around, and the grid of slick, empty roads between the low yellow buildings races by. He takes a few steps forward, unsure of where to go. His eyes pan down the steep slope to the building site, and he starts running towards the next building.

* * *

Joona speeds along the avenue, slamming on the brakes when he reaches two lorries blocking an entire crossing. The traffic lights are green, but the road is at a standstill. As cyclists and pedestrians weave their way between the vehicles, frustrated drivers blast their horns.

The commanding officer reports back from Manvir's villa on Riddarvägen to let Joona know that there is no need for him to come over.

'The house is empty. I repeat, the house is empty,' he says.

'Hold on, I told him to hide in the bathroom on the top floor,' Joona replies.

'There's no one here.'

'This makes no sense . . . Check the garage.'

'He's not here, and neither's his car.'

'Listen to me. Send every available unit to the House of Science.'

The lorries start moving just as the lights turn red, and the cars on the intersecting road start surging forward from both sides. With his hand firmly on the horn, Joona pulls out into the opposite lane, crosses the street and steps on the accelerator.

74

Without stopping to look back, Manvir hurries along the edge of the former hospital building now housing the Institute of Astrophysics.

He rounds the corner and pauses to catch his breath, leaning against the wall. He clamps his hand to his mouth and attempts to cough as quietly as he can.

There are three blind windows on the end of the building, facing out onto the trees straight ahead.

Manvir's eyes scan the narrow patch of grass, moving over to the dense greenery, the glossy, dripping leaves.

His legs are trembling, his heart thudding in his chest.

The minute he has caught his breath, he'll run into the trees and up to the top of the hill. From there, he can scramble down the steep slope to Roslagsvägen and stop a car.

The rain patters against the dark leaves.

Manvir knows that Joona was right. He pictures the model of the planet outside the House of Science and starts thinking about Miranda inside, wearing her little lab coat and safety glasses.

A bird rustles in the dense bushes.

Manvir feels a sudden weariness, his body heavy yet oddly light and numb.

His fingertips start tingling.

He releases the safety on his Sig Sauer and walks slowly towards the corner, peering back towards the AlbaNova building.

There is no one there.

The footbridge across to the rotunda gleams in the darkness.

The road, the grass, the old buildings with their tall chimneys: all are quiet.

The rain is getting heavier, pools of water forming around the blocked drains.

Manvir's pistol trembles in his hand, and his back feels cold, damp with sweat.

This can't be happening.

He hears the leaves behind him rustle again, and he shudders.

His fear is so deeply embedded in the sense of unreality that he feels oddly slow.

A twig snaps by the edge of the trees, and he hears light footsteps on the wet grass, almost like a hare on the run.

He should move, he thinks, taking a few hesitant steps.

Someone is approaching him, and rapidly.

Manvir doesn't have time to turn around, doesn't hear himself cry out and doesn't notice the loud gunshot, but as the echo ricochets between the buildings, he realises that he has fallen and is lying face down on the strip of tarmac by the granite base of the building.

He understands he has been shot in the back, just like the other victims. He has no feeling in his lower body, and is unable to move his legs.

His nose and teeth struck the ground when he fell, and when he turns his heavy head he sees that his pistol is lying in the gutter, no more than ten centimetres from his hand.

There is a loud roaring sound in his ears, like a raging storm.

The pain breaks through the first wave of endorphins, and it feels like he has been impaled on a spear, hauled up from the ground.

Manvir blinks and sees a shadow approaching. Mara moves across the sodden grass like a spider darting towards a fly in its web.

'Mara,' he gasps. 'Listen to me, you don't have to do this. I know you're angry with the police, and I understand that, I agree with you, but I had nothing to do with Jurek Walter.'

His breathing is rapid between the waves of pain, and he notices that one of his hands has started twitching.

'I have a family,' he shouts, the rest of his words coming out as no more than a whisper: 'I have a young daughter, do you hear me? She's only a child, just like you were when you went out in the boat . . .'

Manvir has to close his eyes. He knows he is losing too much blood. He composes himself and forces his eyes open again.

Mara's dirty trainers are right by his face, damp shoelaces are trailing on the ground, her upturned trouser legs muddy.

She bends down and picks up his pistol, then moves around him, tugging at his clothes. When she finds his phone, she disappears from sight.

Manvir's blood trickles down into the gutter, and the heavy raindrops form pink bubbles as they hit the pool that has formed around the drain.

75

The blue neon sign lights up the rain above the old fast-food stand, flashing by like a daub of paint as Joona accelerates up the steep slope.

He has his Colt Combat on the seat beside him, the safety disabled, and it jumps up into the air as he speeds over the crest of the hill.

Joona drives straight across the roundabout and pulls up in front of the House of Science, grabbing his gun, opening the door and leaping out of the car.

The grid of streets glisten beneath the street lamps, but the old hospital buildings themselves are bathed in darkness, the area quiet.

Water drips from the trees around the model of Venus.

Joona notices a lit cigarette on the ground beneath the protruding roof to the back of the lab building and feels a searing pain building behind one of his eyes.

In the distance, an engine revs.

Joona starts running along the main road towards the AlbaNova building.

The vehicle is getting closer, and he hears the gears screech.

Joona pauses and raises his pistol as Mara's pickup comes into view, racing down one of the parallel roads.

He gets no more than a glimpse of it between the buildings, and then it is gone.

Joona turns around and runs back to his car, jumping in and tearing away. He swings left and follows Mara at a high speed.

By the school, a large moving van reverses out in front of him, blocking the road. Joona swerves to one side and drives diagonally across a lawn, between a couple of oak trees and through the blooming dog roses onto the other road.

His windshield wipers clear away the damp leaves.

He continues down the steep hill on Roslagstullsbacken, towards a small footbridge over the train tracks.

Mara must have turned right. The road to the left is nothing but a temporary gravel track leading towards the cranes and bulldozers in the building site.

A sharp bend swings into view in front of him, a broken umbrella blowing along the pavement in the wind.

There is gravel from the construction site on the road, and Joona's tyres skid sideways as he turns right.

The back wheel swings up against the kerb, and his pistol clatters into the footwell.

Joona steps on the accelerator and catches a glimpse of Mara's pickup between the recycling station and a red industrial building in the distance.

His wheels thunder against the road surface.

He is approaching a blind corner, the railings separating the road from the train tracks flickering by on his left.

He can hear sirens in the distance.

As Joona steers into the bend, he sees an old woman with a walker in the middle of the road up ahead. He swerves and passes her on the wrong side, braking and skidding, gliding across the road before he manages to straighten up and accelerate again.

He picks up some speed on a short stretch of road blasted into the rock and then turns off onto Körsbärsvägen, bouncing up onto the pavement and scraping against a parking meter before swinging back down onto the road.

Shards of plastic from one of his brake lights scatter across the ground behind him.

A thin man in slim-fitting clothes is pushing his bike over the crossing, and Mara's pickup hits his back wheel, sending the bike careening into the wall of a building.

The man staggers back with an astounded look on his face as Joona races by.

The sirens are louder now, and his migraine has started to unfurl in his brain like some sort of dark orchid.

Joona is no more than a hundred metres behind Mara as they approach Valhallavägen, but the pickup disappears behind a cluster of trees.

Blue lights sweep across the facades of the buildings.

Joona turns sharply, driving up onto a traffic island and bumping the give way sign just as the first three patrol cars arrive, blocking the road in front of him.

He tries to get past on the inside, but one of the cars backs up and forces him to slam on the brakes and turn the wheel.

His tyres screech.

He watches his colleagues draw their weapons and take cover behind their bonnets.

His car spins around, crashes into one of the patrol cars and comes to a halt.

Glass rains to the ground.

More patrol cars come speeding in.

The rain looks blue in their pulsing lights.

Uniformed officers rush forward with their guns drawn just as Joona's migraine hits him with full force, but he manages to dig his ID out of his inside pocket, opening the door and holding it up.

He stumbles out and braces himself against the side of the car.

'He's police,' someone shouts.

'You missed her, a Ford pickup,' Joona pants, trying to see something through the blinding halo filling his field of vision.

'Which way?' a policeman asks.

Joona squints through the bright ring of light, the flashing blue glare of the cars and the reflection of the street lamps on the wet asphalt.

'To the right, I think. She was probably trying to lose me in the tunnels,' he says, slumping to the ground.

'Is he hurt?' one of the officers shouts.

'Road blocks, helicopters,' Joona whispers, closing his eyes.

He sits perfectly still and listens to their frantic messages over the radio, cars racing off after Mara with sirens blazing, but he knows it is too late.

The pain hits an unbearable peak.

Joona holds his breath and time grinds to a standstill.

He fills his lungs.

The pain starts to level out.

Joona still has his eyes closed, but he hears the officers' voices, the sound of the helicopters.

His wet shirt is clinging to his torso.

He finds himself thinking about Master Fauster's system of train tracks, and Mara's pattern is suddenly crystal clear.

She has taken inspiration from both Fauster and Jurek.

Like a spider, she is creating a pattern. She leaves her victims' bodies at various cemeteries so that they will form a giant M once it is complete.

An M for Makarov, or a W for Walter, Joona thinks.

76

Forests, lakes and fields race by in the darkness beneath the helicopter, and Joona catches a glimpse of the brightly lit nuclear power station and the glittering Gulf of Bothnia as they turn. The enormous reactors look like three dusty blocks of marble in a quarry.

His migraine faded away completely around forty minutes after reaching its peak.

Mara Makarov managed to escape, slipping away in the network of road tunnels beneath the city.

It was late, but Joona arranged a meeting with Petter, Greta and some of the command group at the NCU.

The atmosphere in the room was terrible. Everyone was shaken, anxious and afraid.

On the basis of the find sites in Kapellskär, Hallstavik, Funbo, Lillkyrka and Sandtorpet, Joona drew a large M with nine points – three per line – on a map.

The base of the letter covers a distance of 100 kilometres, and they used the existing points to identify a number of possible locations that would enable Mara to complete her M: Fiby Urskog Nature Reserve, the church in Forsmark, the mine in Ramhäll and the motorway close to the Moraberg exit in Södertälje.

Patrol cars and ambulances were immediately sent out to all four locations.

When Joona heard that a muddy Ford pickup had been caught on a traffic camera just south of Uppsala, he requested a helicopter. Forsmark Church is around an hour north of Uppsala, and if Joona's thinking was correct then that was where Mara was heading.

The first reports from the other sites began to arrive during the flight there.

Nothing had been found around the Iron Age graves in Fiby Urskog, but the officers were waiting for the dog handlers to arrive to perform a second search.

A team from the NCU is currently en route to the mine in Ramhäll.

There was nothing of note to be found in the middle of the motorway, and the sniffer dogs didn't pick up any scents from the verges or ditches.

Each of the previous find sites could be considered a grave in one way or another. Joona isn't entirely sure of Mara's logic, but the motorway is the only location that doesn't fit the pattern.

Strictly speaking, the mine in Ramhäll isn't a cemetery either, but a worker did die there following an accident in 1846, and the man's body was never recovered from the collapsed mineshaft.

The helicopter swings in over the small farming community of Forsmark.

A straight road cuts right through the community, leading from the church to the manor house – a depressing illustration of the two centres of power in the area.

The helicopter hovers above the churchyard, the sound of its rotor blades deafening.

There is a police car blocking the entrance by the church hall and an ambulance waiting on the road in front of it.

The helicopter sways as it comes in to land, tearing leaves from the trees and landing softly on the gravel in front of the church. Sand and dust swirl up into the air, and the branches bend in the downwash.

Two uniformed officers are waiting on the steps outside the church, and they clutch their hats to their heads to stop them from blowing away.

The rotor blades slow, spinning with a muted heaviness, and large clouds of dust swirl through the lights illuminating the facade of the building.

Crouching down, Joona hurries over to the two officers. Both are tall, broad-shouldered men, one with a neat black beard and tattoos on his neck, the other with strawberry blond hair and freckles, a wad of snus beneath his lip.

'We just got here, but it doesn't look like anyone's dumped a body,' says the man with the beard.

'Check the trees,' Joona tells him, setting off around the right-hand side of the church.

The redhead follows him along the edge of the nave. The neatly raked gravel crunches beneath their feet.

Joona glances back and sees the bearded officer walking straight towards the ambulance, pausing to peer up at every tree along the avenue.

The whole scene is quiet, as though in a trance.

But the pattern can't be a coincidence.

Joona can hear his colleague's heavy breathing behind him.

In the pale, reflected glow of the facade lighting, a number of gravel footpaths snake away across the short grass, between pruned boxwoods and rows of headstones.

They keep moving.

There are five large ash trees behind the church, and Joona shines his torch between the branches, up into the crown of each of them.

The leaves rustle, and the red-haired officer flinches when a pigeon flaps up into the air.

He hooks the tobacco from beneath his lip and flicks it into the flowerbed by the church before setting off after Joona.

Beyond the graves, there is a small caretaker's building with a tiled roof. From where they are standing, it blocks the view of the road beyond.

Joona cuts across the grass, and the light from his torch flashes in the small window.

The tap on the outside of the caretaker's building is dripping into a bucket, and there is a wheelbarrow, a hose reel and a shovel leaning against the plastered wall. A number of old grave wreaths have been thrown onto the compost heap to the rear.

They move past the building and in among the trees.

Their torch beams sweep across the pale trunks, causing long shadows to dance between the trees.

Joona rounds a small boulder covered in moss and can just about see the cemetery wall through the undergrowth.

Behind him, there is a loud crack as the redhead steps on a branch.

They pause by the overgrown foundations of an old building and scan the area. Over by the church wall, there is a large oak. Its branches are hidden behind the other trees, but Joona notices some sort of diagonal line glittering in the light of his torch.

There is a faint rattling sound somewhere in the distance, almost like someone dropping coins into a metal bucket.

'What was that?' the officer whispers.

Joona forces his way through a thorny bush and steps over a fallen birch, pulling back a low branch and shining his torch up ahead.

His left hand tightens around his pistol.

A rope has been tied to a fallen tree trunk on the ground, looping up over a sturdy branch on the huge oak.

'Get the ambulance over here,' Joona shouts to the other officer as he makes his way forward.

Up above him, a large sack wrapped in plastic, white fabric and tape is hanging from a thick branch.

'What the hell is this?' the redhead whispers.

Mara must have backed in from the main road and pulled right up to the cemetery wall. Despite using the handbrake, it looks as though her pickup skidded back as the winch dragged the bag over the wall and up into the tree.

The cable cut a deep groove into the branch, and she secured the heavy bag with a number of criss-crossing ropes.

'Hurry!' Joona tells him.

A few pieces of bark fall from the branch, and one side of the bag bulges slowly outwards. The fabric and plastic both seem to strain, and a couple of the ropes tense and shake.

'He's alive!' Joona shouts, turning and running back.

'Oh God . . .'

The officer fumbles for his radio, screaming for the others to bring the ambulance over. He pushes through a thicket and trips over the fallen birch, immediately getting to his feet again.

Joona rushes through the old foundations and between the trees, over to the caretaker's building. He grabs the hose and pushes the nozzle onto the tap.

The red-haired officer emerges from the trees and calls for his colleague in a shaky voice as the ambulance headlights sweep across the church and out across the gravestones.

The bearded officer comes running with his weapon drawn, and the ambulance rolls out onto the grass and pulls up in front of Joona.

The paramedic behind the wheel is a thin man in his thirties, with a blonde ponytail and moist lips.

A nurse emerges from the back of the vehicle and comes around to join them. She is in her forties, with short hair, sharp eyes and thin lips.

'Every second counts now,' Joona says as they start taking out their protective gear.

The two police officers follow him as he drags the hose into the woods, doing their best to make sure it doesn't get caught on anything.

The caretaker's building is no more than twenty metres away, but it feels like an insurmountable distance.

When they eventually reach the tall oak, Joona drops the mouth of the hose to the ground and tells them which ropes to cut and which to wind twice around the other tree trunks in order to lower the bag to the floor.

'Careful now,' he says as they slowly start to let the ropes out.

Little by little, swaying from side to side, the sack drops lower and lower.

Joona moves forward and guides it down to the ground. Through the thick plastic, he can feel the heat of the chemical reaction inside.

The paramedics have almost reached them, ferns brushing against their legs and dry twigs breaking underfoot. They are carrying their equipment on a stretcher, and both are wearing protective masks and thick rubber gloves.

Joona tears back the fabric and plastic and slices open the sealed rubber sack.

The stench is unbelievable, the powerful fumes making their eyes water.

The nurse folds back the top half of the bag, and the red-haired police officer shines his torch inside.

He starts whispering to himself, the torch shaking in his hand.

Despite the fact that there is nothing but a wet, bloody mess where the man's face should be, Joona can tell that it is Manvir.

The chemicals have dissolved virtually all tissue. He has no eyes or lips, and nothing but two holes where his nose should be.

His chest is sunken, but he is still breathing raggedly, and his hands and feet look like lumps of jelly.

'We're going to need a lot of water,' says the nurse.

Joona grabs the hose and starts rinsing off the corrosive substance. Manvir bellows, his arms trembling.

The nurse gives him a shot of morphine, and the paramedic starts crying as he peels away the scraps of clothing from Manvir's body.

Manvir makes a rattling sound as they move him onto the evacuation sheet, and they work together to lift him onto the stretcher and carry him out of the woods and over to the ambulance.

'We'll take the helicopter instead,' Joona shouts.

They run across the cemetery with the stretcher, out onto the gravel and over to the grass.

* * *

The sky is streaked with pale dawn light when the doctor comes out into the waiting room at Uppsala University Hospital to tell Joona that Manvir died on the operating table.

Joona slumps down into one of the chairs and has just closed his eyes when he feels his phone buzz in his pocket.

'Joona,' he answers.

'Sorry if I woke you.'

'Saga?'

'I'm ready to hand myself in if the offer still stands,' she tells him, her voice hoarse.

'Of course.'

'Do you think I'm doing the right thing?' she asks after a brief pause.

'Yes, I do.'

'OK, so you'll come alone, drive me to custody and take me in through the staff entrance . . . You can interview me without a lawyer present and I'll answer all your questions, and then you can decide whether I need to be remanded in custody or not.'

'I'm on your side,' says Joona.

'Are you?'

'Yes.'

'There's a cylindrical parking garage at the end of Rörstrandsgatan,' she says. 'Drive around it, the whole way, and then pull up by the wall at exactly twelve o'clock,' she says, ending the call.

77

Saga passes Karl's phone back to him and peers down at the pink parking garage. It looks like an oversized hatbox has been dumped beside the rusty tracks at Karlbergs station.

The only way to reach the garage by car is to slowly make your way through the crowds of people out for lunch in the area, then down the steep slope.

Up against the rounded wall of the structure, there is a small side building that is protected from all sides. That is where Karl will be waiting, wearing a black windbreaker with the hood up.

Saga went down there last night and cut an opening in the fence.

If Joona keeps his promise and comes alone, Karl will crawl through the hole and get into the car to give him further instructions.

Whoever arrives first always has the upper hand, a fact that is addressed in both Sun Tzu's *The Art of War* and the *Wei Liaozi*.

If anything seems off, Karl will run down into the tunnel beneath the roads and the tracks, take off his black jacket and join the crowds of people on the other side, making his way up towards the bridge over to Kungsholmsstrand.

Saga herself will remain where she is, behind the huge bags of construction waste where she has a clear view of the parking garage and the road leading down to it.

Just before twelve, she will prop open the door to building forty behind her.

No matter what happens, that is where she will go, through the stairwell and out onto the other side, making her way through nine courtyards until she reaches 29 Tomtebogagatan on the opposite corner of the block. She will then follow Norrbackagatan for a few hundred metres and take cover in the garden behind Günter's hot dog kiosk.

That is where Karl will take Joona.

'How's it going?' asks Karl.

'I'm just thinking, looking for weaknesses,' Saga tells him, gripping the whistle in her pocket.

'The one thing you can be sure of is that it won't turn out how you planned,' he says with a grin.

'I hope that applies to Mara Makarov too,' she mutters, mostly to herself.

'Well, I think it's good that you're turning yourself in, either way. Though I do have to admit that the past few days have been great. I've had the time of my life.'

'I never would have managed it without you.'

'You're talking about the music and the food, right?' he says, unable to hide his happiness.

'That too.' Saga smiles.

'I knew it.'

'Seriously though. You saved my life, and I'll never forget that.'

Karl looks down, blushing, and then turns away.

Saga goes through the plan in her head one last time, from the moment when Joona pulls up at the rear of the garage to her entering custody, but she can't see any real flaws.

Worst case scenario, she fails to convince her colleagues of her innocence and they hand her over to the Prosecution Authority.

She still can't work out how she could have ended up in this mess.

Whenever she thinks about the fact that she is on the verge of handing herself in, she feels a dizzying sense of distance from her own life. She feels lost.

Without warning, a memory from childhood rears its head. Her parents had separated, but her mother invited her father over for dinner. She had dressed up for the occasion, set the table and was pacing around the room as they waited for him to arrive. And as their food got cold and they realised he wasn't going to show, her mother did something strange.

Thinking back now, it feels like a dream.

Without a single word, her mother had stripped off and then undressed her young daughter.

Saga was only six at the time, and she thought it must be a game when her mother started dressing her in her own clothes. Underwear, tights, dress and heels.

Everything was grotesquely big on her.

Still without saying a word, her mother fastened her pearl necklace around Saga's neck, clasped her emerald bracelet around her wrist and pushed her wedding band onto her slim finger.

She then left Saga in the middle of the floor, wearing her best clothes, as she walked out of the house and went naked into the woods.

* * *

It's three minutes to twelve and Karl is in position behind the side building, with the taped-up box Saga gave him between his feet.

The street is bustling, though no plain clothes officers seem to have turned up so far.

Saga feels her heart rate pick up when she spots Joona's black BMW rolling down the steep slope. It swings around to the left of the garage, disappearing for a moment before coming back into view at the rear.

The car pulls up to the wall at exactly twelve o'clock.

The driver's side door opens, and Joona gets out.

Saga watches as Karl picks up the parcel and crawls through the hole in the fence. Joona must have heard him, because he unbuttons his jacket and turns around.

Right then, something catches Saga's eye.

A group of teenagers carrying rainbow flags are walking down the footpath, blocking her view.

Her eyes anxiously scan the railway tracks, the windows and balconies.

She can hear a drumming, whirring sound approaching, and she pulls the whistle from her pocket.

Joona opens one of the back doors.

Karl takes a step forward.

A car drives down the ramp.

More teenagers stream past the garage, carrying drums and large balloons.

Saga's eyes sweep across the residential building opposite. The door is open on one of the balconies on the top floor.

A large banner full of messages of love and flowers unfurls and flaps in the breeze.

Karl is on the wrong side of Joona's car.

The glass door on the balcony catches the light.

Saga raises the whistle to her mouth.

Between the balloons and placards, she sees Karl put a hand on the roof of the car and then turn his head towards her at an unnatural speed.

She blows the whistle right as a cascade of blood spatters across the side windows and doors.

Karl drops to the ground.

The crack of the rifle echoes between the buildings, and she sees a wisp of smoke seep through the railings around the balcony opposite.

Saga hears a helicopter approaching.

Her heart is pounding, and she turns away, crosses the road and hurries in through the door she propped open earlier.

78

Saga's entire body is shaking as she runs through the stairwell and out into the yard on the other side. In front of the low green building in the middle of the courtyard, a skinny man in a crumpled jacket is smoking a cigarette.

'I'm looking for . . .'

'A Cheshire cat,' he says.

'Right,' Saga replies, clambering over the fence into the next yard.

She cuts across the concrete and climbs up onto a bicycle leaning against a wall, hopping over the top and onto the grass on the other side. She hurries past a set of white garden furniture towards a low fence, clambering over it and pushing through the raspberry bushes into the next yard, where three girls are playing with a skipping rope.

Saga stops to throw up into the gutter beneath a drainpipe, spitting and wiping the vomit from her mouth with the back of her hand.

The girls have stopped skipping, and they stare at her as she runs over to a red gate.

Saga scales it, scraping her stomach as she lowers herself down on the other side.

She had known there was a risk of a large-scale response – that was why she sent Karl to meet Joona – but she had never imagined they might actually shoot. Snipers were supposed to provide backup; they were there in case things went wrong, in case it developed into a hostage situation.

What just happened was an execution.

She hurries past a laundry building and climbs a fence into another yard a metre or so higher than the others.

On a small wooden deck on the other side, she spots a barbecue and some faded plastic furniture.

Saga drags the table across the patio, clambers up onto it and hops over the last dividing wall into the shady yard on the other side.

She lands on a patch of damp grass, stumbles forward through a bush and manages to regain her balance.

The roar of the helicopters is more distant now.

Her right ankle is aching, her stomach cramping anxiously.

She limps forward, opens the steel door and makes her way into a pretty nineteenth century stairwell with green marble walls and red flooring.

She quickly walks over to the heavy wooden door, reaching for the handle as she squints out through the etched window onto the street.

Saga immediately takes a step back as a police van races by outside.

She waits a few seconds, then slowly opens the door and peers out.

She has managed to bypass their cordon, she realises. There are police cars blocking the street to the right; she can see the officers' backs, their protective vests and their weapons.

She turns left instead, walking calmly along the pavement. In the distance, she can see the sand-coloured Norra Tornen apartment buildings.

There is a police car driving straight towards her, without either sirens or blue lights. The driver's side window is open, and she can see a hand holding an e-cigarette hanging out.

Saga pauses in a doorway with her back to the street and pretends to be searching for her keys.

Through the glass in the door, she can see an older woman walking towards her.

The patrol car pulls up directly behind Saga, and she hears a call come in over the radio: an order to shoot to kill.

The door buzzes and swings open, forcing Saga to take a step back.

The patrol car rolls off down the street, tyres crunching, and the old woman gives Saga a quizzical look.

Saga turns away and hurries up towards the crossroads.

She can hear more sirens in the distance.

There are people eating lunch outside all the restaurants and cafés, and off to her right, behind the queue of people at Günter's, she can see five police cars.

Beneath the sweeping blue lights, the officers are busy pulling spike strips across the road.

People have stopped to film them on their phones, and one of the officers shouts for them to move back as he cordons off the area.

The roar of a helicopter echoes between the buildings.

Saga turns left again, hurrying away from the roadblock.

There are more sirens behind her now, and it takes a real effort not to break into a run.

She is approaching a building covered in scaffolding, and she watches as a lorry with a tailgate unloads a huge stack of plasterboard to the pavement and then retracts its support legs.

Saga glances back.

She sees a helicopter hovering above a rooftop, a sniper leaning out of the door. A moment later, it swings up into the air.

The lorry pulls away from the kerb and Saga runs over to it, jumping up into the back and pulling a sheet of grey plastic over herself.

It drives away from the roadblock, slowing down to do a U-turn when it reaches the end of the street.

Saga shuffles over to the edge and jumps down.

She lands at an awkward angle and feels a searing pain shoot up through her ankle.

The lorry accelerates back the way it came.

Saga walks over to the pavement and takes cover beneath one of the tall trees as she brushes the plaster dust from her clothes.

There is heavy traffic on the criss-crossing lanes of the motorway and the bridges over to Solna.

She hears a loud bang, followed by the sound of breaking glass, and Saga flinches and feels an odd tenseness in her neck as she turns around.

An old man is busy dropping empty wine bottles into a recycling bin.

Sticking close to the buildings, Saga starts making her way down Norra Stationsgatan. A police officer in uniform comes out of a shop around ten metres ahead of her, and he stops and looks in her direction.

The bell above the shop door rings behind him.

Saga ignores him and turns calmly towards the entrance of a car repair garage, but from the corner of her eye she sees him fumbling for his gun.

In one fluid motion, she reaches beneath her jacket and pulls her Glock from its holster. She spins around, takes aim and fires.

She feels the recoil in her elbow and shoulder, and the combustion gases make her hand burn.

The bullet passes straight through his thigh muscle, sending a shower of blood and bone fragments across the pavement behind him.

The loud crack echoes between the buildings as Saga rushes towards him.

The officer drops to the ground, landing on his shoulder and crying out in pain. A gold tooth catches the light in his open mouth.

'Don't kill me, please,' he gasps, pressing his hand to the wound.

She can see the blood pulsing between his fingers, a growing pool on the ground beneath him, and she snatches the pistol from his holster and tosses it beneath a parked van.

Just as she reaches out to take his radio, the bell above the shop door rings again.

Saga reacts instinctively, turning and sprinting across the road.

A car swerves and blasts its horn.

Behind her, someone fires a warning shot.

Ducking down, she runs along the fence. The ground shakes as a bus thunders by.

Locked tyres skid, brakes squeal, and the car starts to spin.

Saga is still running when she hears another crash. Metal crumples, windscreens break, and shards of glass scatter across the road.

She drops the radio and pushes her Glock back into the holster, running as fast as she can along Tomtebodavägen.

There is so much adrenaline pumping through her veins that she can hear it roaring in her ears as she races out onto a bridge over the Klarastrandsleden, heading towards the Karolinska Institute campus. Above her head, the curving motorway bridges block the sun like two enormous canopies.

She can hear sirens approaching.

The filthy metal barrier is nothing but a blur at the corner of her eye. Flickering bars in front of roads, rockfaces and rusty train tracks.

Saga is short of breath by the time she reaches the other side of the bridge and sees the blue lights sweeping across the brown brick facade up ahead.

She turns and runs around ten metres back, jumping over the railing and scrambling down the steep sandy slope on the other side. A set of rotten wooden steps gives way beneath her, and Saga drops with them in a cloud of dust. She lands flat on her back and hits her head on the ground, crashing down through the weeds and the rubbish until she reaches the rusty fence at the top of the drop down to the train tracks.

She manages to get back onto her feet and runs in beneath the bridge, blood trickling down her neck from the gash on the back of her head.

Panting for air, she takes cover against the abutment.

Three police cars race overhead, sirens blaring.

The air smells like rubbish, and the ground is strewn with cigarette butts, empty beer bottles and spray cans.

There are huge concrete columns everywhere, like pale tree trunks rising up towards the sky, and dust swirls through the shafts of sunlight between the high bridges.

A steady stream of traffic surges out of the tunnel up ahead.

Saga hears a helicopter approaching, and she continues down the slope, following a yellow cable pipe. A broken dining table lies in pieces in the gravel around the pier columns.

She knows she has no real choice, but she still hesitates for a moment before running towards the entrance to the road tunnel.

Saga moves quickly along the narrow strip of ground to the left of the lane, the wind from the cars speeding by tugging at her hair.

A lorry blasts its horn, and she presses up against the wall as it thunders past.

Sand swirls up into her face.

She spits and keeps going, not stopping again until she comes out the other side.

The first part is over.

Around fifty metres up ahead, multiple lanes come together in the new tunnels beneath a glittering tower block.

The shadow of a helicopter sweeps over the fast-moving cars.

Its engine seems to roar, the sound hitting her in the chest before fading away.

She waits a few seconds, then runs as fast as she can into the next tunnel.

79

Saga is going against the flow of the traffic, her left shoulder scraping against the concrete wall.

Every hundred or so metres, there is a huge tube-shaped ventilation fan on the ceiling, and the sound is deafening, like a series of waterfalls.

The string of lights on both sides of the tunnel makes the walls seem puckered, as though she is inside some sort of enormous intestine.

If her thinking is correct, she is just over half a kilometre from Norrtull.

The air is heavy with exhaust fumes.

Discarded face masks lie in the dirt by the wall.

A large lorry is approaching at high speed, and Saga watches it overtake the cars in front of it, yellow warning lights illuminating the roof of the tunnel.

The trailer behind it is full of huge lumps of metal that look like parts of a wind turbine.

She presses up against the wall with her cheek to the rough concrete, trying to make herself as flat as possible.

The blinking lights surge forward.

She holds her breath.

The lorry thunders by, its heavy load making the ground shake. The wind tugging at her clothes is so powerful she has to take a sideways step.

An empty McDonald's cup swirls up in the dust.

Saga keeps going, stepping over the frayed remnants of a burst tyre and not stopping until she reaches emergency exit twenty-four, coughing and spluttering.

She opens the metal door and makes her way into a stairwell that smells of excrement and rotten food. The floor is covered in filthy plastic bags, mattresses, cans, sooty scraps of foil and empty sweet wrappers.

A bearded man wearing layer upon layer of loose clothing, his trousers damp with urine, is asleep in an armchair.

Further up the stairs, a woman with a croaky voice is shouting at someone, hitting the metal railing with her hand so that the sound bounces between the walls.

Saga grabs one of the full plastic bags from the floor and unties the handles. It is stuffed to the brim with tiny dresses and knitted bibs.

'I want my fucking money,' the woman shouts.

'Shut your trap,' the bearded man mumbles, his eyes still closed.

Saga tries another bag, emptying it onto the floor. She tosses a pair of bleached jeans to one side and finds a blue and red polka dot raincoat.

'I'll kill them,' the woman says, voice trembling as she starts making her way down the stairs.

Saga grabs the raincoat and sneaks back out into the tunnel, continuing against the flow of traffic.

A black rat darts along the ground in front of her, disappearing into a vent by the floor.

Saga pulls on the raincoat as she walks.

Just after emergency exit twenty-three, the tunnel forks in two, and she takes the road to the left.

A plastic bag has caught on one of the fans, and is fluttering like a tattered flag in the breeze.

The driver of a lorry blasts his horn at her as he thunders past. Dust swirls down from the trailer, and through the cloud left hanging in the air, Saga realises she can see daylight up ahead.

She slows down as she approaches the mouth of the tunnel, smoothing her clothes and tucking her hair beneath her hood.

The Norrtull interchange is one of the busiest in Stockholm, with cars surging forward from all directions, but there is no sign of any police presence.

Saga runs through the traffic, straight across twelve lanes, in the shadow of the E20 bridge.

When she reaches the footpath by the grassy embankment, she slows down. There are people out jogging, walking dogs and pushing buggies. Preschool classes in neon waistcoats walking hand in hand towards Haga Park.

Between the trees up ahead, she can see the glittering water of Brunnsviken.

Saga walks down the shady footpath past the Stallmästaregården restaurant and hears several sirens race by on the motorway.

Behind a wall that looks like it is on the verge of collapse, a tarmacked ramp leads down to the restaurant's service entrance.

She feels like a rat as she makes her way down the ramp and squats behind a row of bins by the loading bay to catch her breath.

There is an old tin of paint on the ground, piled high with cigarette butts.

Five trolleys with mesh sides and small wheels are lined up by the yellow wall.

She desperately tries to gather her thoughts. The idea that Joona might betray her had never really crossed her mind – though of course it was a possibility. Either way, she has missed her chance to clear her name and explain everything from her point of view.

The realisation hits her like a bucket of icy water: everyone at the NCU must be convinced she is involved in the murders. If they weren't, they never would have made the decision to neutralise her when she attempted to hand herself in.

80

Joona storms down the corridor at the NCU, past glass-walled offices and meeting rooms. Posters advertising the police choir, job vacancies and professional development courses flutter in his wake.

One of his colleagues from the International Unit is in the pantry, eating microwaved dumplings from a plastic tub.

'What's going on?' he asks when he sees Joona's face.

Joona ignores him and keeps going, shoving a mail trolley out of the way and marching straight through to Morgan Malmström's office.

He tears the door open and strides in. Greta, Petter and Morgan are sitting around the coffee table, and all three turn and look up at him with frightened eyes.

'You gave me your word,' Joona tells Morgan.

'We're in a meeting here,' the boss replies. 'Perhaps you could—'

'*Turpa kiinni,*' Joona swears in Finnish, turning to the others. 'Did you know about this?'

Petter looks down, and Greta folds her hands in her lap before she replies. A few strands of grey hair have come loose and fallen across her face when she meets his eye.

'Yes, we did. And we also agreed to keep you out of it.'

'The situation had changed,' Morgan explains. 'Saga Bauer is suspected of killing Manvir Rai; we couldn't risk allowing her to get away again, but . . . But the fact that one of the firearms officers discharged his weapon when he did was a mistake; he hadn't been given the order. The special prosecutor's office will be looking into it.'

'I'm holding you personally responsible for this,' Joona snaps, pointing at Morgan.

'Ultimately, of course, I am,' he replies, unable to hide the fear in his eyes. 'But it was a high pressure situation for all involved. I'm not trying to defend myself or the marksman, but everyone was convinced the man coming towards you was Saga, a suspected police killer. He was there at the agreed time, with a new parcel under his arm. Did you really expect us just to let her get away again? The clock was ticking.'

'Hold on, what did you say? A new parcel?' Greta asks.

'All I know is that the task force took care of it,' Morgan replies, giving her an uncertain glance.

'What the fuck,' Petter mutters, getting to his feet.

Greta calls the operative commander and quickly explains the situation, unable to hide the irritation in her voice.

'So, as you can understand, we need it right now,' she shouts.

'This is bullshit,' Petter mumbles, moving over to the window.

He rubs his bumpy scalp and swears to himself.

'Morgan, what did you mean, "let her get away again"? When was the first time?' asks Joona.

'There was an earlier operation at Saga's apartment,' says Greta.

'An operation?'

'I made the decision to have the National Task Force go in,' Morgan explains.

'You said it was just a search.'

'Joona, two more police officers have been seriously injured. We know them – you do too. This is personal. They were our friends, our colleagues,' Greta tries to explain.

'Someone always knows the victim,' Joona grumbles, taking out his police ID and throwing it into the bin.

'Your request for leave is granted. Your security pass will stop working an hour from now,' Morgan says calmly. 'Leave your weapon on my desk.'

'I need it.'

'I'm giving you a direct order to leave . . .'

Morgan trails off as Joona turns and strides away. They hear his footsteps fading down the corridor.

Greta helps herself to an apple from the bowl on the coffee table, but rather than take a bite she pauses with it in her hand. Petter is staring down at his phone, and Morgan gets up to close the door.

'The man who turned up in Saga's place was called Karl Speler,' he says, taking a seat. 'He grew up in South Africa, trained to become a journalist here in Sweden and worked for *Expressen* for eight years before he was fired.'

'What's his connection to Saga?' Greta asks.

There is a knock at the door, and Otis the forensic technician rolls into the room with the parcel in his lap.

'This came by helicopter,' he says, pushing his glasses back onto the bridge of his nose.

Morgan gets up and takes the small box from him, setting it down on the coffee table.

Petter returns to his seat and pushes one of the armchairs aside to make room for Otis's wheelchair.

Greta pulls back the tape, opens the flaps and shrieks as a clown in a red and yellow silk costume shoots up out of the box. It bounces on its spring, arms outstretched as though desperate for a hug. Its eyes seem to be staring straight ahead, and its red mouth is curled into a grin. There is a small scrap of paper taped to its chest, and on it someone has written: *I trusted you, Joona.*

81

After seven hours behind the row of rubbish bins, Saga gets up, stamps her feet and rolls her shoulders.

She managed to doze off twice with her forehead against her knees, though she immediately woke up again, heart racing.

She simply can't afford to lower her guard.

A man in a grubby apron came out to smoke on the loading dock five times, walking right over to the edge to drop his cigarette butt into the tin.

Saga isn't sure whether he spotted her right away, but when he came out for the third time he left a glass of water and a cheese sandwich before heading back inside.

She wolfed both down, then returned the glass and plate to the loading dock and took up her hiding place behind the bins again.

The next time he came out, he dropped his spent cigarette into the tin and, as though talking to himself, announced that the bins would be emptied within the next hour and that a security company comes by to check the doors every evening.

Saga walks up the ramp, past the weeds growing through the cracks in the wall.

The constant rumbling of the traffic grows louder as she comes out onto the footpath.

Her legs are numb after sitting still for so long.

There are far fewer people out and about now.

At several points during the past seven hours, she found herself longing for life to go back to normal, and her eyes welled up at the thought of taking Nick and Astrid to ballet again.

She takes off her raincoat and gazes down towards the shadowy waters of Brunnsviken. There is a fence around the marina, with five rows of barbed wire at the top.

The lack of sleep over the past few days tugs at her like some sort of powerful undercurrent, and she waits until a jogger has disappeared from view before making her way down onto the scrappy beach.

Three brown ducks calmly paddle away.

Saga spreads out her raincoat on the ground and looks up at the faded signs about security firms, alarms and CCTV. She then takes off her shoes, socks and trousers and bundles everything up in her raincoat, clutching it tight as she walks out into the warm water.

She wades around the edge of the fence, the smooth pebbles slippery beneath her feet.

There is a brown mahogany motorboat moored nearby, and Saga grips the line and lifts her bundle of clothes up onto the jetty. She then grabs the wooden planks with her free hand, swings one foot up onto the mooring rope and manages to clamber up.

The tall fence surrounds both the marina and the large patch of gravel used for bringing the boats ashore during winter. Around fifty boats are currently moored along the various jetties, white and yellow buoys bobbing on the rough surface of the water.

There is no sign of anyone.

Saga wipes the water from her legs and notices that the cut on her knee is bleeding. She then grabs her bundle and starts walking along the jetty.

The area is quiet.

By the little yellow huts, there is an outdoor seating area. The club's flag is fluttering on the flagpole, and she can also see a rusty lifting device and a number of trolleys.

Saga pauses in front of a large white motorboat. It must be almost twenty metres in length, with an enclosed cockpit and multiple sundecks.

She pulls on a rope, and the boat glides slowly towards her. The buoy by the bow drifts in with it until the line pulls taut. She jumps on board with a soft thud, ducking beneath the railing at the stern and pausing for a moment before untying one corner of the cover and crawling in.

She is in the dining area beneath a sun canopy, and through the glass doors she can see a dark kitchen and a table with eight chairs.

The sliding doors are locked.

Saga takes out her gun and uses the butt to break the lock, then she opens the door and steps inside.

The walls and kitchen cupboards are all clad in mahogany veneer, and the hardware looks like brass.

She walks through a TV room full of plush leather sofas and makes her way into the bathroom. She pees in the dark, takes a quick shower and then dries herself off with a towel from the linen cupboard before getting dressed again.

Saga heads back to the TV room. Between the bottles of spirits in the bar, there is a large demijohn of water, and she lifts it out of the holder, takes a swig and carries it through to the kitchen.

The fridge is empty and switched off, but she finds a can of tinned ravioli in the pantry and eats it cold.

Once she is done, she makes her way into the bedroom, slumps down onto the bed and stares up at the dark grey sky through the skylight, thinking about Mara and what her next step should be.

Saga had thought she could trust Joona.

She had told Karl that if he heard her blow the whistle, he should drop the parcel and run down to the tunnel as quickly as he could.

If Joona had brought a response unit with him, she would have spotted it from a mile away, but a hidden sniper was virtually impossible to detect before it was too late.

She still can't understand why they had made the decision to execute her on the spot.

82

Saga wakes with a start. Someone is shining a torch straight at her through the skylight.

She rolls onto the floor without a sound and crawls over to the wall by the wardrobe.

There are voices and footsteps on the upper deck, and she can feel their vibrations through the hull. Whoever it is opens the sliding door at the stern.

'We'll call the police unless you come out right now,' a man shouts.

Saga gets up and starts moving towards the voice, pausing when she reaches the door into the kitchen and one of the two security guards points his torch at her.

'The owners said I could stay here,' she says.

'No they didn't.'

'Look, I haven't taken anything,' Saga continues, holding up both hands. 'I just needed to get a few hours' sleep.'

The men step forward into the kitchen, the beam of their torch swinging across the walls and cupboards. The older of the two has a potbelly and a shaved head, and the younger has his black hair tied up.

'You broke the lock,' says the older man.

'That was an accident. I'll leave now.'

'Why shouldn't we just hand you over to the police?' asks the younger guard.

'Because I haven't taken anything, and—'

'This is breaking and entering,' he interrupts her.

'I'll call it in,' says the other man, pulling out his phone.

'Don't, please.'

'And why should we be nice to you, huh?' asks the younger man.

'Enough, Marko . . . I'm making the call.'

'Give me one good reason,' he says, taking a step towards her.

Looking her straight in the eye, he holds out his baton and uses the tip to trace her hip. He keeps going, down her leg and around her knee, up the inside of her thigh.

Saga parts her legs, and when he looks down she takes a step forward and hits him with a firm right hook to the cheek.

His baton clatters to the floor between her feet, and he staggers back and drops to one knee with his hand on his face.

'You bitch,' he groans.

Saga moves quickly, twisting her hips and kicking him in the neck, sending him sprawling across the floor. He lands on his stomach just as the older of the two men brings his baton down on her spine.

Saga stumbles forward, using the dining table to steady herself. She turns around and ducks just in time to miss his baton, which swings through her hair.

She jabs at him with her left fist.

The younger man is now on all fours, still moaning to himself.

His torch rolls away beneath the table, casting a bright crescent of light across the floor.

The older guard approaches Saga, holding out one hand and using the other to aggressively jab at her with the baton.

His phone is on the worktop, a hazy blue dome of light hovering above the screen.

Saga pauses, allowing him to get closer, then she hits his hand with a single jab. All the boxing combinations she has practised over the years are still there, thanks to muscle memory; she doesn't need to think to get the upper hand over him. Saga goes in with a straight left, but instead of moving her feet the way he expects, she takes a long stride forward with her right foot, ending up beside him.

She delivers a hard right hook, hitting his cheek with such force that his head snaps away from her, lips shaking and saliva spraying through the air.

The guard goes down like a felled tree, landing heavily on his shoulder. His temple hits the floor with a loud thud, and he doesn't get up.

Saga kicks the other man in the ribs, grabs the glowing phone from the counter and holds it to her ear as she makes her way outside.

'Hello? This is regional command,' a woman's voice says down the line.

Saga ends the call as she climbs up onto the afterdeck. The guards have left a gangway between the jetty and the deck, and she crosses it and then pulls it back, calling Randy as she hurries across the gravel. The gate is unlocked, and she leaves the marina and is running up towards the tunnel beneath the railway when he answers.

'Randy,' he whispers.

'Call me back on this number in ten minutes.'

She hangs up and turns off the footpath, running across the grass past the Wenner-Gren Center, over the road and into Vanadislunden Park.

Two of her knuckles are bleeding, and she sucks them and holds out her hand to study the wounds when she reaches a street lamp. They don't need stitches, but they could probably do with being taped.

Saga keeps going through the darkness, crossing another lawn. She has reached the playground by the time Randy calls her back.

'Hi,' she answers as she walks along the path.

'I heard what happened,' he says in a low voice. 'It's insane, I don't understand.'

'No, it—'

'I've been suspended. They found my number on Karl Speler's phone.'

'I'm so sorry, Randy,' she says.

'It's fine, don't worry; I'm just happy about what you said when—'

'Is Linda there?' she interrupts him.

'She's asleep.'

'I don't want to get you mixed up in this, but I don't have anyone else I can turn to, and I really do need somewhere to hide.'

'I'll see what I can do. But you should know that another postcard arrived.'

* * *

Randy is in the dark kitchen on the ground floor of his house, and he walks over to the window, pauses and imagines he can hear the sound of bare footsteps coming to a halt on the linoleum floor behind him.

He covers his phone, pushes back the curtain and peers out into the dark garden. In the reflection in the glass, he can see that the hallway behind him is empty.

'What? From Mara?' Saga asks.

Randy goes through to his small office and sits down.

On the desk in front of him, there is an electricity bill from Vattenfall and an insurance document for his Volvo.

Through the window, he can see the parasol and the plastic sun loungers on the patio.

'Yeah, it came yesterday.'

'Yesterday? I don't understand, who found it?' Saga asks.

'It came here, it was in our mailbox . . . Linda brought the post in, and when she saw it was for you she threw it in the bin.'

'You can't stay there,' Saga blurts out.

'Relax,' Randy tells her. He can feel a cool draught around his ankles.

'But Mara knows where you live, she knows—'

'It's fine, don't worry. I'm sure she just wants to communicate with you,' he says, looking out at the willows swaying in the breeze.

'What did it say?'

'Hold on.'

He pulls the door shut as quietly as he can, though the lock still clicks when he lets go of the handle.

He and Linda had an argument about his suspension last night, and she snapped that she had no intention of being Saga Bauer's mailwoman.

'What? What are you talking about?' he asked.

In the end, Linda had admitted to throwing a postcard for Saga in the bin. Randy immediately got out of bed and dug through the rubbish to find it, and by the time he got back Linda had hidden his phone to stop him calling Saga. She kept arguing, accusing Randy of all sorts of things, and eventually he fell asleep with a pillow over his head.

At some point during the night, Linda had left his phone on his bedside table.

'What does it say?' Saga asks again.

Randy opens the top drawer, lifts out a box of receipts and picks up the postcard.

The image on the front is a black and white photograph of a fire-bombed city. Ash and sooty debris are visible in the foreground, and there are fires everywhere, the sky full of smoke. In the background, the camera has captured the wreckage of the old city, the ruins of cathedrals and baroque palaces. The caption underneath reads *Königsberg, 1945*.

'It's a message for you,' he says, turning the card over.

* * *

As she listens to Randy, Saga walks over to a bench beneath a large tree and sits down.

'There are now only two white bullets left,' he reads.

'We know that.'

'Joona will meet my family soon,' he continues. 'There are three Russian words after that, and it's signed *Mark av Omaar*, with two As.'

'OK,' she says, quickly working out the anagram. 'What's on the front?'

'A photograph from the end of World War II, a city called Königsberg. It's almost completely destroyed.'

'Can you send me pictures of both sides?'

'Sure.'

'It would be really good if you could find out what the Russian means, too.'

'I'll be in touch again as soon as I—'

Randy stops talking as the door to his office opens. Saga hears Linda screaming at him, and the call drops.

The phone screen goes dark in her hand.

She gazes out along the footpath towards the closest street lamp. The pool of light beneath it illuminates the tarmac, grass and low bushes, but outside of that bright circle everything is jet black.

Saga remembers the day Mara's psychologist got in touch to tell her everything his patient had said: that Jurek Walter had kidnapped her family and was holding them prisoner in a place that may or may not be called *Moyaveyab*.

But it doesn't exist – or not in Sweden or Russia, in any case.

The police found Mara in the middle of the motorway close to Skärholmen, and they took her to the Karolinska Hospital in Huddinge before she was eventually admitted to the facility in Ytterö.

At the time of Sven-Ove Krantz's call, Saga was deep in the chaotic investigation into the murders that suggested Jurek was still alive. A storm that would soon grow into a hurricane and tear her life apart.

She collapsed, mentally, and never got a chance to dig any deeper into the things the psychologist told her.

Then, once Jurek was dead, she was signed off work and Joona was suspended while the internal investigation was carried out.

Police officers, sniffer dogs and forensic technicians searched every location in Jurek's complex system. They found many graves, but no survivors. Neither she nor Joona were on active duty when the decision was made to deprioritise the preliminary investigation.

Saga thinks back to the drawing of skulls and bones she found hidden in the biscuit tin at the farm. Mara had labelled it 'My Family'.

She shudders, pulls her feet up beneath her and lowers her chin to her knees in an attempt to keep warm.

Does Mara mean that Joona will meet her family once he is dead too, or does she mean that he'll meet their remains in the location where Jurek kept them prisoner?

Saga suddenly feels wide awake.

In order to avoid the metro in the centre of town, she decides to walk to Årstaberg, catch a train to Skärholmen and then start searching the motorway around the spot where the police found Mara.

83

Randy wakes to the sound of slamming kitchen cupboards and realises he is lying on the sofa in front of the TV.

He is wearing pyjama bottoms and a faded T-shirt, and the itchy pink blanket has fallen to the floor.

Thin shafts of morning light spill in through the closed blinds.

Linda stormed into his office while he was talking to Saga last night, and started screaming until her voice broke. He realises now that he never got round to sending the pictures of the postcard like he promised.

He sits up, steels himself and goes through to the kitchen.

Linda is sitting at the table with a cup of coffee and a bowl of lactose free yoghurt, reading the news on her iPad. She has already done her makeup and blow-dried her hair, and her black leather briefcase is on the chair beside her.

'Morning,' he says quietly, pouring himself a mug of coffee.

She ignores him, but he sits down in his usual seat and starts reading the *New York Times* news summary.

'Another love letter?' she snaps without looking up.

Randy puts down his iPad and takes a deep breath. 'We've talked about this, Linda. I haven't cheated on you and—'

'You're such a fucking fraud,' she snaps. 'Sneaking out of bed in the middle of the night so you can come down here and whisper to that whore. I mean, who does that? You're fucking sick.'

'It was about work.'

'In the middle of the night?'

'Yes, she was—'

'You don't even have a job, remember. They fired you because of—'

'I haven't been fired, they've just put me on administrative leave while—'

'Leave?' she retorts, getting to her feet. 'You've clearly taken leave of your fucking senses, because there's only one thing going round and round in your head.'

'Calm down.'

'You've been lying to me this whole time. I don't understand how you could be so cruel, so mean,' she shouts, tears streaming down her cheeks. 'We *live* together. I've really put everything into this relationship . . . Do you understand how this makes me feel? Do you? Completely worthless. I've always struggled with my self-confidence . . . how could you do this to me?'

'I might not have been the best at managing your jealousy, but—'

'Oh, fuck you,' she screams, grabbing her bag from the chair. 'Fuck you. I never want to see you again!'

'This has gone way too far now . . .'

'Just shut up!'

'OK, OK . . . Why don't we talk once you've calmed down—'

'I don't care about you, I don't care what you do, you can run off to your little whore as far as I'm concerned,' she says as she storms out into the hallway.

Randy remains where he is at the table. He sips his coffee and hears the front door slam, so hard that the framed photograph shakes on the wall.

He knows that Linda will walk over to her car, sit down behind the wheel and compose herself with her lips pressed firmly together. She'll dry her eyes and fix her makeup, then she'll start the engine and back out of the parking bay.

She is convinced he isn't over his relationship with Saga, but he has no idea what being over her would actually entail. Randy loves Linda, but that doesn't mean he either wants or is able to cut Saga out of his heart.

He has thrown away all the pictures he ever took of her, though he did keep the negatives. That way he can still make new copies if he ever wants to.

Since she called him from Karl Speler's phone, he hasn't been able to stop thinking about what she said, that he was the one.

He knows she said it, but he can hardly believe it actually happened.

When Linda gets home from work this evening, she'll act like their argument never happened. Randy has been through it all so many times now.

He gets up and goes into the office, picking up the postcard and taking a picture of both sides, then sending the images to Saga.

He hesitates for a moment, then forwards the same pictures to Greta, goes back into the kitchen and rinses out Linda's bowl. He fries two eggs and serves them on a slice of toasted sourdough with a little ketchup and Worcestershire sauce.

As he eats, he thinks about how he can help Saga find somewhere to lie low. He is a member of a photography collective with access to a basement darkroom. It's still a bit too early, but he'll give the chairman a call and request to book the space for a couple of days in an hour or two.

Randy heads upstairs to brush his teeth and wash his face. He studies his face in the mirror above the basin.

His eyes look tired, his mouth dry.

A splash of water rolls down the glass, across his reflection, making his features melt and run.

A sudden noise puts him on high alert for a few seconds.

It sounds as though someone is throwing thumbtacks down the stairs.

He rubs his head and goes through to the bedroom, where he puts on his watch and opens the wardrobe, pulling on a pair of clean boxers, a black T-shirt and blue jeans.

Randy knows that Saga will do everything she can to track down the killer and save Joona, no matter the cost.

How could anyone seriously think she is involved in the murders?

He drags the stool over to the wardrobe and climbs up onto it, moves a white Stetson and takes down the cigar box from the top shelf.

He then sits down on the edge of the bed and opens the lid.

A dog starts barking in one of the other houses further down the street, and the neighbour's Rottweiler soon joins in.

A gust of wind makes the bedroom window shake on its latch.

Randy gets up and looks down at the street through the apple tree. A car with a roof box drives slowly by and disappears.

The branches sway in the stiff breeze, and he catches glimpses of the neighbouring houses through the leaves.

His eyes follow the gust of wind as it makes its way through the neighbours' small gardens, and it suddenly occurs to him that he didn't lock the door behind Linda. Then again, why would he have? They never lock the door during the day.

He turns back to the cigar box and carefully lifts out one of the developed strips of film. It contains four half-frame negatives, the same subject in each, taken roughly one minute apart.

Saga, lying naked on her back in the middle of a seven-point star made of cherries.

He had mounted the camera on the ceiling in the studio in order to photograph her from above, and these images may well represent the happiest moment of his life.

They ate pizza straight from the box before he got to work rigging the camera, setting up the lights and reflectors, measuring and setting out the cherries.

In the negatives, her lips and nipples look white, her slim body dark grey with pale, glowing contours. The space between her fingers seems to be glowing, but the white sheet beneath her is black.

He stares down at the brilliant darkness between her legs, a white triangle with concave edges, a Bankoff circle drawing in his gaze.

As always, Randy took twelve pictures and then they started to make love on the bed in his studio. He remembers kissing her breasts, her stomach. He remembers licking her softly, between her legs, over and over again.

So incredibly warm and smooth.

She held his head in one hand, parting her thighs even further and pressing herself against his lips.

84

Suddenly, the window shakes again. In the bathroom, the wind is roaring through the vent.

Randy can hear something downstairs.

It sounds like someone is pushing the hangers along the rail in the hallway.

Linda must be back, he thinks, heart racing. He carefully puts the negatives back in the box, pushes the lid on, climbs up onto the stool and tucks the box behind the hat.

Maybe she changed her mind while she was sitting in the car, realised that it wasn't such a big deal for him to talk to Saga after all.

Still perched on the stool, he turns towards the window and peers out at the street.

The sun has disappeared behind a cloud, making all the colours look deeper.

The wind seems to be getting stronger with every minute that passes, and the treetops tremble, bowing in the breeze.

He hears a soft knocking sound from the ground floor.

It's just the branches of the willow tree brushing against the windows, he tells himself.

Randy climbs down from the stool, carries it back over to its usual place and lifts his shaver from the charging station.

The tapping on the glass starts again.

He shaves as he wanders out of the bedroom, turns out the bathroom light and walks down the stairs.

The whirring of his razor is so loud that he can't even hear the steps creaking under him.

He reaches the bottom and walks along the hallway to the kitchen.

The razor makes a scraping sound as he shaves beneath his nose.

He pauses and switches it off, listening to the wind whistling around the house. The rustling and knocking of the branches against the windows.

He switches the razor back on and walks into the kitchen.

Forty minutes, then he can call the chair of his photography collective.

In the garden outside, the bushes blow in different directions, the branches of the willow whipping through the air.

The gale howls through the extractor fan.

He shudders and turns around.

The door to the cleaning cupboard has swung open.

Randy walks back down the hall. The hose from the vacuum cleaner is bulging out, and he pushes it back in and closes the door.

He holds his breath and pauses for a few seconds before switching the shaver on again.

The sound is deafening the closer it gets to his ears.

He peers back over his shoulder. The kitchen seems even darker now; maybe it is about to rain.

He hears a creaking sound from the cleaning cupboard, and a cool draught blows around his ankles.

He switches off the razor and turns back towards the hallway.

Up in the bedroom, the window rattles again.

Just as he steps out into the hallway, the front door swings open and thuds against the wall.

The framed photograph of Linda drops to the floor, sending shards of glass across the hall.

There is a small cardboard box on the doormat.

Randy immediately knows what it is.

Mara Makarov no longer has an address for Saga, but she knows that Randy is still in touch with her.

The door slams, making the bell chime softly.

Randy hurries over, grabs the box and turns the lock.

He runs through to his office and sets the parcel down on his desk. Documents and bills fall to the floor.

With shaking hands, he manages to pick one corner of the pale brown tape loose. He tears it off, folding back the flaps and lifting out a ball of paper that he slowly unwraps.

He holds the little figurine between his index finger and thumb, and for a moment it feels as though everything has gone black.

He blinks, angling it towards the light.

The figurine is him.

I'm the next victim, he thinks, blood roaring in his ears.

He fumbles for his phone, but his hands are shaking so much that he can barely enter the code.

Randy tries to calm his breathing and sets the phone down on the desk in front of him. He uses his left hand to steady his right, and forces himself to slow down.

He brings up his call log and dials the latest number for Saga.

'Hello,' she replies, her voice neutral.

'It's me, it's Randy. A new parcel just arrived, here at the house . . . I'm the next victim, I've got the figurine right here, and—'

'Randy,' Saga interrupts him. 'Do exactly as I say: get out of the house right now. Don't stop to grab anything other than your wallet, phone and car keys. Don't get changed, don't lock the doors, just go!'

'OK,' he says, getting to his feet. 'But shouldn't I—'

'Are you leaving?'

'Yes.'

Overcome by a powerful sense of unreality, he walks down the hallway. The door to the cleaning cupboard has swung open again.

'Shouldn't I call command?'

'They won't make it in time.'

He hurries past the cupboard and grabs his bag from the hook, pushing his feet into his shoes. He then unlocks the door and runs outside.

The wind whistles through the trees, tugging at the leaves. His bike has fallen over, and the garden basket is lying on the neighbour's lawn.

'Have you left?' Saga shouts.

'Yes, I'm walking along—'

'Hurry,' she interrupts him. 'Get into the car and start driving, keep driving. Don't tell anyone where you're going, just pick somewhere you have no connection to, somewhere you've never been before, never mentioned. Call or send me a text later, so I know you're safe.'

She ends the call, and he starts running along the street, towards the apricot-coloured row of houses.

Dust, leaves and rubbish swirl along the tarmac.

The car park between the grey buildings is virtually empty.

Randy runs over to his Volvo, and is short of breath by the time he stops to dig the keys out of his bag, his hands shaking so much that he immediately drops them. As he bends down to pick them up, he checks underneath the car.

There is a small, blonde doll's head on the ground by one of the tyres.

He grabs the keys and straightens up, unlocks the door, jumps in behind the wheel and starts the engine. He tears out of the parking space, turns right onto Vibyvägen, and accelerates away.

85

Saga's heart is racing after Randy's call. She is in the middle of
Västerbron, walking along the right-hand pavement so that any cars
passing her approach from behind.

In the bay below, she can see white breakers on the waves.

The stiff breeze tugs at her hood.

Saga nipped into a branch of Naturkompaniet earlier and took a
whole armful of clothes into the changing room. She picked out a
moss green windbreaker, tore off the security tag, stuffed it under her
sweater and then left the shop.

She double checks that the security guard's phone isn't locked and
realises she will have to find some way to charge it within the next
few hours.

A police car with blue flashing lights appears behind her, and she
pretends to be looking at her phone as it races by.

It takes a real effort to keep trudging on with her head down rather
than looking up to watch it drive away.

After a minute or two, she stops and turns her back to the traffic.
She peers out through the wire railings, across the water to the dense
tower blocks on the islands.

Her fingers are cold as she enters Joona's number and lifts the
phone to her ear.

'It's me. I'm just calling to say that a parcel arrived at Randy's place.
He's the next victim. I told him to get into the car and drive somewhere
he's never been or mentioned to anyone.'

'Good, you did the right thing,' says Joona.

'I think the figurine and the wrapping are still at his house, but I
don't have any way of getting over there.'

'Saga, I'm sorry about—'

She hangs up. Joona calls her back, but she doesn't answer. Instead she keeps going across the bridge, heading towards Långholmen and Hornstull.

As Saga walks and the wind tears at her jacket, she tries to convince herself that Randy will be fine so long as he does what she said: gets as far away from Stockholm as he can and lies low until this is all over.

That will deal a blow to Mara's plans – and with a bit of luck, that blow could also bring her to her knees.

There must be a way to stop her.

Saga decides to start by going to the motorway in Skärholmen, searching for *Moyaveyab*, the place where everything began. The place where Mara plans to lure Joona and then shoot him in the back with the last white bullet.

86

Joona turns off and pulls up on the street outside Randy's house. He gets out of the car and walks over to the front door. The blustery wind is tugging the branches of the willow tree in all directions. He rings the bell, opens the door and steps inside.

A framed photograph has fallen from the wall, and there is glass all over the floor.

Joona looks around and walks quickly down the hallway into the kitchen.

The table and the workbenches are both empty, the wind roaring through the extractor fan.

He opens the door to a small room off to one side and sees bills and receipts scattered across the floor. The cardboard box is on the desk, the metal figurine lying beside the crumpled sheets of paper it came wrapped in. It looks just like Randy, Joona notices as he unfolds the larger sheet of paper.

A branch breaks outside, thudding down against the window frame.

The sheet of paper is a page torn out of the kind of road atlas people used before GPS was invented.

The back is blank, but the front is a map providing an overview of the greater Stockholm and Uppsala area, showing all the main roads and junctions from the 1950s.

Joona studies the map and tries to work out whether anywhere has been marked. He switches on the desk lamp and holds the page up to the light, searching for pin pricks, but can't see anything.

The other piece of wrapping is a thin sheet of paper. On it, a short note has been written in old-fashioned handwriting.

The question I commendably answer below: as nature transforms sulphur and <u>iron</u> ♂ into gold, may we not wrest from nature its ~~well-preserved~~ secret and do the same?

Joona reads the short text twice and realises it is a reference to August Strindberg's alchemist period in Paris.

Sulphur and iron become gold.

The editing marks are old, but the word 'iron' has been underlined twice, seemingly at a later date. Probably by Mara, he thinks.

The alchemical symbol for iron is the same as the symbol for the male sex and the Roman god Mars.

Joona studies the map again.

The Sweden Solar System's model of Mars is in Mörby centrum, but Mörby centrum hadn't been built in the 1950s, and as a result it doesn't feature on the map.

This is no use.

He needs to think like Mara.

Alchemy, iron, Mars.

Joona sits down and notices an insurance letter for a Volvo on the floor.

The Volvo logo is yet another version of the symbol for iron.

Mara is planning to kill Randy in his own car on one of Stockholm's roads.

The wind picks up a sun lounger from the garden next door and dumps it on the lawn outside.

Joona gets up and calls Randy. It rings for a moment, then goes through to voicemail.

He tries again, needs to warn his colleague, tell him not to pull over if someone tries to hail him or beckon him over to the side.

87

The pavement on the motorway almost seems to flow in beneath the front of the car as pylons race by on the right-hand-side.

Randy's heart is still racing, but his adrenaline levels have started to level out since he got onto the motorway.

He did exactly what Saga told him to do, without stopping to think for himself. He ran out to his car and tore away, past the old yeast factory and the Co-op supermarket his father still insists on calling Obs!, a name that hasn't been used for years.

He overtakes a concrete mixer and sees a man in hi-vis clothing standing on the roof of a white industrial building, talking on his phone.

Randy tries to make sense of the fact that Mara Makarov has picked him as her next target.

It feels incomprehensible, surreal.

He just can't understand why.

What he really wants is to drive straight to the station, pull up outside and run in, but he also knows that is probably what Mara expects him to do.

Saga told him to get away from Stockholm.

He pulls into the exit lane as he approaches Kista and then continues onto the E18.

Randy finds his mind drifting as he drives. His argument with Linda and the little figurine keep swirling around in his head.

He can't remember any details of the packaging.

Saga told him to go somewhere he has no connection to, somewhere he has never been before, never spoken about. Does that make this road too obvious, too big?

He has no idea, but he decides he should probably try to be a bit more random in his choice of route, and he leaves the motorway when he reaches Bålsta, following Enköpingsvägen onto road 263.

He is safe now; he just needs to keep driving.

A sense of calm spreads through him at last.

Randy follows the narrow country lane as it winds through the enormous nature reserve. Meadows give way to birch trees, gradually growing denser, with more and more pines and spruces on both sides.

He slows down on a bend and accelerates out of it.

Up ahead, he can see a car parked on the left-hand verge. The bonnet is open, and its yellow hazard warning lights are flashing across the tarmac and the tree trunks.

An older man in a crumpled suit is walking through the ditch with a reflective warning triangle in his hand.

Randy slows down and opens the window, pulling up just before he reaches the man.

'Do you need any help?' he asks. 'I'm a police officer.'

The man pauses and runs a hand over the thin white hair on his scalp.

'It's the battery.'

'You got any jump leads?'

'Yup.'

Randy swings across the centre line and comes to a halt in front of the other car, pulling the lever to release the bonnet catch.

The man sets out his warning triangle and turns back.

Randy gets out and lifts the bonnet.

The wind is howling through the trees, sending pinecones falling to the dry ground. The man opens his boot to take out the leads.

Randy tries to peer in through his windscreen, but with the pale sky reflected in the glass it's almost impossible.

Is that someone sitting in the passenger seat?

The man rummages through the boot.

Randy moves over to the ditch and squints in through the side window. He thinks he can make out a small, grey face through his own reflection.

The man returns with the cables in a plastic pouch.

'Very kind of you,' he says.

Another vehicle appears around the bend as the old man takes out the red cable and leans in over Randy's engine.

'Positive to positive,' he mumbles, clamping the leads into place.

The vehicle approaching them is a white van with a broken headlight.

Randy feels a sudden wave of unease as he realises his phone is still in the bag on the passenger seat.

The old man clamps the other end of the lead to his own battery and takes out the black cable.

'Negative to engine,' he mutters, turning back to Randy's car.

The van slows as it gets closer, and Randy moves up onto the grass verge beside his own car.

The wind makes the old man's hair stand on end.

At the edge of the wood, the branches creak as they blow against one another.

The van rolls by. There is a child in the backseat, filming through the window on her phone.

'You can start the engine now,' says the man.

Randy gets into his car and watches the van disappear into the distance. He turns the ignition and leaves the engine ticking over.

The old man is standing in the ditch, wiping his hands on the tall meadow grass.

The person in the passenger seat opens the door half-way, but they don't get out.

After five minutes, Randy turns off his engine and the old man disconnects the cables in the reverse order.

He gets into his car and starts the engine without any issues, holding out a thumb through his open window.

Randy reverses away from him, drives back over onto the right side of the road and hears the old man honk his horn in thanks as he accelerates away.

Randy still has no idea where he is going, but he decides he might try to make his way past Uppsala on the country lanes and then find a small hotel he can check in to somewhere.

As the countryside opens up once again, Randy takes a right at a roundabout and turns off onto the 55.

The tank is almost empty, he realises.

After around four kilometres, he spots some buildings up ahead, the red roof of the petrol station glowing like a beacon.

88

Randy slows down and has just turned off towards the petrol station when he realises he isn't sure he has his wallet.

He pulls up around ten metres from the pumps.

On the other side of the deserted forecourt, he can see a small wooden building. The windows are dark, and around the empty seating area outside there is a banner reading *Pizza, Kebabs, Burgers*.

As he rummages through his bag on the passenger seat, he is relieved to find his wallet inside.

His hand bumps his phone, making the screen light up, and he sees he has five missed calls from Joona Linna.

Randy has just taken his phone out of the bag when something darts behind the car.

He catches the movement out of the corner of his eye.

He looks up and checks the wing mirror.

There is a crow on the tarmac behind the car, pecking at a plastic bag.

The downy feathers on the bird's head flutter in the breeze, and it flaps up into the air as a lorry thunders by on the main road.

Randy looks out through the windshield again. On one of the pillars by the pumps, a sign with a picture of a crossed out cigarette shakes in the wind. Rubbish and dust swirl across the forecourt.

Right then, the car rocks.

Randy turns back to the side mirror and sees the crow pecking at the plastic bag again.

It felt as though the ground beneath him shook as it landed.

He has just unlocked his phone to call Joona when the car shudders again, and he looks up at the mirror.

Another crow has landed behind the car.

Randy unfastens his belt and twists around to get a better look through the back windscreen, but instead finds himself staring straight at another person.

He gasps.

There is a young woman sitting in the back seat of his car.

Mara Makarov, he realises.

Her eyes are dark, her cheeks dusty.

He gropes for the door handle just as a loud crack drowns out all other sounds.

The seat seems to slam into his back.

A small, dark hole has appeared in the windscreen, surrounded by a larger circle of cracked white glass.

Randy feels hot blood spill down the left-hand side of his torso.

Tiny shards of glass glitter on the bonnet.

His ears are ringing.

The car door swings open and he slumps out. His shoulder hits the ground, and one of his feet gets caught beneath the seat.

His telephone lands on the tarmac without a sound.

Randy manages to untangle himself, losing his shoe in the process, scrambling away from the car and getting to his feet.

The two crows flap up into the air.

The bullet has passed through the side of his abdomen, and it feels like he has burnt himself. Randy clamps a hand to the exit wound and starts running. The back door of the car opens behind him.

The pain hits him as he runs over to the deserted fast food kiosk, searing upwards with every step he takes, making his nostrils flare and his eyes water.

From the corner of his eye, he sees Mara following him with the red pistol raised.

All sounds seem to dull slightly.

Gasping, he staggers into the toilet at the side of the building and locks the door.

This can't be happening, he repeats to himself.

The ringing disappears, leaving behind the sound of roaring waves in his ears.

Randy can hear the flags flapping in the wind, footsteps coming to a halt on the other side of the door.

'What do you want?' he asks, his breathing rapid. 'What have I ever done to you?'

The handle turns, and the lock creaks as she pulls on the door.

'Mara, I know you want revenge for something, and I'd be happy to listen if you—'

Right then, he hears a car engine outside, tyres crunching as it pulls in to the petrol station.

'I might be able to help, are you listening? I can—'

Mara's footsteps move away, and Randy clambers up onto the toilet lid with a whimper to peer out through the small window.

A yellow car has pulled up by one of the pumps.

Two of its doors are open.

A young woman in a pair of blue jeans and a brown leather jacket is standing in the pale light beneath the flat station roof with a small girl in a pink dress.

Mara approaches them with the pistol in her right hand.

The girl clearly needs the toilet, hopping from one foot to another.

Mara stops in front of them and says something.

The woman looks frightened, and she rummages through her bag and hands Mara her phone, says something to the girl and then ushers her back into the car.

As Randy struggles back down to the floor, blood spurts onto his right shoe. He unlocks the door, leaves the toilet and pulls the door shut behind him.

He tiptoes around the rear of the kiosk and watches the yellow car pull back out onto the road.

Mara is nowhere to be seen.

The banner strains in the wind, and one of the red parasols has fallen over between the tables.

Randy leaves a trail of blood across the forecourt as he runs back over to his car. He jumps in behind the wheel, groaning loudly in pain.

He sees Mara stride around the corner of the building.

Without pausing to close the door, Randy starts the engine with shaking hands.

She walks calmly towards him and raises her pistol. He puts the car into gear and releases the handbrake. She steadies the gun with her other hand.

Randy stamps on the accelerator. The open door hits a lamp post and slams shut.

Mara pulls the trigger.

There is a sucking sound as the bullet hits the windshield.

It passes straight through his chest, and he slams into one of the pumps.

Petrol floods across the ground beneath the car.

Randy's head hits the wheel. He opens his eyes and coughs, spraying blood onto the dashboard.

Mara is getting closer.

He tries to reverse, but the engine makes a metallic screeching sound, like a teaspoon in a blender.

The petrol is still swilling across the tarmac.

Mara studies him with dark, inscrutable eyes.

Randy jams his hand down on the horn, blasting it for as long as he can manage.

She opens the back door, and he watches in the rear-view mirror as she takes out some sort of plastic jerrycan.

Blood bubbles up in his throat with every breath he takes.

She moves over to him and opens the driver's side door.

Randy is choking, coughing up more blood as she lifts the heavy jerrycan and pours a murky liquid onto his chest.

A sharp, chemical scent fills the car, and he feels a burning sensation on his abdomen and between his legs.

Randy is on the verge of passing out, but he manages to reach forward and start the engine again.

Mara drops the empty jerrycan to the ground and moves back.

He lowers his hand to the gearstick and feebly tugs at it.

The engine dies.

She stares at him, takes a step back, raises the pistol and shoots him for the third time.

The bullet passes through his body and hits something metal.

That tiny spark is all it takes to ignite the petrol fumes.

It sounds like a parachute unfurling as the ball of fire envelops the car and the pumps.

In the few seconds before Randy loses consciousness, he is back with Saga. His old studio is like a negative, a world of inverted light and dark.

'The love of my life,' he whispers.

Beneath the black glow of the lights, her lips and nipples look white. She straddles him and lets him push inside, embracing him, leaning forward, steadying herself on his chest as she kisses him.

The contours of her face are pale and shimmering, and her mouth is full of light as she groans and closes her eyes.

Randy puts his hands on her hips, completely oblivious to the huge storage tank beneath the petrol pumps exploding.

The blast throws shards of glass and twisted metal in all directions, tearing off much of the flat roof above the pumps.

A fifteen-metre fireball surges up into the sky, brilliant and golden, quickly folding in on itself.

The steel pillars slam into the ground, and sheets of red aluminium land in front of the fast food kiosk.

A column of jet black smoke chases the flames into the air, twisting back on itself in the gale.

Fresh petrol continues to feed the flames, throwing them upwards with ferocity inside the swirling black cloud.

89

Saga sits down at a computer in Årsta Library. She has her back to the main entrance, but she has studied the emergency evacuation map and is keeping an eye on the doors through the reflection in one of the windows.

Randy still hasn't been in touch. She hopes that is a good sign, though she can't help but feel increasingly anxious with every minute that passes.

Joona has called her three times.

She logs in to her emails and sees that Randy sent her a message that morning.

Hearing the door open, she looks up. An old man on crutches makes his way inside.

She quickly opens Randy's email containing the photographs of Mara's postcard. Just as he said, the image on the front is a black and white picture of Königsberg in ruins. She clicks on the second image and reads the text on the back:

Saga Bauer,
There are now only two white bullets left. Joona will meet my family
soon.
ИДИ В МОЯАВЕЯБ!

Mark av Omaar

Saga opens Google Translate, switches the keyboard language to Russian and, though she already suspects she knows what it says, starts typing one letter after another.

A blue light dances across the sloping concrete ceiling in the library. A police car has pulled up in the square outside.

Saga watches as the translation pops up on the screen:

GO TO MOJAWAYAB!

She turns down the volume as low as she can, then clicks on the small microphone icon beneath the Russian and leans in to the speakers. A tinny woman's voice says: 'Idi v Moyaveyab.'

The door opens behind her, and she watches in the reflection as a uniformed officer comes in to the library. Saga quickly logs out of her emails, deletes her search history and follows the officer's movements in the glass. As he begins making his way up the stairs, she calmly gets to her feet and turns towards the entrance.

There is another police officer standing outside.

Saga slips in behind a bookcase and makes her way over to the far end of the library. She pushes past a group of school children, breaks the seal on the emergency exit and opens the door.

The fire alarm starts howling as she runs away from Årsta centrum.

She doesn't slow down until she reaches the trees by the community gardens, wiping her mouth with the back of her hand and forcing herself to walk calmly as she tries to gather her thoughts.

Mara probably saw a sign for MORABERG after escaping from Jurek. It was the only landmark that she remembered. In her confused state, she mistook the Latin letters for Cyrillic, reading R as Я and G as Б. As a result, she thought the name was МОЯАВЕЯБ.

What she kept trying to shout was 'Go to Moraberg!' but the muddled combination of Cyrillic letters, pronounced 'Idi v Moyaveyab', meant her message was completely incomprehensible.

Moraberg is an interchange with a large shopping centre, just off the E20 to the east of Södertälje. It also happens to be the only location from Jurek's system where they didn't find any remains or trace of him.

Saga checks her phone again. She still hasn't heard from Randy, and with her heart pounding anxiously in her chest she sits down on a park bench to call him.

After five rings, a woman answers.

'Hello?'

Her immediate thought is that it must be his girlfriend Linda, but then she recognises the voice: Greta from the NCU.

'Hello? Who is this?' Greta asks.

Saga hangs up, gets to her feet and calls Joona.

'What's going on? Where is Randy?' she asks, hearing the fear break through in her voice.

'I'm so sorry, Saga.'

'No . . . No, I don't understand . . . Greta answered his phone and—'

'She's at the crime scene, a petrol station just north of Enköping.'

Saga's throat tightens, and her eyes well up, making it difficult to see.

'Is he dead?'

'Saga, I want to—'

'Just tell me,' she interrupts him.

'They haven't managed to put the fire out yet, but his car has been completely gutted and they've found charred remains.'

'I don't understand, Enköping?'

'Mara must have been hiding in his car from the moment he left the house.'

'Of course,' she whispers.

'Saga, I don't know what you've done, but it's starting to get dangerous for you and—'

'I know, I can't do this anymore . . . I confess, I did it, it's all my fault.'

'Don't say that.'

'But it's true, I killed them all, I couldn't stop it. You're the only one left.'

'Saga, I know you.'

'No, you don't,' she says, ending the call.

She buries her face in her hands for a moment, then composes herself, dries her eyes and starts walking briskly through the park.

She tried, she fought, and she failed. It was her job to save nine people's lives, but she hasn't managed to solve a single one of Mara's riddles in time, and now Randy, Verner and Margot are all dead.

In a daze, she walks along the narrow footpath across Årstafältet Park.

The wide expanse of grass seems to float by.

The gravel crunching beneath her feet sounds as though it is coming from another world.

Saga comes out onto a road flanked by tall tower blocks, and she continues heading south.

Everything she touches ends up tainted then dead.

She drops the phone between the bars of a storm drain, crosses the road and comes to a halt in the parking area outside Hägersten Police Station.

The door has been propped open, and two officers in uniform are kicking a football against the drab wall.

She wouldn't care if they shot her when she walked inside and set her gun down on the counter, she thinks.

It's all her fault.

How could she have failed to save Randy?

Mara's riddles continue swirling through her mind.

On the postcard she sent to Randy, Mara wrote that Joona would meet her family soon, and she rounded off her message by writing 'Go to Moraberg!'

There is little doubt in her mind that Mara was referring to Jurek's system, to the coordinates that pointed to a spot in the middle of the motorway east of Södertälje.

But there was no trace of Jurek there, no remains of any kind.

I'm right back at square one, Saga thinks. Nothing I've done since I received the first postcard three years ago has brought me any closer to stopping her.

It's all been a huge waste of time.

All I've managed to do is convince the others that I'm involved in the murders.

What choice do I have now but to hand myself in and hope that my name is eventually cleared?

Saga tries to steel herself for what is about to come: the shouting, the guns, the handcuffs.

She lowers her eyes and listens to the ball thudding against the wall, the officers' quick footsteps and their heavy breathing.

She starts walking towards the police station.

The ball rolls towards her, and she kicks it back.

The officers wave in thanks, both grinning.

Maybe she never stood a chance of stopping Mara, Saga thinks as she continues towards them.

Maybe Mara's riddle was always impossible, just like the problem involving the seven bridges of Königsberg.

Saga pauses. The problem might be *theoretically* impossible, she thinks, but it is perfectly possible in reality, in three dimensions.

In real life, you could swim or walk underneath the bridges.

Her heart rate picks up.

The answer to Mara's real riddle is that her family were at Jurek's last location all along.

Not on the motorway, but beneath it.

Saga knows that the police scoured both sides of the road with sniffer dogs. They didn't find any doors, entrance points or culverts.

She has studied the plans herself, detailed drawings from when the motorway was first built, while they were carrying out the blasting and excavation work.

But their bodies must be there somewhere.

That's the answer to the riddle.

Mara has only one white bullet left in her Makarov, and Saga is the only one who can save Joona.

If I fail, it's over, but only then, she thinks.

She turns her back on the police station and starts walking away.

Saga knows precisely who she needs to talk to. She needs to track down Jackie Molander.

90

As Joona leaves Randy's house, he thinks back to his conversation with Saga. He hopes she hands herself in soon, because otherwise he will have to start hunting her.

In order to thwart Mara's plans, he needs to understand exactly how she and Saga are connected. That is the key. He gets into the car and calls Greta to find out if anything else has come to light.

'You're no longer on the case,' she says sternly. 'I can't just start giving out information about an ongoing investigation.'

'I don't have time for this,' Joona replies.

'It was your decision to—'

'Greta,' he interrupts her. 'I know you're upset, but I'm the one Mara has picked out as her ninth victim and I need to try to stop her before it's too late.'

'OK, but only this once. We found one white bullet casing and two regular. Forensics have just got to work, but so far everything suggests that the victim is Randy. From what I've seen, the fire seems to have been unintentional. He drove into a pump as he was trying to get away, and the fumes ignited ... Mara and Saga didn't have time to dissolve the body. He probably burnt to death,' she rounds off in a heavy voice.

'Have you found any sign of Saga there?' asks Joona.

'Yes, and we're going to go in hard; we'll neutralise them both if we have to. You know that, don't you? And you—'

'Your boss gave me his word,' Joona interjects. 'He said I could bring Saga into custody and give her a chance to explain her role in all this.'

'Don't call me again,' Greta snaps, ending the call.

Joona starts driving, slowing down at a crossing to allow two young boys with their arms around each other's shoulders to cross the road. Once they are clear, he sets off again, turning into the next block.

If Mara really was hiding in the back of Randy's car, then her pickup is probably still parked somewhere nearby.

He drives along the rows of apricot-coloured houses, past small gardens with outdoor furniture and empty guest parking spaces.

Jurek never did anything without reason, Joona thinks to himself. His system was a means of structuring his memory, a thought palace. It was never about communicating with the police, never a case of playing games or setting riddles.

Perhaps the same is true of Mara?

He continues onto Lantgårdsvägen and drives through an area of grey and white houses.

In a parking space outside one of them, he sees a caravan and a car beneath a protective cover.

A bearded man with a baby in a sling is walking along the pavement.

Joona systematically works his way around the area, speeding up slightly when he reaches Mäster Henriks allé. Between the tall trees up ahead, he can see a low fence, white paint peeling, around a large and well-tended lawn.

He slows down, turns left and passes a woman with a walker as he drives towards the parking spaces.

In the shade beneath a mighty oak, there is a Ford pickup with a powerful electric winch.

Joona parks his car across the road, blocking the entrance, and unholsters his gun as he gets out.

The wind tugs at the treetops.

The tyres and fenders on Mara's pickup are caked with dry mud, and the pale sky makes it impossible to see in through the windows.

Joona approaches the vehicle diagonally from behind.

In the bed of the truck, he can see two plastic drums, a number of tension straps and a tightly rolled tarpaulin.

The hook on the end of the winch line sways in the breeze.

The back window has been patched up with silver tape.

Joona sees himself reflected in the filthy glass by the driver's seat, and he reaches out and tries the handle, but the door is locked.

Through his own reflection, he can make out the wheel, the curve of the seat, the handbrake and the gear stick.

The butt of his gun knocks against the window as he leans in and uses his hands to block out the light.

Mara has left the last box on the driver's seat.

He takes a step back and breaks the window with his pistol, causing small chunks of glass to rain down on the seat inside.

The woman with the walker stares at him for a moment before turning back the way she came in a wide arc.

Joona reaches inside, opens the door and lifts out the parcel.

It feels heavier than the previous boxes.

He runs back over to his car, opens the boot and sets it down inside. He starts tearing off the tape, only to realise that he should probably be more careful this time.

Joona grabs his knife from the glove compartment, cuts a small hole in the bottom of the parcel and peers inside.

The box is full of soil.

He cuts away the entire bottom of the box and slowly pours the earth into a plastic bag.

A small tin figurine appears, silvery grey against the dark soil.

He picks it up and blows off the dirt. With that, he suddenly understands everything.

91

Joona is driving along the E20 towards Södertälje at 140 kilometres an hour, planning to make a brief pitstop in Hågelbyparken.

He needs to talk to Bo F. Wrangel.

Joona is now convinced that the location of the final murder is also the last point in Mara's enormous M: in the middle of the motorway to the east of Södertälje.

The very same location also appeared in Jurek's system of coordinates, the only spot where neither human remains nor any trace of him was ever found.

They searched a huge area, cordoned off the motorway and used ground-penetrating radar to search for cavities beneath it, but all without success. There were no plans or maps that even suggested there might be any hidden structures beneath the road, but given the fact that the ninth box contained nothing but soil and the little tin figurine, Joona is working on the assumption that the underground space is there after all.

Bo F. Wrangel was Joona's commander during his basic military training at Karlsborg Fortress. Wrangel led exercises on the large, dusty patch of gravel outside, and he was always incredibly despotic, picking out favourites and others he wanted to harass.

He often liked to pretend he couldn't understand Joona's Finnish accent, forcing him to do 100 push-ups in front of the others as punishment every time.

Joona was frequently mocked because of his Finnish background, with the others claiming he stunk of vodka or telling jokes about the Finnish Winter War and the refugee children sent to Sweden.

For the past eleven years, Wrangel has worked for MUST, the Swedish military intelligence and security agency, and is now in charge of the Armed Forces' various secret facilities.

After Jurek's death, Joona himself didn't take part in the search for surviving victims, remains, relics or depots. He was suspended while they investigated his role in the violent developments in the Netherlands, and it wasn't until much later that he finally got an opportunity to go through all of the material from the huge search effort and the exhaustive forensic work.

He remembers having the same thought then as now, and that he got in touch with MUST to check. After all, if there were any secret spaces beneath the motorway, they had to be military in nature.

Wrangel listened to what Joona had to say and then replied, with a hint of amusement, that the Security Service had already asked the same question.

Joona didn't have the necessary clearance to request material from MUST, and nor could he escalate it with anyone higher up, but he did share his suspicions with his superior at the time.

The highest level of classified information in Sweden is known as 'Top Secret', and it covers anything that might be critical to national security. Either there must be another, more classified level that not even the Security Service had access to, Joona explained to his boss, or Wrangel simply didn't want to help.

It wouldn't surprise him if his old commander continued to use his position to wield power over others.

Joona has no idea whether the NCU or the Security Service ever raised the issue with the head of the Ministry of Defence. All he knows is that the search was never resumed.

But now, with the arrival of the ninth figurine, Joona is utterly convinced that there must be some sort of space beneath the road in Moraberg after all.

He has just turned off onto a narrow, cracked road alongside a field of rapeseed when the first sting of a migraine hits him.

A drop of ink in a glass of water, swirling and expanding.

Not now, he thinks, pressing two fingers to his left eyelid.

He passes a full car park and swings in between two gateposts, down an avenue of trees and pulls up on the gravel in front of a grand yellow building.

It is the second day of a large budō meeting, and devotees of various Japanese martial arts have gathered from across Europe to train and compete.

Joona spoke to his former colleague Anja Larsson, who now works for the office of the Commander-in-Chief of the Armed Forces, and she told him that this was where Wrangel would be during his week off.

The man has a black belt, tenth dan. He runs Bujinkan Danderyd Dojo alongside his day job, and has been teaching advanced level ninjutsu for many years.

Above the doorway to the manor house, banners printed in Japanese flutter in the breeze.

There are people everywhere, many of them dressed in white, walking down footpaths and over lawns, stretching, practising footwork or just chatting in groups.

Joona pulls up in front of the broad stone staircase, switches off the engine and closes his eyes. He feels the pain start to recede.

He puts on his sunglasses, gets out of the car and runs over to a middle-aged man in black who is busy showing off some sort of antique weapon on a chain.

'Do you know where Wrangel is?' Joona asks, buttoning his jacket with shaking hands.

'They've already started,' the man replies, pointing across the park.

Joona runs down the gravel path around the main building. He can feel that the pain is about to flare up again, and he slows to a walk.

The migraine hits him with full force a moment later, blinding him.

He reels to one side, fumbling for something to lean against. His foot hits loose earth, and he slips and cuts himself on the roses before regaining his footing.

Joona stands still, rubbing his lips and listening to his own strained breathing, until his vision gradually begins to return.

Over the loudspeakers, he hears a voice announce the next event.

Excited voices and laughter spill out through an open window.

Joona makes his way back onto the path and stamps the soil from his shoes. He hurries forward, feeling a pulsing pain shoot out from his eye with every step.

He passes a group of serious-looking women with wooden swords and makes his way in among the trees.

On a patch of grass up ahead, a number of black-clad men are sitting in a ring in the sunlight, hands resting on their thighs.

Joona strides over to them, his migraine dazzling him with a searing halo of white light.

In the middle of the ring, Wrangel is standing in his black costume, a matching belt tied around his waist. His trousers are laced around his calves, and he is wearing soft shoes with high tops and separate big toes. He has stubbly grey hair and warts on his cheeks.

A man in his twenties is standing opposite him with both palms turned upwards.

Joona doesn't hear what Wrangel says, but he watches as he takes a step forward and delivers a sudden blow to the younger man's throat.

The man cries out and staggers away with tears in his eyes. The others part to let him out of the ring, and he slumps onto his side in the grass.

'Wrangel, we need to talk,' Joona shouts, pausing on the edge of the circle.

The next man gets up. He has a shaved head and a pink scar behind one ear, and he rolls his shoulders with a look of embarrassment and fear on his face.

'Do you remember my question about the motorway over by Moraberg?' Joona continues, stepping forward into the ring.

'Ah, we have a volunteer,' says Wrangel.

'You lied to me,' Joona continues, stepping in front of him. 'But now—'

A new wave of pain stops him in his tracks. He presses two fingers to his eyelid again, trying to keep his breathing calm, fully aware that he should be lying down in a dark room somewhere.

The young man with the shaved head returns to his place in the ring, and Wrangel clears his throat.

'I'm going to demonstrate a variant of Mawashi geri,' he says.

'Could you just give me a minute?' Joona asks, smiling at the absurdity of the situation.

Wrangel moves straight towards him and launches a kick from the right. Joona raises his hand to block it, but Wrangel's foot changes direction and hits him on his left cheek, knocking his sunglasses to the ground.

The students clap.

Wrangel moves back and gets into a strange, low position with one hand over his throat and the other open, pointing straight ahead like a rifle's sight.

92

Beads of sweat glisten on Joona's brow. The pain quickly climbs to a peak, radiating outwards across his face.

'I don't . . . have time for this . . .' he stutters as his vision all but disappears again.

His head feels like it is crackling, and he holds up a hand, blinking hard. He can just about make out the pale sky above the treetops.

Wrangel says something, and a shadow darts across the grass. Like the sun passing behind a cloud.

He lunges forward, and Joona feels a kick to the ribs, staggering backwards but managing to maintain his balance.

The migraine makes him lose consciousness for a split second, and he comes round as both knees hit the grass and he hears the men in the ring clapping.

'God . . .'

Joona leans forward, steadying himself with both hands before getting up.

His legs are shaking, and he clenches and unclenches both fists and feels the blood tingling in his fingers.

'There's no need for this, it's—'

He groans in pain as the black ink in his brain begins to retract.

'*Tobi geri taihen*,' Wrangel says calmly.

He runs forward and swings his left knee upwards, powering off his other leg and lashing out with his right foot.

A few torn blades of grass fly through the air.

Joona remains where he is, making himself wider and trying to push Wrangel's foot away as his leg straightens out.

The underside of his shoe scrapes Joona's cheek as it passes, and he delivers a right hook to Wrangel in blind panic.

His knuckles make contact with Wrangel's chest, and the older man wheezes as the air is knocked out of him.

Joona's punch hits him hard, and Wrangel lands flat on his back, his head hitting the ground. He quickly shuffles back with wide eyes and unsteadily gets to his feet.

The migraine has shrunk to a black pearl behind one eye, and Joona tries to blink away the last of the blindness. He grabs his sunglasses from the grass and puts them back on.

The students get up, shifting anxiously.

'Can we stop playing games now?' asks Joona.

'*Omote shuto.*'

Wrangel darts forward with his arm outstretched, his entire palm facing Joona.

He fakes a low kick and then lashes out with one hand.

This time, Joona is focused on what is happening. His years of training, of Krav Maga, enable him to react without thinking.

He moves softly, taking a step forward to neutralise the force in Wrangel's blow, swinging around and ramming an elbow into his cheek.

Wrangel's head snaps to one side, beads of sweat following his movement.

Joona catches a waft of coffee on his breath.

Wrangel drops down and grabs Joona's jacket in an attempt to maintain his balance. He grins, his teeth smeared with blood, and delivers a weak hook that hits Joona in the throat.

Joona sees Wrangel's pupils contract as his field of vision shrinks and his knees turn to jelly. He refrains from hitting him again and simply prises Wrangel's hands away and lets him drop to the ground.

Wrangel lands on his hip, hand fumbling up to his cheek. He rolls over onto his side and is in the process of trying to get up when Joona tears his black belt loose, winds it around one foot and drags him away.

The students move to one side as Joona pulls him across the grass and into the shadow of a tree. Wrangel's arms are flailing, his jacket riding up, and he tumbles onto his stomach.

'For God's sake,' he pants in confusion.

446

Joona pauses and lets go of the belt. He can feel the afterglow of the migraine swelling behind his eye, sending sparks of pain flickering out across his vision.

Wrangel is still slightly stunned as he turns over and lowers his head to the ground. He has grass stains on his chin and his pale belly.

'I need answers,' Joona tells him.

Wrangel props himself up on his elbows, spits blood onto the grass and then straightens his jacket. He looks up.

'Who the hell do you think you are?'

The wind scatters a couple of dandelion heads, sending the fluffy white seeds sailing through the air.

'You know what I'm talking about. You lied last time I asked,' says Joona.

'That's what happens when something is classified.'

'Then I'm begging you,' says Joona. 'This is incredibly important, people's lives are on the line, but—'

'I don't care.'

'You might care when both your legs are broken.'

'Is that a threat?'

'Absolutely.'

Several of Wrangel's students have started slowly moving closer, and Wrangel glances over to them, sits up and licks his lips.

'There are no fortifications in that area, but even if there were I wouldn't tell you about them.'

'You've got that the wrong way around. There is a fortification of some kind, and you're going to tell me about it right now,' says Joona.

'I'll call your superior if—'

'What superior?' Joona snaps. 'I'm here on private business, I don't give a damn about the consequences. Get up and we can continue where we left off . . .'

One of the dandelion seeds lands on Wrangel's eyebrow.

'I don't owe you shit,' he says with a smile.

'Class will continue in four minutes,' Joona tells the students standing closest to them.

'What the hell are you thinking?'

Joona steps forward, grabs one of his legs and starts dragging him back over to the others.

'Stop, for Christ's sake.'

447

'Last chance,' Joona tells him, dropping his foot.

'OK, OK, what the hell, it's not worth it,' Wrangel mutters, sitting up. 'I'll tell you if you promise to leave me alone.'

'Talk.'

'The structure you're talking about is part of the Southern Front,' Wrangel continues, spitting out another gob of bloody saliva. 'As you know, the front was a military fortification line built to protect Stockholm against attacks from the south.'

'I'm aware of it,' says Joona.

'Fine, but are you aware of Colonel John Bratt?' Wrangel asks, burping quietly.

'I'm in a hurry.'

'He actually began his career as an officer in Karlsborg, but this was over 100 years before our time. In any case, Bratt was the head of the Association for Stockholm's Permanent Defences. He built trenches, batteries and forts, and by the start of World War I the Southern Front stretched all the way from Tullinge to Erstaviken; it was so big it needed forty thousand soldiers to man it fully.'

'But Moraberg is to the south of the Southern Front.'

'This is where the classified part comes in, Linna . . . Bratt was an expert strategist, and he pushed through the construction of an under-ground fortification south of the Southern Front. That way, he'd be able to bring down the enemy from behind, through trench warfare.'

'Where, exactly?'

'Both the Southern and the Northern Fronts have lost their military importance, but a decision was made to keep that particular reinforce-ment secret. That's why it doesn't appear on any maps – other than ours, of course.'

'How do I get in?'

93

Saga ran to Årstaberg station and caught the 41 train to Tullinge.

She is now walking down Alice Tegnérs väg, past the grand villas with their big gardens and new cars parked in the driveways. Over the fences and through neat hedges, she catches glimpses of trampolines, goalposts and swing sets.

Four years ago, when Jackie Molander was sixteen, she and two of her friends were arrested by the Security Service on suspicion of having trespassed on a military facility on the island of Muskö.

Saga conducted the initial interviews, but the case was eventually handed over to a colleague.

Jackie's mother had died five years earlier, and her father had started a new family. Saga recognised herself in the rebellious young girl and struggled to see their actions as anything other than an ill-considered case of urban exploration.

Her colleague was just about to hand the preliminary investigation over to the prosecutor when Saga managed to delete the CCTV footage from Muskö.

She is now walking alongside a white fence, past a junction box, gazing over at a large red house with white corner panels and window frames. On the lawn outside, there is an inflatable wading pool beneath the apple tree.

Several pieces of clothing have come loose from a clothes line and caught on the bushes nearby.

Saga opens the gate and follows the path up to the house, stepping over a tricycle.

She rings the bell and hears excited shrieking and the sound of quick feet before a middle aged woman in a faded sweater and tracksuit bottoms opens the door.

'Is Jackie home?'

'Who should I say it is?' the woman asks, giving her a confused look.

'Saga Bauer.'

The house smells like something is baking, the television is on, and there are two young children running around with cushions. Behind the woman, Saga can see that the place is decorated with rugs, rustic wooden furniture probably bought at auction, ceramics and textile art.

The woman has just turned around to climb the stairs when Jackie appears on the landing. She is wearing a pair of white trousers and a black vest with the words *Anti-Fascist Action* emblazoned across the front. Her head is shaved, and her arms are dark with tattoos.

'Saga?' She sounds surprised.

'Can we talk?'

'Sure, come on up.'

Saga takes off her shoes and heads up the stairs.

Jackie's walls and floor have been painted with chalk paint, making it look like bare concrete. Other than an unmade bed and two over-flowing wardrobes, the room is empty.

'So this is how the other half lives,' she says, gesturing to the space around her.

'How are you doing?'

'Good,' Jackie replies, lighting a cigarette.

'I need your help with something,' says Saga.

'Anything.'

'There's an underground facility in Södertälje that I need to find.'

'OK.' Jackie nods and takes a long drag.

'That's your area of expertise, right?'

'Absolutely.'

'Do you have a map?'

Jackie sits down on the bed, balances her cigarette on the edge of an ashtray and picks up a grubby computer from the floor. She opens Google Maps and enters 'Södertälje' into the search bar. Saga takes a seat beside her and points to the motorway. Jackie zooms in, and Saga shows her the exact spot.

'Right under the road,' she says.

Jackie tugs on the ring in her lower lip and stares at the map for a moment or two.

'Nah, I don't think there's anything there.'

'There must be, I know there is,' says Saga.

'Is it military?'

'I have no idea, but probably.'

'Probably,' Jackie repeats, opening a VPN programme.

'What are you thinking?'

'First I need to tunnel the connection . . . and now I'm logging in to a forum to see if I can reach out to a friend,' she says as her fingers dance across the keys.

'It's kind of urgent,' says Saga.

'Yeah, I can tell . . .'

Jackie waits for a moment, picks up her cigarette and pushes it between her lips, then types something else.

'Is there any other way?' Saga asks, starting to feel stressed.

'Yeah, maybe . . .'

'So should we try—'

'Hang on, we're in,' she interrupts Saga.

'Ask about the motorway by Moraberg.'

Jackie writes something, waits, adds something else. The light from the screen shifts across her face.

'OK, you're right,' she says. 'Pim is pretty sure there's something there, but the entrance is miles away . . .'

'Ask her for the coordinates.'

Jackie types something, and the answer arrives immediately.

'No coordinates . . .'

'Come on,' Saga whispers.

Jackie waits for the next response.

'It'll be OK,' she says after a moment. 'You can count on Pim.'

Saga's heart is now racing. She really doesn't have any time to lose. She knows that the Spider's last package is due. Joona might already have received it, and might be tempted to head down below the motorway.

'Could I borrow your phone to send a message?'

'Yeah, sure . . .'

Without taking her eyes off the screen, Jackie unlocks her phone and hands it over to her. Saga enters Joona's number and writes: *Don't go to Moraberg. It's a trap!*

94

Saga borrowed a compass, headlamp, hacksaw and small rucksack from Jackie, then ran back to the station and caught the train to Södertälje, stealing a bike from outside the yellow station once she arrived.

Jackie told her there were probably other entrances Pim wasn't aware of, but that this one involved an incredibly long ladder and a narrow passage south.

Saga turns off onto Österhöjdsvägen and rides into the forest.

She pedals as fast as she can, but the whole thing still takes longer than she has time for.

There is a huge water tower at the top of the hill, a cylindrical reservoir with a ring of concrete pillars around the base.

Saga brakes, walks the bicycle into the brush and lets it drop to the ground.

Her thighs are burning after the uphill ride.

She runs back over to the water tower and stops dead when she spots a short figure in white sports clothes standing at the base.

'Pim?' she says, slowly making her way forward. 'I'm Saga.'

The girl studies her blankly. She doesn't look much older than fifteen, with a thin, pale face, a crooked nose and icy blue eyes.

'I'm the one who needs to go down into the tunnels,' Saga explains.

The base of the water tower is covered in graffiti.

'My friend Jackie said you could help me,' she continues.

Pim presses a hand to her flat chest, hesitates for a moment, then gestures towards the trees.

'Is it over there?' Saga asks. 'Is that where I need to go? Roughly how far?'

Pim wanders past the columns, hops down to the ground and makes her way in among the trees. Saga sets off after her. After around fifty metres, they scramble down a steep rockface, turn off to the right and come to a halt in front of a rusty metal hatch on a concrete plinth. There is a broken padlock lying in the bilberry bushes to one side.

'Is this the way in?' Saga asks, moving forward.

She lifts the heavy hatch and sees a ladder leading straight down into the darkness. A couple of small grey moths flap up in the stale air.

'It would be great if you could wait here and close the lid once I'm inside,' Saga tells the girl.

Pim grins, baring her crooked teeth.

'Can you do that?'

The girl's eyes seem to glaze over again.

'Just so I can see the ladder while I . . .'

Saga trails off as Pim turns and starts walking back in the direction of the water tower. She watches the young girl go, then lowers her rucksack to the ground and takes out the headtorch, shining it down into the hole. Thousands of criss-crossing spiderwebs gleam in the light for the first twenty or so metres, but after that all she can see is darkness.

She pulls the rucksack back on, switches the headtorch to the dimmest setting and tightens the strap around her head.

Moving carefully, she climbs inside.

A few small rocks tumble down beneath her, clinking against the ladder and then vanishing into the void.

Saga grips the concrete plinth and tests one of the rungs before reaching up and closing the heavy metal lid above her.

She is immediately plunged into darkness.

Her headlamp casts a dinner plate-sized circle of light onto the wall in front of her, sending black spiders scurrying back into the corners.

Saga starts making her way down the ladder, clinging onto the grooved rungs as she tries to find a solid foothold, counting every step.

The cobwebs make a soft rustling sound as she pushes through them, and she feels the sweat trickling down her back.

The acoustics change, becoming increasingly oppressive the further she climbs.

As she slowly starts to feel more comfortable, Saga speeds up.

Eighty-three, eighty-four, eighty-five.

The next rung is missing, and her left foot bumps against the one below and slips.

She clings on for dear life, and her shoulders crack as they take her full weight.

Saga's mouth hits one of the side rails, her knee the other. She quickly regains her footing and stands still for a moment before setting off again, moving more carefully this time.

The air around her gets colder and colder, but she keeps climbing.

The sounds are now so deadened that she feels like she is going deaf.

All she can hear is her own breathing, the crackling spiderwebs and the soft ringing tone her hands make on the ladder.

After two hundred rungs, Saga pauses, hooking her arm around the ladder. She turns up the head torch and looks down.

She is only around ten metres from the bottom now, and she hurries down, quickly reaching a concrete floor strewn with loose earth and old leaves.

Tiny white insects swirl through the beam of her lamp.

Her fingers are cold and stiff as she brushes the cobwebs from her hair and clothes.

There is only one way for her to go now: along a straight tunnel, around two and a half metres in diameter.

She can't hear a single sound.

In order to avoid giving herself away, Saga turns down the headtorch. She then takes out her pistol and starts walking.

The passageway is monotonously straight, and the glow of her torch stretches no more than three metres ahead of her; everything else is bathed in darkness.

She thinks back to the drawing in the biscuit tin, the skulls and bones.

My family, Mara had written.

And on the third postcard, which Mara signed with an anagram of her own name, she wrote that Joona would meet her family soon.

They must be down here somewhere.

Mara must have realised that Joona was the only person who could stop Jurek and that he abandoned everyone to their fate before he did so, in order to save his own daughter.

That's why Mara's family is dead. Saga is convinced that Mara plans to lure Joona down here somehow. He has probably already received the last parcel, solved the riddle and set off.

She just hopes he got her warning in time.

If not, he is likely already in the tunnels somewhere.

Mara wants to shoot Joona in the back and then string him up directly beneath the motorway, in Jurek's original location.

She is obsessed with patterns and riddles and wants her own constellation to come together with Jurek's, like some sort of passage to Hades.

Jurek will take his revenge from the grave, and Joona will get to meet Mara's family.

After around three hundred metres, Saga reaches a heavy steel door that seems to have to be raised manually using a hand crank.

The door is hovering roughly twenty centimetres above the floor, and Saga tries to turn the hand crank to lift it higher, but it refuses to budge.

The cogs have probably rusted together.

The door must weigh at least half a tonne.

Saga takes off her headlamp and kills the power, plunging the tunnel around her into darkness.

She reaches out and finds the door through a layer of cobwebs, then drops to the floor, takes off her rucksack and lies flat on the ground.

She holds her breath, listening through the opening.

She can hear a dull thudding sound somewhere in the distance, almost like water lapping against a hull.

Perhaps it is just the ground above her.

Aiming her pistol through the gap, she adjusts the headlamp and switches it on.

Light spills through onto the other side, illuminating a pair of feet no more than a metre away from her.

Saga's finger trembles on the trigger, but she quickly realises it is just a pair of old wellington boots.

Her heart is pounding.

Around five metres behind the boots, there are two rusty oil drums on the concrete floor.

Saga uses the barrel of her gun to brush a couple of large cobwebs away. She feels her heart rate level out again, rolls over onto her back and turns her head to one side in order to try to shuffle under the door.

The cold underside of the steel door presses down on her temple, and as her ear draws level with it, she hears an ominous creaking sound.

The door would crush her head if it dropped even a few centimetres.

Saga uses her feet to push herself slowly through the gap, trying to make herself as flat as she possibly can.

She feels the pressure on her chest, and the buttons on her jacket scrape against the metal.

She makes it to the other side, reaching back through the gap and groping for her rucksack, pulling it underneath and rolling away.

Saga quickly gets onto her feet, aiming the gun down the tunnel ahead of her.

The corridor is deserted.

Pale insects scuttle away.

She aims over the top of the oil drums, standing perfectly still.

There is no one there. Nothing but a rusty can of spray paint that has been left on the floor, cocooned in white cobwebs.

Grey moths flutter through the beam of her light.

She can hear the groaning through the rock again, as though it is taking a deep, slow breath.

Saga speeds up, keeping her gun trained on the floor.

The narrow beam of light reaches no more than five steps ahead of her, spiderwebs brushing against her face.

She reaches an intersection and pauses up against the right-hand wall. She removes her headlamp, powers it off and then stands quietly in the darkness, listening.

She should turn the brightness up as far as she can before she switches it on again, she thinks. Use it as a guide light by holding it beside the barrel of her gun, so that the beam follows her line of fire as she secures both sides.

Her eyes are starting to adjust to the darkness, and she can see a faint, pulsing glow somewhere off to the left.

At first she isn't sure it is really there – it could just be the lingering glare of the torch – but the light continues to sway softly across the concrete wall.

It dances along the corridor to the left, spilling around the corner and into the passageway straight ahead.

Saga realises that whatever it is must be somewhere to the right, that it is moving in such a way that its glow spills back and forth around the corner.

She dries her clammy palms on her trousers and adjusts her grip on the pistol.

This is it.

She slowly makes her way around the corner with her gun raised.

Ten or so metres up ahead, the tunnel opens out into a larger space. She can see a flickering candle pushed into the neck of a wine bottle.

Saga moves as quietly as she can, and a little more of the space becomes visible with every step she takes.

On the floor by the candle, a dark pool of blood catches the light.

There are drag marks stretching off to the left, and someone is moving around in the room up ahead, causing the flame to tilt in different directions. The walls seem to lean and buckle in its flickering glow.

She needs to move much closer to the end of the tunnel in order to get a better view.

Saga hears the soft patter of bare feet, and she stands perfectly still, ears pricked, but she is unable to localise the sound.

It could just as easily be coming from behind her as in front.

She slowly moves closer.

Her eyes are drawn to the trail of blood, following it over to one side, where it disappears around the corner.

She takes another step forward, and a piece of glass crunches beneath her foot.

Saga stops dead and holds her breath.

All is quiet.

The other person seems to be holding their breath, too. Listening.

Without making a sound, Saga fills her lungs.

A heavy spider moves across its web.

The candlelight sways, and the greenish shadow of the bottle moves in an arc across the floor.

Someone is moving, and fast.

It sounds as though their footsteps are climbing the walls.

Saga keeps going.

The footsteps are on the floor again.

She hears someone groan in pain.

Saga reaches the end of the passage and peers in to the large room on the other side. It's square, with four doorways: one on each wall.

The dancing candlelight flickers around the space like a beating heart.

They are probably right beneath the motorway now, and Saga can see a large shape lying in a pool of blood off to the left.

The wristwatch Joona's daughter gave him is lying broken on the floor.

Her heart starts racing.

In the dark doorway closest to her, she notices a cautious movement, grey arms and legs catching a hint of reflected light. Mara Makarov slowly moves forward with the red pistol trained on the body on the floor.

Her finger is already on the trigger.

Saga knows that Mara will kill Joona if she fires her pistol, that she will shoot him before her own bullet can neutralise her.

Her hands are shaking as she takes aim at Mara's chest, moves her finger to the trigger and pulls it halfway.

95

Joona runs through the darkness, almost without a sound. His migraine finally disappeared around ten minutes ago, leaving him with an icy clarity.

He passes through a thick clump of cobwebs and continues down the passageway, towards the flickering candlelight in the room up ahead.

In the soft glow, he can see a heap of blankets in a pool of blood.

His watch, which disappeared three weeks ago, is lying on the floor.

Joona has already released the safety on his Colt Combat, and he is holding it out in front of him with the barrel angled down.

He reaches the entrance of the tunnel just as Mara emerges from a doorway with her red Makarov trained on the blankets.

Joona swings to one side with his own pistol.

Saga is standing in one of the other doorways with her Glock ready to fire when Mara turns her gun towards her.

Saga squeezes the trigger.

Joona has the perfect line and fires his Colt. There is a loud crack, and the recoil hits his shoulder like a piston.

The empty case is ejected from the chamber.

His bullet hits its target.

Blood sprays across the wall behind Saga.

The casing flies through the air, glimmering softly.

Joona turns his pistol towards Mara, but she has already disappeared into the darkness.

His gunshot echoes through the underground space.

Joona darts forward through the cloud of smoke.

The casing clatters to the floor.

The flame bends to one side, turning a shade of pale blue.

Saga falls, hitting her head on the wall and slumping to the floor.

* * *

Three black helicopters sweep in over the silvery-grey water in the narrow inlet.

Their shadows seem to chase them across the surface, and the dull roar of the rotor blades echoes between the steep shorelines.

Six operatives from the tactical unit are hanging from an SPIE rope beneath the last of the helicopters. All are wearing helmets and body armour, carrying assault rifles with mounted lights.

As the Kiholmssundet lighthouse comes into view, the helicopters climb through the air in unison as though they were tied together. They pass over the power lines, bank to the left and then follow the clearing through the dark green forest.

They round the northern edge of Södertälje and peel apart as they approach the motorway.

The first swings out over Torekällberget, reducing its angle of attack and moving in above the water tower. A powerful side wind makes the helicopter veer to the left, but the pilot manages to compensate for the movement using the foot pedal.

Its searchlights sway uneasily over the looming concrete structure.

The pilot hovers above the aerials as the six operatives are winched down onto the flat roof of the tower.

They quickly secure their lines and jump backwards over the edge, rappelling down to the ground like sluggish shooting stars, unclipping themselves and running to take cover.

The second helicopter swings in above the motorway, hovering overhead. On the outside of the cabin, a sharpshooter is strapped into place, feet on the landing skid.

The third helicopter makes a wide turn around the Fornhöjden area of Södertälje, causing the SPIE line of operatives to swing out beneath it.

From up in the cabin, the flight engineer tries to minimise the motion with one foot on the line.

The roar of the engine deepens as the RPM drops and the pilot sinks towards the ground inside the barbed wire fence.

The trees and bushes bend in the powerful downwash.

461

They come in towards the driveway outside the boarded-up building, and the bottom operative hits the ground, unhooking his carabiner from the D-ring and then holding the line steady for the others.

Right then, the tail rotor collides with the top of a birch tree.

There is a rattling sound, and the line is torn out of his hands.

The second operative is thrown to one side, and shredded leaves rain to the ground.

The helicopter sways, but the pilot manages to hold it steady.

One by one, the operatives safely hit the ground, unclipping themselves, running back and taking their positions.

The land, owned by the Swedish Armed Forces, was adapted to accommodate troop transport vehicles during the cold war, but the underground network was never brought into use.

The entrance is hidden behind a large garage with tall folding doors.

The six operatives run forwards in pairs.

The lock on the main door has been drilled, and the squad leader gestures for the others to spread out to the sides.

* * *

The flame flickers, flares and glows yellow again. The room seems to grow, the concrete walls no longer moving.

A pool of blood blossoms beneath Saga.

Her Glock is on the floor around a metre away from her, and Mara's footsteps fade down the dark passageway.

Saga's eyelids flutter.

Joona pulls out his knife and drops to his knees in front of her, his cheeks slick with sweat. Saga opens her eyes, her breathing unsteady, and stares up at him in confusion.

He slices open her jacket to get at the bullet wound on her shoulder. Her blood is pulsing out in quick spurts.

'Joona, what the fuck . . . I'm not involved,' she pants.

'I know.'

He cuts her T-shirt open and twists the material into two firm rolls, using the strap from her headtorch to make a kind of makeshift tourniquet. Saga groans in pain and looks up at him.

'So why . . . why'd you shoot me if you—'

'I'll be back soon,' he says, getting to his feet.

'Be careful. If you follow her into a room, she ends up behind you.'

Joona runs down the dark tunnel after Mara, towards a faint light up ahead. It stretches out along one wall, making the concrete look wet.

The patter of her bare feet fades into the distance.

Joona was singled out as the final target in Mara's series of nine murders, but that was nothing but a trap, another strand of her web.

Time and time again in the footage from the psychologist's sessions with Mara, she asked about Saga, but she never mentioned Joona.

Not once.

That was what made him realise he couldn't be her final target, regardless of what her postcards claimed.

This isn't about him; it's about Saga.

96

Joona runs soundlessly down the dark passageway, sticking close to the wall. He reaches the next room and swings around the corner with his Colt Combat raised.

A bright light blinds him, but he manages to catch a brief glimpse of Mara before she is swallowed up by the shadows once again. It all happened so fast that he didn't have time to shoot.

He keeps going.

The cold rock feels like it is closing in on him.

There is a torch on a stool, its beam pointed straight at him. On the floor around it, he can see tins, water bottles and an outdoor stove, all covered in cobwebs.

He makes his way into a pitch black tunnel, trailing the fingers of one hand along the wall as he walks.

The sound of Mara's footsteps disappears into the distance, and it almost sounds like she has managed to slip into one of the cracks up by the ceiling.

Joona hears a soft tearing sound as he walks through a spider web.

He reaches a door, fumbles for the handle and pushes it open.

Jurek was the one who broke and created Mara Makarov, but he also taught her how to be pragmatic.

She read the entire classified investigation and decided what form her revenge would take.

Master Fauster taught her the practicalities, how to kill and to avoid leaving a trace, but it was Jurek who remained her mentor, Mara his apprentice.

In line with his mentality, her riddles and communication with the police were never narcissistic; both served a higher purpose.

Everything she shared, whether it seemed unintentional or not, was part of her plan to lead everyone involved in a specific direction.

The door swings open, and Joona finds himself peering into a small room with a lamp shaped like a deathcap mushroom.

The floors and walls are bathed in soft red light.

He pauses to listen, then steps forward and secures the left-hand side before swinging around to do the same on the right.

There is another heavy steel door up ahead, and he sees Mara slip past it.

He hurries after her, coming to a halt by the side of the door. He can hear her quick footsteps on the other side, followed by a dry rattling across the floor.

Joona pulls on the heavy door, and it swings open without a sound.

A faint glow lights up the dull steel from inside.

He has reached the mid-point of Mara's giant M, he realises.

Joona moves through the doorway and quickly secures the space.

There is no one here.

She has already escaped into the next room.

There is a lantern on the floor in front of him, but it is putting out almost no light at all.

Joona slowly makes his way forward, keeping his gun trained on the closed steel door on the other side of the dark room.

He pauses.

At first, it is difficult to make sense of what he is seeing.

In the middle of the square room, the lantern has been placed on top of a pile of skulls. The battery is about to run out, but its weak glow is still bright enough to illuminate a pale yellow circle of bones on the floor.

There are hundreds of them, eight people's worth, and they have been arranged symmetrically, each body stretching out from the hub of skulls like the spokes in a wheel.

Each jawbone is followed by a row of cervical vertebrae, collarbones and shoulder blades.

Taken together, the bones resemble a snowflake, its outer tips made from tibiae, feet and toes.

Joona steps carefully between them, his gun still pointed at the door up ahead. He accidentally knocks a thigh bone, which wobbles and hits a hip bone with a dull thud.

He hears the sound of something brushing against metal and fixes his eyes on the door handle.

After Mara was discharged from the psychiatric clinic in Ytterö, she managed to get hold of the NCU's material surrounding Jurek. She used that information to make her way back to this underground facility beneath the motorway, where she found her entire family dead.

Saga had access to the exact same information two years earlier – when Mara first reached out to her through the psychologist – and could therefore have managed the same if she had tried.

With one key difference: Mara's family would still have been alive back then.

That is why, in her eyes, Saga is responsible for their deaths.

Eight people died because Saga didn't do everything she could while Mara was locked up in Ytterö.

Mara made the decision to start murdering people close to Saga, those she had been in conflict with, in order to make her seem increasingly suspicious.

She left traces of Saga at the crime scenes, DNA and chemicals on her motorbike, horse hair in her rucksack.

The whole of Mara's complex web was created with the express aim of leading to this moment beneath the motorway.

Her plan was for Saga to be killed by Joona or arrested and convicted as a serial killer.

The lantern on the pile of skulls grows weaker, causing the circle of light to flicker between the bones.

This is the ninth find site, and there is no doubt that it is a grave.

Mara has pieced together the eight skeletons belonging to her family on the floor.

Joona realises he needs to take out his torch before the light disappears completely, and he aims his gun at the door straight ahead.

The red glow of the mushroom lamp from the previous space reappears as the lantern dims again, causing his shadow to stretch up and over to the steel door.

Water trickles from a rusty pipe, following the lumpy calcium deposits down to a small drain on the floor with a soft babbling sound.

He takes a step to one side to avoid standing on a child's breast-bone, and as his shadow swings across the wall, he notices a spiderweb glitter between the handle of the closed door and the frame.

An icy wave of adrenaline pulses through him.

The door behind his back starts to move.

He turns around and lunges back, bones crunching beneath his feet.

Time almost seems to grind to a halt, heavy and soundless.

The door is about to close, the chink of light from outside getting narrower and narrower.

Joona hurls himself forward, jamming his pistol into the crack just in time. The heavy door dents the barrel, but the door isn't locked.

He quickly gets back onto his feet, head ringing.

He managed to scrape both elbows when he threw himself forward, and he can feel blood trickling down his leg from his right knee.

Joona flings the door open, and the twisted remains of his Colt Combat drop to the concrete floor.

Mara is standing on the other side, pointing her red Makarov at him.

Her eyes are wide.

Her face is dirty, and she is breathing quickly through her half-open mouth. The muscles in her slim arms look tense.

'It's over, Mara,' Joona tells her, holding up both hands.

He moves slowly towards her, and she takes a step back, still aiming straight at his chest.

'I saw the last figurine,' he says as he takes a cautious step forward.

Her eyes flutter as she turns the gun on herself and jams the barrel into her mouth.

'Wait, listen to me . . . It was Jurek who did this to you and your family; it wasn't your fault. Do you understand that?' Joona asks, holding out both hands in an attempt to calm her.

Mara's eyes well up, and he can hear her teeth chattering against the metal.

'Jurek poisoned everyone around him; he got into their heads and took up residence there, even long after his death.'

Her finger has turned white on the trigger.

'Don't do it, Mara. I've never shared Jurek's last words before,' Joona continues, noticing something change in her eyes. 'I could have arrested him, but I made the decision to kill him instead. And when he realised what was about to happen, he whispered something in my ear. Something I've heard every day since. Do you want to know what he—'

Joona lunges forward and grabs her right forearm, using his other hand to push her head back and knock the barrel of the gun out of her mouth.

The back of her head hits the wall, sending a spray of saliva down over her chin.

Joona pulls her arm up behind her, knocking her off balance and kicking her legs out from beneath her.

For a split second, she loses all contact with the ground, and her hair flies up over her face.

Joona maintains his grip on her arm, twisting it upwards as she falls.

Mara gasps, though she should be roaring in pain as her shoulder is ripped out of its socket.

Joona manages to prise the pistol out of her hand, shoving it into his shoulder holster and rolling her over onto her stomach. He uses a cable tie to secure her hands behind her back, then sits her down against the wall.

'Right before Jurek died, he looked me in the eye and whispered "Our souls will trade places now – you'll fall and I'll be left here,"' Joona tells her.

She groans as a wave of pain washes over her. A trickle of blood runs from her lip, and she looks up at Joona with dark eyes.

'He knew what he was doing. He wanted me to know that I'd change if I executed him,' Joona explains. 'He wasn't afraid of dying, he just wanted me to think that I'd become like him . . . And his words have followed me ever since, they've made me doubt myself. But if I was like him, bound by nothing but my own dark desires, I would have killed you right here and now.'

Joona pulls her pistol from his holster and unloads the last white bullet into his palm, holding it out to her.

97

Saga is lying in bed in a room at the Karolinska Hospital in Huddinge, a sterile dressing on her shoulder.

Joona's bullet shattered the top of her humerus, but the surgeon managed to stabilise the fracture and stop the bleeding.

The morning sun filters in between the pale pink curtains, across a copy of *Fermat's Last Theorem* on the bedside table and over to Saga's bruised shin.

There is a knock at the door, and Joona comes into the room. He looks down at her as though she were his younger sister, then reaches out and strokes her cheek.

'How are you doing?' he asks.

'You know it hurts when you shoot people, right?' she says.

'I'm really sorry, but I didn't have time to do anything else.'

'What happened?'

Joona sets down the ninth figurine on the table beside her. The sun gleams on the dull grey metal.

The model is of a young woman with messy hair. She is standing with her feet wide apart, her arms by her sides, and she is holding a pistol in her right hand.

There is no doubt about it. Mara Makarov was the ninth victim.

'I thought the last figurine would be you,' says Saga.

'Me too, but the whole thing was actually about you and her, no one else,' Joona explains.

'But the postcards, the threats against you . . .? I don't understand.'

'It was just part of her web.'

'And I got caught in it.' Saga sighs.

'Mara managed to find her dead family using the same material you had access to, so her reasoning was that you should have been able to find them, too – while they were still alive.'

'That's true, I know that. It's my fault they're—'

'No, it's not, it's not your fault. It's Jurek's fault, but Mara placed all the blame on you . . . She wanted you to be convicted of nine murders.'

'I can understand that,' Saga mumbles.

Joona pulls a chair over to the bed and sits down. Saga picks up the small figurine and studies it from every angle.

'Beneath the motorway,' Joona continues, 'when Mara turned to you, she never had any intention of firing her pistol. She just wanted you to shoot her.'

'So the whole thing was really just an elaborate suicide plot?'

'Yes.'

'And you shot me to stop me from killing her,' says Saga, setting the figurine down.

'Because otherwise you would have been convicted of the murders . . . Or the last one, at the very least,' he says. 'Among the blankets on the floor we found a letter describing how you'd threatened her into not taking her story to the media.'

'She'd planned everything,' says Saga.

'Mara blamed you for failing to save her family, but more than anything she blamed herself. She was the one who managed to escape from the bunker, and the rest of her family probably thought that meant they'd be saved, that she'd come back with help. But she was so weak after all that time in the darkness that she just walked and walked without really registering where she was.'

'Other than a sign for Moraberg . . . That was what she kept repeating to the psychologist, but he couldn't understand her,' Saga says quietly.

'If she hadn't had a mental breakdown and ended up in hospital, her family would have survived.'

'Pretty heavy burden to carry.'

'And that was why she thought she deserved to return to the place where the others were held and die there too.'

'How did you find the space beneath the motorway?' asks Saga.

'The nine burial sites formed a huge M or a W, with a base of 100 kilometres . . . And when I saw the ninth figurine, I realised that the murder site and the burial site would be the same.'

'Because Mara wouldn't be able to move her own body.' Saga nods.

'Exactly. And by following her pattern, I knew where the last site would be.'

'You're learning,' she says with a smile.

As Joona suspected, in the wake of the incident in the bunker, Mara revealed her plan, and there is little doubt she will be convicted of the murders.

They spend a while discussing the victims, and Saga turns pale when they touch upon Margot and Verner, but it is only when they get to Randy's desperate struggle to survive that her face crumples and tears start spilling down her cheeks.

'Why does everyone have to die?' she whispers.

'Sometimes it feels like . . . the price is just too high.'

'Yeah.'

'Jurek still colours my thoughts . . . Sometimes I still think that I'm like him,' says Joona.

'You aren't.'

'It's just that . . . it all feels so much harder. After every case, it's like I have to walk back across a bloody battlefield.'

'I know.'

'I have to stop by every single body and relive their fear and suffering, the grief they're leaving behind.'

'I can't stop thinking about the victims either,' Saga whispers.

Joona meets her eye.

'For a long time now, it's felt as though I'm making the world a darker place,' he confesses.

'But you're the best,' she says.

'No, you are. We should work together more often.'

'We really should,' she says with a smile, drying the tears from her cheeks.

Saga remains in bed, staring at the ceiling once Joona gets up to leave. She hears him exchange a few words with the officers stationed outside, and then his footsteps fade down the corridor.

She closes her eyes and thinks back to the long ladder, to the way the darkness seemed to close in on her, and eventually dozes off, only waking when she hears the sound of raised voices outside.

'Let go of me! I have to—'

'Take a step back, please,' says one of the officers. 'We need to see valid ID and—'

'I have a right to see my girlfriend! I need to—'

'Calm down,' says the other officer. 'If you don't calm down and take a step back—'

'What, are you going to shoot me?'

'No one is going to shoot anyone, but we'll have to arrest you if you don't do as we say.'

A moment or two later, the door opens and one of the officers comes into the room with an embarrassed look on his face.

'Someone called Karl Speler is here to see you,' he says.

'You can let him in,' Saga tells him with a smile. 'But I'm definitely not his girlfriend.'

Karl comes into the room with his pointy teeth bared in a grin. With the enormous bandage around his head, he looks just like the poet Apollinaire.

He is wearing a black T-shirt with the words 'Tangerine Dream' printed on the front, and is carrying a large bouquet of red roses.

'Has anyone ever told you that you look like a princess?' he asks.

'Nope.'

'The bullet took out a chunk of my temple,' he says, gesturing nonchalantly to his head.

'I don't think it made your new hairdo look any better,' she says, holding back a smile.

98

Joona and Valeria are sitting at a table in Wedholms Fisk, eating grilled turbot. The dining room is quietly elegant, with flickering candles and white tablecloths. There are only a few other diners left, and the staff seem to move through the room without a sound.

'I've started to think that everything we do, even the things we don't . . . it all gets added to the balance, it determines who we are,' he says.

'Yes.'

'And that nothing in this world ever really disappears, even if we sometimes wish it would.'

Joona typically tells Valeria about the more complex, intense cases once they are finally over. It's part of an unspoken agreement they have: she allows him to disappear into his work without asking any questions, but once things start to clear back up, he lets her in.

As they ate their starters, he told her all about the figurines, the riddles, the time pressure and the hunt for the killer, and by the time their mains arrived, he had recapped the traps, the solution and the showdown under the motorway.

'They'll give Mara a thorough psychiatric assessment, but I'm not sure . . . I never really thought of her as mentally ill in that sense. I'm not convinced she was even while she was committed,' he says, lowering his cutlery. 'She was tired and undernourished, traumatised and desperate . . .'

'And she had a story that seemed too far-fetched to be real.'

'Mara hoped Saga would be able to save her family, and with everything the psychologist told her and all the material we had on Jurek, she could have done it. Saga knew the patient had seen a sign reading 'Moyaveyab' not long after she escaped, and if she'd just realised it was muddled Russian and looked into it, she would have realised it was Moraberg. And since she already knew that Jurek's system pointed to that exact spot . . .'

'OK, I think I understand. There was a chance, no doubt about that,' says Valeria. 'But the fact that – how can I put it – that she didn't manage to spot and solve a riddle . . . that's hardly a crime.'

'No, it's not, but once Mara was discharged, she decided to turn everything on its head, to see whether Saga would be able to solve the riddle before it was too late.'

'So the whole case was like a trial? If Saga found the bunker in her attempts to save herself, she would be proving herself guilty of letting Mara's family die?'

Joona sips his wine and thinks that Mara was forced to be like the Pied Piper of Hamelin, getting everyone to follow the sound of her flute to the decisive moment when she would be reunited with her family and see that justice was done.

'Mara created riddles, falsified motives, evidence and clues, and all so that Saga and I would be one step ahead of everyone else,' Joona continues. 'She wanted us right behind her, working separately, each with our own riddle to solve . . .'

'Because she was convinced that, when it really came down to it, Saga would shoot her in order to save you.'

'No one knows how they'll react in an extreme situation. It all happens so fast that there's no time to think,' he says.

'But you were a hero.'

'No . . . far from it.'

He sits quietly for a moment, his gaze darkening.

'Are you thinking about his whisper again?' Valeria asks quietly.

'I don't know, maybe it's unforgivable . . . The fact that I killed Jurek, pushed him over the edge, I have to live with that for the rest of my life. Some part of me fell from the roof with him that day, and some part of him stayed with me. But we didn't swap places, I didn't become Jurek.'

'No, you're you, and I love you more with every day that passes.'

'I find that hard to believe.'

She reaches out and puts her hand on his, looks him straight in the eye.

'Don't worry,' she says, her voice solemn.

'What do you mean?'

'My answer is yes,' says Valeria.

'Yes?'

'If you ask the question,' she says, trying to hold back a smile.

Joona gets up, reaches into his inside pocket and takes out the ring, dropping to his knee in front of her.

Epilogue
Thirteen months later

From up above, the complex looks like two huge crosses, surrounded by a forest that is ablaze with colour in the autumn light.

Helix is a large, modern facility built to cater for specialist forensic psychiatric care.

Saga Bauer rides between the red maples and golden birches, parking and hanging her helmet from the handlebars.

The dove grey facade of the main building is bathed in warm sunlight, slanting in over the treetops. From where she is standing, the six-metre high wall and electric fence surrounding the facility are both hidden from view.

Saga makes her way inside and reports to the reception desk. The décor is so bright and airy that it almost feels like she is checking in to a luxury hotel. The receptionist verifies that her visit has been approved by the head doctor, then hands back her ID.

Saga moves through security, and is given a receipt in exchange for her phone, bag and all loose objects.

A burly nurse with sad eyes and a personal alarm hanging around his neck comes out to meet her in the waiting room.

He takes her down a number of long corridors, swiping his key card and entering various codes as they make their way to H1, the highest security wing.

A few years ago, an OPCAT investigation was launched following rumours of inhumane, torture-like treatment in Helix.

'All visitors must maintain a distance of at least four metres from the patients, which means all physical contact is forbidden. You may not give the patient anything, nor take anything from them. All conversations will be filmed for training purposes.'

A female guard with eczema around her mouth conducts another quick search, and then the centralised security office buzzes them in through two locked doors.

They make their way through the staff area, which has a reinforced window out onto the patients' rooms. The majority of the patients are lying in beds with their eyes open.

'The most common diagnosis here is some form of schizophrenia,' the burly carer whispers. 'And everyone is treated in line with the laws governing forensic psychiatric care, with periodic discharge reviews and comprehensive restrictions.'

'Why are you whispering?' Saga asks.

'Some of the hallways here lack soundproofing.'

They walk past the isolation unit, through a set of locked doors, pausing in front of another reinforced door with a sign reading HELIX OMEGA.

'It's haunted here. I swear,' the carer whispers. 'Though if you ask some of the others, they claim it's a spider, crawling through the cracks in the walls.'

The lock whirrs loudly as the central security office opens the door.

'This is as far as I come. She's in room three,' the guard says quietly, attempting a smile. 'It'll be fine, there are emergency alarms, and we'll be watching every second.'

Saga steps inside, pausing in front of a board setting out the various safety regulations. She hears the door swing shut behind her.

The sound echoes down the corridor, and then everything is quiet.

This ward, reserved for extremely dangerous patients in long-term isolation, was not mentioned in the OPCAT report. The patients are kept under constant surveillance, whether they are sleeping, using the toilet or taking a shower.

The hallway leads past three rooms with four-layer reinforced windows and steel doors.

The lights glare against the vinyl flooring.

Saga glances into the first cell as she passes.

An overweight man is lying in bed on top of the restraint straps, masturbating absently.

There is a slot for food and medicine in the thick concrete wall, with automatic hatches that cannot be opened at the same time.

Other than the low hum of the ventilation system, Saga's footsteps are the only sound she can hear.

The second patient is a young man with chapped, bitten hands. He is crouching down beside the glass, watching her with a big smile on his face.

The few pieces of furniture in the patients' rooms are all bolted to the floor, and the beds have neither sheets nor headboards. The toilet seats and lids have also been removed, in order to reduce the risk of self-harm.

Through a small, barred window with adjustable metal shades, Saga can make out a gloomy inner courtyard.

She pauses to compose herself before making her way over to the last of the rooms.

Mara Makarov is calmly sitting on a chair, staring down at the floor. She is wearing a pair of nondescript tracksuit bottoms, but her upper body is naked. The wall behind her is covered in complex mathematical equations.

Her head is shaved, and Saga notices that she has old scars and new-looking cuts all over her torso.

Saga hesitates for a moment, swallowing hard before crossing the red line and moving right up to the glass.

'Mara . . . I believe your doctor told you I would be coming,' she says into the microphone.

'There are no gods in mathematics,' Mara mumbles, her voice almost inaudible. 'Nothing but darkness . . .'

'Do you know who I am?'

Mara looks up and meets her eye through the glass.

'At the heart of every system, a milk white bullet shoots towards each of us at the speed of light squared, and because of time dilation, we're all doomed to meet before we're ready.'

Her shoulders and arms are still muscular, and her upturned palms are both grey.

'What happened to your family wasn't my fault. I think you know that, deep down,' says Saga. 'It was all Jurek Walter's doing. He was the one who took you to the bunker, and if he hadn't been stopped they would have been buried alive . . . Still, I do agree with you on one point, that I should have found them. I'm sorry I failed. But that doesn't mean I killed them.'

Mara stares up at Saga with her lonely eyes.

'Do you want me to say I forgive you?' she asks.

'It makes no difference what I want. I've always struggled to forgive myself, but I'm starting to think it might be possible for a person to do that after all.'

'Is it?' Mara asks, her eyes still locked on Saga.

'Yes. But it's a process that might never really be over,' Saga replies. 'That's what I came here to say, that everyone makes mistakes, that ultimately we all bear responsibility for each other's lives.'

Water drips slowly from the recessed showerhead, and a rip-proof blanket has been dumped in one corner.

'Am I mentally ill?' Mara asks, looking up at her again.

'My opinion is irrelevant.'

'Not to me.'

'You're here because of a serious psychiatric disorder, but that's a legal term, not a diagnosis. Your psychiatrists have mentioned a faltering grasp of reality, with delusions and confusion, marked obsessive compulsions and a low level of social function.'

'Yes,' she sighs.

'I'll never be able to accept your methods, but I do understand your pain, your logic . . . And I know that you're incredibly intelligent.'

Mara chews on a cuticle and looks up at Saga. 'You're back on duty,' she says.

'It was a long process,' Saga replies, surprised that Mara would know this.

'As an operative detective with the NCU.'

'Good guess.'

Mara gestures back over her shoulder towards her calculations.

'What else have you worked out?'

'That you're dating a boxer called Rick Santos,' she replies.

'How did you find out about that?'

'It's just maths.'

Saga studies the equations. The tiny letters are so tightly packed that the white wall looks black.

'How long will you stay here?'

Mara simply smiles in response, then gets to her feet and turns away from the window, moving over to her formulae on the wall.

Saga studies the wounds on her back, muscles trembling as she raises an arm and strokes the letters and numbers.

'Have you managed to work anything else out?' Saga asks her quietly.

'Yes.'

'What?'

'That you'll succumb to your own darkness soon,' Mara replies without turning around.